SCIENCE AND SORCERY III
More Weird Tales from the Far Side of Imagination

by Jeffery Scott Sims

THE HORRORS OF THE BLACK SWAMP!

I found myself in a place of utter darkness, and yet light seemed to radiate from me, so that I could see nearby objects. I was splashing through a shallow, weedy marsh, on what might have been a path enclosed by denser growth, damp moldering trees and fat, clinging shrubs. I could smell the place, smell it in a dream. The odor was like a compound of everything detestable and unclean, the reeking odor of decay, of death, of excrement, of vomit. The liquid, oily slush underfoot teemed with vermin, and larger, shadowy creatures rustled, not quite out of sight, among the nearer bushes. I was terrified, yet nothing could have prevented my pushing on; and I seemed to know where I was going. The trail served to an extent, but there came occasions when I would deliberately, yet without conscious thought, crash my way painfully through the dank growths. It was as if I followed a homing beacon.

"The sense of delicious horror mounted as I proceeded, growing extreme when I began to hear the sounds. I detected a thumping and bumping, and a grumbling of many voices—low, unpleasant voices—gabbling in rough unison, and punctuated by shrill cries. It sounded like a crowd in motion. I passed through a wall of bent, twisted trees to behold a freakish sight: a clearing, a wide circle of stinking muck, and within the circle a small island, a dryer patch of ground where a vast, unimaginable horde of monstrosities swayed and danced and chanted around a dimly seen central mass. I waded through the ooze, without the slightest hesitation, climbed up onto the island to join them. There, in close proximity to the beings, I quivered with disgust and loathing; I felt nauseated, and in one or more fashions I think I soiled myself; yet I joined them willingly.

"They weren't human. Many—most of them—might once have been so, but except for their general outlines all had long ago departed from any state of passable humanity. I thought they'd been dead for centuries, then dug up and animated—that gives you some idea what they were like—but whatever had happened to them, they were far gone down the road to decay. Some were dry and brittle, others as liquid as the swamp. They jostled one another, and as they did so bits and pieces broke or sloughed off. They kept on dancing, however, and through their moans and their sobs they laughed. Others moved among them: things that had never been human. I can't describe them, although I remember they wore curious drab vestments and bore corroded iron crowns on the sodden lumps which might have been their heads. It occurred to me then that they were priests . . .

From "The Man Who Sought Blug"

Science and Sorcery III: Eighteen tales of terror and weird mystery, exploring the shunned boundaries of the unknown!

CONTENTS

SLICES AND DICES OF LIFE

There ought to be an art associated with the creation of short story collections. Obviously the writing of the tales is a given, but with those in hand, how to proceed to the next stage? That depends on the goal, and off the top of my head I can think of three plans for a literary collection: a grab-bag, an amorphous mass of stories of all kinds; a themed project, with all stories relating to a specific central concept; and an assortment of diverse pieces, offering hopefully pleasing variety within a chosen general framework.

With this third volume in the *Science and Sorcery* series I'm shooting for the third option, and have put together a package meant to cover many bases while serving up constant thrills. This book intends to provide a hefty batch of, over all, spooky tales, my métier. Given the title, you can expect some science and sorcery mixed in there, but those are broad categories granting considerable leeway. What you get from these stories is a wide range sampling the span of my career, from straightforward supernatural horror, to paranoiac mystery, to science fiction, then on to fantasy and the classical weird tale. Long and short, too, to suit your taste, from novella down to near flash size. Let us preview what's in store should you dare to further turn these pages.

To begin at the beginning, the volume starts off with a private viewing of "Langley's Painting," a massive tale notable for containing an early appearance—by correspondence only—of Professor Anton Vorchek, who provides vital background information to the puzzled hero. What is so puzzling? Well, terrible things happen to people who see the titular artwork. It makes them miserable for certain, and some fail to survive the experience. The artist Terrill Langley may explain why, if he lasts long enough.

"Office Consultation," short and sweet, dabbles in philosophy, dealing in existential matters. I caution against too deep a consideration of the central premise, for the result can be awkward; in fact, totally annihilating.

"Night Flight" takes you on a routine journey that turns dark and mysterious. Check your ticket before you go, for indications are that this is a one way trip.

The hero of "The Man in the Globe" simply can not get over his good fortune, so proud of the honor bestowed upon him. Do not rush to envy him, however, for as so often the case in life (and this sort of story) all is not what it seems. Too much of a good thing should be cause for suspicion; accept that they are out to get you, and just maybe you'll learn the reason before you're through.

A creepy wax museum can be all kinds of exhilarating fun. It may be something more, as learns the hero of "The Chamber of Horrors." What inside such a place could transform thrills into terror? No, not the well-worn gambit of horrid displays come to life. The fright factor can be something much more personal.

If you must go shopping late, pray you don't find yourself "Alone with the Night Crew." They're a special breed, operating within a unique establishment. Their people skills, to put it mildly, aren't what they once were.

Dive into pure fantasy with "Kardowan," a zippy tale relating the efforts of a nobleman of yore to restore his fortunes at the expense of the whole world. To achieve his evil designs he seeks a mighty ally, not pausing to realize that this unusual comrade is also mighty dangerous. This tale constitutes a sequel of sorts to my novel of ancient Dyrezan, *The Journey through the Black Book*.

All American family meets lost Indian idol, and the results aren't happy, for they have awakened "The Mad One." Legends tell hideous stories about this thing, and believe it that they don't exaggerate.

Here's a quick detour into straight science fiction "In the Time Vault." Take a smug, self-aggrandizing criminal, mate him with futuristic high tech, and what comes out of the mix? Perhaps not quite what he had in mind.

Rushing back to the spookies, a long lost diary tells of the incredible mystery surrounding "The Gold Sphere," a strange artifact that opens the door into an unknown world. The hero brazenly embraces unbelievable hazards in order to uncover eons old secrets, but the menace doesn't end with him.

"The Guardian at the Gate" maintains his constant and necessary vigil without adulation or reward. So long as he's left alone to do his job, all is well, but when matters become complicated by a less aware interloper, all bets are off. The stakes couldn't be greater.

"The House at the End of the World" is a ruin now, uninhabited and forgotten, but in former years it was the center of big doings, crazy delvings into forbidden knowledge that might rock the cosmos. Sit down by that great wreck and listen to the tale, as told by one who knows.

Professor Vorchek contributed to the first story here; he stars in the remainder of the short tales, often accompanied by his lovely assistant Theresa Delaney. In "A Simple Solution" he goes it alone, playing Sherlock Holmes in a weird case of supernatural murder. Be sure that clever Vorchek gets his man, but how does the good professor choose to administer justice? Why, he keeps it simple, of course.

Vorchek goes serious climbing on "The South Face of Medicine Man Mountain" with that most hapless of breeds, his graduate student. Neither the annoying student, nor anyone else for that matter, understand why the professor wishes to scale that difficult peak, which happens to be sacred to the local Indians. Since primordial times they have passed down the most frightful legends about that place . . .

Vorchek and Theresa accept invitations to "The Big Sedona Bash," held in that cosmic-minded city by a rich fellow even more so minded than his neighbors. With money no object, he's gotten hold of a single page of the rare and dreaded book of the medieval wizard Jacob Bleek. The proud owner can't imagine any harm coming from playing around at the party with his new acquisition. Vorchek can.

Vorchek and Theresa are in Egypt managing an archeological dig where they uncover the fabled tomb of "Yardreela." The fables about her, dating back thousands of years, are pretty grim. Of course there couldn't be any truth to them; Yardreela is dead and gone . . .

Pity the hero of "The Man Who Sought Blug." He's got everything this world has to offer, and should be deliriously happy, yet he's miserable with self-loathing. He's come to Vorchek and Theresa for their aid on a religious problem. Yes, that's right; you see, this poor guy seeks an extraordinary god for a very special brand of worship, and only a smart chap like Vorchek can swing it for him. Oh, but you just can't believe how nasty it is!

As a big bonus, I'm topping off this book with a republication of my creepy short novel, *All Expenses Paid*. Think of the marvelous possibilities of a free stay at a scenic resort hotel, all the amenities, the devoted staff; what could possibly go wrong? The answer merely involves a little matter of life and death.

There ends this collection on a truly ghastly note, I assure you well worth waiting for. I hope you enjoy reading the stories in *Science and Sorcery* III as much as I did writing them. Should these tales please you, I have many more available.

Have fun!

Jeffery Scott Sims
June 26, 2019

LANGLEY'S PAINTING

L angley, they say, is missing and presumed dead, the victim of foul play. I have no compelling reason to dispute that; the facts appear to speak for themselves. The trashing of his apartment living room, the vandalistic destruction, the bloody smears on the wrecked sofa and similar splashes on the walls and floor, seem to tell the tale. Those close to him, including myself, can testify that in his final days he went in fear of his life. The only remaining mystery attached to the apparent crime should concern the identity of the culprit. Killer or killers unknown; and yet, given time, we may choose to believe that the forces of the law will bring the case to a satisfactory conclusion, all questions answered, justice upheld.

Well and good, if it works out that way; but speaking frankly, I have my doubts. Certain press reports, for what they're worth, indicate puzzling factors, which may demand explanation in vain. I've read that all of the doors and windows were locked and bolted from the inside. The crime scene is located on an upper floor of a big building, full of people at all hours. How did intruders enter without leaving any definite traces of themselves? How did anyone, living or dead, manage an exit? The exact time of the supposed crime is known. Neighbors heard something—according to all accounts, they were terribly aware that something dreadful was happening—but they saw nothing. I'm not sanguine about the ongoing investigation, and wonder whether the police officials are qualified to illuminate a tragedy of this kind. There is too much they don't know, or most likely won't accept if they do. I know many things others don't, or that others only suspect, about Langley's last days. He confided in me, more so, I think, than to anyone else. I haven't been especially forthcoming about what he told me, nor is it clear to me that I should. What purpose would it serve? At the very least I can write down what I learned and deduced from various sources, and decide later what to do with the information.

Already, even before the body is found (it won't be; take my word on

1

that), the eulogies are starting to come out, and so far the public releases have been uniformly favorable. We've lost the great Terrill Langley, artiste extraordinaire, composer in oils of daring and exotic images—that fine fellow—ah, yes, that clever painter chap . . . He might have appreciated a bit more such talk in life, although I don't doubt the sincerity of those statements. In private, however, in conversation and commiseration with his associates, I detect sinister undercurrents. No one actually comes right out and says so, but there are those—more than a few—whose manner is oddly gleeful when they refer to his suspected demise. Unimpressive, you say? To be sure, those familiar with the art world know it to be rife with jealousies, antagonisms, and rivalries, professional and personal clashes which even the grave can not still. I'm perfectly aware of that—despite my best intentions, I've gotten involved in a few teapot tempests, and how they do drag on— but that isn't what I mean. Just this morning I talked to a guy who could barely contain his joy. He's glad that Langley is gone. He dwelt lovingly on the possible mechanisms of death. That isn't normal behavior, not even in Langley's circles.

If I'm right about the existence of this simmering hostility, is there an explanation for it? I'm afraid there is, and it doesn't involve his personal quirks, though they were legion: his overweening vanity, his smug self-absorption, his shabby treatment of friends and, especially, women. There are a couple of girls out there who will always hate his guts, but nobody cares about that sort of thing around here. It has nothing to do with his private morality or his social opinions; as far as those went, he was about average for the crowd he ran with. Langley never had a good word for his own country, despised the "narrow-minded bourgeois" attitudes of anyone who wasn't high-minded like himself, and confidently affirmed that the reigning political order was ripe for demolition. He enjoyed seeing the important and the proud knocked off their perches, and secretly seemed to think that some people—to the extent that they differed from himself—possessed way too much freedom to act and speak. His vociferously voiced views on current politics were tritely popular, following all of the safely subversive talking points of the day, and he rode a hobbyhorse—I can't quite recollect what it was about—maybe something related to global warming. Yes, he was that sort of character, and whatever you might think of his type, he didn't lose any points for it among his cronies. None of that is the way to the answer. No, it all has to do with that ultimate painting of his, Langley's self-proclaimed masterpiece, which was going to put him on the map once and for all, and raise him to the highest ranks of the artistic elites. Maybe it did that, or maybe it should have, but regardless, I can't say that it did him much good. In fact, I think it led directly to his death. I will state for the record that I hope it got him killed, because—given my insider's knowledge of the events leading up to his vanishing—I get the sickening feeling that the whole truth could be so much worse. And therein lies my tale.

I first met Terrill Langley seven years ago, when he was already an up and coming artist, but nowhere near the status he later attained. Along the way I learned a few details of his earlier life: a troubled childhood somewhere in Idaho (I could find the state on a map, but wasn't fully aware that it was inhabited); a father who didn't encourage his creative leanings, a mother who did; difficult high school years, and then a scholarship to a local college for, of all things, mathematics (he was good with figures, if his grasp of money was any guide); throwing over the scholarship at the earliest opportunity in order to enroll in art classes; finally dropping out when he thought he'd accumulated sufficient technical skill, and fleeing to San Francisco, the home of everything weird and outrageous, where I found him two years after he arrived. I don't know how he'd survived up to that time—it certainly wasn't on the proceeds from his paintings—but he'd managed to ensconce himself in a cheesy loft in a wretched building populated by similar types, and there he did a lot of lazing around and a sufficiency of creative dabbling.

I saw that pathetic place somewhat later. We met at a seasonal open air art fair down by the bay, not too far from the big bridge, from which I'd gathered infrequent finds, and where he had presented a couple of his recent efforts for public perusal. Both were semi-expressionistic studies of obscurely menacing landscapes, with something in them to catch the eye, although the human figures in them didn't quite measure up to the overall standard. I made a creditable remark to the fellow standing next to me, who turned out to be Langley himself. Concluding that I was intelligent and worthy of conversation, he embarked on a long harangue about his work's "meaning"—the sort of desperate earnestness I've heard many times from many people—but he was young, lively, and really did know a thing or two. I didn't buy, for, like most men in my position, I write more than I purchase, but I was impressed, and I remembered.

I won't say that I was right about him, because one never can forecast this business, but I wasn't surprised when Langley began to produce ripples in the local pond. A few months later I saw another work in a little gift shop at the foot of the Hill; not a fancy place, but in an upscale section of town. The price asked was ridiculous, yet the picture had merit, and I took the opportunity to hunt him up. He looked shabby then, like his lodgings, and thin. He couldn't have been eating much. In his offhand way he was pleased to see me, perhaps more so by my offer to treat him to lunch. Others had noticed him in the meantime—I believe Hoskins had already published his small piece in *The Benchmark*—but Langley was actually keen to talk to me. From that time I saw him more or less frequently until the end, and remained generally aware of his doings.

3

SCIENCE AND SORCERY III

I recall one statement of his from that coffee klatch long ago: "I want to paint that which the eyes can not see." That was Langley to the core, the kind of professional gab that almost made sense, coming from him. I never figured out just what he meant, I don't think, but that may be my lack, for he discoursed on the subject in painstaking detail throughout the years of our association.

"Painting is a medium," he told me another time, "for the presentation of images and ideas. Second-raters focus on the one, or on the other. Masters handle both with equal facility. Yet I say, there are images within images, and ideas within ideas. Think of reflections bouncing endlessly between two mirrors, an infinite series. I want to paint that, to burrow down through all those levels, to open all the doors, and to reveal all that lies within. There is a way to do that—I am convinced—and I'm willing to spending my life learning it and finding it."

On a separate occasion I asked of him, "Haven't all artists felt that way? Every man has his own vision, and some are driven by internal forces to broadcast it. Aren't you merely expressing the age-old need for the creator to create?"

"A producer of rubber ducks could say that much," he retorted. "I mean much more than that. Let us not speak of interminable variations on the aspects of superficial appearances. Every child can make a stab at that by kindergarten. Every artist in history, no matter how grand, has simply built upon that universal capacity. They keep doing an admirable job of scraping the surface. That isn't what I have in mind. I intend to dive deeply below, to get behind consciousness and matter; to see through the illusion of commonplace reality."

And so forth. I've wondered where Langley got his fancified notions on art. Perhaps from one of those avant-garde courses he took, although he refused to give college classes any credit for developing his ideas, as opposed to technique. More likely he got them from books, for Langley read a great deal more than any other painter I've met. He had a sizable collection, many of them paperbacks, but a number of bulky, worn hardcover tomes. No novels, no outright fiction at all, but rather eldritch artistic studies, mathematical volumes, overly complicated works on optics and physics, and then those which I would only classify as strange. These books, by authors whose names meant nothing to me, dealt with wild supernatural or supernormal phenomena, and the nature of "true reality," and related subjects that we peasants can't be expected to understand. Langley ate up that stuff, and I guess events have shown that he took it very seriously indeed.

Of course I didn't worry about it at the time. I couldn't help but notice that, for all his big talk, his productions, however unusual—in a time and place where the unusual is the norm—didn't live up to his aspirations. His efforts resembled, in most respects, the endeavors of those who had gone before him. I once wrote that his works compared favorably to the wilder conceptions of Torquelle and Dereida (which the artist brusquely appreciated). He created imaginative dreamscapes, concocted moody other-worldly visions, and fashioned startling juxtapositions out of conventional scenes. I liked a lot of it, but I wasn't bowled over by any of it. He wasn't perfect, not by his own lights. He had difficulties with the shape and lines of the human torso; he couldn't capture the form, which caused him grief at first, until he contrived to make that a signature feature of his work, transforming weakness into strength. Oh, he could be slick when he wanted to be. I figured Langley was yet another clever mind worth watching, a man who could provide items of interest, perhaps have his day in the sun, maybe make a financial success of himself if he really buckled down. I must say, he did entertain me more than the run of the mill.

During those budding years I kept in touch regularly, but I was a busy man, with plenty on my plate, and there were other possibilities and hopefuls who also absorbed my attention. Langley kept going, somehow, and single pieces found their way into fairs and anthology exhibits. He received comment—I commented—and he managed to keep his head above water which, for a fellow in his line, is no small feat in and of itself. He didn't disappear, which was the main thing; others fell by the wayside, as most do, but he persevered. I gave him high marks for that. Eventually I broke down and acquired, for a respectable sum, a Langley original, *The Prophet's Secret*, offered to me by the artist as his best work thus far. I say it's the best of his early period. I own it still. Picture a barren, rocky plain by night, strewn with leaning or toppled antique columns and other shattered vestiges of lost greatness, and a low, featureless mound rising in the center, upon which sits a bearded elder in flowing tattered robes. He looks a bit goofy and disjointed, but his woebegone expression and mad eyes are sincere. Above all the blue-black sky swarms with fiery stars and swollen planets, so bright as to cast faint shadows. What did it mean? Who cares? I didn't ask; I liked it.

Langley's salad days were approaching. His next big step brought him the fame and notoriety he craved. He showed me the new picture when it was almost complete, at the same time requesting me to pull strings in order to guarantee a proper presentation. I warned him that the painting was grotesque, obscene, and nauseating; and I assured him that it was daring, original, and stunning.

He grinned widely. "Do you think they'll go for it?" It was the first and last time he cared to ask such a question.

"Everybody will scream," I replied, "but they will eat it up." So he pushed it to completion as quickly as he could, and within weeks there debuted, at the prestigious Stanfield Gallery, *The Turd Race at Oswiegan*.

SCIENCE AND SORCERY III

Artists love to throw dynamite, as long as they can get away with it. Langley got away with it. He handled it cagily enough. He placed the painting—a two by three, larger than his previous efforts—inside an ornate, gilded wooden frame, suggestive of tradition and class, had it set up as the centerpiece in the main hall, and appended below a gold leaf sign (at his own expense) which fully explained the scene's lurid historical background. "A True Incident on the Ninth of October, in the Year Nineteen Hundred and Forty-Three, at the Infamous Nazi Concentration Camp," ran the subtitle, followed by these words:

"The camp commandant, Obergruppenfuehrer Otto Schoerner, conceived a sportive festival by which to amuse himself and his men. Dozens of Jewish inmates were taken to a limestone quarry and forced, under the watchful eyes of armed guards, to run a relay race, utilizing rules of Schoerner's devising. Each participant was made to carry chunks of human excrement in his mouth, to rush at breakneck speed across the impromptu court, and transfer his mouthful to the next man, who then continued the relentless cycle. As each victim of this ordeal wilted from horror or revulsion, or collapsed from underfed weariness, he was immediately shot. The victor—the last survivor of the game—was feted at a Vitellian feast, then led, amidst cheering and jibes, to the gas chamber for his execution."

There you have it. The painting was shortly snapped up by a Middle Eastern collector and lost to sight, but I've got a professional photograph which does it justice. Langley made use of an off-colored, somewhat impressionistic style, not his standard, but well done. He imagined the high-walled grotto in shades of blue and gray. The sunless sky lowered in sickly, roiling yellow. On the floor of the quarry three contestants still stood erect, dressed in rags, frozen in agonized postures of staggering, corpse-like motion. They clutched in their clenched jaws what, at a glance, appeared to be rough cigars. The central figure stood closer to the viewer. The look on his face did not bear long perusal. Several bodies lay scattered about the cracked stones, their limbs sprawled in non-anatomical angles (good old Langley!), the terrain nearby specked with ominous dabs of crimson and yellow. Above and to the left, on a rocky shelf surmounting the scene, a group of spectators stared down and observed with evident mirth. There were camp guards aiming rifles, and in their center a tall officer, clearly the commandant, resplendent in his black uniform and full Nazi regalia. He seemed gravely pleased rather than jovial, and about his head there hovered an aura—one might call it an unholy halo—or luminous emanation, of a somber greenish hue, framing the cold pale face.

Well, howls of protest ensued, most of them valid, all of them pointless. Langley had created an insult, a mockery, a travesty; probably so. He deftly countered the criticism by publicly discussing his "pictorial statement against bigotry and intolerance," which it may have been. The usual suspects bought that line and simmered down, with a few lingering grumbles and carping complaints about "going too far." The local art society kicked him out, then took him back when no one was watching. The practical effect of the episode was the enhancement of Langley's artistic stature, and the geometric increase of his fame. Suddenly, whatever might be said about him, people who counted—lots of them—took him seriously. He no longer received comments in back pages of the journals; he got write-ups and cover stories, he got interviews and television guest spots. He became a known quantity far beyond the Bay area, and outside his accustomed circles. An historian hosted a documentary about that concentration camp, called *One Small Corner of Hell* (a title which I considered greatly superior to the original, although the originator scathingly disagreed), which performed adequately in the ratings. During filming the producers recorded a few minutes of Langley opining, and a shot of *Turd Race*. In the end they cut out the painter, but kept the painting, which could be seen behind the opening titles and concluding credits.

Turd Race packed the gallery. The Stanfield hadn't seen such crowds since their blockbuster Egyptian exhibit of some years back. All kinds of folks wanted to see the picture, and condemn it, and brag about having condemned it. Langley would drop in occasionally, wait to be recognized, then expound on his theories of art, which everyone sagely approved, and no one understood.

Success didn't go to his head, but it sure made a difference in his life. Langley got rich off that painting, or near enough. He earned more at one swoop than he had from all his earlier productions. He moved out of that proletarian garbage dump of his and took a long lease on a snazzy apartment at the top of the Hill. He started keeping company with a generally better class of people, including women—even a Hollywood starlet for a spell, which helped maintain his place in the public eye—although he still abused the latter dreadfully. He ate right, or lavishly, for the first time since I'd known him, and gained twenty pounds.

Langley enjoyed his new life, and made the most of it. He no longer had to struggle to sell his wares. Customers came to him, or to dealers, asking for the merchandise. Also, he experienced the new sensation of working with paying clients. Langley, of all people, got into the portraiture racket. There were those, with spare change in their pockets, who wanted their pictures painted for posterity by the famous artist. He obliged. I thought he was wasting his time in an area not his strongest, and I never heard of his clients fully appreciating the end products. The portraits commonly contained unusual, quirky elements, not entirely suitable to the medium. Only by chance did they flatter. I suspect that most of them ended up hidden away in back rooms. Langley didn't mind. He had money in the bank.

He was far from satisfied, however, with his situation. It took me a while to realize why, and when I did, I could only feel sorry for him, just a wee bit. As I had already surmised, he was a classic auteur, and could not be content unless the world accepted him on the basis of his own self-evaluation, a boon which is granted to few. They didn't appreciate him, they didn't comprehend him, they didn't see him for what he was; those terrible "theys," who made life both possible and oh, so frustrating. How many times have I heard that lingo! Each new client brought forth a new diatribe from the embittered artist. I always listened patiently, and my heart always bled, but not a lot.

To give Langley his due, that wasn't his major concern. As I eventually learned, he was far more frustrated with himself. I heard it all at a dinner meeting at the Karbala, in the spring, several months after his big smash at the Stanfield. He treated, because he needed to sulk and talk. In his view, he was just marking time with his artistic career, and had not yet begun to achieve his desired goals. He wondered if it were still possible, or whether he ought to throw over the whole thing and find himself an honest job. I didn't believe his noise for a minute—this was merely a typical mood swing—but in the spirit of avuncular friendship I sought to dissuade him.

"Terrill, think rationally, if you can—that only requires practice—and you'll realize how extraordinarily well you're getting along. All of my other contacts envy your success. You set out to excel at creating weird art, and you've done it. You're the only painter with anything as daring as *Turd Race* on your resume. No one can top that now, and many an age will pass before anyone does; unless it's you, of course."

"You obviously didn't pay attention," he said. "I haven't taken one step toward my artistic aims. They continue to elude me. I'm not even clear in my own mind as to what I'm driving at. My recent stuff . . . oh, it's clever, but not ground breaking. I could pat myself on the back and say that I've pushed the conventions of the form to their logical limits, but that means nothing. Tomorrow I might paint a pretty girl with a bowl of chicken livers on her head, call it *Hope* or some silly thing, and gain the same glory."

"No, that would just be silly. Your plan, as I recollect it, is to present what the eyes of others don't see—"

"That's my point!" he cried. "Not others, but any eyes, including mine. It isn't a question of my vision. I have no interest in providing a 'unique perspective'. I want to portray the world as it really is."

I threw my hands in the air. "You've lost me. Unless you're speaking of absolute realism—which isn't your style—I don't understand you."

He mused. "Absolute realism; that's good. Yes and no—no, because I'm not referring to style—yes, because I seek the ultimately real. It's out there, behind a secret door, and there must be a way to open it."

"Terrill, you place me in a difficult position. I'm close to accusing you of working too hard and needing a rest."

"You may be right, but it doesn't signify. What I need to do is stop mixing oils, and catch up on my reading."

"Stop painting?"

"Cut back, so that I can concentrate. My reading list has grown. I've acquired new books, some of which may contain answers." I knew he meant his swelling collection of volumes devoted to the occult and the bizarre. Previously I had encouraged his passion, since it helped him generate ideas. I wasn't so sure now. "Most of it," he continued presently, "is basic fare, the sort of popular rubbish true believers feed upon. That doesn't do me much good. On the other hand, there are, or have been, intelligent, learned men, hands-on philosophers, who have sought to unveil the mysteries of the universe. Genuine seekers of the unknown, compilers of the supernormal, men who drove past theory into the realm of concrete investigation. Their books are hard to find, and if found, hard to afford. I've got money now—more than I know what to do with—perhaps that will make a difference to my studies. If I know what they know, mightn't I be able to capture, in my mind and on canvas, images of that knowledge?"

It wasn't my place to argue. The conversation ran on at greater length, but Langley added nothing of importance. It sounded to me like he intended a crash course in wasting his time, but my chief concern—then, and for a considerable period thereafter—focused primarily on how his obsession might affect his career. I decided not to badger him, and counted on him not to throw a good thing overboard.

During the next two years I had occasion to wonder if my worst fears had been realized. Langley virtually disappeared from my life, and from the public eye. He shortly stopped accepting portrait clients—which suited me fine—but then largely gave up on commissioned projects altogether, which disturbed me. He turned out the rare piece on spec, and received generous payment when he did so. Increasingly strange dream-world scenes, with the emphasis greater on the grotesque, and lesser on the trappings of humanity, constituted his total output for this period. These assured me that he was still in the running, but that was all. My colleagues knew less of his daily doings than I did. Those with weaker associations to him asked me if he had dropped out of the game.

Langley and I crossed paths, by chance, at the annual Barbary Coast Festival held on Alcatraz. I attended to revel in the historical reconstructions and costume shows; I found him mooning around the mural wall, apparently lost in contemplation. I spoke to him, but he proved uncommunicative. He did tell me that he had commenced his binge buying and reading of books, and was out that day taking a break from wearisome study. The mural didn't impress him. He deplored the crowds. No more would he tell

That winter I determined to visit Langley in his lair. I dropped by, unexpected and unannounced, curious as to the sort of reception I had coming. I needn't have worried about that. He welcomed me into the apartment warmly enough, bade me make myself at home. He seemed cheerful, bright-eyed, even ebullient. He informed me that he had recently received a grant from the NEA, which had made his situation easier still (and from which he subsequently produced a total piece of crap; he laughed about it later). The quality of his living conditions, though, had declined to a tragic level. His rooms, new and pristine when last I saw them, now looked all too lived in. The artist's chaos reigned supreme. Most of the disorder stemmed from the piles of old books, ragged manuscripts, and unbound papers scattered over the colonial furniture or heaped upon the plush rugs. He brought refreshments, cleared space on the sofa for me, then did the same for himself on an opposing armchair.

He immediately launched into a recital of his current activities. While he did so, I surveyed the scene. From what I could make out, we were surrounded by exceedingly odd reading material. I took in some of the titles: *Ancient Heresies*, *The Paradoxes of Saint Montague*, *The Death Vision of Pseudo-Plutarchus*. Those were old tomes. On the coffee table before me stood a stack of relatively newer works, probably anthropological or scientific, such as *The Customs of Shunned Tribes*, *Developments in Organic Light Sensitivity*, and *Holobiologia*. I can't tell you how many books there were. Whatever it all meant, Langley had his hands full.

Ah, but at that moment he was explaining. When I had sufficiently tuned in I heard him saying: "This is the real, the hard-core stuff. I began reading as soon as they started coming in, and it wasn't long before I hit pay dirt. Each of these offers something useful, a little part of the puzzle. In many cases, the old writings are more helpful than the new. I've got a rare one over there, on the counter, written by hand in medieval Greek. I needed the right kind of dictionary for that, and you can't find those just anywhere.

"With all this, I required a key to tie it together, to make sense of the big picture. I found it. Let me show you." He strode to a closet, extracted a small, frayed, leather-bound volume, and returned with it. He didn't hand it to me. "This is none other than *The Catalogue of Truths*, composed by the infamous Jacob Bleek."

"This is the key that ties?" I asked innocently.

"Indeed. You wouldn't believe what I had to go through to get hold of this copy. There aren't many in existence, and I've always heard that they're all incomplete. The original was never professionally published, you know. I sought the most intact version I could find, in order to maximize my chances of striking gold. I had to go outside the usual channels to track it down—funny how people won't even discuss Bleek, if they can avoid it—and it cost me a fortune, but it's going to be well worth it."

Langley grew pensive, then lay the book down and pulled a sheet of newspaper over it. "Perhaps you think I oughtn't to have done it?" It was difficult to come up with a coherent reply, since I hadn't the slightest idea what he was talking about, so I mumbled something noncommittal about being careful.

"Precisely!" he cried. "It's a question of caution, not fear. I have nothing to worry about. It's only information. Bleek figured it out long ago, he brought the strands together. These"—he indicated the other books—"are the strands. They're necessary, because Bleek, in his wisdom, assumes too much. He already knows this other stuff. With him, I can connect the dots, and raise his conclusions from the theoretical to the actual. Bleek's truths realized by me, in oils. How does that grab you?"

"It's beyond me," I admitted. "Where does it get you, Terrill?"

"I can bring my dream to fruition. I shall create, without any special tools, an image of pure reality; not the world as I see it, or you see it—or an ant sees it, for that matter—but as it really is. Not a subject, not a theme, not an episode, not a style, just truth unvarnished. Absolute reality, before your very eyes, without pretense.

"You are generally aware that our view of the universe around us is inherently limited. Our optical system operates within a narrow range of the spectrum. We use high-tech cameras and other devices to extend that range. We know that many creatures see in different portions of the spectrum, and their understanding of the world is quite different from ours. Now, my first step was to conceive the possibility of observing the entire color spectrum at once.

"That may sound grandiose enough for you, but years ago I discovered that it's merely a question of technical wizardry. Science is capable of handling that end, and may have done so already. That still restricts us, however, to the currently accepted light range, broad as it is. Armed only with that, I could play games with colors, but not much else. My most cherished fantasies run a great deal farther.

"I know, with a moral certainty which admits of no doubt, that there exists an invisible world, the world of the hyper-normal, if you will, that lies beyond and encompasses the dimensions we recognize, within which Einsteinian space-time makes up the merest fragment. I've read the foundational works on the subject. It's there. In our usual human circumstances we can't touch it, can't sense it in any way. We can't see it, because—once we posit the hyper-normal—we must allow for the corresponding existence of the hyper-spectrum, an observable range far surpassing that previously known. It may be that no gizmo can ever reveal it to us, for any machine the experts can construct lies wholly within conventional space-time. It would be as materially limited as they are. On the other hand, perhaps they will tinker something in a thousand years. Who can say? I'm not willing to wait!

"No machine can reveal it, but the right kind of prepared human mind can; my mind. That's what I've been doing with all this reading—training myself to see in the full range of the hyper-spectrum—the ultimate act of the creative imagination. It requires knowledge, skill, and will power. I have to force myself to look at an everyday object—that lamp, for instance—and see it in all its extra-dimensional forms, within the broadest conceivable band of light and color. It isn't easy. At first I wasn't convinced that it was possible. I couldn't make it happen, not from just wanting to do it, until I had so expanded and released my brain that the images began falling into place of their own accord."

This sounded like squalid drug mouthings to me, a potential weakness of which I'd never suspected him. When I gently questioned Langley on the matter, he grew indignant. "These aren't hallucinations," he said, "chemically stimulated or otherwise. They're real glimpses of the hyper-normal world. It comes to me fairly easily now. In the beginning it gave me a headache to see properly, but not anymore. You've know of those specially designed pictures, that show a stereoscopic image when you stare at them a certain way, an image that springs out when you focus just so. Well, it feels like that. I have to make the effort, but I've developed a knack for it, and as time passes I'm gaining more control over the visual process. Increasingly I'm seeing purely through the comprehensive awareness of my mind, rather than with my eyes.

"However, even that isn't enough for me. I haven't embarked on this artistic odyssey in order to paint a still life of a multi-dimensioned lamp. A presentation of absolute reality demands an absolute subject. I must understand what I see before I can paint it. That's the reason for the anthropology texts, and . . . some of this other stuff here. Pretty wild some of it is, difficult to absorb. I've had trouble grasping critical points. Perhaps a lingering unwillingness has held me back; certain conceptions regarding the true nature of the universe are so vast, so incomprehensible, so *frightening* in their implications, as to give me pause. The more I understand, the more I'm filled with awe. I have moments when I'm not sure that I want to follow Bleek down the road he traveled. What lies at the end is immense."

He sat silently for a while, then added, "There may be a religious component to my quest. I didn't expect that. It's never been important to me before, and I don't know how to deal with it." And that was all I learned that day.

LANGLEY'S PAINTING

During the ensuing period of many months I heard no more from or about Langley. There was no trade mention of fresh productions. He wasn't recognized out and about in his usual haunts. The grapevine eventually informed me that he refused all new clients. I popped by his place once more, but no one answered the door. I called a few times. On a single occasion he picked up the phone. He was home but, as he made rudely clear, not officially in. I asked him what he was doing. Working on his grand project, he told me. Had he actually begun the painting? Yes. Might I see it? No, positively no. Why not, pray tell? This time he responded with more than a brush-off.

"It wouldn't mean anything at this stage. Until I complete the picture—until every detail is in place, each curve and angle formulated and captured—it won't have the desired effect. It would just be a picture. This time you must wait." Click, disconnection.

So he would have it. The whole business intrigued me, naturally. I keenly wanted to be the first to make a public announcement about his ongoing magnum opus, but if that wasn't going to happen then I refused to accept such treatment. I did my best to put Langley out of my mind, a task made simple by his reclusiveness.

Now I must bring my account of events up to a point about two months ago. I'd still heard nothing of Langley, and he knew and cared nothing about me. I'd temporarily landed in France—Paris, of course—where in my high-minded fashion I agreed to act as one of the experts on an art panel overseeing a formal prize competition. The details don't matter (it was another one of those), but while there I enjoyed the scenery in company with an aspiring local sculptress, a sweet, pretty young thing, who'd convinced herself that my guidance could be beneficial to her career. I got what I wanted; regretfully, I can't say the same for her. She had talents, to be sure, but not in the line of sculptural expression. At any rate, she kept me happily overseas far longer than originally planned.

One crisp morning, while jotting down notes, alone, at the Louvre for what might become a magazine feature, I ran across Leonard Chockinaw. This uninspiring poseur from Modesto, who must have called in some big favors to get an art column in three newspapers, had just flown into town in order to "vertically insert" himself, as he told me, into the refreshing Old World culture. He intended to "hunker down" and "embed" himself among charming surroundings until he managed to pull himself together. In response to my minimal politeness he assured me that he wasn't physically ill, only shaken, and needed time to recuperate. I'd always thought this empty-headed dolt (in the old days he shouted the praises of nine day wonder Andrew Pindar, who gathered his watercolor materials from sewage treatment plants and called the stinking result social commentary) unflappable, but for once in his life he had something on his mind.

He said to me, fretfully: "Since you're so thick with Terry, I guess you know all about it."

"Terrill Langley?" I exclaimed, somehow smothering my surprise. The artist had never wasted time on this hack. "What's he to you?"

"He's put out a new one. I saw it last week. A crazy thing; I don't like it."

In this manner I received my first intimation that Langley had finally completed his epic work. He called it, I now learned, *Cosmic Kaleidoscope*.

I swallowed my distaste and invited Chockinaw to dinner, which represented a major disruption of my intended evening engagements. At the Maison that night he explained everything, and this is the gist of what he said:

The painting began its display the previous Friday at the renowned Radetsky Salon. That was bound to impress. It opened without the customary preliminary fanfare. An interesting development, that. The artist didn't show. Langley had pulled that stunt before, and it meant nothing. First reviews were mixed, subdued, rather querulous. So, they were playing it cagey with an original item; standard critical practice. Chockinaw had much to say concerning the mounting hostile reaction, but I dismissed his words. I'd heard it before with *Turd Race*. Besides, this clown wasn't capable of reporting, much less judging, the opinions of others.

Impatiently I listened, until he got around to describing his own experience with Langley's painting, which he viewed the day after opening. Here his tale took an unexpected turn, and fully commanded my attention.

"It's a large painting," Chockinaw said, "his biggest yet, a four by six. He placed the canvas inside an ugly chrome steel frame. I don't get that. If he'd been smart enough to ask me, I'd have advised differently. Then again, maybe it doesn't matter with this one. I don't believe anything could make it right.

"How do I put *Cosmic Kaleidoscope* into words? When I first saw it, across the gallery, I wasn't sure what I was looking at. It seemed a jumble of clashing images. The picture is a mess, I can tell you, just a bath of muddy oils; chaotic, like *Guernica*, but not as clever—no thought, no higher significance—ugliness without meaning. Somehow, though, he slipped in forms and figures in a way you wouldn't expect.

"I saw that up close, however. I've never denied that Terry has technical skill. He's done something to the image—I haven't seen this before, maybe fancy varnish—that makes the picture appear to develop, like a photograph, as you approach. The closer I got, and the longer I stared, the more I saw. Portions seemed to detach themselves from the whole—no order to any of this—and catch the eye.

"And then in a flash I saw it all—or just one part—I don't know; it leaped out at me, as if I'd entered a room rather than stuck my nose into canvas. The scene came at me from all sides, it overwhelmed my vision. It hurts to think about what I saw."

It took a generous dose of expensive Moselle to move Chockinaw forward. Then he said, in a low, whispering voice, "It ought to be a crime. What he's done goes beyond pornography. I've looked at that stuff—for professional reasons—but this beats anything I've seen. How could that man cram so much depraved, detestable, debasing foulness into one painting? Bosch is a joke by comparison. Terry's strong point has always been human figures—he does funny things to them—but here he's gone around the bend. A great sweating, slobbering heap of sexual excess, without purpose. I sensed a sick joy behind the physical distortions, the pain and cruelty, the ecstatic wallowing in human shame. He doesn't leave anything out, and he invents new combinations of flesh and fluids. There's nothing cosmic about it, it's all lowly and degenerate sadomasochism. He must be hiding something horrible inside him . . . and yet, upon viewing the picture, I haven't been able to escape the feeling that what I saw was inside me, coming from within me, that it wasn't in the picture at all. Ridiculous, you say—I'm a great guy, everyone knows that—but I haven't felt good about myself since."

As soon as I could tear myself away from my maundering companion I wired home for press clippings and a copy of *Evocative*, the weekly periodical, in order to get the straight story on Langley's painting. The artist's vague declamations hadn't prepared me for this. From Chockinaw's distraught account I gathered that I should expect something on the order of *Turd Race II*, with an enhanced dwelling on nastiness. If so, what an amazing let down! On principle I rejected the notion, considering my source, but no matter how wrong he'd gotten it, could the poor fool have missed the point that completely?

My situation annoyed me throughout the following day. Here I was, on the opposite side of the planet, while Langley released his extravaganza—without my being in the thick of things—and possibly damaged his career. A regrettable outcome, if it happened without my wise and pertinent comments. I refused to speculate until I learned more, but the time passed slowly, and I wasn't in the mood for fun and games. Even Clarisse couldn't cheer me up. When the afternoon paper came I sent her away, for I read a small item which further got under my skin in the worst way. I had misjudged the man. I didn't know Chockinaw had it in him—I didn't know he had anything in him—and a mild clutch of guilt seized me as I realized how disturbed he must have been. Last night, shortly after I left him, Chockinaw had hanged himself.

The materials I'd sent for arrived. The newspaper references were sparse and unrevealing. They established that *Cosmic Kaleidoscope* existed. The latest issue of *Evocative* contained one long paragraph on the subject, in which the glib, anonymous editorialist seemed to be struggling mightily to write around the painting, without quite coming to grips with what it objectively conveyed. He wrote nothing that corresponded to Chockinaw's lewd description, but he didn't offer much else, either. He did have this to say:

"We hope that Terrible Terrill hasn't run off the rails with this one. Always a fantasist and explorer of dark themes, this time he attempts to merely disgust his audience, rather than awaken honest, if suppressed, feeling. Also, he abandons even the pretense of realism. All art, no matter how outré, must be grounded in reality, in the true experience of humanity. It remains to be seen whether this complex and striking painting, however brilliant its execution, meets this bedrock definition of art." And thanks for nothing, I thought, whoever you are.

It wouldn't serve my interests to remain in France. I had to be at the scene of the action. A few calls, a few apologies—good luck, Clarisse—and this not so old man went west, in a hurry, on the next available flight. I landed in California whenever, and once back in the groove everything turned strange.

The Radetsky was closed this day. I phoned Langley, without success. No matter; I'd follow up with him later. I called Hoskins, who tended to make sense in the best of times, but he told me nothing. He refused to discuss the painting. He sounded angry. I didn't pester him. I tried to contact Morton, another straight shooter, but only reached his wife, who informed me that he was late—as in the late Morton—my colleague was dead. She didn't tell me how it happened, and I didn't press, but I gathered that it was a recent and sudden occurrence.

Whatever in hell was going on, it certainly wasn't a happy time for my gang. Now I called Winslow. He wanted to talk, he was glad to talk. His voice quavered. He said something odd over the telephone—"It doesn't always pay to think too deeply"—then invited himself to my home for an extended session. He appeared, looking worn, more nervous than I remembered him. We commiserated the losses of Chockinaw and Morton. Concerning the latter, he would only say: "If he had to do it, why did he do it that way?"

He gave me his impressions of Langley's painting, and he showed me something. It was a photograph of the picture he'd snapped for a feature, which he now declined to write. I looked at it. Taken from a moderate distance (not too close; against the rules of the salon), it captured the familiar wall of honor, with the harshly framed oil as the centerpiece. I glanced up at Winslow, mystified. He shook his head in sympathy. The photo revealed nothing. I saw an oblong of inky darkness, a sheer black canvas. I could not discern a hint of detail. He verified my unwilling suspicion that this wasn't an accurate image. Somehow, through some kind of unprecedented lighting effect, the camera had entirely failed to carry out its function.

As stated, he gave me his impressions—he described the painting at consummate, professional length—but at first all I could think was how dissimilar his version was from that of Chockinaw. A little of it harked back to the generalities I'd heard, the bits about confusion and disorder, but after that Winslow might as well have been telling me about a different picture. According to him, there was nothing overtly or suggestively sexual about it.

"In retrospect, I can't guarantee you that I viewed the entire painting. Perhaps I missed something. I don't think so. If anything, I saw too much. Such a large canvas, so many elements intertwined, themes flowing like rivers—the magnitude of it all!—I could have overlooked this or that portion. I'm convinced that I took in its essence, and that's enough. *Cosmic Kaleidoscope* is a ghastly work, the most intensely vile production I've seen or heard about. It's evil. Yes, that's what I mean. We must create a new category, Evil Art, in order to understand Langley's intention. Talking about it gives me the creeps. When I saw it, I felt as if he had painted it solely for my benefit, that it spoke directly to me and only me. It wasn't a picture, an object, before me, but images in my mind, images of forgotten nightmares and forbidden memories. He can't portray men accurately to save his life— he stopped trying years ago—but that doesn't matter in this case, because now he invents monsters. A fine hand he's got for it, and superb technique. I grant him this: he's mastered the medium. He paints monsters. I look here, I look there, they're springing out at me, those creatures. I believe they were grouped around some central figure, an uncongealed shape in the background. I didn't think about that until later, so I only recall a fleeting suggestion of looming shape in . . . yes, in dreary, filthy circumstances. There was a lot of dirt. Raggedly clothed shapes stood or crouched up to their skinny ankles in mud. The creatures crowded around, as if worshipping the central monstrosity. I see them as in life, right down to the straggly hairs on their arms; those that had arms. Some resembled the medical freaks I saw a long time ago in an old book. They were relatively easy to view. There were things that might once have been human, but had decayed to an extent incompatible with their apparent liveliness. Other things might pass for human at a distance—or in a dark alley, sneaking up behind you—but their faces gave them away. No human soul animated those faces; none ever had. Mixed in among them were still others, twisted fantasies of horror, which looked like nothing in this or any sane world. Anything faintly human would have recoiled from them in panic, yet they seemed to be the leaders of the pack. Others deferred to them. All of them were hideous. I couldn't stand their touch when they crawled on me."

"Winslow, look at me. They didn't do that."

17

"So you say. You're right, but I was there. They came out onto me, they got inside me, they became part of me. They wanted me to join them. For one terrible, sickening moment, I considered it."

As he left I had to ask: "You won't do anything rash, will you?"

"No", he replied, after a long breath, "I won't. I wouldn't think of it. I'm not that type, thank God. Thank God I'm not that type. I 'd never have the guts to do it on my own." Thus spake Winslow.

I hunted through back issues of the morning *Examiner* until I found an account of Morton's death. Stale journalistic language, carefully sanitized; and yet, what I read so revolted me that I couldn't finish the story. Nobody did it that way.

I now had access to all of my local channels of artistic information, and I tried to get a better understanding of *Cosmic Kaleidoscope* from the mass of reviews. I gained little from the effort. They were just more of the same. No one seemed quite sure how to deal with the picture, although none of them were quite willing to admit it. The thin descriptions varied to an extraordinary degree. Each reviewer, I concluded, felt uncomfortable with his task. I read no especially harsh critiques—certainly nothing like I'd heard from Chockinaw and Winslow—but I sensed that all wasn't well in the Langley fan club. They might bend over backward to avoid saying it, but these guys simply didn't like the painting.

Word spreads fast in my circles. Within twenty-four hours Langley telephoned. He welcomed me back, boasted of achieving his goal, and apologized with mock contriteness for opening the show without me. Once done, he hadn't been able to bear the thought of holding off the exhibit for a minute. He sounded triumphant, also tired and edgy, and confessed to exhaustion. He planned to get away for a while, leave town, commune with trees in the north country until the furor subsided. Then he would return to reap the rewards.

I commented on what I'd been hearing, without specifically mentioning the freaky stuff. That drew a sarcastic laugh from him. He argued that it wasn't a problem of personal interpretation. The human brain, he pointed out, hadn't evolved to perceive hypernormal reality. It stood to reason that an artwork incorporating such principles would be seen askew. In transmitting the visual data, neurons might misfire, which with some individuals could upset the electro-chemical basis of the mind. Their subjective experiences, drawing upon their ingrained mental templates, might upset them. Weak types, or the excessively analytical, had better keep their distance.

Cunningly I asked him to describe the picture—in his own words, which I could publish—no go. What, then, did the title signify? He didn't bite. I really must see it for myself. View it with an open mind, but maybe not too open. Don't get in a tizzy over it; it's just a painting. Remember that.

He hadn't heard about Chockinaw. No great loss, Langley said. What of Morton? Most unfortunate, Langley said. He must run. He didn't know how long he'd be gone. I'd hear from him when he returned; sorry to have missed me.

Lousy timing, that. Of course I ought to see the thing before I fussed more about it. Here, however, is a marvel: in the days to come I discovered various excellent reasons for not visiting the Radetsky. The salon was too far—all the way across town—and I couldn't spare the time; I had a hefty backlog of work (I can't recall what); I had to catch up on my correspondence. The latter took a while, for I had plenty, and I dragged out the process of perusal and response. I remained alert for more reports, but nothing new appeared. It was my mail that got the ball rolling again, as eventually I came upon a curious letter which bore directly on the matter of Langley's painting.

It had arrived without return address on the envelope or the single hand-written, closely scrawled page inside. The writer identified himself at the top of the sheet as one Anton Vorchek, professor. The name meant nothing to me, but he knew of me and, so he seemed to think, of my current concern. I transcribe the body of his letter, which I have with me still, in its entirety:

> I have recently enjoyed the public display of the new painting *Cosmic Kaleidoscope* by the artist Terrill Langley. My examination of the relevant literature reveals that you have written more about him and his work than any of your peers. I presume that indicates uncommon interest on your part, for that is my justification for writing to you. I have already noticed that the work generates unusual reactions from viewers. It had an extraordinary effect on me. I must take the liberty of telling you why. It is fair to admit up front that I do not count myself as an expert on art. My expertise extends to other, esoteric realms, and on account of this my explanation shall partake of the purely scientific.
>
> This is the only work of art I know which may be evaluated according to a rationalistic yardstick. From the first glance I deduced, not artistic skill—of which I know little, unfortunately—but mathematical brilliance. I find no reference to this talent in any publication on Mr. Langley, including your own, but it must be so. The painting reeks of number. I admired the interplay of the carefully ordered planes and angles. So much did I admire that I risked, while no one observed, measuring some of them with a tape which

SCIENCE AND SORCERY III

I always carry. Among the complex facets I discovered calculated mathematical concepts; for example, *pi*, Angstrom's and Avogadro's numbers, even the Celician Helix. The appearance of the Helix mystified me, for it implies a daring course of study I would expect only from a dedicated researcher into old and forbidden subjects. At any rate, the result is that the separate pieces of the picture (or puzzle!) fit together to create an escalating series of images, sliding, clashing, weaving into one another in an apparently chaotic, but actually well-orchestrated fashion. The painting is aptly titled, in more ways than one. The faceted images appear to change depending upon the angle of view. As in mathematics, alter one factor and the entire equation alters. The trick, in this case, is to find the right angle from which the totality of the grand design may be perceived.

I accomplished this, but not via standard math. The Helix was my clue. Mr. Langley has intruded an element of hyper-normal dimensionality into his painting. Surely this must be deliberate. The odds against a chance occurrence of this kind are . . . shall I say, literally cosmic? I hope to learn, one of these days, how he did it. He may possess useful knowledge. That young man is a true pioneer, in his field, and in mine.

Having determined the special qualities of the painting, the tremendous moment of realization unfolded. I saw, with the eyes in my head, the surface planar structure of the images begin to warp and curve as I gazed into the abyss of the hyper-dimension. The true picture flashed out at me: a vast, ghostly spiral, like a distant galaxy, only containing no particulate matter, but rather composed of a shimmering, homogenous substance. The spiral caught the light of the exhibit hall and appeared to pulsate at meaningful intervals. I describe a painting, and yet I can not speak of the image in static terms. I sensed that the spiral rotated about its axis, so fast that its motion was subliminal. There was a nervous energy suggestive of rapid movement. This continued, perhaps accelerated, until I detected a hint of form developing from the glowing central mass. A globular shape, perfectly round, with something in the center—another, smaller globe, darker—I examined this focal point closely. Then I knew. An eye staring into mine, an enormous, all seeing eye, peering out of impossible cosmic depths directly into and through the vibrating matter of our trivial universe. The great eye of Xenophor, which no man may behold; the awesome, soul-incinerating eye of the Ultimate Master, the Creator and Destroyer; this I beheld!

At last I have looked upon His face, as I always dreamed. I shall withdraw, hopefully into safe obscurity, with the lingering remembrance. Your artist should be made aware that unforeseen consequences may ensue from exposure to stark meta-reality. That which is gazed upon may gaze back in return. The dominant force that hungers in the eternal night may choose to take unto Itself that which dares to draw Its attention. If, incredibly, Mr. Langley lacks understanding, then all may be well. Otherwise, the fates may deal harshly with him. I envy him. I pray that he does not deserve my pity.

Forgive the unsolicited communication. The craving to write overwhelms. Best wishes to you and yours.

Sincerely,

VORCHEK

Say what you will: a crank, the maddest of hatters, a candidate for medical incarceration; and yet the epistle of Professor Vorchek frightened me. Sure, I couldn't figure out half of what he wrote, and I disbelieved—wanted to disbelieve—the other half, but the contents of his letter struck me with eerie familiarity. A lot of it sounded like statements Langley had made to me in the past. Perhaps neither of them knew what they were talking about, but they were certainly on the same wavelength. And what of the professor's fantastic description of the painting? Another independent report, similar in some ways to what I'd previously heard, strikingly different in others. Something incredible was happening.

I had to nerve myself to the decision, but a morning came when I found myself entering the Radetsky Salon, promptly at opening hour, determined to view Langley's painting for myself. Once again my timing was bad (and thinking back on it, I have no regrets), for it turned out that the big opportunity had passed. Without prior notice the Radetsky had canceled the exhibition. I didn't realize that at first. I checked in the main hall, where I expected to confront the thing, and then in the ancillary galleries, without success. The handful of patrons present didn't gather in front of any one picture in particular. Signs told me nothing, and I definitely didn't observe anything out of the common way. When I finally stooped to speaking with a docent, however, I got an earful.

"*Cosmic Kaleidoscope*? The Langley piece? That's off. We're getting rid of it. It's been taken down, and he can claim it whenever it suits him. We've had too much trouble with that one; the picture, I mean." Nobody cared for it, she said. There had been bizarre episodes—unpleasant scenes— associated with the painting. People didn't behave themselves in its proximity. They, the management, weren't going to stand for that. This was a high class establishment.

So they still had it on the premises? Yes, but not prepared for public view. It was already packed for shipping, and they really couldn't be troubled . . . Well, I threw my weight around. I insisted on seeing the man in charge, whom I knew to talk to, emphasized Who I Was, and he grudgingly gave way. Still advising against it (with an air of genuine concern, I thought), he led me into the cluttered basement workshop, indicated the offending item among the artist's tools and more kindly regarded canvases, and then, unexpectedly, left me alone with it.

It wasn't boxed, but they'd wrapped the painting in heavy burlap and tied it tight. I used a sharp implement to cut both cords, and began working the burlap back from a fold at the top left-hand corner. The multi-layered wrapping didn't reveal its secrets easily, but I finally got off enough to uncover the end of the ugly frame—dull, unadorned metal—and a portion of the picture the size of an 8 ½ by 11 page. The lighting in that subterranean room wasn't up to exhibition quality, but I had no difficulty viewing the painted surface.

It takes longer to write the words than to live the experience. What happened next lasted maybe two seconds, five, ten. Keep in mind that I'm only seeing a small sampling of the whole. I observe a multitudinous swarm of tiny, immediately indecipherable shapes, painstakingly figured into a jet background. The ground appears featureless, but just for a moment I sense something deep within it as well. With my focus removed from the foreground forms, I'm strangely able to make out more clearly what they are, or seem to be for a brief moment. People, or hunks of anatomy—I see arms, legs, heads, all the parts—but no definite impression of natural combination. They swim in liquid; no, a thick, sluggish gel, through which they struggle. Every mouth is opened wide, crying out. Oh, but initial error undercuts my analysis. I've missed the point. These details must be imagination, for I begin to discern a broader image cleverly constructed upon them. Taken together, they compose a shape which fills the corner of canvas: a white, greasy, doughy face, unlined, infantile or fetal, with blank, fishy eyes. The loathsome face thrusts itself into my own—

I dropped the flap of burlap. The tenacious image remained in my mind, even after I exited the room and hurriedly departed the Radetsky. You will ask, why didn't I look at the rest? What right have I to speak, on the basis of a partial view? I can ask myself that now. It didn't matter to me then; I couldn't have made myself look at the rest, not for a king's ransom. Langley's painting terrified me. There was more to the moment than my eyes had recorded. Something within the image had touched unfathomable recesses of my mind, grim and alien places I had no wish to explore. I shivered and sweated until I got home, and it required several stiff drinks to restore my composure.

What happened to me had happened to others, with greater intensity. Perhaps no one could view the thing with indifference, or—can I say this?—with their sanity entirely intact. Men destroyed themselves on the basis of what they saw in or learned from Langley's painting. I didn't, but hateful dreams plagued me (and, irregularly, continue to do so). The artist had achieved something unprecedented; he had captured in oils a representation of a primal power with which we may co-exist happily only so long as it is hidden from our sight.

Langley returned. Not knowing his whereabouts, I had been phoning at intervals, fruitlessly, and then he answered. His voice put me on my guard. He sounded bad. I guessed that the holiday hadn't helped, but it was more than exhaustion I was hearing. This parody of his normal tenor contained anger, nervous irritation, and panic. His manner cut short the customary niceties. I told him I'd seen the painting, and had to discuss it with him. He indicated little interest in the subject. I brought him up to date, as he obviously didn't know, on what had become of the showing at the Radetsky. He couldn't care less. Did he plan to collect the piece? No, he didn't want it near him. They could burn it with his blessing. I insisted on arranging a meeting. I'd come to his place and kick down the door if he didn't cooperate. He fought, but my obstinacy beat him down. He relented. I could come by. However: "I have to know it's really you. Identify yourself so there's no mistake. If you don't, I won't let you in."

In a pensive frame of mind I set out for my penultimate conversation with Langley, and the last time I ever saw him in the flesh. I knocked at his door and loudly called out my name. It required several attempts before I got results. After a pause I heard locks tumbling and jingling. The door opened, and the tenant quickly ushered me in. There stood Langley; or, more accurately, there cringed Langley. He resembled an inmate of Oswiegan. Before he apologized for his appearance and explained, I knew he hadn't been eating or sleeping. This was human wreckage, not the proud and arrogant man who'd amused and baffled me for years. The interior of his apartment complemented his condition. I saw unkempt squalor, with no visible trace of books, papers, or artistic materials. After the barest formalities he motioned me to a chair, threw himself down on the sofa, and began to speak in earnest.

"I knew it would hit some people hard. *Cosmic Kaleidoscope* was meant to shock. A public display of ultimate reality must stagger the limited mental capacities most employ to orient themselves to the universe. They would be tempted to cram the images into their own subjective conceptual frameworks, with unpredictable consequences. I expected that. I welcomed it, but please don't think evil of me. My intentions were pure. I believed that my visual revelations would benefit mankind. 'Ye shall know the truth, and the truth shall set you free.' Isn't that the bill of goods we've been sold by every major thinker in history? I took it seriously, and through my chosen medium of expression tried to relate that truth.

"I told you all the technical stuff before, but I could have put it to you differently. I desired to behold the face of God, and to show that face to the world. It's there, underlying all things, always, and every intelligent man has craved just that one fleeting glimpse, if only to assure himself that life makes sense and has purpose. I eventually arrived at this understanding, through my studies, of the need within me. Who was I to know that the burning bush blazes too hot, and too brightly?

"I didn't run away. From my standpoint, everything was fine when I left. I rented a cabin by a creek among the redwoods and took it easy, as contented as a baby. I'd kill time leisurely while the painting did its work, and return to applause and acclaim. It was after I found solitude—after I disconnected myself from trivialities, alone with my thoughts—that the disturbing influences crept through.

"They didn't bother me while I was preparing the piece. Maybe my passion drowned out the discordant notes. Maybe they hadn't started then. Now . . . it began with the nightmares. In sleep the force penetrated my brain. I would sense an *awareness*, a vague ghost of consciousness, which seemed to turn in my direction out of an infinite distance. A spotlight of thought, barely visible, focused upon me and grew brighter. I felt that it was searching for me, probing across the dimensional gulfs. Every time this happened it came nearer, and grew more oppressive. A sensation of weight beat down on me, accompanied by a rhythmic throbbing like a vast machine in relentless operation. Sleep became a chore. Slumber brought no rest.

"Soon I fancied that I could hear the pulsing during waking hours. Before long I knew it wasn't fancy. The sound—but it wasn't; I stopped my ears, and it didn't make any difference—the sound took on the characteristics of a humming, strumming voice. Something was speaking to me, or I overheard it speaking to itself, whichever might be the case. It wasn't language of a kind I could recognize, but it was speech, and at some level I understood it. The encroaching presence was talking about me."

At this point I felt a subject had to be raised, although my heart wasn't in it. I suggested the possibility of overwork, stress, emotional adjustments. He violently rejected the notion, as I knew he would, and went on, now almost in tears.

"All this was bad enough, but I first felt doom when I began to see things. This phase commenced with a rearrangement of visual data. Common combinations of optical input would momentarily assume unusual forms, there and gone again, then popping out somewhere else. It happened in everything. The angles of the walls and ceiling, a picturesque clump of trees, the pattern of white water flowing over blue stones, changed. I know why. In flashes I saw their hyper-dimensional aspects. I was beginning to think and see in those terms, without trying. Either I had trained myself too well, or something was forcing the expanded view upon me.

"I'm pretty sure the latter explanation is correct, considering what happened next. In the same sporadic fashion, coming at me so suddenly and for such short duration that I tried to ignore them, I began to detect minor *intrusions* upon the normal visual scheme. A tiny pinhole of extraneous light would open up within a scene, and it would grow, encroaching upon my vision. Have you ever heard of the migraine illusion? It's commonly associated with that affliction. I've suffered from migraines since childhood, and I've come to recognize that strange, shimmering speck of radiance which travels with the turn of the eye. I've fantasized about its deeper meanings, if any. Well, this was a lot like that, only the image didn't move with my eyes. The light grew out of a specific spot in space. I could look away and avoid it, but when I looked back it would still be there, only larger. Eventually it would vanish. However, it returned with greater frequency, and stayed longer. Soon it formed a veritable hole in the landscape, through which I could discern hints of hypnotic form and motion.

"Accept this: a gap was developing between our dimension and that other. In a way, that is what I set out to do with *Cosmic Kaleidoscope*, to break down the barriers and see across to the far side, in a controlled manner. Now it started happening unbidden, and it never entirely goes away anymore. As I speak to you, I'm aware of splinters and shards of unearthly light and indefinable shapes just beyond your right shoulder. I can look through, only because something on the other side is looking through at me! It's found me, and it's studying me, and when it's finished the examination it will come."

Here I interjected a comment with untoward results. What he was saying recalled to mind the odd letter of Professor Vorchek. My mysterious correspondent had written a peculiar word—a name—which meant nothing to me. I spoke this word to Langley.

"Heavens, no!" he shrieked, in paroxysms of terror. He ground his face against the backrest of the sofa. "Not that! Never speak that word! I struggle every minute to keep it out of my mind. I don't dare say it aloud! I pushed the door ajar, just to snatch a peek, and He forces it open and strides through. He beckons, and He demands. I refuse. Better death a thousand times over than eternity with Him. Don't you understand that my only hope is to render myself invisible? If I can sink my mind low enough, banish all telling thought, then I might escape. He may deem me insignificant in His sight. That is my only chance."

No more of a coherent nature could I gain from him. I advised him to get out and mingle with people—which I do think could have ameliorated his condition—but he wouldn't do it. He bade me leave, and made clear that future visits would be discouraged. I begged him promise that he would telephone me, at any time, if he needed help. He didn't sound interested.

There is very little more. You already know how the tale of Terrill Langley and his painting concludes. I never saw him again. I did hear from him once more. He called, on what I came to realize was the last night. I wish I could report another thrilling conversation, but there wasn't much to it. It mainly consisted of desperate, hopeless queries for information on my part. I knew the voice right away, even though he was screaming. There were other sounds, waves of noises reaching a crescendo over his shouts, but I couldn't identify them. I determined that he wasn't alone, that a visitation of some kind had taken place. All his precautions had been in vain. He said, if I heard him rightly, "The translation begins. Pray for my soul." He said something more that I couldn't catch, and then silence. There just wasn't any connection at all.

I contacted the authorities, who had already been informed by Langley's neighbors. They heard it all, more than I did, but they couldn't tell the police anything more useful than I. Several people, as it happened, were able to speak of his shy, furtive behavior since returning home in the days before the end. A number of them deduced or guessed that he was afraid of someone. I was willing to say that much, but no further in my account would I go. I don't expect that my additional input would have been appreciated. Nothing the police took down could aid them in explaining what they found, and didn't find, inside his apartment.

What became of the painting, you ask? I have it. The Radetsky tried to unload it, but without diligence, and there were no buyers. It would interest me to know the specifics of those sales sessions. I agreed to assume responsibility for it—acting as a kind of informal executor—until final disposition could be made. I don't know when that will be. Langley's painting resides in the back of a closet, a big walk-in affair, where the picture stands on its end against the wall, still wrapped and tied in burlap. Suits hang on racks, obscuring the package. I've never had it out, and I'm not sure that I ever will. As time passes, perhaps I shall wonder more and fear less. Perhaps I shall untie the strings and unpeel the wrapping, ever so carefully, if only to catch another glimpse of that marvelous painting.

Most likely, not.

OFFICE CONSULTATION

Good morning Mr.—Smith, is it?—John Smith. I'm glad to see you. From reading my records, I gather it's been a while since your last check-up. How are you doing today?

Not very well, I'm afraid, Dr. Cadwallader. That's why I asked for this appointment, you see. I'm pleased that you could see me at such short notice.

No trouble, I assure you. Happy to oblige. Now, what seems to be your problem?

It's difficult to explain. To put it in a nutshell, I'm increasingly unable to come to grips with being.

Indeed? Mr. Smith—John—John, why don't you sit up on the table, and I will check you out. Let me see. Your eyes look fine—your ears—yes, looking good. Open, if you will—ah—well, nothing in there that isn't supposed to be. Bear with me a moment—pulse appears normal—unbutton your shirt, please—all right, your heart sounds steady. Being, you say? Being what?

It's the general principle of being which troubles me, Doctor. Being me. Being anything. The more I think of it, the less I can fathom it, and it scares me.

At times we all have such concerns. I wouldn't let it bother me, if I were you.

But "being" is the central fact of my life. It is important.

I suppose so—

Dr. Cadwallader, I'm concerned that this may be developing into a serious life issue for me, and therefore a medical issue. You see, I read this book on probabilities, and it suddenly occurred to me just how improbable I am; how unlikely is the fact of my existence. Here is this boundless, eternal universe, with all of these stars and planets and trees and things—none of which have anything to do with me—and yet here I am, the product of a chaotic, meaningless genetic heritage, the terminus of an age-old, ongoing game of cosmic chance. I try to put all of the factors together, in order to understand my being, to make sense of the fact, but I simply can't do it. As a matter of probability, I shouldn't exist. The odds against it are astronomical.

And yet, John, you are here.

But am I, Doctor? I am an organic creature which eats other organic substances, breathes oxygen, requires liquid water (which presupposes an acceptable temperature range), light for seeing, eyes to collect the light, a sun to provide it, which can't be too close or too far away; and a thousand other details which are just so, and which must be just so if I am to exist, much less survive to talk about it. Not very likely, wouldn't you say?

What you're arguing applies to all of us, to everything.

I don't have time to discuss everybody's problems. Doctor, I have attempted to calculate the possibility of my existence. I'm not very good at this, but I've come up with some rough estimates. The numbers aren't too impressive.

I guess they wouldn't be, John, if you approach the problem that way. Still, the unusual does occur.

Not to me. My life is excruciatingly dull and uneventful. I've a bland, milquetoast personality. There isn't much to me in the best of times. No, Doctor, something is wrong. I worked out the betting odds. Do you gamble?

Whenever I get the opportunity.

I don't, and I certainly would never accept a bet like this one. The odds against me run past the trillions, the quadrillions, into numbers I don't even know to exist. If the numbers don't exist, what chance have I got?

As long as you've got your health—

I don't know that I do. I don't know that I have anything, or am anything. Let's stick with the gambling analogy for a moment. At the casino a man may play against the odds for a time, and even be fabulously successful at it. He may experience a winning streak. However, in the end the laws of chance always catch up with him. If he doesn't get up and walk away from the table in time, he loses. He may lose everything. Do you follow me, Doctor?

Of course, John. In life, though, we all eventually lose.

You mean die. I'm not talking about that. That's comparable to leaving the table. Forget that. I'm talking about losing the game because the odds against you pile up too high. Sooner or later, chance must be balanced. When that point is reached, what will happen to me?

Nothing will happen.

But it must, you see. If every fiber of my being is composed of energy wavelengths—as the best scientists assure us—and the actuality of those wavelengths are determined by quantum probabilities—surely you know that . . .

I'll take your word for it.

Then, Doctor, when the odds begin to run too heavily against me, I'll start to go. That is what's happening to me now.

On what basis do you deduce that?

That's the proper question, Doctor. Ever since I first began reading up on this problem, the signs of my coming nonexistence have been multiplying. The pattern commenced with little things, not so different from past experience. People started to notice me even less than usual. They paid even less attention to what I said, or acted, for a second, as if they didn't know me. Then it got worse.

How so?

My landlady showed my apartment to a young couple, to whom she intended to let it. She forgot I was there!

A mistake, John.

At work—I'm employed at a small real estate office—a new man was assigned my desk. They forgot it was mine!

They placed him there by accident.

So you say, Doctor. Listen to this. Only yesterday the electricity was cut off in my apartment. I called the utility company. They didn't know what I was talking about.

The curse of bureaucracy—

And my phone is disconnected. It isn't listed in the phone book. I never had an unlisted number. It isn't that. My connection to the world—my role within it—is disappearing.

There must be alternative explanations.

I know the explanation. I need help, and fast. Doctor, just this morning I went to work, like I always do. I got there early. Others began to arrive. They didn't know me. They asked why I was there. My desk was gone—the configuration of desks had changed—there was no space in that office for my desk. As far as they knew, there never had been. I left there, called you, and came straight over.

All right, John, I grant that it sounds like a troubling situation. We must do something.

I'm so happy to hear that.

Next door is a colleague of mine, an eminent man, a specialist. I'm going to ask him to join us for a little talk.

What sort of specialist?

Well . . . a mental specialist.

SCIENCE AND SORCERY III

No! Doctor Cadwallader, I'm not insane. These things are really happening to me. I'm about to cease!

I'm not referring to insanity on your part—your part—John, John, yes, that's right, John Smith. Catchy name... John, he is an authority on various weighty concerns. A talk with him would do you good. He may be able to help us work through your syndrome.

I don't see how. Okay. I'll talk to him, if you think it's any use. You're going to fetch him now?

Right now.

I have one small favor to ask. May I come with you?

That won't be necessary—

I'm terrified of being left alone, Doctor. I can feel my time running out, but I keep thinking it won't happen as long as I have people around.

I must speak to him privately. Don't worry. His office is just on the other side of this wall. Look: I'm stepping out into the hall now. Give me thirty seconds, and I'll bring him back with me.

Please hurry.

. . .

Well, Roger, here is the fellow I wanted you to meet. Mr.—Mr.—why, where did he go?

Too bad, Bob; looks like your patient ducked out on you.

How could he have passed us? There's no other way out of this room, and we would have seen him.

Never mind. What did he want, anyway?

What did who want?

Wasn't there someone . . . no, I suppose not. Bob, you asked me to your office for some reason.

So I did. What was on my mind? Something important, I thought. I—oh, yes, I know. I was thinking: since I have no appointments this hour, and you don't seem busy, we might do lunch.

Let's do.

NIGHT FLIGHT

Glen Fallow arrived at the airport in what he hoped was a sufficiency of time, parked his car in the expensive garage, checked in his single bag, collected his boarding pass and dashed for the gate. He thought himself lucky to have caught a flight at such short notice, even one scheduled for the middle of the night; this promising business proposition had cropped up out of the blue, and as much as it discomfited him and disarranged his evening plans, he couldn't bring himself to pass it up. It was a big deal by his standards, and however well it might actually pay off, it couldn't do his finances any harm.

He noted that the terminal wasn't so busy at this time of night. All the better; no fear, perhaps, of being bumped or irretrievably delayed. It still took a ridiculously long spell to wend his way through the tedium and effrontery of security, and by this time Fallow was counting the minutes. They fussed about everything: his belt buckle, his fountain pen, his bottle of cough medicine. They insisted he sip the medicine. Well, he was due for that anyway. Then, with a shrug on their part, he was clear, walking quickly, and reached the gate presently. Only a handful of people were standing around or sitting there, and boarding hadn't yet commenced. As he walked up an official appeared and started processing the passengers. That was perfect timing.

Within a couple of minutes he had taken his seat, by the window. Fallow didn't look forward to the trip. It would be a long flight, and he was traveling coach. He had paid extra in order to ensure that he got fed properly. Everything cost extra with the airlines these days. Also—this could be helpful—he had booked himself onto one of those wide-bodied, double-aisled airliners. There was a screen not far before him, on the bulkhead between the aisles, for an in-flight movie, so maybe it wouldn't be too bad. He might even catch a wink of sleep, which he badly needed.

31

SCIENCE AND SORCERY III

A few late-comers trundled in with their on-board luggage, and then the still small number of passengers were advised by the frumpy flight attendant to buckle up. Flight attendant; there was a tiresome phrase which suggested more than it was meant to do. Fallow remembered the old days, when air travelers were graced with pretty stewardesses. Those were the good days. Those days were a long time ago, back when he could always afford to go first class, and when he expected to be happily retired by now. It hadn't worked out that way. He still had to earn a living, even though he didn't feel so well any more. Nowadays he fretted about his health a lot, yet he had to keep going. Too bad for him.

Engines hummed, raced, the body of the plane heaved. Then it began to roll. In the darkness, punctuated by countless bright spotlights, the plane taxied across anonymous concrete to a darker region, then did nothing for a spell. Soon it began to roll again, faster and faster, and presently Fallow felt the elevator sensation of take-off. Somewhat later a casual voice announced itself as the captain, and thoughtfully explained that the ship was in the air and on the way.

Fallow watched the lights of the city as they swept out from under him and dwindled. After that he saw only a small number of isolated glows below, and even fewer in the sky, the brightest stars which could barely be glimpsed through the thick safety glass. Now there was nothing for him to do. He wished that he had thought to carry his reports and other relevant papers with him, instead of packing them away. He had been in too much of a hurry to think of it. He didn't need to look at them, anyway. Morning preparation over breakfast, when he reached his destination, would bring him up to speed.

The movie came on, which he could listen to with headphones. He put them on. As it happened, the film was a reasonably current theatrical release, rather popular in some quarters, but not his cup of tea. He didn't have much use for new movies. Their stories and styles tended to be crude, and the modern crop of actors were too coarse for his tastes. He watched the thing aimlessly, for a while, and then wearily removed the headphones. He noticed that most of his fellows were watching the picture with the appearance of interest.

He flipped through the magazines in the back pocket of the seat in front of him. There wasn't much to them. They mainly dealt with travel prospects to places he was never likely to go, although in some cases he might have wished to do so. In his entire life he had, not once, ever taken a long trip for pleasure, and the short trips had been few and far between. One of these days he ought to bite the bullet and treat himself. One of these days . . .

Had he dozed? He didn't think so; nothing in his surroundings had obviously changed. The movie seemed close to its conclusion, which surprised him. Perhaps it wasn't very long. Something was different. He felt out of sorts, as if something had gone wrong in his life or situation. It wouldn't be the first time he'd thought that, but it struck him more forcefully now. It might be that such a long, quiet trip provided him with too much opportunity to think. He must remember to avoid late night flights in the future.

The film did end, its credits scrolling interminably. Shouldn't the meal be due by now? Some of his fellow travelers were nodding off already. He wondered if the airline held off as long as possible, a clever savings measure. They charged for food, but didn't have to feed the sleepers. Pretty smart of them, if so; Fallow's eyes felt heavy. He closed them. A short relaxation would do him good.

He opened his eyes. This time he sensed that considerable time had passed. He had slept, without deriving much by way of refreshment. He glanced out the window. A few sparkles above and below, otherwise nothing. Another movie was running. He didn't pay attention at first, but soon certain strange features of this item drew him.

This wasn't a new movie at all. Whoever chose these things must be scraping the bottom of the barrel, on the dubious assumption that no one would care at this hour of the night. Judging from its cinematic style, and the clothing and hair styles of the actors, this picture must be several years old, dating, he would guess, to the early 'Sixties. It was a color film, but age had treated it badly. Whoever picked it had grabbed hold of a poor copy. The color looked washed out, and the images looked cruelly used. Everything appeared too dark. There was lots of dirt and hair on the picture, and numerous rough jumps or bad splices. He couldn't figure out anything concerning the plot from staring at the screen. A conventional hero, a pretty girl with big hair, and an older bearded guy were engaged in exaggerated conversation. Large, shiny machines loomed behind them. It might be a laboratory, Hollywood fashion, which could indicate a kind of cheap science fiction story.

If so, Fallow wasn't familiar with this one, and he knew a few. As he watched, he began to realize what a peculiar movie it was. The acting was terrible. Did somebody pay these people? They stood there like puppets and moved their mouths, seemingly at random. He surely couldn't read their lips, not with those odd, wagging motions of their lower jaws. Their eyes appeared to stare at nothing. They held their bodies rigid. It gave him the creeps.

The scene flickered messily, then changed. Now the man and the girl were driving in a rear-projected car, through drab desert scenery. They spoke excitedly, mouths flapping like rubber. Were they puppets? No, of course not, but in certain respects they didn't look real. He supposed that the awful film quality was fooling him. That had to be it. Now they were climbing into a prop plane and roaring off of a landing strip surrounded by a barbed-wire fence and official warning signs: No Trespassing. It must be government. Fallow slipped on his headphones.

The picture was lousy; the audio was worse. He could scarcely decipher their garbled, continuous conversation. This didn't appear to be a foreign film, but he wondered if the soundtrack was off kilter. He knew they were speaking English, but knowing that didn't help him much at all. They seemed to be talking about people or beings known as the "Bursters," who must be pretty rough customers. Fallow guessed that they were alien invaders of a particularly horrid sort. Another aircraft, which didn't appear to be a plane, flashed by, and then chaos broke loose. Colored lights flooded the scene, and the plane began to spiral out of control. The girl pointed at the attacker, her arm stiff as a board. No, she wasn't real, nor could the others be. They were realistic mannequins, or animated dead people. What a sickening thought! And yet, having occurred to him, it seemed frightfully accurate. These actors moved as if their fleshy frames were directed from outside themselves. The weight of their limbs even seemed to resist movement. This was more than poor acting; it was film style conceived by a lunatic. Why would anybody make a movie like this?

The bearded man reappeared, only to burst. He blew up with a jarring popping sound, and fake green goo spouted from his mouth. He thrashed like a dying fish on a line. The other characters responded weirdly, slumping on stiff spines as if propped up from behind. The hero cursed the Bursters. Fallow removed his headphones. He'd had enough of this. The show bugged him. He ought to demand part of his ticket money back, just to let somebody know how he felt. Speaking of which, he felt awful. The movie had made him sick. He did his best to direct his attention elsewhere, and before he knew it the movie had come to an end. Rather abruptly, so he thought, the final credits appeared—merely a title card, "The End," and the screen went black.

He caught the eye of a fellow across the aisle, one of the few passengers still obviously awake. Fallow jocularly alluded to the film which had just concluded. The man hadn't been paying attention, so didn't get the joke. Oh well . . .

Fallow nodded again. The act of awakening informed him that he had slept, for this time he felt no sense of passed time. It was as if the lights had flickered momentarily, which alarmed him for a brief period before he fully regained consciousness. The plane sounded fine, a steady droning. He peered out the window, but saw only darkness now. They might be overflying barren territory, or perhaps clouds had moved in.

The man across the way had left his seat. Fallow leaned into the aisle to see if food was coming yet. It wasn't. No attendants were visible, nor anyone else in motion. Except for the engine noise, it sounded frightfully quiet. He couldn't even hear the rustling of magazine or book pages being turned.

The lady two seats in front of him must have slumped down in sleep, or she was in the rest room. Whichever, he couldn't see the back of her head any more. There had been someone else ahead of him—a young couple— who also had disappeared from view, or perhaps changed seats. They weren't there now. Ahead, to the right, another traveler must have changed his place, unless he were crouched down, resting. It occurred to Fallow that he couldn't actually see any other passengers.

He twisted his head to observe the few people behind him. Now this was most curious. He saw no one. It was impossible to lie down in these seats, and they couldn't recline far enough to hide their occupants altogether. The vista, such as it was, really gave the appearance of his being completely alone. That suited him just fine, but it was odd.

Fallow got up. It would do him good to stretch his legs. He stepped into the aisle. He still couldn't see anyone, which he should have been able to do, standing. What a weird development. It looked like everyone had shifted to another compartment. He walked down the aisle a little ways, toward the tail, in order to confirm his suspicions. He was right: all these seats were empty. He walked back a few rows. He squeezed along the row in the center, looked both ways down the second aisle. Still no one in view. No question about it, he had the compartment to himself.

How had this come to pass? The crazy thought came to him—not that this could be true for a minute—that he had slept much longer than he would have considered possible, and that in the meantime the airplane had landed and disgorged its passengers at their destination. He had somehow been overlooked, and now the plane was flying on to God knows where. He might end up a thousand miles from where he wanted to go. It would take hours, a day, to get back on track. Such a complication would kill his deal for sure, and—though he hated to admit it—that business was critical to him.

However, that hadn't happened, of course. In some inexplicable fashion he was failing to comprehend the true, trivial, situation. Perhaps everybody had moved up ahead to view an interesting sight in the sky. It could have been a brilliant meteor. Couldn't that have been seen from any window on the proper side? Well, maybe not. Fallow walked forward.

He passed through both of the front compartments, finding them entirely devoid of passengers. It was downright creepy. Here he was at the boarding door, and facing the door to the pilot's cabin. What to do? These days airline officials were leery of anyone who approached the cabin, but under the circumstances he had a right. He'd paid his money, and he was a citizen. He needed to talk with those inside. He knocked, tentatively.

Nothing happened. He knocked again, three raps this time. Still nothing happened. He put his ear to the door. He heard nothing but the sound of engine vibration. He called out, politely, to the occupants. Then he called louder. The door did not open. Despite his concern, which began to be tinged with frustration and flecked with anger, he chose not to try pushing on that barrier. He didn't want to create an incident at this stage.

He walked back toward his seat, shaking his head. Along the way he noticed that the overhead luggage, or at least some of it, was still in place. They wouldn't have all got off without their belongings. He stopped at his seat. He asked himself, with a nervous chuckle, if he were actually sitting there, asleep, dreaming this. He didn't think so, but at the moment he couldn't come up with a better explanation. It was either that, or everybody was hiding in the bathrooms.

He went on, through the rear compartment, to the men's rest room. He might as well make use of it; he didn't expect to find anyone inside. Nor did he, but what he found there puzzled him exceedingly. When Fallow opened the door a harsh, acrid smell assaulted his nose, a rancid, unclean odor. A terrible sight assailed him as well. The tiny room looked like a disaster area, as if it hadn't been cleaned in ages. He saw mold on the walls, piles of waste paper in the corners, and the sheen of liquid on the floor. This was the greatest shock yet. He backed out of there and pulled the door shut behind him.

Okay, so something wasn't right. In fact, something was wrong, to a greater extent than he could fathom. No public airliner should have a rest room like that. Was he still on the same plane? Was that the answer? He attempted to concoct a scenario by which, during his doze, he could have been transferred, for whatever warped reason, to another flight, one not intended for the public. Needless to say, he could not imagine such a thing. Perhaps if he had been heavily drugged—that seemed possible—terrorists had sneaked aboard, at a signal had risen and thrown everybody but him off the plane to their deaths, and were keeping him as a hostage, for their own nefarious reasons. The thugs were in the cabin now, laughing at him, planning a dismal fate for him. Soon they would emerge . . .

And soon he would wake up. Fallow was scared, a little bit, but he wasn't stupid. He had to find an answer. Where, though, could he go from here? He was at the rear of the plane. There couldn't be anything past that. On the other hand, what was this? He hadn't noticed that before. It appeared to be a stairwell.

There shouldn't be stairs on an airplane. No, wait; there could be. Why, that must be it. He had boarded the flight so fast that he hadn't realized that this was one of those jumbo jets, a big double-decker with two levels. He was on the top, all the others had gone below. The airline must be throwing a party for their guests down below. Everybody was invited, but he had been asleep, so they left him alone. Most considerate, despite the heart ache the mystery had caused him.

The staircase spiraled down. Fallow descended. The metal bannister seemed rickety, and the stairs creaked ominously, which didn't please him. Also, the light visibly darkened before he had proceeded more than a few steps. It wasn't supposed to be like that, but he wouldn't worry about it now. All that mattered was finding people.

At the bottom he came to the lower level, exactly as predicted. Perhaps exactly wasn't the right word; it was gloomy down here, and he heard no one, saw no one. He hadn't gone far before he knew he'd missed the boat, or the party, or whatever he expected. This level was just as empty, and even spookier. He found no evidence that anyone had been here, not even luggage in the overhead bins. In addition, the seats looked ratty, poorly maintained, as if the area were seldom, if ever, used.

At the front of the plane he came to another door, precisely like the cabin door on the level above. Fallow pounded furiously, and cried out, without attracting attention. When he ceased making noise the silence, save for the ever present hum of the engines, closed in. He pressed his face to the nearest window. There simply wasn't anything out there to be seen. Blackness without, twilight within. He ran down the length of the fuselage, eager to return to the brighter level from which he'd come. As dreadful as it had been, he missed it now.

He ascended the stairs two at a bound, gasping from the exertion. He reached the top, feeling oddly safe for a moment. Why safe? Nothing menaced him, not yet. This was a nightmare, or a ghastly mistake, nothing more, yet fear kept bubbling up in his mind. He ought to feel better for being back where he belonged. Doubts, however, crept in. It wasn't as well lighted up here as he remembered—it didn't look much different from regions below—and something else had changed. At first he couldn't identify the problem, then it hit him. The luggage was gone. Every trace of former occupancy had vanished during his few short minutes downstairs.

Not possible, he told himself. This was another error on his part. He wasn't where he thought he was. He'd run up to the wrong level, passing his own. That could be it, if the explanation weren't so utterly ludicrous. Who ever heard of a triple-level airplane? There wasn't such a thing. He knew that. Could he be the victim of the all-time craziest practical joke? It infuriated him to think that someone might be doing this to him deliberately. It terrified him, too.

He spied a big door of unique shape at the end of the compartment. It resembled a hatchway. One more item he had overlooked, apparently. He wondered where it led. Surely not to the outer air; there would be a hands-off warning sign. Strangely, this door wasn't labeled in any way. It had a handle. All he had to do was pull that, and the door should open. Don't think of it. It was sheer foolishness even to consider it. The consequences were incalculable. Fallow pondered the matter, turning over in his mind all of the really sound objections to even touching it. He pulled the handle.

The throbbing of the engines abruptly intensified, causing him to jump. Within the dark compartment he discerned crates, boxes, and smaller containers. This was the baggage hold. He supposed it wasn't insulated for sound, which was why it sounded like he were listening to the motors through a sea shell. All of the luggage had to be in there. For that matter, all of the passengers had to be in there. It didn't look like a happy place, but Fallow had no choice. He forced himself across the threshold.

This area was a shambles. Boxes and packages were strewn at random, as if a hurricane had blown through. Suitcases had burst open, spilling their contents. The items seemed very old and worn, more like a collection of garbage. There was more to the confusion than disorder, however; the chamber was dirty. Dust lay thickly over all surfaces. His shoes slid on the gritty, slimy floor, and a miasma clogged his throat. He detected a weak stench, which didn't appreciably differ from that in the bathroom. He dreaded the live vermin which he imagined crawling about his feet, not that he'd seen any. Nor would he look too closely. He heard nothing creeping in the murk—he was fairly sure that he heard nothing—but he wouldn't stop to listen.

The compartment extended rather farther than he would have believed possible. It was more of a tunnel than a room. The space shrank as he progressed, the walls and ceiling narrowing, pressing upon him. It continued ahead of him, still narrowing, as far as he could make out in the encroaching blackness. That couldn't be right, either. He felt a strange craving to see to the end. He turned. The oblong of dim light from the hatch was very far away, and appeared very small. If he kept on in this direction, he would lose the light altogether within moments. That he could not risk. He would rather die than get lost in this seemingly endless darkness. If he wasn't already dead, of course.

He retraced his steps.

That solution had begun to occur to him. As one plausibility after another had failed him, the possibility of an impossibility had suggested itself. Fallow didn't know much about such things—he doubted that anyone did— so he wasn't prepared to reach categorical conclusions. He was quite certain now that everything had gone wrong for him (whatever that signified), and he increasingly assumed that what had happened to him was beyond any human power to solve. Perhaps this was death, or he had been taken away from the real world to another place. It didn't matter what he called it. His dilemma was real, it might be permanent, and he had better get used to it.

So thinking, he re-emerged into the passenger section of the plane. This level looked subtly different from its previous appearance. It might not be the same one. Not possible, but it didn't matter. This sort of plane might possess infinite levels. Developments had prepared him for that eventuality. He walked down the aisle to his seat, if it was the same one. The number seemed right, but he wasn't sure anymore. He sat down, as he presumed he should. There wasn't any point to wandering. He wished for company, then thought better of it. Be careful what you wish for, he reminded himself.

He noticed movement on the movie screen. Vague, formless nebulosity swirled there. The image snapped to black, and then the screen brightened. A picture show began. Oh, yes, this looked like his old favorite. They were running it again. This time he watched the opening titles. So it was called "The Bursters." He didn't recognize any of the names, but he would remember them. This time he could see it from the start, and gain a better idea of what was going on. Perhaps this knowledge mattered to someone.

Far ahead Fallow heard a door opening, and the jostling of metal. With languid carelessness he craned his head into the aisle. Hard to see through the gloom, but he could discern a flight attendant wheeling a food trolley his way. Personal service; he liked that. He heaved himself into the aisle seat so that he could better observe. Here she came. She—it—no, he didn't want this, or need it. He wished he had back the frump, rather than this misshapen thing. It didn't look especially human from a distance, and he feared that it would look rather less so up close. As it dragged itself toward him, shoving its rolling burden, he turned away and bowed his head. That same stench filled the air. He closed his eyes. He knew the sounds of the thing stopping, of the tray being folded down before him. He felt the tray press his stomach. He heard something—a semi-liquid sound—deposited on the tray. The trolley and its dreadful mistress receded, but he still heard something close before him. Something moved feebly, sluggishly, on the tray.

He would eat. He presumed he had to eat, and there was no good reason to put it off. It pleased him, he assured himself bitterly, that they chose to feed him. He had very little else to do, and Fallow suspected that this was going to be a long flight indeed.

THE MAN IN THE GLOBE

Allen Gerrold suffered an unnerving experience when he arrived for the gala dinner. It was being held, as it turned out, in what he couldn't help considering as the wrong part of town: a grimy, low rent, semi-industrial area; dark, with a faint haze of chemical smoke in the murky air. Despite explicit verbal directions, he had begun to dread getting lost. As he pulled into the lightless parking lot another car had charged out of the gloom, veered sharply toward his vehicle, almost clipping the bumper, then raced away; not before, however, the driver had shrieked to a halt, leaned out of his window and shouted, "Makes you think, doesn't it?" Motorist and car then vanished as quickly as they came.

It distressed him that what might well prove to be his big night should start in such a fashion. Still, he had arrived, and his fortunes could only improve as the evening progressed. Gerrold parked his car with all the others in the silent lot. The other vehicles were much grander than his. This must be the place, even if no one was in sight, and the building wasn't quite what he expected. A nondescript pile which had seen better days, it appeared to date from the turn of the century; the previous turn, that is. He approached the only visible door with diffidence. Then it was thrown open from within, light blazed out, and all was well.

"Your name, please?" inquired the elderly, extremely well dressed guardian of the gate. "Ah, yes, Mr. Gerrold. Mr. Benchley said you were expected." Gerrold liked that. The greeter ushered him into a low hall which immediately opened upon the main room.

Given the shabby, anonymous outside aspect of the structure, the interior positively dazzled him. The vast space before him teemed with elegant people and elegant furnishings. Perhaps a former ball room or theater from the olden days, freshened and refurbished. The ancient gas fixtures now glowed with electric light, including the baroque chandeliers overhead. Painted images adorned the ceiling, too worn with age to be made out except as sweeping surfaces of color. The expansive hard wooden floor (with nary a creak) had been given over to numerous small, cozy dining tables, where some—guests, members?—were already seated. Mainly the ladies; the wives of important men, no doubt. Others, mostly sharp looking or distinguished men, stood or strode about the tables, engaged in swirling conversations. Ornate oak-mantled doors graced both sides of the room. Through the one which stood open he spied a busy kitchen. Beyond all loomed the high stage, stretching from wall to wall, scaled by short flights of steps at both ends. Heavy ruffled curtains, crimson with sprawling gold tassels, concealed the performance area.

"Who are you?" demanded a brash voice as he drifted uncertainly into the room. The owner of the voice, a stocky young fellow with drink in hand, broke away from his clique and confronted the newcomer. "Gerrold? Gerrold. The name's Blakefield. Pleased to meet you. Of course, Benchley told us all about you. I'm glad you made it. Very glad. Your first time, eh?"

"It is," Gerrold replied.

"No problem. Come right in. Join us, or find a seat. There's one for everybody. Hey, Benchley!"

Mr. Benchley approached. Gerrold felt relief at finding someone he recognized; his superior at the firm, the man who had invited him, in fact.

"Gerrold, it's a pleasure to see you," said Mr. Benchley, extending a firm hand. An older, heavyset man, he exuded quiet assurance and avuncular good will. "I am so happy you came. I hoped you would, but it wouldn't do to count on such an important eventuality. Still, here you are, and that gives me great hopes for a fine and productive evening. I am sure that all of our members will benefit from your appearance."

The reference to members meant something to Gerrold, but had only done so since the morning of the previous day. Until that time he had never heard of the Global Visions Society. Called to the boss's office, he had entered with trepidation. Gerrold hadn't been with this outfit long, he had just lost the important Markland account (through no fault of his own, he was ready to insist), and he dreaded a dressing down, at least. Nothing of the sort happened. Mr. Benchley airily dismissed the subject, which his subordinate had hesitantly broached, and embarked upon a glowing description of this unknown club.

"A gathering of movers and shakers," he explained. "Businessmen, philosophers, government types, all getting together in order to think big thoughts and discuss grand ideals." They were an eclectic group, who pushed a number of advanced ideas concerning various contemporary issues. He assured Gerrold that the Society had performed some very good work, behind the scenes, in a quiet way. "Of course we don't spend all of our time formulating policy," Mr. Benchley went on. "We at Global Visions make things happen, play a part in the world. And then, there is the aspect of bonhomie to consider. A delightful atmosphere of camaraderie reigns at our annual meetings, of which I am fortunate to be the host this year. When all is said and done, we like to amuse ourselves."

Then he tendered the offer to attend, which Gerrold accepted happily. It couldn't hurt, and it might do him a lot of good to rub shoulders with the bigwigs. Mr. Benchley cautioned him to dress appropriately for a gala occasion, which led to his renting of a tuxedo for the first time since high school. If observation served him, he gathered that no one else here needed to rent.

Duty called Mr. Benchley away to other attendees, but not before he considerately directed the young man to the drinks table. There Gerrold fortified himself, as he saw virtually everyone else had done before him. He needed to put himself at ease and make himself comfortable, for he wasn't accustomed to moving in such circles. As far as he could tell, everybody here knew everybody else. He strove to catch their words without appearing to do so. Their conversations weren't private, and he awaited an opportunity to join in and become one of the boys, but the esoteric subjects formed a barrier to easy entry. In small knots and clusters they pontificated, debated, or exchanged views on vast, weighty matters. Here the topic was the utility of religion in an international economy; there it was education as a tool for industrial planning; behind him, someone spoke passionately on the fate of the individual in a rationally organized future. Gerrold really didn't know where to begin. He felt dampness forming under the tight suit as he pondered the prospect of remaining odd man out for the entire evening.

An angel saved him. "Mr. Gerrold, isn't it?" A very pretty, classy girl accosted him. "How do you do? I'm Leonora Forsythe. This is my first time here. My father is the medical director for the state hospitals. You've probably heard of him. We've all heard about you recently."

"I'm glad to make your acquaintance, Leonora. You may call me Allen. What could you possibly have heard about me?"

"Come sit with me. Dinner will be served in a moment." Well, this was more like it. They crossed the room and sat down by themselves at a table ornately laid for four, front and center before the hidden stage. She didn't take her place until he held her chair. "Oh, Mr. Benchley—a great friend of my father—told us lots and lots," she continued. "He said you were aiming to be an up and coming associate of the company, that maybe you even hoped to be a partner one day."

"He said that?" Gerrold hadn't previously sensed that degree of respect from those above him. They thought him up and coming, partner material.

That must explain his presence here tonight. "He flatters me."

"He said you would be simply perfect for this evening's festivities," Leonora gushed. "I agree with him. You will make a superb star attraction."

"How about that," Gerrold muttered vaguely. While he attempted to frame half a dozen questions in his mind which would elicit more information, a ponderous fellow approached, with a large black cigar clamped between his teeth and a withered woman at his side. They took seats at the table.

"It's time to eat," said the man.

"Father, Mother, this is Mr. Gerrold."

"Allen, please."

"You're going to entertain us tonight," Mrs. Forsythe cried.

"Gerrold," Mr. Forsythe grumbled. "Yes, I've heard a thing or two about you. Entertainment is hardly the word for it, my dear. This is serious business, and I expect Gerrold to so treat it."

"I assure you I will," their guest said hastily, "and it's nice to meet you both. I get the impression that something special is required of me tonight, but I don't know what it is. Nobody has told me anything."

"Nothing is required of you," Mr. Forsythe growled. "You can do what you like. If you choose to cooperate, however, the meeting will be a memorable success. Benchley made a big deal out of how we could count on you."

"Dinner is served." An army of white coated waiters, laden with dishes and trays, descended on the tables one at a time. Gerrold noted with glee that they came straight to his table first. That might be an honor due to his hosts, he reflected, but he cheered himself by thinking that the honor was his own. He didn't quite recognize the courses—they looked Frenchified—but shame at his ignorance kept him from asking. The portions were small, but it was pretty good stuff. Tasty wine flowed freely. During the meal conversation rarely rose above small talk, most of it confined to the other three, although Leonora made a point of addressing him at intervals, mainly to praise the food.

Throughout the dinner Gerrold attempted to remain chipper, but a gnawing concern nagged at him. From the elusive comments he feared that they all did want something from him, and he knew, with mounting, dreadful certainty, that what they wanted was a speech. The very thought sickened him. He did not excel at public speaking; he was terrible at it, and tried to avoid the embarrassment at all costs. It pained him enough when he had a chance to prepare for the miserable moment. An impromptu presentation— on what subject, anyway?—would devastate him. He knew from experience how foolish he could sound. Please, God, he pleaded silently, anything but that. He would tolerate anything the night had in store, if he didn't have to stand up and talk in front of all these people.

It was actually a relief when nature began to demand attention. He excused himself and wended his way among the tables toward the clearly marked bathrooms. It seemed as if all eyes were upon him as he proceeded.

"Where do you think you're going?" He turned at the harsh voice to see a man springing quickly from his chair. Fairly young, self assured, hard looking, he strode right up into Gerrold's face as if to bar the way. "Trouble with the service?"

"Is there a problem?" Mr. Benchley asked pleasantly, appearing from nowhere. "Mr. Gerrold, is there anything we can do for you?"

"I'm just making a pit stop," he stammered.

"Certainly. We have every facility. Jones, meet Gerrold. Jones, in addition to his vocation as a highly esteemed policy chief for the administration, works as a consultant for the Society."

"I thought it was him," Jones said decisively. "I didn't want him cutting out on us before the big time. We'd all regret that. Hi, Gerrold. It's a thrill to have you here."

"It's a thrill to be here." Gerrold attempted to control his cold tone. "Haven't we met somewhere?"

"I doubt it, but I count it a privilege now. You could be important to us. You have no idea how important you are capable of becoming."

"Thanks for the kind thoughts. Pardon me, gentlemen."

"Don't be too long or you will miss the fun," Jones called. He and Mr. Benchley whispered among themselves as their guest hurriedly broke away. Gerrold wouldn't swear to it—he granted that a mistake was possible—but Jones strikingly resembled the man who had cut him off at the parking lot entrance. The hot eyes, the strong jaw, the ferocious stare, all fitted. Surely it was him... but it couldn't be more than a chance resemblance. The harrowing experience had been fleeting. Of course it wasn't him. That wouldn't make any sense, any more than his paranoiac sense that many pairs of watchful eyes followed him as he crossed the floor to his destination.

Gerrold entered the men's room, a bright, polished affair of glass, metal, and tile, rather different from the old-fashioned dining room. He took refuge within a closed stall. Scarcely had he settled himself and begun to concentrate upon immediacies than he heard the startlingly noisy entry of several others. The rest room door opened with a crash, bodies seemed to blunder about against the walls and each other, and what sounded like a murmur of conversation, caught in media res, ran unchecked. Within seconds it appeared that the other stalls were full, and that the urinals and the faucets at the counter were all in operation.

They continued to chatter among themselves. A stream of running water muffled the words, but now they were talking back and forth across the room, and he picked up snatches of intelligible speech.

"—Well and good to save the world, but we must confront the issue of fate," a faceless voice opined.

"—Reality determined by the clash of opposites—" said another, perhaps in response.

"Black and white, rich and poor, daring and cautious, life and—what?"

"—Critical moment comes to us all—"

"How to act?"

"—Decision to be made—"

"—Stands outside of the world, looking in—"

"—Or is sealed within it—"

"—False move, without hope of escape—"

"—Human condition—"

"Checkmate."

Gerrold flushed the commode. At that instant came a clatter of metal panels, more sounds of bodies against bodies, hurried footsteps, the swinging of the door. When he exited the cubicle he found the room absolutely empty. An overlooked faucet still poured, the water spiraling fast into the drain. He shut it off.

What had just happened spooked him. He couldn't shake the crazy feeling that the bizarre episode had been staged for his benefit. Something about those words got under his skin. It wasn't their meaning, not exactly— he couldn't be sure if he had determined their meaning, from the bits and pieces he overheard—but rather the manner of their being projected. Yes, what he heard had sounded like a recitation, a catechism, of mysterious significance. Something to do with the club? Involved members might have their secret words or phrases of importance. Perhaps they had been rehearsing for a later event.

He departed the shelter of the bathroom. Most of the diners' attention now focused on the stage, where Mr. Benchley stood before the curtain speaking, reading glasses perched on his nose, a sheaf of papers in hand. So the meeting had finally come to the point. Gerrold rejoined the Forsythes. Dishes and utensils were being collected by the efficient waiters. He hadn't finished, but he didn't make a fuss about it. The wine and the goblets remained.

"I thought you'd taken out a lease on that room," said the father with a frown.

"Everything is fine, dear," the mother soothed.

"I was afraid you were going to miss the good parts," said Leonora.

THE MAN IN THE GLOBE

"Not for the world," replied Gerrold.

These good parts, if such they be, proved somewhat tedious. Mr. Benchley was in the process of reading some brief personal messages from members who hadn't been able to attend. Some of them were off in far corners of the globe, masterminding public works of vital import to regional health, education, and welfare, and regretted being unable to tear themselves away. All made a point of offering special wishes for a rewarding meeting. There were quite a number of these, and Gerrold grew restless. He was not alone.

"All right, already," muttered Mr. Forsythe, still scowling. "I don't want to be here until dawn. Let's get this show on the road."

"It's always done this way," Mrs. Forsythe observed.

"Benchley just likes to hear himself talk. Now last year—" He stopped as Mr. Benchley cleared his throat and shifted gears.

"So much for preliminaries," said the speaker. "Ladies and gentlemen, the Global Visions Society exists to foster a cohesive approach to solving the ills which plague our world. We combine unity of purpose with a broad spectrum of method. Conceptual acuity, harnessed to good old practical diligence, enables us to make our mark. GVS stands for action! The lessons of the past, filtered through the experience of the present, constitute the hope of the future—"

And so on. Some members of the audience—Leonora, for one—seemed rapt by the performance, while others, such as her father, exhibited signs of impatience. Gerrold didn't derive much benefit from the speech. It sounded to him like conventional after dinner maundering, the sort of thing he still feared they expected from him.

"What exactly does the GVS do?" he asked quietly of the girl beside him.

"Absolutely amazing things," she whispered back.

"Such as?"

"Instill a rewarding frame of mind," she said, barely paying attention to him.

"—Bold, forthright advance into the new millennium. We will not be left behind. We will not keep pace. We do not follow; we lead, by example. All ideas are on the table. Our strength lies in choosing our servings with care. Mere action, for the sake of action, is not our way. That is foolish, wasteful. It is the mark of the beast. We choose to march, not wander. The compass of talent and skill points the direction—"

"I trust that the clock points him in the right direction," Mr. Forsythe quipped. Gerrold, much to his distress, felt a growing need to use the bathroom once more. It wouldn't be good form, of course; also, now that he thought about it, he didn't want to go back in there again.

"—Broad strokes, but with due consideration for the critical details. No half measures at GVS! Where others give up, there we pick up the ball. What they call accomplishments, we call the bare beginnings. Civilization progresses through unswerving determination to identify and achieve rational goals, with rational means, for rational ends." Mr. Benchley stopped. A weighty pause ensued. He placed his hands behind his back, then brought them forward gradually into an attitude of prayer. His gaze swept, by degrees, the entire gathering.

"Is this it, Father?" asked Leonora.

"At last," Mr. Forsythe responded. Gerrold sat erect and waited.

"Let me be clear about one thing," Mr. Benchley said presently. "We are not pie-in-the-sky utopians. We deal with the real world as we see it, as we find it. We don't kid ourselves about the difficulties, the costs. We are realists. We face reality!"

"We accept reality!" thundered the group in unison. Gerrold jumped in his seat.

"We seek the truth!"

"We know the truth!" roared back the crowd. To Gerrold, they seemed to be reciting a prepared script. He wished he knew the words.

"Great hardships go hand in hand with great achievement. In order that most may rise, some must fall. It is an inevitable consequence. We act to minimize the pain, but we can not wholly escape it. Is there anyone here unwilling to pay the price?"

"The price shall be paid!"

"And that leads us," Mr. Benchley solemnly intoned, "to our little morality play, the sacred tradition of Global Visions. Here, once every year, we remind ourselves of the price man pays for advancement. Ladies and gentlemen, behold the world!"

The speaker gestured with his right hand. Other, unseen hands began hauling on invisible cords which pulled aside the crimson curtains. Scattered applause accompanied the rustling movement. The interior of the stage lay revealed. There Gerrold saw a remarkable thing on the hardwood floor: a giant cement globe, perhaps six feet in diameter. The smooth, even polished gray surface was marred by painted black lines symbolizing latitude and longitude. Crude splashes of dull brown portrayed recognizable representations of the major continents. The Americas faced to the front. A thick circle of metal occupied the position of the North Pole. It was a weird object. If solid, he wondered how they had been able to move it onto the stage. Somebody had gone to a deal of trouble.

"This is our special globe," Mr. Benchley indicated, "the image of man's habitat. Man is of the world, man is in the world. If all present agree, we must fill it."

"We agree!" All in the audience, save one, screamed the words.

"As you know, we have with us tonight an important guest—" A wave of clapping and hammering of goblets on tables ensued as all eyes turned toward Gerrold.

This is it, he thought. There was no question as to what was coming, and he couldn't readily evade it without ruining his possibilities. He tried to think of engaging platitudes which might satisfy these people. From what he'd heard so far, they couldn't really expect too much from him. He just had to come up with something to fob them off for a while.

"Mr. Gerrold, would you join me, please?" More applause as their guest rose. Leonora touched his hand, looked worshipfully into his eyes and breathed, "I am so proud of you." Thus fortified, he made his way onto the stage.

"Thank you, thank you," said Mr. Benchley, offering his hand in a hearty clasp. "You enjoyed the dinner?"

"I did, very much."

"And the gracious company?"

"Marvelous company."

"Mr. Gerrold, you have it in your power to do us a great service. You honor us by your presence, and you may honor us further by your willing participation in our grand ceremony. I hasten to assure you that the choice is yours. If you refuse, that is the end of the matter."

"I'm not inclined," Gerrold said hesitantly, "to refuse anything to you good people. It's good of you to have me here. I'd be happy to say a few words, if that meets with your approval." Tittering laughter emanated from the crowd.

"Ah, but sir, at this moment we emphasize action over words. We desire you to act for us."

"He's already accepted," called a harsh voice. Gerrold recognized it at once.

"Only in principle, Mr. Jones," Mr. Benchley noted in return. "Our guest deserves better. Now, Mr. Gerrold, I put it to you bluntly: will you be our Man In the Globe?"

"I don't understand—"

"Come closer." Through an inviting smile and gentle pressure on the shoulder he steered the young man to the curious ball. "The sphere is hollow. This iron portal on top is a door which allows entry. There is plenty of room inside for a single man. I'm asking you—in the name of the Global Visions Society and everyone gathered here—to climb inside."

Gerrold was aware of the hush that had fallen upon the entire room. He heard only a dull thumping sound, perhaps blood pounding in his ears. "Inside?" His eye caught Leonora's. She nodded eagerly. "Well, what then?"

"We will take it from there. If you play your role, we will play ours."

"I want to cooperate—"

"Do you?" The elder man asked the question in all seriousness. "The decision is yours. Do you indeed?"

"Yes."

"Excellent, Mr. Gerrold. You have chosen appropriately. We shall never regret it. Let's get going!" Mr. Benchley lifted the iron ring—which now could be seen to be a lid—from its circular groove, and propped it against the globe. Gerrold still wasn't certain how to proceed—the opening was an inch or two above his head—but his thoughtful host had planned carefully. That worthy fellow drew from behind the round mass a folding stepladder. He arranged it fastidiously by the sloping side. "Up and in you go."

Gerrold mounted the ladder slowly. At the top he could easily reach the opening. He peered inside. He saw only darkness there. He looked up and about quickly. The lights of the room seemed brighter, dazzling.

"Don't fear for your comfort," Mr. Benchley advised. "We wouldn't overlook that detail. The interior is padded with soft velvet. Also, please note the air holes drilled into the top around the entrance. You need have no worries on that score. "

Gerrold nodded, and clambered down into the globe.

Mr. Benchley retrieved the lid, climbed up and laid it into place. Then he removed from his jacket pocket a set of metal screws which, with deft motions, he used to fasten the lid securely. He came down, folded the ladder, and carried it to the side of the stage, placing it just out of sight. He then returned to the globe, faced the audience, and called in a stage voice, "Mr. Gerrold, can you hear me?"

"I hear you," replied a little mouse's voice.

"Then listen well. You rest within—comfortably, I trust?"

"I'm all right," said the mouse.

"Very good. You rest within a complex representation of our world, a magnificent piece of engineering. The outer shell is composed of concrete, reinforced by steel: durable, unbreakable, everlasting. An inner shell of light material—well padded, as you know—surrounds you. But there is much more."

"Indeed there is!" cried the crowd.

"We stand for progress, achievement, enterprise. These are facets of the world in which we operate. We act to enhance the lives of as many of our fellow men as possible. No one knows, better than we, what that requires.

THE MAN IN THE GLOBE

We accept the glory of success, we acknowledge the penalties of failure. There is no perfect system."

"Not all can be saved," intoned the group.

"Not all. There are occasions in which, for the sake of the many, the one must be sacrificed. We advocate life; we recognize—"

"Death!"

"All decisions have been made, all choices accepted. We will pay the price, through you. Do you understand me, Mr. Gerrold?"

"I don't," squeaked the mouse. "What's going on?"

"You confront the final aspect of the human condition," said Mr. Benchley. He snapped his fingers and, from the wings, a man appeared, carrying a small, boxy apparatus—sporting an ostentatious red button—from which depended a bulky coil of thin wire. He attached leads to two screws, handed the box to the speaker, and left the stage to join the onlookers. "There is one more feature of this globe which I must bring to your attention. Packed within the inner and outer shells are several shaped charges of TNT, strategically emplaced so as to bring about an implosion. In order to illustrate the power of fate in human affairs, I shall now detonate the charges."

"Let me out," demanded the voice from within, now sounding strangely tinny.

"You shall attain a state of release," Mr. Benchley said, as he strode away, unrolling the coil.

"Let me out, let me out!" shrieked the little voice.

Mr. Benchley descended the stairs. He awaited the collective nod from the audience. It came.

"Let me out, let me out, let me out—"

Mr. Benchley pressed the red button.

There followed a crash of muffled thunder. The globe rocked. Black smoke and traces of flame geysered from the air holes, or vents, as they might be styled. The crowd exploded into a pandemonium of cheering, which lasted for many minutes as the smoke cleared. The globe, its upper surfaces marred by soot, otherwise stood as before, solid, eternal.

"Ladies and gentlemen," Mr. Benchley merrily boomed, "this meeting of the GVS is adjourned. Until next year!"

THE CHAMBER OF HORRORS

It was one of those gray, tiresome, out-of-kilter mornings—there were so many of those now—when nothing looked or felt or smelled or tasted right, and Abernathy, scarcely having risen, decided that there was no way he would make it to work this day. The job didn't matter to him, save when the bills came due, and it had been made clear often enough by his boss that Abernathy didn't matter much to the job, so, once again, why bother? He'd cut out before when he felt like it, with little more than recriminations and warnings as result, and yet another skip couldn't hurt. He loathed the job, despised everybody with whom he was forced to associate. He would amuse himself this day, loll pleasantly or wander aimlessly as suited. He had no one else to whom he must answer; the typical state of affairs. He made the call at the proper time, got an angry earful, warmer than usual. Had he pushed too far this time? If so, he'd deal with it later. He just didn't care right now.

Wallowing in bed didn't satisfy. After a while without so much as a doze Abernathy got up, dressed in whatever he could grab, and fled his dingy, stifling apartment. Rent was coming due—that day's pay would count—later, later he'd sort out the difficulty, or add it to the pile. Now he wanted out, to do something, see something, anything that wasn't the grinding norm. He hopped into his old, growling compact car and trundled away, down the street and into the main traffic artery. Lots of drivers whizzed dutifully by to somewhere. Abernathy just drove. He might stop off at the store for badly needed household supplies, or at the grocery to replenish his TV dinners and canned goods, or go nowhere. He chose the latter, and went there as fast as his tired vehicle would carry him.

Truly this was one of those mornings. There were no clouds or haze that he could see, but the light of the sun seemed subdued, and the fleeting images of terrain appeared distorted, changed in some subtle, displeasing manner, as if he had driven out of the familiarly known into another realm, where an attempt was being made, for his sake, to mimic conventionality, with mediocre success. Just past the turnpike, where the houses disappear, giving way to patches of scrubby trees and vacant lots, he saw the place. Abernathy slowed down to stare, couldn't see clearly, pulled into the drive to check the place out. He shuddered to a halt at a parking slot in the otherwise empty lot, got out and scrutinized the small, oblong building. The thing stood there right before him, yet his vision wouldn't cooperate in the perusal. What sort of place was this? He hadn't noticed it before. Then a shadow passed from his eyes or brain and he saw clearly, as through binoculars, this one feature of the landscape to the exclusion of all else. "The Chamber of Horrors Wax Museum" read the big sign over the door.

It was one of those. It must have been knocked together and put up fast. Abernathy had visited such places as a youth, guessed what he could expect, debated. It didn't seem a popular attraction, judging from the absence of other patrons, but he thought it might give him a kick, like a blast from relatively carefree olden times, to tour the silly thrills and chills of a phony phantasmagoria. The screen door whined at the pressure of his hand, he passed inside to the office, loafed before the empty desk where he was supposed to pay. Cheap, ratty posters bragged of marvels within, "Sights to Curdle the Blood!" No one showed to offer him a ticket and demand his money. After an irritating period of silent stasis he wandered through the curtained opening beyond the desk, brushing aside the silky fabric like cobwebs, telling himself that the proprietor could catch up with him later.

He walked down a short, dark hall, wooden floorboards creaking underfoot, entered the first dimly lighted chamber. Yes, he remembered well this kind of thing. The quite large room contained a meticulous recreation of an old-fashioned car, with many holes poked through it, with traces of generic outdoors scenery clustered about, while half in and half out of the car dangled two fair mannequins, covered in unsightly blemishes, in postures suggestive of extreme physical distress. "The Killing of Bonny and Clyde" announced the exhibit sign, which also provided, in smaller text, a smattering of gruesome historical details. Abernathy read of the number of bullets fired at the wayward pair, the number of bullets that struck home, the caliber of bullets employed. Oh yes, he'd seen this one before, long ago. He'd even seen the real car, or so he'd been told; that had been a big part of the draw. Maybe this was it too, although nothing said so. Perhaps it had been scrapped in the decades since, or finally ensconced in a proper museum.

He passed from there with a shrug down another short, gloomy hall, into a second, smaller chamber, opening upon a pitch-black alcove fronted by a legend, "The Hanging of Joshua Logan." Good Lord, he remembered that one, too. He pressed the button and the interior light flashed on, revealing in all its waxy glory the famous scene of a man accidentally decapitated by his clumsily handled execution, with red soda pop or something similar spouting from his severed neck. Beyond this Abernathy proceeded to more chilling amusements: "The Immolation of Juliette," an episode in the life of the Marquis de Sade, offering for the gawker's edification a savage-faced man gloating over the burnt corpse of a young female, from which faux flames flickered; "The Closet of Bluebeard," "Interrogation by Torquemada," and so forth, all very interesting in their own way, all quite familiar from previous waxen presentations. Abernathy supposed that all these places were pretty much the same, perhaps even rotated among themselves the identical exhibits. As long as the dummies and props were maintained, he mused, they could be milked forever. Not, though, unless he paid, and it puzzled him that no one showed up to confiscate his cash. It was a ridiculous way to run a business.

But what was this? The next frozen image wasn't exciting in the least, nor did it possess the veneer of historical respectability. Entitled "The School Bully," it portrayed a passable playground scene in which a tough little punk brutalized a smaller classmate. Instead of delectable blood and guts it afforded a capsule view of common, sneering callousness and helpless misery. It didn't impress, and it turned off Abernathy, who didn't sympathize with the victim in any way. The child looked soft and weak. Abernathy recalled what passed for his great days in grade school, when he'd rounded on such saps for the sheer joy of it, before he'd been sent to the special school. That was after his mother dropped out of sight, and the county hacks had no choice but to act "on his behalf." Suddenly the scene galled him. He imagined himself as the bully. The wax figure even resembled him a bit, as he appeared in old family pictures, back when he still sort of belonged to a family.

The next was similarly bland and irritating. Called "The Firing," it showed a red-faced, enraged young man being unceremoniously drummed out of what the setting suggested was a labor job, with the three other characters in the scene sporting saddened, weary, yet firm expressions. Abernathy hated this one. That might be him in there. How many times had he faced termination at the hands of officious buzzards, solely because he wouldn't knuckle under to their unfair regulations and dictates? Real men make their own rules, keep their own hours, work as hard as they feel like it. He wasn't a slave, and he'd spit in their faces before he'd allow them to treat him like one. Anyway, it was a lousy scene. What kind of a dump was this place? Something about the fake people in "The Firing" stirred memory, but he surely hadn't come across this lame exhibit before.

Another jaunt down another narrow corridor took him to "The

Ceremony." This one, for all of its lack of imaginative appeal, stopped him dead in his tracks. Really, it gave him the creeps to look at it, although there was nothing overtly hair-raising in the scene. The weirdly lighted, oddly shadowed grouping presented two people, man and woman, standing side by side in a nondescript office before another man reading from a book. The female half of the couple, despite a stab at finery in her dress, looked frowzy, while the male half appeared in unbecoming walk-in clothing. That woman—my God, that woman—it was her! That wax dummy was a very good likeness of Jenny, his deplorable selection for his one ghastly attempt at matrimony. It wasn't just resemblance; it was a perfect recreation of that squalid little tramp. Out of all his mistakes (not that there had been many, he insisted to himself, refusing to accept responsibility for what others had done to him) she was the worst, the worst too of all the rotten, self-serving women he'd carelessly known. He could never forget that pinched, cold face, the sharp features, the narrowed eyes and drab hair. Something of her callous, naturally hostile personality exuded from the glossy wax. Their so-called marriage hadn't lasted long, but too long as it was, enough to give him stomach cramps to think of it, long enough to produce a girl whom both parents detested, and with whom the other got stuck after Abernathy finally threw them both out. That had cost him, though he'd never forked over more than he could get away with.

Then there was the younger man, captured at the infamous moment of muttering "I do." Abernathy stared, blinked, laughed aloud, drew back. He couldn't believe it, but it was true. That was him. Without question, this tableau represented a wretched scene from his own life, one in which he was the clownish star of the show. He tried to laugh again, but that strange gurgling sound died in his throat. He couldn't stand it, wouldn't accept it. Someone, somehow, was playing an incredible practical joke on him. Someone—it terrified him to even consider who it might be—had set up all this for his special viewing. He thought of the unseen proprietor of the museum, quaked at the thought.

He turned, fled back down the passage, took a wrong turn (he guessed, for if there were turns or detours, he hadn't noticed), ended up before another scene from the life of Abernathy, this one still more recent, more insulting, more insinuating; a picture of his life as it was now, in all its weary uselessness, entitled "On and On." He dodged away from that, raced into enclosing darkness, emerged before another, equally horrible, then hurtled down more mysterious tunnels, round and round—how could that dinky building hold so much nastiness?—shocked and dazed by more waxy glimpses, more hateful insights into his life, before he encountered one with a difference.

THE CHAMBER OF HORRORS

This presentation, simply labeled "Despair", did not reveal an awkward or embarrassing moment from the life he'd lived. He was not yet the aging, hollow-cheeked, gray-haired, shabby shell sitting morosely hunched over a bare table, leaning on skinny arms, with a half-empty bottle of rot gut at his elbow and a brimming glass in his hand. Not yet had he developed the blind, haunted stare, the pasty complexion, the flaccid, soulless expression. He wasn't that, but Abernathy knew, of a certainty, that he would be, in time. It was an image of his ordained future.

He lunged into the scene, smashed the wax fake of himself to bits, broke the table, trod the remnants underfoot. Having performed this rite, the last spark of passion sputtered out. It didn't matter. He could smash every one, as he had the eggshell of his existence, but in this place he presumed there could and would be more. He just wanted out now, out at any price. He shouted, crying out for the secretive owner to appear. He staggered away, down the black hall, into another room, steeling himself for another assault on his soul. But no; this one was different still, very different; rather than an attack, it presented an answer. This was "Resolution."

He didn't appear in the scene, such as it was, this time. Obviously he was meant to use his imagination, of which he possessed a sufficiency. Of course, there was always a way, and this one made sense. A shadowed alcove, with a dais inside, and a shiny pistol lying atop. He brushed aside the framing curtain and picked up the weapon. Not wax, nor plastic, but hard, cold, genuine metal, heavy, solid; this was the real thing. He held it up to his head, idly brushed his temple with the barrel. Abernathy pondered, smiled grimly, pictured to himself a final scene entitled "Decision."

ALONE WITH THE NIGHT CREW

After a tedious and uneventful day, followed by a tiresome and unrewarding evening, Haredon wearily rose from an unrefreshing doze, convinced that sleep would not come this night. The universe consisted of his sparsely furnished, one room apartment, or so it seemed as he flicked on a lamp and gazed about in the yellow glare. It always looked like this. Nothing had obviously changed, yet he sensed an alteration far behind the background fabric of being. Perhaps it was the feeling of greater solitude. No sound penetrated the white-washed walls, nor light gleam through the thick curtains. Having washed his face and rinsed his eyes, he nibbled on something still edible in the refrigerator and pondered how to pass the time until dawn commenced his daily cycle anew.

He had reading material on hand, but it was all old stuff, and too much of the current moment already felt stale. Perhaps the television offered time consuming pleasures, although Haredon had no guide to aid him. He turned on the machine and clicked through the accessible channels. Quite a few presented only blank screens or hissing electric snow. In others, manically joyous announcers hawked vital and unnecessary products to gullible possessors of credit cards. He flashed past these. Here was something different, a movie which, although already getting under way, was immediately familiar to him. Despite being an old black and white film, he might as well watch it.

This was that family favorite about the decent young man in a decent small town, a fellow with an adventurous streak who suffers a series of unfair disappointments throughout his honest career, faces disgrace, contemplates suicide, and receives a visit from his guardian angel who soon sets him straight as to what's important in life. Haredon knew it by heart. At first he paid more attention to the film quality. A poor copy, this, with many scratches and dirty, badly maintained splices, as well as a muddled sound track. The conversations among the angels were virtually inaudible. Also, when he could decipher the speeches, their words weren't exactly as he remembered them. Come to think of it, quite a few details weren't quite right.

Apparently this wasn't the movie he had in mind, although it was very similar. The earnest hero appeared—not the expected Oscar-winning actor, but a young fellow much like him—and in short order the heroine did likewise—not the pretty Oscar-winning actress, but it might have been her sister. Developments didn't play out as recollected. Single scenes were recognizable, but the whole was structured differently, and there was the recurrent suggestion—at first he dismissed this aspect, then couldn't escape it—that the hero was getting just what he deserved. The dreadful events mounted, frustration built to the breaking point . . . yet the angels, from what Haredon could make out of their dialogue, were oddly unsympathetic. Certainly there was an element of gloating in their tones. When the guardian finally appeared, he laughed too much at the nastiness around him. His laugh was nasty, too. That face, recalled as full and jovial, here appeared fat and sly. Was he trying to save the hero, or convince him to give in to fate?

At that point the picture blanked out and a droning hum commenced, evidence of a technical problem at the station. Another minute of this and the viewer, now thoroughly dispirited, switched off the set, not really caring to see any more of that one. He wondered if he'd been watching a bad dream. So, what then? He would not sit here all night. He might as well put the dead time to good use and run errands. He dressed casually and set out in search of 24-hour stores.

Driving through a still, airless night, with no stars in the sky and without identifiable landmarks below, Haredon kept an eye out for grocery and department stores. His usual shopping haunts had closed hours ago, so he continued down the anonymous lane, looking for tell-tale clusters of lights. No one else was about, which seemed odd, although he couldn't blame them. Except for occasional bright flickerings at extreme visual range, which inevitably disappeared, he saw no evidence that others were sharing the road or the cosmos with him. The trip lulled with its boredom. He couldn't pick up anything on the radio. Then an eye-catching display loomed on the right, the facade of a big, long building sporting several wide windows with light inside. This could be it. He pulled into the broad, largely empty parking lot.

Fair-Mart, the garish sign read in throbbing neon. He knew the name, that of a major department store. He remembered reading something about a destructive fire one long ago night, accompanied by considerable loss of life, which had closed the place down. It had been a major news item at the time. Evidently the store had reopened, and not much the worse for wear, although he'd visited more wholesome establishments. It had a seedy appearance about it, and the few vehicles out front looked abandoned rather than parked. The lights within weren't quite bright enough to reassure him. He briefly entertained the notion of driving on and looking elsewhere, but didn't know what options he had. Every place might be the same at this hour. Besides, he only required a few cleaning supplies. This shouldn't take a moment.

The door didn't open automatically for him. As he pushed inward, Haredon spied sooty stains on the concrete just outside. Within, he confronted a long row of vacant check-outs, with no cashier on duty, and beyond that endless aisles flanked by merchandise. He didn't approve of the dim lighting. A cost cutting measure, perhaps, but he'd begun to doubt whether the store was open for business after all. No one was in sight. The solitude galled him. On the other hand, a tinny radio was faintly spewing an ear-grating pop tune somewhere far away, and over that could barely be heard more pleasant music piping over the store intercom. Somebody must be here. He chose not to call out, not yet.

Not knowing his way around, Haredon skirted the registers and set out down the broad aisle which bisected the sales floor. Most counters sported signs promising great deals and substantial savings. Peering down the cross ways, he saw numerous cardboard boxes piled in front of the metal shelves and, tucked here and there, huge stacks of boxes precariously jumbled atop wooden palettes. This was evidently stocking time, when the depleted shelves were filled for the coming day. He saw no one actually doing that, but supposed they might be gathered elsewhere taking a break. Working the night shift, in the absence of many customers to impress, must be a pretty leisurely occupation.

Turning left into another wide lane, he presently came upon shelves of household goods which contained the items he sought. He collected a heavy box of laundry detergent and a spray bottle of kitchen cleaner. Both were needlessly dusty. He tried to think of what else he could buy, as long as he was here, to save himself a later trip. He spotted paper towels in the next aisle. Good, but his hands were already full, and he hadn't thought to acquire a shopping basket up front. Fortunately, quite a few were scattered about, some filled with flattened cardboard boxes and rubbish, others empty. Haredon chose one—the first rolled badly, so he settled for one that squeaked—deposited his stuff and moved on, dodging the occasional palette stack in his way.

In short order he'd gathered half a dozen items, which his cash in pocket would just cover, so he made for the front check-outs. The store seemed more expansive than he would have expected. There was a sense of having traveled a considerable distance, and throughout it all he hadn't met up with a fellow human being. He passed by a glass counter displaying dozens of watches. All were stopped, all set to the same time: 3:46. Every digital specified A.M. As long as he watched, the numbers didn't change. How strange.

Getting back took rather longer than coming in, but eventually the registers hove into view. No one was there, still. He trundled down the row, noting that one check-out was actually open for business. The computerized screen glowed greenly. He stood there for a time, then ostentatiously looked around, then drummed his fingers on a metal display, then—with curious trepidation—called out loudly, "Is anyone here?"

No one appeared, no one replied. Finally Haredon felt creeping upon him the first symptoms of annoyance. He wished to speak with the manager, set him straight on business policy and deliver a lecture on customer relations. Even late at night somebody must be in charge. The muted, muddy sounding music continued to play. He didn't recognize the tunes, although they occasionally approximated popular songs he knew. He waited longer, grinding his teeth, wondering what to do. He couldn't justify this absurd feeling of helplessness. Walk out or find help? It would serve them right if he opted for the former. He called out again, with a less cheerful tone of voice. Beyond the large front windows he saw nothing but uninviting blackness. By this time he would have expected to see a hint of dawn, or something, anyway. He glanced at his watch. 3:46; now there was a freakish coincidence. With sudden determination he grabbed the spray bottle from the cart—just to look official, as if he had a right to be here—and marched up the nearest big aisle in search of someone to whom he could swap his money.

To the extent that he thought about it, Haredon intended to circumscribe a square, ending up at the exit door, and if he hadn't received satisfaction by then, to be on his way in a theatrical huff. He proceeded past a long series of stands and racks containing cheap, generic clothing, toward the back of the store, into the gathering gloom. Indeed, there was less illumination than before, perhaps only in this corner of the building. Remote walls and surfaces were difficult to make out. The unstocked freight claimed more floor space here, with the contents of some boxes dumped and scattered, a hazard to navigation. A right turn, then onward to the region where he'd shopped before. But, no; not realizing how, he found himself in the toy department. Large stuffed animals stared at him, their fake fur stiff as brush bristles, their glass eyes gleaming feebly. He was about to turn again when someone passed across the aisle far ahead of him.

Haredon scurried after, just fast enough to show purpose, not so much as to feel silly. Rounding a bend tiled with shoe boxes, finding no one, he advanced to the back wall of the sales floor, discovering two swinging doors which must lead into the stock room. He poked his head through and called out, "Hello?" It was extremely dark in there, but he didn't care for what little he could see. The interior, of problematic size, resembled a battlefield. Boxes and packing cases were scattered everywhere, with no sense of order, some of them smashed and spilling out their contents. An acrid odor, like that of damp charcoal, hung in the air. A human figure stood to one side . . . only a life-size cardboard cut-out of some fleeting celebrity. He could discern wisps of sound, as if through a long tunnel, an indistinct mumbling and grunting, and a dull thumping. Something about the sound distressed him mightily, and he backed away, without even the consideration of entering. The doors swung and flopped together loosely.

That was enough, or rather, too much. Fair-Mart would have to survive without his trade. All Haredon wanted to do now was clear out. Back he went, past the glaring furry animals and plastic space ships, then down a short aisle stacked with bags of dog food, some of them busted and dribbling brown pellets on the untidy floor. Something darted away from a heap of bags, immediately lost to sight beneath a mound of litter. A cat? No, more likely a mouse, but if so, a well fed specimen. Shadows loomed on the wall above the next aisle—this place offered more shadows than merchandise— but these shadows shifted as if with volition. He stopped. Yes, someone, a number of someones, were moving over there, and quite close too, without a trace of sound. Did he care anymore? He pursued, but refused to dash after them. Around the corner, and he saw them, for a moment, before the dark shapes disappeared into yet another aisle. He couldn't make out anything through the dimness but thin, stooped forms, shambling jerkily out of sight.

Of course he couldn't be certain from such a quick glimpse, but if the images burned into his mind were in any way accurate, it didn't say much for the quality of personnel on the night crew. He had the impression of rough, shabby characters, with something more than a little wrong about them. They walked funny, for one thing. It must be hard to get good help after regular hours. Most likely they possessed faulty personal skills. At any rate, he wasn't keen on having any dealings with their sort.

Sticking to the current aisle should bring him back to the front doors. He followed this path, still carrying the spray bottle with him, just in case he found a cashier waiting for him. By now someone might have wheeled his cart away. That would be fitting. He unexpectedly entered a large, semi-enclosed chamber crammed with gardening supplies. The place was terribly dirty, as if it was never cleaned. The rancid smell from ruptured bags of loam didn't help matters. A rustling noise close by unnerved him. The heavy bags were strewn across the floor. A pile of dark, earthy material had been pushed against one side of the lane. Quite a heap it was, more like dried sewer mud than anything healthy for growing plants. Was this any way to run a business? Something protruded from the pile. It looked like—it was—a piece of splintered bone.

Haredon backed out of there, scraped his shoes on a patch of thin carpet, and took off the way he'd come. A left turn led him into an unfamiliar aisle, which he wouldn't have thought possible at this stage. Surely he had covered the entire sales floor by now? Whoever designed such retail outlets obviously knew how to maximize space. It wouldn't seem so alarmingly cavernous, though, if it were filled with customers. He quickly walked past a lot of soap and shampoo displays toward a broad open area which he assumed was the front of the store. Unfortunately, he was once again in error. He entered a hitherto unknown plaza containing centralized stands of televisions and other electrical appliances. One set bore a fractured screen. It was beyond his powers of guessing how he could have missed this before. It troubled him, more than he cared to admit, that he didn't know where this region lay, relative to where he wanted to go. His internal compass had failed him. He gazed about helplessly, but it was so dark that he couldn't recognize anything. He glanced up at the ceiling, saw nothing save discolored, sooty paneling and water sprinklers. He could use a drink now, of something.

Across the way he could barely make out an indeterminate figure, which caught his eye only when it suddenly moved and vanished behind a counter. That surprised him, because it didn't seem like the sort of shape which ought to move. It happened very fast, to be sure, but he'd been looking right at it, and he couldn't summon up a picture of sufficient humanity to satisfy him. Haredon suppressed an irrational desire to back away, inwardly cursed himself for a fool and rushed after the presence, wanting only directions to the door that would get him out of here. Any door would serve at this stage. He was tired, tired of wasted effort and this gloomy place.

He zipped around the corner, finding no one, but detecting the tread of heavy, clumsy feet just ahead. It sounded still nearer—at last he was gaining—then stopped, now very close. Once more around an obstruction, a towering palette stack which almost blocked the aisle, and this time he found someone waiting for him on the other side.

Before he could quite calm down, or think clearly, Haredon found himself a considerable distance away from the point of confrontation, sans the spray bottle. He must have set it down or dropped it during what he could only term his panicky flight. Even now his brain struggled to function, shifting gritty gears while trying to make sense of the situation. Nothing could excuse his actions. Objectively, what had happened? He'd come face to face with one of the night crew, those people who shun the light of the sun and most of mankind as well. Presumably they had their reasons for living and working as they did. This particular fellow didn't have much to explain. Haredon thought hard. A possible answer came to him, one just conceivable. There had been a fire here, once upon a time. He hadn't paid much attention back then, but recalled reports of deaths, and presumably terrible injuries and disfigurements. The poor guy he'd bumped into must be a long-term employee who had—just barely, by the look of him—survived that tragic fire, and here came an unfeeling late night customer with nothing better to do than humiliate the unfortunate sufferer.

Yes, that explained everything. Of course it did, for there couldn't be any other explanation, none he cared to think about, that is. That dreadful hunched, sagging form, propped motionless like a sales dummy, the soiled, cast-off clothing, the stench—so like that of decay—and that face, which he would never forget, no matter how he tried. Darkened, pinched, taut, more bones than flesh, with collapsing cheeks, and eyes which he could not recall save as dark, empty holes. There must have been something in them; they seemed to stare into his soul. Yes, Haredon had it down pat now, he had it all figured out, so there was no need for icy sweat, his heart could stop pounding like a trip hammer. Only—sweet Jesus, why was he thinking this?—he didn't believe a word of it!

He focused desperately on his surroundings. With an effort, he made out cans and plastic bottles of household liquids, packages of paper products. Under the circumstances, it was almost like homecoming. He knew these aisles, having shopped them what felt like ages ago, and knew the way out from here. All he had to do was remain calm, walk in that direction, take a left into the broad lane, then straight to the front. He would be rid of this ghastly place forever within one minute, home in fifteen. There he would be safe, or—the weird idea crossed his mind—he would wake up, but he would be out of this.

That first corner was just twenty paces away in a straight line. Skirting all the junk on the floor, more like forty. Someone had slipped over here since his original visit and made a bigger mess. There the wide central aisle, so poorly illuminated that he couldn't see to the end of it. Without doubt, the lights were failing. The store couldn't pass for open anymore, nor did it need to, now that he was inside. What an ugly thought. Haredon was overcome by the creepy sensation of having been lured to this place, by powers who had achieved their objective, and were now abandoning all pretense.

Some evil movement was afoot. As he advanced down the ever lengthening aisle, he heard furtive whisperings and mutterings at far remove, but from all points, especially ahead of him. The store apparently harbored a large nighttime population after all. Whatever the reason for their previous concealment, they were switching to new tactics now. They didn't want to kid him anymore. He had seen something he shouldn't, or the time had come to reveal it, and the underlying reality of his situation was seeping out. He halted and shut his eyes, realizing that any moment would bring fresh information which he couldn't stand. He didn't want to be here, he didn't want to know he was here. Just to block out the surrounding images for a second brought useless relief.

He opened his eyes. Haredon saw motion in the aisle, before him, coming his way. Several dark shapes, no longer shy, lurching awkwardly toward him, not quickly, but with inexorable purpose. Barely able to hold themselves erect, leaning clumsily on one another, but representing a menace which he couldn't deal with or struggle against. Before they became clearly visible he darted into a cross aisle and ran.

It did no good to think. There couldn't be any question of cause or justification. Who was he to these people, or they to him? They wanted him, that was all, the only fact of the world that mattered. Whatever his ultimate fate, he couldn't allow it to happen like this, at their hands. He must flee, dodge and hide until escape opened to him. It meant more than anything not to have to gaze upon them again.

Easier said than done, he feared. The current mumbled song from the hidden intercoms lapsed into squeaking, squawking noise, a sound beyond static, as if of an alien language significant to those who could understand. At the same moment a twisted shape, loathsomely incomplete, suddenly thrust itself from behind a toppling stack of boxes, leaping out to cut off its prey. Haredon turned abruptly, not daring to see, noting the ungodly stink of putrefying flesh as he stumbled into the adjoining corridor. He thought he heard words behind him, or something vaguely like speech, deliberate intonations, nothing he could make out or wanted to hear. No tongue still human could produce such sounds.

He had to get out of this narrow tunnel of terror before something closed in ahead to shut him in. He came out the other end where, as predicted, they were waiting. Two blackened forms approached from the left. To the right he went. Another ghastly sound—that unhealthy, sobbing rasp—his breath. A kaleidoscope of sound: shuffling, stumbling, wheezing, grunting, orchestrated to music which no longer passed for intelligible or sane. Insufficient light to cast shadows, yet shadows all the same: tangible, shifting darkness resolving itself into hulking, degenerate shapes, following him, reaching out for him.

All reason left behind with his pursuers, Haredon planned or calculated nothing, but merely ran in as straight a line as he could, tapping his last reserves of adrenaline, down a broad aisle, enough space to each side that nothing could easily grab him as he passed. He ran for a hundred miles and a hundred years, into the unknown, going nowhere, without destination, incapable of standing still. So dark now, little boy in the closet dark, under the bed dark, alive with awful stick figures that should lie down and stay still, but refused to do so. The faintest radiance ahead, oozing over the top of obstructing shelves. He paused, started one way, spied movement, turned the other, saw the check-outs as if through mist before him, the windows, oblongs of blackness, the door.

Something manned the nearest register, not that it mattered anymore. Haredon charged through, pressing his shoulder against the door. It didn't give—that insane, choking laugh, which horrified him so, exploded out of his mouth—he read the word on the glass, transposed. *Entrance*. Pushing away, sensing withered hands at his back, turning, rushing down to the next door. That beautiful mirrored word of hope: *Exit*. He hit the door flying, and it opened wide onto the night.

And there he stopped. It didn't occur to him to continue. The last moment of truth, the final revelation, had come. Outside he saw . . . nothing. This wasn't the dark of night which should have led him back, fearfully, to the safety of his apartment and the real world. There was no parking lot, no cars, no road, no wider world beyond. It wasn't night, not even the perpetual night of 3:46 A.M. It was only absence. He wasn't held back or restrained in any way; there just wasn't any place to go.

He backed away, allowing the door to swing shut, forever. Haredon turned, head down, so that he could see as little of the surrounding presences as possible. They jostled incrementally closer. One bent, corroded shape broke from the pack and advanced decisively, one hand outreached. Perhaps the night manager wanted words with him.

KARDOWAN

Kardowan, exiled wizard and nobleman of mighty Dyrezan, sojourned long and bitterly in the barbaric kingdom of Thallia, nursing black grudges while dreaming of restoring his former glory and wreaking fiendish vengeance upon those who had cast him out. They had rebelled against his greed, his cruelty, his unslakable thirst for domination; yet was he not deserving, as the greatest mage among an empire of mages? In his bold and reckless grasp for power—which led to the downfall of his house and his casting from the seat of civilization—had he not sought merely his just due? Kardowan thought so, and he had not yet grown accustomed to brooking dissent on that point, nor was he likely ever to do so.

Kardowan lived well, for he had absconded those many years ago with much loot, but he dwelt in Thallia only as a big man among the lesser, boasting hollowly to the crude denizens of that bleak land. He fantasized of more, unimaginably more, nor would his heart beat easily until such time as he could translate his fevered cravings into brutal reality.

He first learned of the Oracle of Nemphine from an itinerant native priest, a secret adept of the Nemphine order who blabbed of hidden mysteries, his tongue loosened initially by wine, subsequently by torture. After disposing of the remains Kardowan pondered what he had been told. In a cave at the top of the shunned Saracel Valley, deep within the mystic fastness of the Kurkian Mountains, brooded the ancient Oracle, seat of wisdom and fabled mouthpiece of the most high Gods, perhaps a direct link to none other than majestic and terrible Xenophor, Lord of All Things. There, in that stronghold of cosmic knowledge, might a man learn the truths of the ages, including those (he reasoned) of vital personal significance. So Kardowan determined to go there, and from the lips of the Oracle—if it had such—to wrest the answers and receive those boons which would arm him with the power to restore his fortunes and make him triumphant over all the world.

Kardowan expended the balance of his gold horde to raise a private force of desperate warriors, convicts and wastrels who would follow him anywhere for generous hire. He gave them much, promised them more (for are not promises cheap?), and set out on the lengthy and dubiously charted journey to the Kurkian range. On that trek great and mysterious perils hailed him and his band from all sides, and there were casualties among his dark crew, not always from sane causes, but that counted for nothing, so long as they cut their way to the mystic mountains and found the shunned valley. Find the Saracel Valley they did, forging their path upward into a desolate region of boulders and volcanic spires, a lifeless, empty land where it seemed that no man had ever trod, though formidable presences lingered and lurked to pounce when they might. Yet came Kardowan in time to a sheer cliff face of brooding basalt, and there espied a large, circular cave mouth adorned about its portals with grisly carvings and flanked by hideous onyx statues, twin representations of multi-armed, multi-headed entities that surely never walked the earth. There the priests of Nemphine came forth from within the black opening to warn away the troop, threatening them with death or worse if they tarried. Kardowan mocked the threat, at which the priests blasted his men with fiery enchantments, reducing them to sputtering sparks and smoking ashes. Yet Kardowan laughed, for he was a cunning sorcerer, and had taken measures against artful opposition, and his conjurations protected him from that obvious and predicted doom. Then he muttered the spell which had saved him when despairing treason rose against him in Dyrezan, and with the thought those feckless priests were twisted and ruptured, reduced to rancid ooze beneath his boots.

Kardowan entered the cave and, lighting again a torch that had fallen from the withered hand of a destroyed priest, advanced into the gloom. On the walls of the tunnel he beheld chased into the smooth stone the peculiar and abhorrent images of deities or demons, culminating in a grand mural of many colors depicting the horrific visage of great Xenophor, He of the Million Eyes, who knows all and sees all, Master of Time, Master of Creation and Destruction. Kardowan quailed from that loathsome painting, yet it pleased him that it should be there, indicative of the averred boundless power of the Oracle.

After a seemingly endless walk along that corridor, past those dreadful pictures and many a disturbing side burrow, he attained the chamber of the Oracle. There he required no torch, for the room and its affects glowed of their own sickly yellow light. There, atop a marble dais framed by marble pillars, gleamed the Oracle stone, a purple gem the size of a man's head, from which flashed a weird flickering radiance. Those strange flashes brightened as the stone spoke. It said, "Who dares desecrate these halls, sanctified to Great Xenophor the Powerful, Xenophor the Merciless; who dares stand before His rage?" Came the answer, "I, Kardowan, do so dare, for I would share with Xenophor Most High the power and fury He possesses that I desire above all things." Said the Oracle, "Consult, O man, the priests of the Order of Nemphine," but Kardowan laughed, saying, "Excellent advice, I am sure, but I have slain them all, so I will speak directly." And the Oracle laughed and said, "What wilt thou?"

Kardowan said, "Give me power to terrorize my enemies, and riches to humble them, and pleasures to offend them. Tell me how to achieve these rightful goals. I ask for my just due."

Spoke the Oracle, "This may be. Thou could be favored of the harsh All Seeing, comely in His inescapable sight. Prove thy worth with these three acts: curse a friend; wound a love; outrage a people. Go, and do these three things, then return to claim thy just reward."

So Kardowan went forth from the Oracle, and hazarded alone and curiously unopposed the shunned valley and the evil mountains, making his way back to Thallia where he undertook to accomplish his telling deeds. Thusly he fared. There was an old man of Thallia, a goodly man and naive, who had from pity embraced Kardowan when first he fled to that barbaric land. This man, asking nothing for himself, welcomed the stranger when the people would have killed him, protected him until that society accepted his presence. This man Kardowan now denounced for black witchcraft, forging lying evidence as to his crimes against the citizenry, who believed the lies and slew the old man. Then there was a young lady of Thallia for whom Kardowan feigned an attraction, gulling her with false claims and poetic effusions and expressions of spurious love. These she at last accepted, and bestowed her heart on him, and the nuptial day was set, and all her family came together for the ceremony, and before them all Kardowan stood up and forsook her with abysmally untrue and scandalous charges, forever breaking her heart. Then, as they objected to this hateful treatment, and would stir up anger against the cruel suitor, Kardowan fulminated a conspiracy with the savage hill tribes against the folk of Thallia, and there came upon them needless fire and rapine and wailing misery. These tasks performed, Kardowan fled before those who would avenge his horrors, vowing to pay them for their righteous hatred once he came into his own.

Without incident he found his way again to the dead valley and the dark cave, presently standing amidst the sickly glare before the twinkling Oracle, to which he bragged of his enormities. "I have so acted," he said, "as to please my master Xenophor, and to fulfill the demands of the Oracle. The deeds are done. Look out into the world, survey the wreckage of hope and body that trails me. Now, truly, give me my just due."

And the Oracle said, "Thou hast indeed prospered as promised. Surely thou art favored of Xenophor, like a deserving child unto Him. This Oracle sends your message in all its particulars. If He deems it fitting, great Xenophor will respond."

So He did. The Oracle chamber rocked, the walls shook, the ceiling groaned. Indeed, that shock ravaged the earth for a hundred leagues around. The Oracle said, "He has heard, and He delights in the news. Such is His strange joy, O man, that He would not relinquish thee, but shall offer thee the greatest boon He may bestow: to take you unto Himself, body and soul, to writhe and shriek forever within His substance. This is your just due. Though mortal men should ever speak your name in fearful whispers, you will know, until the end of time, the peculiar joy which is Xenophor's."

Kardowan objected; he pleaded; at last he screamed for mercy, but that final request necessarily made no sense at all, nor did the Oracle deign to answer. In a gust of hot wind Kardowan vanished from before the Oracle, never to be seen again by living man, yet to endure always, especially beloved of He who lords over a crazed cosmos.

THE MAD ONE

Kerry found the stone.

Not that he sought it; rather, it seemed to find him, judging from the way it suddenly caught the toe of his walking shoe. The stone protruded from the muck surrounding a shallow, bug-infested pool in the otherwise dry arroyo where it looped behind the steep slope of the lonesome, rocky hill, the hill which rose in solitary silence above the sere lowlands with their scraggly shrubs and stunted trees. To Kerry's eyes it seemed only a black cylindrical lump, veined with gray and flecked with green, half buried in the gooey silt and ooze. So it seemed, at first.

Kerry had wandered away from the summer place earlier that morning, when the sun grew hot and indoors games became unbearable. His father sent him outside—the cabin, cramped and lightly furnished, could not accommodate the entire family when awake, and his parents were busy writing about some Arizona Indians. Their eight-year-old son did not know much about that (his conceptions concerning native Americans were formed largely by old westerns on television and the original prints his father hung on the walls of their regular home in the city), and momentarily enjoyed the thought of exploring the nearby wilds. Soon, however, he sorely felt the lack of companionship; all his friends were miles away, Mom and Dad had settled into their usual routine, which excluded him, and even Ralph, the family collie, was kept penned behind the house for fear that he might run afoul of dangerous animals. The semi-desert landscape, and the few tumble-down, abandoned farms from the olden days, fueled his interest for a time, but by noon Kerry solemnly regretted, in the manner of all little boys, leaving those people and scenes which were familiar and entertaining to him.

Shuffling along the precarious banks of the seasonal stream, bored to distraction, Kerry stumbled upon the black stone. Shrouded in shadow as this particular spot was, with the overhanging bluffs thoughtfully blocking the sun, the utter blackness contained within the rock nonetheless caught his eye and drew a curious glance. After a moments childish contemplation he detected something not quite right in its shape and structure, something which hinted at more than the natural

73

processes whereby stone gets chiseled and polished in creek beds. Kerry stooped low on the hard packed but crumbling bank, attempting in vain to grasp the object. Failing this, he seized a thick branch which had fallen by the water, prodded the stone. He could move it with some effort—which meant there was not a lot more buried under the mud, iceberg fashion—so he began hauling it up onto the shore. It slid through the tacky ooze, and when well within reach Kerry tossed away the stick to grab for his prize. The salvage operation took only a moment more, and he was very careful not to get his clothes muddy (Mom would appreciate that). He regarded the stone.

A strange thing, he discovered. What he had appeared to be a carven figure of some kind, about a foot in height, six inches across, representing a person with a hideously leering face. It resembled a bust, although Kerry did not think of it that way; to him it was a *head*, and not a very pleasant one at that. The features were unfamiliar and rather frightening, nor had he ever seen an expression like that on anyone he knew. The mouth stretched wide, with the lips parted to reveal sharp, needle-like teeth, dozens in a row; the nose straight and narrow, with thick, flaring nostrils; the blank eyes bulging from their sculptured sockets a good half inch beyond the rounded cheeks. The boy suppressed a shudder, gave thought to throwing the thing into the murky water.

He did not do so. It occurred to him that this must be one of those Indian artifacts his father was always on about, and which he so desperately hoped to find in this wilderness area. Indeed, only days before, when they had just arrived, Dad had shown him the old stones on top of the barren hill behind him, the stones arrayed in a loose circle and obviously very old. This head reminded him of those stones; it appeared ancient and weather-worn, chewed by the grit of the sporadic stream into which it had fallen—or been cast—ages ago. Perhaps it belonged up there. Dad would surely want to see it.

And yet, as he realized this, Kerry felt an obscure compulsion, obscure because it was not normal for little boys, and most assuredly not for him. Adventurous young men do not, as a rule, abandon their trophies, but this was now exactly what he intended to do. He felt the need to return the stone, to replace it in the crude circle on the hill. How he knew it should rest there was beyond his unformed intellect, but it seemed the only thing to do.

So he scampered up the hill, pushing through the sticker bushes at the base, clutching the black stone as he crossed the lifeless and dusty hilltop. At the crest he found the broken and scattered circle, a shapeless altar within which he placed the forgotten idol. As he did the child heard a low humming sound which seemed to come from within his ears rather than without; reminiscent, yet utterly unlike the sound he heard in shells at the beach. It meant nothing, for Kerry Williams was entranced by the restored head, resting now on the shoulders of an oblong slab.

Diana Williams, staring about her with set mouth and nervous eyes, paused once again from her labors. Typed papers lay on the plain coffee-table before her, on the uncomfortable old couch to either side, on the floor by the empty, disused fireplace. Several sheets bore her heavily penciled editing marks, as did those in her lap. Through the doorway, in the room which served as their bedroom at night, she could detect the constant, muted chatter of her husband's typing at his laptop, now and then breaking off as he leafed through his stack of notes for new and precious bits of information. Ralph barked throatily, unceasingly, as he dashed to and fro across the backyard.

Damn that dog! Whatever the source of her growing distress, she supposed that it involved also the dog. The queer tension and the stabbing headache had started about the time Ralph began vociferously sounding off, and the stupid animal had not shut up since. Such a normally well behaved beast, it seemed a shame to allow one infuriating outburst to disturb her so, but there it was. Neil ought to do something, he knew how to deal with pets better than she, and certainly he could take a moment to deal with it, before she shut the mutt up permanently . . .

Now what did that mean? Diana realized she had spoken the harsh thought aloud, and glanced back into the bedroom to see if she had attracted Neil's attention. No, he kept banging merrily away, grinding out the learned document which would earn him a doctorate if it should please his stuffy, godlike department board. Neil struggled so hard to meet their demands, timetables, and strictures, facing their inevitable carping criticism like a true gentleman. Funny thing, but she had never conceived of his historian overlords in such a dismal light before. Trying to blot out the thought, an inrush of other troublesome conceptions suddenly plagued her, screwing up her mild and pretty features in an earnest frown, and the pain intensified. It knifed through her cerebrum, actually blurring her vision. Was this a migraine? Impossible, she never . . .

Knife . . .

She massaged her aching temples, morosely pondering her husband's situation. His intentions were grand, his passion for the field tremendous. Neil's Indian studies had led him to this deserted region—an unknown and little documented tribe of north-central Arizona had caught his fancy, and she had to admit that the sparse clues indicated some exciting possibilities—and forthwith they had set off, family and dog, to dwell here for the summer while he perused old records and explored the expansive, unpeopled landscape for more evidence. His work was important, and she realized it could make him a big name in the scholarly halls of history and anthropology. Oh yes, he stood on the verge of a major find, and he surely needed all the help required. The interminable proofreading, the corrections, the advice she had to offer as an English major; that did not appear so much to ask. In keeping with her abilities Diana found comfort and pleasure in furthering her husband's career . . .

The pain jolted her. There swam into her mind's eye a hideous image, a dreadful dark face which slavered and taunted her in a language not her own, yet which managed to make itself understood. The hard, black lips exploded forth in a torrent of guttural hatred, deluging her throbbing brain, bringing together all the disjointed ruminations of the past half hour. The knife . . . the knife . . . Then the face winked out, even the memory borne into sealed catacombs of the mind.

Her husband's career? Oh my, his career, his work, so necessary, above all else. *His* career, *his* work. What happened to her life, her hopes, dreams, expectations? All that lost, the infinite possibilities, the gateways to her own glory slammed shut forever. All for him, with his eternal rat-tat-tat on that cheap laptop, the piddling through old and pointless papers, the grubbing over bones and useless relics. What was she doing in this wretched place? He didn't care, he couldn't care, so wrapped up in his own plans while she vegetated. Had he forgotten that he had a son? Kerry, who wandered alone now amidst treacherous ravines, surrounded by vicious creatures and lurking pitfalls. What sort of man would desert his own son, send him away into the wilderness, an alien environment in which he could not cope if danger threatened. Even now little Kerry might be trapped in a cave, or pinned underneath a toppled boulder, or . . . Desertion? Diana suddenly realized—it struck her, like a shot in the night—what the future held in store for her. Neil would climb to the top on her back. He would make it, for ruthlessness does have its advantages, and in the end he would discard her as he discarded a broken arrowhead. Such was her future, indisputably coming; could she doubt it any longer, when Neil was willing to consign the child to an early death? It must not happen. Options narrowed, but choice remained. She listened, could hear nothing. More notes, then. She leapt to her feet, moving noiselessly, with deliberate tread, into the kitchen. Proceeding straight to a certain drawer, she removed the long, heavy-handled butcher knife. Diana studied the shimmering blade, admiring the sparkles of light in the smooth, polished metal. She closed the drawer. As she turned, Diana detected footsteps.

Neil Williams continued to plug away at his rough draft, though he was distracted by Ralph's continuous baying, the low but persistent buzzing in his ears—an audial nerve infection?—and his grinding headache. These irritations had come upon him rather suddenly, slowing production to a crawl, interfering with what began as a fine work session. Now he proceeded with extreme difficulty, his mind cluttered with hazy images, vague impressions which fused into cruel urges when he halted long enough to consider them. He endeavored not to, but it almost seemed as if force, directed from within, was being applied against him.

He shrugged, with an effort returned to work. No doubt exists, he wrote, that the legends, lurid as they must appear to the casual researcher, possess a basis in fact. Recorded tales are numerous, and while many are unreliable oral transcriptions, taken down at a vastly later date, a baffling amount of agreement and authentic detail seems to support these otherwise incredible stories. Natives and white settlers alike relate—

Perhaps he made a mistake in coming here, in leaving Flagstaff and the university, hauling the family out of their daily lives into this forsaken hole. The work called him, of course—his chance discovery of the antique papers, elusively describing the undocumented Indian tribe, had seemed a bolt from heaven, his big opportunity to earn fame and respect—but now he was not so sure. The county records in Prescott told him little, consisting mainly of a collection of horror stories, all hearsay. Earlier Neil had dismissed correspondence as inadequate—he wanted to see the place, get the feel of the shunned region—but those local accounts could not compare with the original reports prepared by the then new territorial government. Even those, however, were secondhand whisperings; could he build an entire thesis from this material?

The early tales, handed down from neighboring tribes, speak of the Mad Ones, an obscure and horrible cult or tribe which inhabited that north-western region of the Verde Valley. Considered devils by other natives, the Mad Ones (their name for themselves lost to history) engaged in wholesale warfare and looting of any peoples who fell within their reach. Several references can be found attesting to their bloodthirsty and diabolical nature; the dismembered bodies of their victims, the severed heads used in mysterious rituals at established periods, apparently connoting some peculiar form of worship; and the catalogue of atrocities visited upon those unfortunates bold or rash enough to dare enter their domain. The truly interesting aspect of these terrible beings lies not in what they brought down upon others—

Half-heartedly scanning the preceding page, Neil's disquiet blossomed in radiating doubts. Not very good, he thought; the writing was poor, uneven, the vital points unclear, the main thrust wavering as his mood changed. Or was it? Except for spelling and other minor grammatical mistakes he always felt satisfied with his composition… but not now. Diana could clean up the lesser errors, allowing him to concentrate on a free-flowing style and concise air, but could she rescue a thoroughly bad paper? Would she even try?

What would she think when she read this rambling, amateurish effort'? Even now, this very moment, she was proofreading the first chapter, probably chuckling to herself, aghast at his feeble and mindless technique; with pity or loathing she considered her husband of ten years who found the culmination of his career in this stinking morass of unconnected musings and jottings. This, then, the final disgrace, the one piled atop the other sad and dispiriting incidents which would lead to the final break—

Neil endeavored to thrust these ideas aside. They did not make sense; Diana was faithful, supportive, loyal and respectful like his son. He wondered what Kerry was up to just now. Earlier Neil had told him to go outside and play . . . or had he *forbidden* it? Why didn't the boy mind his father?

Neil saw the face. It spread from the limits of consciousness, dark and gibbering, shouting insultingly and demanding nameless things. It strangely soothed him, easing the pain somewhat. Determination formed and crystallized. The thesis receded further from his thoughts; as the unheard voice told him, it was of no consequence;

why not throw it away'? Why not, indeed'? He could not be sure that a strong argument did not exist for destroying the paper before it damaged his reputation.

Destroy it before it hurt . . .

Destroy . . .

His leaden fingers moved slowly, as if in a dream. Alphonse Thompson, a minor federal official, came the region on a fact-finding mission in 1874, as the first American settlers entered that wilderness country. He found the abhorrent Indians gone, disappeared, probably wiped out to the last man, woman and child. Reports garnered from friendlier tribes failed to shed much light on the disaster, nor was he able to verify whether the Mad Ones were slaughtered by vengeful enemies, or—as was plainly stated by several eminent neighboring tribal authorities—they destroyed themselves in a cataclysmic orgy of murder and suicide. The latter theory, while realistically unsound, Thompson considered quite seriously (evident, since he took such care to gather the information), and the fastidious scribe offers his interpretation of a religious motive. The Mad Ones, he says, worshiped a horrible deity which demanded gruesome sacrifices and activities on the part of its faithful. This monstrous god brought insanity and violence to the Indians, whose oral traditions dimly recalled an earlier age of peace and benevolence. How they came to worship such an evil being is unknown, but once the religion had fastened itself upon them the tribe was locked forever in a continual state of fear and bloodshed. The reign of terror ended with their downfall, though subsequent settlers generally avoided the region as somehow unsafe, or haunted. Vorchek's recent study presents the unlikely claim that genuine—

Neil stopped. Enough; the paper appalled him, the labor involved constituting a drain of his energies, a waste of his potential. Rapidly, without thinking, he slammed keys, blanked out the digital document, saved the emptiness. He felt an unusual sense of accomplishment. Rising stealthily, he leaned forward to peer into the living room. His wife was there, head back, hands rubbing her eyes. Not working. She had given up on him, as he always knew she would when the going got rough.

He quietly drew open the desk drawer, retrieving the revolver kept there—purely as a precaution, one could not be too well protected in this lonely spot—but the gun had other uses as well. She meant to leave him; he knew that, he had seen it in her face many times, found hints in her subtle conniving against him. Had she not turned the boy against him? Kerry, who even now was out frolicking in the desert, disobeying his strictest orders about leaving the premises? His own son turned against him, and now she would go . . . unless he could prevent it. It was the only way; as a promising young professor Neil had appearances to consider, a career to protect. He could not have her ruining everything.

She was gone! Glancing through the open doorway, he saw the empty couch, the scattered printed sheets. Caught in the act of abandonment, the vicious shrew, the slut, her damned betrayal laid bare for all to see. Over the incessant howling of the dog he detected furtive sounds in the rear of the house. So she hadn't made her getaway yet. Neil chuckled softly to himself. This far, no farther. He advanced gingerly across the den, the cold metal grasped firmly, held before him as a shield and a harbinger of final judgment.

As he approached, Neil heard a drawer closing.

Kerry staggered into the looming cottage, weakly clutching his temples and sobbing from the pain. He wished he could make the agony go away; there must be something he could do, or if not he, then his parents. They were always such a comfort when he injured himself, and this detestable throbbing and pounding in his skull hurt worse than any previous experience. Ralph's loud and uncharacteristic barking did not aid matters. The boy found them in the kitchen, sprawled awkwardly on the floor, and what he saw forced new and greater tears from his swollen lids. His mother lay facing upward, a look of shock and unreasoning fury corrupting her normally calm and loving features. A thin trickle of blood coursed from between her clenched teeth, and her tiny hands, fingers tangled and bent, clawed in frozen distress at an abdomen exposed, blown open, splashed with crimson and seared with ebony burns. His father, spread-eagled across her legs, reposed face downward, his body contorted in the middle, propped slightly above the floor. Below him a widening red pool glistened, while in the small of his back a ragged circle of similar color oozed, a narrow, splotched point protruding from the wound.

Kerry could not comprehend this scene, far more than an eight-year-old could grasp; the presence of death, violent and meaningless, the stillness of eternity. Gazing about the gory room, absorbing the awful spectacle, he noticed the revolver lying beyond his father's outstretched hand. He picked it up; it smelled funny, and he knew what that meant. Kerry did not know what to do, with everything so strange and terrible. Call the police—wait, they didn't have a phone—walk to town, then, all that way, and get help, or— He must do something!

He must do something. Later he did, like a good boy . . . but first he shot the dog.

On the barren hill, not too far away, within the primordial ring of stones, the ancient and forgotten idol stared sightlessly. The blind eyes bulged, the nostrils flared, the wide mouth gaped in what could be described as a grimace . . . or a grin.

IN THE TIME VAULT

Jerry Sloane knew the police were closing in on him, that apprehension could be avoided for minutes at most, but this theoretically bitter knowledge did not disturb his joyful equanimity. Everything had been planned, everything accounted for in his daring scheme. He, Jerry Sloane, the petty thief, the sleazy crook, the two-bit hustler after infertile dreams, had scored and scored big: the Big Time, the heist all the smart-alecky pros talked about, but none dared contemplate except Jerry "Shaky Fingers" Sloane. Despised by the cheapest con artists, spat upon by house-breakers, loathed by those who took pride in this great field of human endeavor—robbery—he had pulled off the greatest criminal caper of all time. He'd stolen the largest, most fulsomely desirable diamond known to man, the treasured Cytherian Star.

And he'd get away with it! Dodging between two campus buildings on the outskirts of the university grounds, eluding the probing rays of police searchlights sweeping the night, he lugged the monstrous gem under one arm as he darted down the covered walkway to his destination. Laughing as he ran, his utter confidence bubbled up from within as he imagined the shocked faces of the authorities when they realized what he'd done. Sloane smashed his revolver through the plate glass door, reached in, turned the lock, entered the main room of this special enclosure. As his pursuers pounded up the walkway he contemptuously dropped the gun on the floor. He wouldn't need it where he was going.

He confronted the Time Vault.

Sloane didn't waste time surveying the scene, and he didn't know enough about science to fully comprehend the magnificence of this fantastic technological achievement, but he knew enough about the Vault to have factored it into his plans.

The Cytherian Star, the only notable relic brought back by the first intrepid explorers of Venus, had been formed by the brutal crushing action of that alien atmosphere, its enormous pressures, far superior to any generated on earth for miles below the surface, compressing the raw carbon over eons until that fabulous crystal was fashioned. After cutting by the finest Swiss jewelers it still remained thirteen inches from side to side, flawless, priceless. But the problems involved in stealing it, the matter of the actual theft, and especially that of disposal, had daunted the cleverest underworld minds, until the lowly Shaky Fingers had hit upon the Time Vault, that most recent of acclaimed scientific discoveries.

Sloane drew open the heavy steel door of the Vault, examined its empty interior, then leaped in as the police clattered up to the antechamber entrance. He heard their harsh commands, demands for surrender. He slammed the huge door behind him and immediately set the controls built into the inner wall which he'd memorized from the popular vidis. The Vault would open again only from the inside—some kind of safety precaution—once the mechanism was programmed for eternity. This he now did. He could open it any time, they never. Simple as that, it was done.

Sloane had read everything he could get his hands on concerning the Vault. Built last year by the famed physicist Merrick of Cal Tech, it functioned as a sort of bubble in the space-time continuum, its unique energy field shielding any objects or occupants from external forces. Radiation, gravity, sound, all universal forces ceased to operate at the edge of the device, yet its chief attribute lay in its absolute negation of the remorseless flow of time. Dead matter would not alter its composition inside, nor would living matter grow old. Once inside, a man could exist forever, alive and aware . . . or so long as convenience dictated.

As soon as the door clanged shut Sloane drifted off the floor, his slight movements propelling him into the air. No gravity, as expected. Outside, he guessed, they were beating on the door, screaming at him to open up, raging over the lost fortune. Let them, he could wait. In zero gravity he felt like a new man. The absolute darkness didn't faze him either. He switched on the flashlight he'd packed, let it burn continuously. The batteries would never run down.

Oh yes, Sloane had made a full study of the Vault and its effects. He could sit out a hundred years or more, take it easy, ponder the question of how he would cope with the future when he faced it. By then, he reasoned shrewdly, the immediacy of his crime should have worn off, and he would be a celebrity when he emerged. He would be famous, loved, a hero, and even if he couldn't keep the stone (that, he conceded, might prove a sticky legal point) he would be set for life on the royalties from talk shows, interviews, books, and of course film rights. Oh yes, he had it all figured out.

Of course time stood still only with reference to the outside world; he would not age, but would experience every moment. One hundred years in a ten by ten steel cube, lit only by a flashlight, with nothing to do, might wear rather thin. No means existed of telling time within the Vault, and the scientific articles (what he could make of them) had stressed the difficulty a human brain would face in marking time without some frame of reference. Sloane just shrugged that off. So what if he stayed a little too long? Two hundred was as good as one hundred years, and he could surely tell the difference over the long haul. That had bothered him at first; was it really possible to sit in the Vault for centuries, millennia, without realizing it? Spooky, but he supposed the eggheads were talking through their hats again. He could handle it. The prize justified a little boredom.

And so he settled down for the long wait. Time passed, he didn't know how long. He instituted a routine of sorts, sleeping whenever the urge overcame him, staring at the light when he required it, flicking it off when that steady glare and sharp disc of radiance became too much for him. That was basically all he had to do. Sloane did not eat, drink, excrete, smoke, talk, read, watch television or do any of the things possible on the outside. In a sense, a disquietingly reinforced sense, it was like being back in prison. Except here he never got out for daily exercise.

This lethargic routine, to be sure, grew old very fast. Maybe it was only weeks, perhaps months. When he envisioned all of the years stretching ahead of him now his throat constricted, his heart raced, his eyes watered. In his mad dash to the safety of the Vault, Sloane hadn't managed to bring anything with which to occupy himself. Possibly he hadn't very carefully thought through this aspect, yet there must be a way to pass the time.

He approached this goal in stages, proceeding rather cautiously and, by his standards, scientifically. Sloane set himself an unbounded schedule: he would first do or think one thing, indulge in all its possible ramifications, and only when he exhausted that would he move on to the next. He started by imagining what he would do when he got out and really began to live. He conjured up visions of fast cars, splendid mansions, fawning worshipers, flashy clothes, boxcar loads of clinging, madly passionate women. He imagined travel, ostentatious wealth, all the grand things in life he had somehow missed.

By straining every fiber of imagination he possessed Sloane supposed he had consumed a number of years. Truly, he couldn't have believed he had so much in him. He wondered why he hadn't prospered before, if he was so clever.

Then he reviewed his past life. This was a grimmer, far less enjoyable subject, but since it required only the application of memory he spent a great deal of time on it. He saw his pitiful childhood, relived his abysmal adolescence, watched himself grow more vile, more cowardly, more spineless as his young manhood progressed, ever impatient of honest effort, ever seeking the main chance, until frustration and misplaced anger ate him up. He followed once more that insistently downward spiral leading to reform school, foster homes, prison, the streets, brightening only toward the end when he conceived the crime of the century, of all centuries.

Years ground by slowly, like dying snails.

He resurrected all the people he ever knew, classifying them according to his own peculiar standards. Not one single relationship, with man or woman, had stood the test of time. Each bond failed when Sloane learned how little others were willing or able to do for him. He hated them all, and was glad they would be dead and buried when he emerged.

He played games. He didn't know very many that could be played inside the head of one person, but he employed them all, and improvised the rest. Each he played painstakingly, over and over again, until the very subject of games nauseated him. He felt the decades creep by, decades of unrefined boredom, tedium so intense he had to grit his teeth and bite his tongue to keep from screaming aloud. He wasn't that far gone, not so soon. The alluring dream of greatness maintained his wavering resolve.

He talked to himself. From the earliest days Sloane had muttered about the future, whispered about the past, cracked jokes and inane stories, but now he evolved complicated monologues on all aspects of his life and human behavior in general. He declaimed at inordinate length, speaking or ranting for days, weeks, until his tinny echoing voice grew hoarse and he must pause for recuperation, or because he sickened of his own gibbering speech. He debated scientific points: why did some bodily functions stop inside the Vault, and not others? How did time affect human beings? It pleased him to think that he would be pardoned, come what may, because the professors would wish to learn of his ordeal. He didn't know why they would, but he knew they would. Profs were always interested in junk like that.

Years, years . . .

In a fit of unreasoning fury he hurtled the flashlight against a bare, smooth wall, destroying it, realized too late how much that illumination had meant to him. By snapping it on he had broken the deadening monotony, had spent probable hours gazing glassily at the Star, dreaming of mind-boggling riches to come. Now it was as if all that was irredeemably snatched away. He shrieked and raged and cursed cruel fate and begged God, some god, any god, to restore the vital light. How long had it been: fifty years, seventy-five, a hundred already? How could he tell? He'd expected trouble, but he could never have foreseen the hazards of estimating time without some reference, not necessarily clocks or seasons, but even mealtimes, trips to the john, punching a card on a minimum-wage job while out on parole, anything.

Those science writers, he sourly admitted, might have had something on the ball.

Sloane tried not to think of it, fearing madness, the slow seeping away of sanity into the impenetrable darkness. More than once his groping hands strayed to the wall controls, reaching out with a will of their own; obeying impulses he didn't consciously originate, and only by a wrenching effort of self-mastery did he avoid setting off the gears that would open the Vault. Not enough time had passed . . . or had it?

If he couldn't be sure enough time had passed, how could he guarantee that too much hadn't elapsed? This nagging worry assailed him for decades, or so he presumed, and the conviction steadily mounted through the years that he had erred tragically.

It hadn't been years, or decades, nor mere centuries. He'd been imprisoned, by self-inflicted torture, inside this damned stifling cube for thousands, millions of years. Already it seemed as if he'd always existed within the Vault. Surely no moderate span of time could engender such a strong sensation? The specter of a world rapidly aging without him rose up before his confusion-plagued consciousness, and once considered took firm hold. The roots of despair burrowed into the silting morass of his mind; he pictured the earth decaying, fading, dying, the race of man passing into history, perhaps all life vanished or otherwise removed. What use then the Star or his wondrous tale of fortitude and courage? Who would care, or be there to care? Did he dare hang on longer for numerous years, when they might well be chasms of time so gigantic and deep that his own species had become one with the dinosaurs?

Sloane's final struggle began, the struggle to master his growing dread, and the battle thundered on in his head for as long again as he had already waited. The details of that memorable war with eternity disappeared into the yawning well of his uncertainty, but eventually an epoch arrived when he knew the time had come; whether a thousand, million or billion years of nightmare stretched behind, he had to end it now and escape this suffocating box.

He fumbled frantically, blindly at the controls. Unseen mechanisms grumbled and throbbed within the walls, a piercing ray of blazing white light erupted from the edge of the door frame. Somewhere, far off, a cosmic alarm spewed forth a shrill whining, which made him think irrationally of the Last Trumpet. Sloane, crawling on all fours, craving yet cringing from the fiercely painful glare, crept like an animal toward his salvation.

Many hands appeared within the inviting crack, throwing the door fully open. Many human forms, silhouetted against the unbearable blaze, rushed into the tiny dungeon, seized Sloane roughly and bore him away while others clustered around the now forgotten Cytherian Star. The wretched man was dragged into the outer chamber, and as his weakened eyes grew accustomed to the light he recognized the room as the lobby containing the Vault.

Nothing had changed, nothing at all, except the glass door had been repaired. The stern-faced figures standing over him were common, everyday policeman of the type he knew so well, and the others within the room were obviously curious laboratory technicians. Everyone was talking, gesticulating, shouting, laughing at the same time, and from fragments of their disorderly conversations the wretched Sloane, would-be super criminal, gathered that he'd been encased within the Vault for a sum total of nine days.

THE GOLD SPHERE

It was Matthias who found the things. We were "treasure hunting," as I like to put it, searching through the ruins of a morbidly ancient, long-abandoned house, with the aid of a metal detector, for silver coins, jewelry, broken milk bottles and whatever other historic memorabilia we could turn up. This, a favorite pastime of ours, had proven mildly rewarding that spring, but nothing could compare to what we found this day.

The house, spotted during a reconnaissance drive through the backcountry of the White Mountains, was situated on State Trust land about four miles north-east of Greer, approachable only on foot across the muddy-banked river in the valley of the South Fork, and appeared so completely deserted and forsaken that we both expected no trouble investigating the site (active owners generally dislike having people digging into their property). Very little of the disintegrating pile remained intact; it looked as if it had come to a sudden end in a storm, Matthias remarking that it appeared far more dilapidated than its apparent age could explain. The ground floor had been totally flattened when the upper story crashed down, the wreckage of both levels so commingled as to obliterate any semblance of their original form. Matthias led the way; it was his detector, and it was he who had introduced me to the intricacies and thrills of this fascinating hobby months before. He possessed an extensive, if trashy collection of relics and tidbits from all over eastern Arizona—being a full-blood Apache he could go places and root around where I never could on my own— and over the years had trained himself as a first-class amateur investigator. He boasted, seldom giving cause for doubt, that he could find anything. He was also something of a kook, always clowning around, concocting wacky schemes for getting rich off his hobby or at least making a profession of it. He claimed to be an expert on the history of the Old West, especially the Indian half, but most of his expertise derived from his willingness to sift through old records (and dirt) for hours, seeking one trivial item he wanted. He did know his stuff, I'll grant him that.

SCIENCE AND SORCERY III

A metal detector operates most efficiently on clear, level ground, so when we began exploring he naturally chose the easily accessible pathways through the debris for our search. Those areas did not yield any treasure, however, just rusty nails and bottle tops, Matthias concluding that others had covered the ground before. Bearing this in mind we shifted our operations to the rubble-strewn interior of the decrepit structure. My friend located a handful of broken window sashes and other domestic materials, then noted a very unusual reading on his machine.

He came across the reading by accident; the detector swung over an unpromising mound of rubbish as it headed toward a better location when the audio alarm exploded noisily in a burst of ear-splitting static. I rushed to his side, asking the obvious questions. I had never heard the device sound off like that before.

"It's not very big," Matthias discerned, sweeping the probe over the spot, "but it gives a strong signal. The thing must be extremely dense." Dense metals, I scarcely need mention, can be incredibly valuable. "Probably just a lead window-weight or something," he muttered, laying aside the detector and pulling a trowel from his kit. "Let's find out."

A heavy square of tar-shingle roofing lay over the site, but the task of retrieval did not consume as much time as we expected. The object was not buried in the ground but merely underneath a loose mass of ceiling timbers, wedged into a crevice between the rotted wood of a commonplace chair and an antique desk. I think we both lost our heads when we found it. Not lead, not even silver (we did unearth two tarnished candlesticks, snapped off at the base, below the crushed desk top), but the alluring glitter of pure, fiery gold. A globe of gold, hollow to judge by its weight, yet so large that my hands could not meet around it! Oh, how we jumped for joy, raved about our newfound wealth, dedicated our lives to seeking the "rest of the fortune buried here." It seemed too good to be true.

In poking around within the desk Matthias found two other items of interest: a scrap of browned parchment inscribed with a meaningless jumble of disjointed words, and a massive leather-bound volume which, upon opening, proved to be the diary of a former occupant. The neat, handwritten black letters on the title page read THE JOURNAL OF JONATHAN PARKER, and below that the boldfaced notation 1943-. The first entry, I saw, was dated December 24, 1943. Matthias thought the written material might be useful to our quest, so he packed up both with the gold ball in his travel bag. It being late in the day we decided to postpone additional exploration for a later date, after he had time to digest and supplement the information in the diary. We drove back to Show Low, filled with hope of future lucrative discoveries.

After three days of absolute and annoying silence Matthias reappeared at my door after work, in an excited state, still carting the goods uncovered at the old house. He deposited them on the coffee table, dropped into a chair as was his wont, and spoke breathlessly, "You won't believe what I've learned. This diary is the strangest thing you'll ever read."

Matthias informed me that he had spent the first night reading the diary, an absorbing process which kept him awake long past midnight. It evidently alarmed him considerably; even now he hesitated before describing its contents. During the last two days he had twice shuttled down to the St. Johns courthouse, gathering the data contained in the county records. He now knew most of the background on that deserted shell of a dwelling.

The house, not always so lonely, was once the home of the Talbots, minor celebrities in that region, and Jonathan Parker was a descendant of that clan. Apparently he was the last, also; Matthias had checked the 1950 census returns and found nothing, nor anything more recent. The original house had been built in 1903 by Joshua Talbot, with a second story added in 1924, whence it passed through his daughter to her son Jonathan. Aside from being fairly well off few facts had surfaced to distinguish them.

The public details available on Jonathan Parker at the county office were meager. Born in 1918, he lived a typical small town life until 1937, when he enlisted in the Marine Corps (a more popular alternative to working for a living in those days). By 1942 the war against Japan had drawn him to the Pacific, where he served as a lieutenant and earned praise and a decoration for his conduct in the early campaigns. On November 20, 1943 he received a severe wound in the leg during the assault on Betio in the Tarawa Atoll, and was shipped home for good at the age of twenty-five. Nothing else appeared in the county documents (aside from tax returns) until 1946, when a Springerville newspaper clipping described the shocking collapse by night of his isolated home, and the unaccountable disappearance of its single tenant, on September 20th. No clues were ever found, to judge from the lack of follow-up in the press. In the course of time, due to lack of heirs, the state had assumed nominal control of the property.

Interesting, but hardly earth-shaking, that. Of course it was Parker's diary that caused Matthias's excitement. Shortly after his honorable discharge and return to Greer the young man, tormented by the bleak vision of a long, monotonous life ahead of him, had turned to antiquarian studies, formerly a lackadaisical hobby, in order to relieve the insidious effects of boredom. According to the diary his more earnest historical delvings disclosed certain dim references, dating back to the last century or earlier, of a hidden tribe of Indians which had taken to caves and inaccessible regions when the white men came.

Now, even I know of those archaic stories, spread by old-timers and devotees of obscure western lore; Matthias had related to me dozens of fairy tales about them as told by Navajo elders. The difference was that Parker clearly accepted the stories at face value and sought by his own means to verify them. He was convinced that isolated pockets of the mysterious tribesmen still existed somewhere, and based on what he had heard they possessed knowledge not available to the modern world.

SCIENCE AND SORCERY III

Parker reasoned, in a roundabout fashion, that if he could find them all his problems would be solved; he might become rich or famous or both, and by practicing the wisdom of the old ones he could change the earth itself, which he had come to despise out of bitterness at his battle infirmity and the lingering ailments he developed in the South Seas.

My companion went over a few basic details which would aid my appreciation of the diary. "Toward the end," Matthias discoursed, "he must have gone round the bend. He really believed this garbage, and claimed he found what he was looking for." Matthias held up the lovely golden ball. "This, if you take his word for it, is the key to all the knowledge and power in the universe. And this paper," he continued, tapping the strangely written she

et, "turns the key." I asked him if the diary solved the mystery of Parker's disappearance. "No," he replied slowly and thoughtfully, "not really. But it is suggestive, in an eerie sort of way. You'll see what I mean." He hopped up from his comfortable slouch in my best chair, declaring that he had to run. "You keep the diary for the night," he offered. "You'll get a kick out of it. I'll take the gold and the paper."

An evil grin crossed his features; 1 asked him what he had planned for the evening. "I'm going to try a funny little experiment," he said, chuckling offhandedly. "Frankly, given what he wrote about these things, I'm surprised they were left to be found by us. I imagine it was an oversight of the gods, not collecting everything they meant to. I'll find out, huh?" And with that impenetrable witticism Matthias left, carrying the priceless object and the document for his presumably zany "experiment." Once I'd seen him off and gotten myself settled I immediately turned to the diary.

THE JOURNAL OF JONATHAN PARKER. 1943-. Leafing casually from beginning to end I saw that it ran from December of 1943 to September of '46, the 20th to be exact; the date he vanished. I skimmed the last paragraph or two, but they didn't make much sense out of context so I returned to the front and began reading steadily.

Most of the windy, intensely written volume was unbearably dull, for the entire first half dealt with reams of dry historical research and cloudy local reports, all pieced together in the space of a year or so. I was briefly humored by the fact that Parker's research techniques paralleled those of my friend. Toward the end it got better, but until the last month it offered nothing but speculation and inflated dreams. One thing which caught my eye, by its absence, was the writer's refusal to complain about hardship or difficulties fostered by his wound; remarkable, considering the numerous travels he undertook on foot. Obviously he was a dedicated man, almost obsessed. Also of interest to me, thanks to Matthias's explanations, was the constant reference to such 19th century characters as Captain William Howard, a once famous Greer resident, and Diego Gavez, a Mexican official of the early 1830s who wrote an enormous report on the Indian tribes of Arizona. These were real people, and Parker claimed to have obtained much of his information from their works. My friend had filled in a lot of their background, leading me to the conclusion that Capt. Howard at least was as much of a lunatic as Parker.

As I said, the diary grew more interesting toward the end, also exhibiting increasing signs of mental confusion and decay, the entries of the last month being especially gripping. They tell the story better than my summary could manage, so here they are, edited slightly in order to avoid redundancy, awkward journalese and occasional extraneous matters.

August 24 (1946). At long last: progress! The journal of the rancher, Mike Powell, holds the key to locating the point of entry. His account, apparently written in the late 1880s, speaks of the opening as on or near his property. Now all I have to do is dig through the files at the county courthouse, check his land title and investigate every square inch of that ground, plus a bit more around the borders. That will be the easy part. After that I must make contact; the very thought scares me to death, but the possible rewards are more than enough to decide me.

August 25. Damn it! Just when I thought I was on to something. There is no Mike Powell listed in Apache County! My impression—based on Howard's description at the turn of the century—was that his holdings lay somewhere to the east of Greer, but according to local records he never existed. I even checked in McNary. Possibly, although I consider this unlikely, his spread actually lay under Escudilla Mountain, in which case I need to check in Eager or Springerville. I plan to drive down tomorrow.

August 27. If at first you don't succeed. . . I got the information I needed in Springerville. A hell of a long way east, but then my info never was too precise. Powell didn't own; he leased his land from the Butlers. The Butler's old territory, once a huge tract, is now divided into seven smaller allotments, two of them presently inhabited. If necessary I'll have to get permission from the owners to snoop around, but the other five should be simple. Simple! I don't even know what I'm looking for! A cave I suppose, but there are an awful lot of them around there. I hope there won't be more than one on a property that size, because that will be the one I want.

August 31, evening. Found the area in a remote stretch of forested ridges and grassland above the valley, and covered two of the lots, without success. I'll keep going until the land runs out. Better luck tomorrow.

September 9. I can hardly believe I'm standing—sitting, actually—in the light of day (sunlight is streaming through my study window). After all I have been through the last week, all I've seen and heard, the tremendous knowledge I've gained, the normal world appears tame and illusory by comparison. I must try to set it all down, if for no other reason future reference, to remind myself it really happened.

The most complete success attainable is mine! On the afternoon of the first—it seems ages ago—I discovered the entrance, an overgrown, partially sheltered cave mouth perched on a limestone knob overlooking a trickling wash, a tributary of the Little Colorado. I spent an hour or so watching it from a nearby ravine, hidden in a clump of bushes, and noticed something rather peculiar which served to verify my suspicions: animals shunned that mysterious opening. On that day, I'm sorry to relate, so did I; my nerve failed me and I left without crossing the threshold. During my meanderings back to town I met up with a group of young boys, and I cautiously asked them about the cave. It turned out that it was fairly well known locally, but not very popular even among adventurous youths. It had a reputation for being haunted, and the boys told me stories they had heard about some kids who went in and never came out. Such tales are not uncommon, but in this instance I was willing to lend it a little credence, anyway.

So what happened was, I put it off for a day. On the morning of the second I returned bearing a backpack containing food, water and necessary tools, resolved to do or die. With my flashlight held before me I entered the fetid, stygian hole, nervously glancing every which way for signs of human passage or habitation. After a difficult, claustrophobic crawl the tunnel widened by degrees; soon I could stand, then walk comfortably. By the penetrating rays of my light I saw that it continued widening into a cavern of mammoth proportions, complete with beautifully colored stalactites, stalagmites and other, rarer crystalline formations. My exploratory travel seemed of infinite duration—I can recall minutely such impressions as the startling brush of a disturbed bat, the repellent silkiness of draping cobwebs, the far away tinkling of artesian water seeping through the rocks—but in reality it lasted no more than thirty minutes. Then all doubts fled, to be replaced by fear.

Shapes rose out of the inky blackness on all sides, springing into view as I screamed and swung the flashlight wildly. Human shapes, closing in, shouting among themselves in an unknown tongue, brandishing stone and metal spears, seizing me firmly by the arms. What can I say? This was, after all, what I had hoped and expected, but despite that I felt only terror. A strange new world, an alien culture, unsympathetic to outsiders; what would they do to me? I was not foolish enough to struggle, and presently they lighted torches, confiscated my flashlight and pushed me along, farther down the descending tunnel.

We walked for hours, miles, and with each step my terror grew. It seemed that dreadful trek would never end; on and on we strode into the earth's bowels, farther and farther from any chance of escape. I noted countless side tunnels opening and branching out as we passed. Without a source of illumination I could never have found my way back even if I could break away, and that was utterly impossible. So on we marched, away from the world I knew and now remembered somewhat more fondly than I had hitherto realized, into the depths of the unknown.

At length we entered a brighter, cooler region where pleasant breezes blew mildly. The dangerous, broken path became smooth and level, and brilliant, glowing globes of an indeterminate nature dotted the receding walls like streetlamps. At last we turned a corner, confronting a high stone wall punctuated by a gate of the same metal forming my guardians' spear-points, which I now recognized as copper. The huge door drew back, we were accosted by two more armed men, and then we emerged into a vast space, clearly inhabited, which was evidently the lost center of civilization I had long sought. Gigantic concentric rings of those burning globes swept round the expansive plain, rendering the place as bright as a moonlit night, and all around loomed dwellings and buildings of stone, a grim, austere city of primeval complexity.

I soon learned and saw much more about that city, but I must take this opportunity to describe it as it first appeared to me, the sudden impact of that first shattering view. It lay in a cavern the likes of which I had never imagined, a great windswept land deep within the earth's crust, the distant end lost to sight, the high rocky ceiling above faintly visible where it reflected the rays of the fire-globes. From the smooth floor rose the city, its outer provinces a closely packed network of tiny huts of stone, crude and savage in appearance. These living quarters extended out to the wall which formed a safeguard at this end. Toward the center the small dwellings disappeared and in their place rose huge monolithic stone buildings and towers, the tallest of the latter crowned with platforms. Most of the architectural designs of these structures were unfamiliar to me, lending that brooding vastness an aura of alien mystery. In the distance however, at the extreme limits of vision, I detected a mountainous bulk which seemed reminiscent of a Central American step pyramid, the narrow top of which joined the uneven cavern roof.

The inhabitants streamed from the huts and walkways, clustering excitedly and calling to one another in a language which was gibberish to me. Most were smiling and laughing and curious to a fault; they swarmed around me, staring and pointing, and my captors, a rather dour lot, did not seem amused. They pushed through the frantic throng, shoving me before them, forcing me down a graded road or wide path which led straight into the heart of the underground megalopolis. After a tiresome hike, besieged by crowds of onlookers throughout the route, we approached a massive cyclopean stone building which I knew instinctively must be a temple or primitive palace. There we halted, I feverishly wondering if this was an altar of sacrifice or something equally grotesque.

An old man shuffled out of the forbidding edifice, lamely hobbling with the aid of a stick. I could sympathize. A young man broke from the crowd to join him and both strode up to where I stood, rigid and wary. The young man especially attracted my attention; he appeared so normal, and then I realized, without surprise, how pale most of these people were. Indians without a doubt—big noses, high cheek bones, lank black hair and so on—but exhibiting all the symptoms of a lifetime shunning the sun. This young man was not like that. Bronzed, strong and confident, he looked like anyone on the upper earth, and. . .

"Your name?" He spoke English! A man, dressed in only a loincloth as did all the men (and most of the women, I hasten to add), here in this forsaken realm, speaking plain, unaccented English! I gave him my name. "Why are you here?" he asked coolly.

I hesitated—the wrong reply might mean the axe for me—bit my lip and answered, **"I come to seek knowledge."**

He muttered incomprehensibly to the old man, who beamed broadly and whispered something in return. The young man also smiled, then announced, "That is the only acceptable answer. Come this way, please." He shouted at the crowd, who began dispersing sulkily, with much moaning and groaning, and the pair led me inside. A luminescent globe resting on a copper tripod in the center revealed a cubic interior, the walls of which were adorned with lurid friezes and gruesome murals, apparently of an historical rather than a religious nature. Several small rooms led away from the main chamber, but there we took seats on embroidered reed mats and waited silently while a number of young men like my interpreter joined us.

Formal introductions followed. The old man was called Kaza-Tora, which roughly translates as "Truth on Wings," which (I later learned) marked him as a tribal chieftain and elder of great significance. The young man had a name about a mile long which I shortened, with his approval, to Willu-See, and I cannot remember what it meant, nor can I recall the names of the others. All were complicated hodge-podges of adjacent consonants and blurred vowels, so I really couldn't retain them.

We got down to business. The meeting initially took the form of an interrogation, with them firing away streams of questions. All of the young men spoke perfect English, so they asked while Willu-See translated for the benefit of the old man. Why was I here? I told them as carefully and as assuredly as I could: how I had researched the old tales for years, convinced of their authenticity, desirous of gaining the knowledge I knew this lost world must possess. That obviously pleased them but the grilling proceeded, in a similar vein and on tangential subjects; did I have any immediate family, close friends? No to the former, and as for the latter I related how my only true friends were all killed in the Pacific, where I earned my red badge. They nodded politely and revealed through their questions that they knew all about the war and what went on up there. I wondered about this, and about the curious aspects of my younger hosts, so when the opportunity arose I put a question to them.

Already they were willing to share information. Willu-See informed me that, for reasons of knowledge and strategic purposes, many of their kind lived among the surface dwellers, carefully concealing their identities and avoiding close contact with them. He and the other youthful types present were examples of those "spies," if I can call them that, observing the world and reporting periodically on current events. This fact astounded and disturbed me. I had never considered how devious are the goings-on in my world, or how little I and others knew of the secret forces around us. All this time they have watched and waited amongst us; for what? I did not know then.

At last the meeting broke up. I was told that I had passed some kind of a test and might be quite useful to them. The old man remained behind, the others filed away chattering to each other, and Willu-See escorted me out, announcing that henceforth he would be my guide and companion. He promised to tell me all about his culture and show me those things not closed to outsiders. He made it clear that I was a free man, subject to the natural limitations of my position (he didn't want me hurting myself by intruding on situations I didn't understand), and that I could expect to return to the surface shortly.

Thus began my stay in the subterranean city of Alta-myan, an incredible visit which lasted seven days. I cannot begin to describe the place, its citizens, or their culture, but I can set down some informal background here. Later, when I break through the bonds of space and time and have mastered what they taught me, I may have time to write up a complete treatise.

I don't know how to begin. An ancient Indian civilization, thriving and growing beneath our feet all these years, the vaguest myth of a handful of obscure tribes, is a reality. El Dorado, the Seven Cities: all have a basis in fact, but the conquistadores never knew where to look! Or did not believe what they were told, most likely. I now know that these people have maintained a highly advanced, continuous civilization for thousands of years, stretching so far back into antiquity that even they have lost track of its founding. Their oldest epics speak of the Years of Wandering—possibly a garbled account of the initial human conquest of the Americas eons ago, a period lost forever to surface anthropologists—and the Time of Fire, a mystifying reference to a great, fabled cataclysm which supposedly devastated much of the primordial American southwest. Their reliable records, complete with names of famous rulers, descriptions of bloody wars and mighty deeds, go back to what I reckoned as 5000 B.C., a period when Europe and the rest of the planet still slumbered in the crude trappings of the New Stone Age.

Of course these people, the Mautas as they style themselves, did not always live underground. A long time ago they began excavating their tunnels and enlarging existing caverns for storage or other matters, but few of the population originally descended into those nighted depths permanently. It was sort of a fashion, I guess, that caught on through the centuries. Even when the Spanish arrived many still lingered in the sunlight, but the advent of that dire threat drove the last die-hards below. I wonder what Cortez and his motley crew thought of the stories they heard. I remember reading once that the first priests in the New World maintained the belief that the local religions bore acute similarities to Christianity—a concept against which the Inquisition took strong measures—perhaps they did hear about the inner world, and thought the natives were speaking of Hell! I don't know, and the passing of time reduced the tales to mere legend.

It was pointed out to me that the Mautas suffered in a material sense from their total isolation. Alta-myan, for example, sank pretty low for a while, shedding much of the veneer of civilization before adjusting to its new environment. I wondered why they refused to face the enemy but, as I subsequently learned, their reasoning was very sound. Even now, however, Alta-myan was only just attaining the level it once held. Other underground cities—for there are several, scattered throughout the continent—maintained themselves despite adversity and reached new heights. The center of this civilization is, and always was, somewhere in northern Arizona, where exotic traces of crumbling ruins bespeak only the dregs left by the withdrawing tribes.

Their social system is fairly simple, basically the standard Indian tribal organization with modifications necessitated by their advanced state of learning. Chiefs rule, although their powers are limited (of course, except during times of emergency such as war this is likewise true of the documented tribes), functioning as a sort of supreme advisor, an arbitrator of laws and disputes. Laws, by the way, are few and basic, at least from what I gathered; here is a society operating on the American equivalent of the Ten Commandments! Then again, this may not be so surprising; they are old and set in their ways, a static, conservative lot. Legalistic taboos are nonexistent but habit enforces the ancient decrees.

The society itself is quite complex, being an agricultural state supporting a form of industry and key centers of learning. The people seemed to have a lot of time on their hands while I was there, but I was assured there was no lack of things to do. Most of the city's sustenance, mainly vegetable and grain foods, is raised within enormous caverns deeper within the earth, the crops consisting of special hybrids nurtured through the millennia to adapt to the lack of sunlight. Hard to believe, but I never actually saw one of their farms so I take their word for it. Considering the miracles they have accomplished I can accept their theories of cultivation on faith. Up until fairly recent years they habitually supplemented their diet with game procured on the surface, but lately the catch has dwindled to almost nothing due to their fear of drawing attention from the hostile dwellers above.

The sole material industry, metallurgy, is unimpressive, resembling that of a Bronze Age culture more than anything else, but this is not remarkable given their emphasis on weightier sources of power. And this is the key to their civilization, the one I dreamed of, this other source of power. The Mautas, through ceaseless centuries of determined delving, have unlocked the ancient secrets of magic. Their strange quest has led them to such heights that I shudder to think of it. I have with me now what I believe will prove their mental superiority once I am able to fully understand it. But I will describe that in a moment.

THE GOLD SPHERE

I call it magic, for want of a better term, but what is it, really? They have this force under their control, an immaterial force which has enabled them to bypass the brutal mechanization which grips my world. Without this power their civilization could not have lasted; it would be one more barbaric culture, floundering in its own inherent contradictions, failing catastrophically as did all the empires of the past. The Mautas can, with a little luck, last forever, and I have decided that it is their deep feelings of immortality (in a racial sense) which led to their abandonment of the surface. When faced with the possibility of awesome conflict they retreated below to await the proper time when they may return without effort. Kaza-Tora stated that the time is drawing near when the outer nations will weaken and die, or destroy themselves with terrible new weapons which can eradicate all surface life. He said his people had known about such infernal devices for ages, but never decayed to the point of using them. I think I know what he meant, although he surely overstated the case, but considering the worsening political climate of the last year I can understand their patient eagerness. Does my willingness to aid them make me a traitor to my kind?

The "magic" keeps the lamp-globes burning, pumps their water, replenishes the air and helps maintain the crops. No machines are utilized. Their ancient chronicles tell of wars fought with the amazing power, but not often; such clashes were infinitely bloody and agonizing. Entire regions of the continent were reduced to wasteland during a prolonged struggle which raged across what is now northern Mexico and the southern U.S. in the 6th Century, and since that time no conflict has been allowed to escalate to such extremes. Apparently they learned something that round. One thing I never could fathom was the source of their fantastic power, although I can recount what I was told, absurd as much of it sounds. This leads me to my return to the surface, and what I brought with me.

On the fifth day of my stay (September 6th, it was) I was summoned from the roomy, though sparsely furnished, lodge where I slept, to the temple of Kaza-Tora. He announced, speaking through Willu-See as always, that I must leave soon, that I had proved myself worthy in accordance to their laws, and that I could take with me a fragment of their glorious knowledge. I listened carefully to everything he had to say.

Kaza-Tora produced an object which looked like a ball of gold. On closer examination I discovered it to be exactly that: gold, not just the color but the precious metal itself. He gave it to me, saying that it was mine. I held it in my hands, running my fingers over the absolutely smooth surface. It was about four inches in diameter but not as heavy as I would have thought. I assumed it must be hollow, and when I held it to my ear and shook it something in the center rattled a bit.

The gold sphere was, he said (here I attempt to render my companion's quaint and flowery translation into something intelligible to the uninitiated), the focus of cosmic energy, one of numerous charms they jealously hoarded, the source of the magic that powered their world. The extraterrestrial energy flowed from the will of Those Who Live Beyond the Rim, a ritualistic title I first decided had a religious significance, but later surmised was meant to be taken literally. The old man invoked the name often, sometimes describing them as gods and at other times as vastly superior beings who had watched over the tribe since the Time of Fire. They were always present but never seen unless one called them up through magic, which only the brave and the foolhardy ever attempted. Kaza-Tora hinted at various marvels and tragedies the great beings had visited on humankind, depending on the type of stimuli employed to raise them. These stories, sounding so much like stereotypical witchcraft, gave me the willies, particularly those relating to the Time of Fire, which began to seem less mystical and more a very real event or period in history. I felt distinctly uneasy holding that yellow orb while my teacher spoke of the dire consequences that could result from misuse. But the old lure of knowledge has proven too strong.

Kaza-Tora said there was a way to acquire wisdom and power from Those Who Live Beyond the Rim through the sphere, and he would do his best to guide me in the necessary steps. With the preliminaries behind us we sat down for two days of concentrated study, he attempting to force-feed me all of the accumulated lore of the sphere: how to make it work, how to speak to those beyond it and what to request of them. It was all intensely complicated and detailed, but the two days passed all too quickly, and my training was less revealing than I cared to admit. How could I ask him about what I didn't understand when I didn't understand the questions? Early on the seventh day (I never could keep track of time while I was down there; I had forgotten my watch and my companions kept no regular schedule I could figure) I was awakened and informed it was time to depart. Kaza-Tora delivered to me a bulky, coarse-grained leaf of written matter which turned out to be a hastily scrawled English transcription of the required formula. I was overwhelmingly grateful. I shook hands with Willu-See, who handed over my flashlight. I jokingly asked if I could look him up when I got back, which raised a good laugh, but of course his whereabouts on the surface is a major secret. I waved to the ubiquitous crowd who flocked again to see me, see me off this time, and with my escort soon put that weird underground city behind me.

Just before we parted the old man muttered a few syllables to my younger, brown-skinned friend. Willu-See spoke the words. "Go now and never return. May the gold sphere bring you joy and wisdom. Prepare the way for our coming. Show caution in how you use the formula of the talisman. No man may look upon the face of Those Beyond and live."

So here I am, back in my familiar home in Greer, the exhausting ordeal over and done with. Were it not for my souvenirs I would dismiss the experience as a dream. I left the cave yesterday afternoon, pausing a long time to get used to the sun again, before trekking back to Springerville. Exhausted, I took a motel room for the night and was out like a light as soon as I hit the bed. I don't know what they thought of me there; I must have been a sight! I slept until check out time, then made my way home. Like I said, here I am, with the beautiful sphere and the lengthy inscribed document, just waiting for my next move. The question is, what do I do with them?

September 10. Having perused this stuff once more, I am at a loss as to how to begin. The formula as written is not quite as I recall it, although I'm not sure what the problem is. Perhaps my memory is at fault. Because of my doubts I did nothing today; maybe tomorrow.

September 11. Still nothing. I think I figured out some of the inaccuracies, mostly mistakes of my own. I should have paid more attention to Kaza-Tora.

September 13. Finally got it right. What I was forgetting was the differences in accent and inflection of various words which the old Indian apparently misunderstood. I might be ready to try it tomorrow, if I can work myself up to it.

To tell the truth, my real problem is a failure of nerve. The more I ponder the prospects the dicier they look to me. An awful lot of risk for an uncertain return; sometimes I think I'm out of my depth, but I know it is far too late to turn back now. Three years cannot be a total waste.

In the warm light of the sun the gold sphere gleams like fire. I spend hours just staring at it, hypnotized. Maybe if I stare at it long enough the answer will emerge.

September 14. A thoroughly bad day. I tried the formula, or at least started to. Early this morning I finished going over the formula, satisfied that any, probably imaginary, discrepancies had been ironed out. The final version which I came up with runs as follows:

[I have deleted the section of the diary containing the formula. This undoubtedly seems a foolish precaution, but in light of subsequent incidents I consider it for the best.]

Around four o'clock this afternoon I retired into the den, closing the door behind me and drawing the curtains. I was not sure what the effects would be, and thought privacy mandatory. I placed the sphere on the desk and lit two tall candles behind it. I drew myself up in the chair, took a deep breath, wiped my brow (yes, I was sweating profusely) and began to read. Almost immediately something happened: hardly had the first sentence escaped my lips when the talisman began to glow, a pulsating radiance which left green spots in my eyes. I stammered, tripped over a tough phrase, doggedly kept going. Then, when I reached the hideous words [deleted] a spooky sensation of throbbing started up, like the house was shaking. I really thought for a minute that it was an earthquake or something; it reminded me of the feeling I get standing near a big engine. Well, after that I simply could not go on. I felt that I was on the verge of death, and one more word might be the clincher. I jumped up, threw down the parchment and ran from the room. A little while ago I looked in and saw that everything was back to normal. But what a fright I had!

I cannot face that ritual again. I haven't been so scared since Tarawa. I just know I'm doing something wrong. If only I knew what was supposed to happen! The tales the old man told me—about Those Who Live Beyond the Rim, and what they do to the unwary and the unprepared acolytes—too much. If I look upon their faces (do they have material forms, or are they made of something else? It's not worth finding out) I will die; or is that the merciful way out? Would death be the best I could hope for? One thing is certain: I no longer harbor any doubts about the reality of this business. What happened today was real.

I have decided on a course of action. The only thing to do is go back to Alta-myan and verify every bit of information before I proceed. Kaza-Tora said never to return, but surely he can make an exception in this case. It is worth a try at any rate. I can ride down later in the week, force myself to endure that rugged hike again, see what comes of it.

What comes? And I thought I had it all figured out. This situation is really not fair.

September 20. This may be the last entry I write in this journal. I should go ahead and fill in the date on the title page, but that would be too fatalistic. Nothing has worked out, and I am down to only one option.

Four days ago I finally got back to the cave. I was warned off a farmer's property once getting there, but I circled around and arrived shortly before dark. With flashlight in hand I entered the mouth, crept down the familiar passage . . . and came up against a solid rock wall! A huge boulder completely blocked the tunnel, and nothing I did could budge it, nowhere could I find a gap. An accident maybe—rock falls happen—yet I can't help feeling it was deliberate, a purposeful attempt to deny me, personally, egress. Is that paranoia? I hope not. I left eventually and made my way back here yesterday morning.

I'm sitting now at my desk, the sphere and formula before me. I have reached a decision, probably a crazy one but I've thought it over carefully. Too much time and effort has been invested in this project to run out now, when I might be so close to discovering the gateway to the universe and its secrets. I could say that my whole life is wrapped up in this, but that is too ironic a statement to take seriously. If I don't go through with it I have nothing to live for. I am afraid, but I can overcome that. All men live in fear, but the truly great pioneers master their fear and carry on, so I shall do the same.

All is quiet now. No wind blows, the air is still and cold, the patch of sky seen from my window quite dark, speckled with stars. The sun departed hours ago. I am about to try the formula one more time. Neither luminosity nor vibrations will stop me this time. If I fail, may heaven help me. If I succeed, I will write it all down below.

THE GOLD SPHERE

There the diary of Jonathan Parker ends, the last few lines jotted neatly at the top of an otherwise blank page. More blank leaves follow. I need add nothing to his account; the increasingly rambling tale speaks for itself, and as for that final, tragic silence at the end, I hesitate to theorize. When I finished reading it that night, far past my usual bedtime, I better understood Matthias's cryptic remark about the diary not settling the mystery of Parker's disappearance, "not really." The matter is settled only if one accepts the tale as the product of a sound mind, and despite everything else I still have doubts, but not many.

Unfortunately there is more to tell, only this involves not the missing (presumed dead) Mr. Parker, but my friend Matthias. He has vanished under inconceivably strange circumstances. I've been questioned by the police about the case, but of course I could tell them nothing. Or could I? I hid the diary while they were here, and I suppose the safest plan is to destroy it. The police wouldn't understand the connection anyway, and that grim volume seems to draw trouble.

Matthias, good old Matthias, joking about his great find—the oversight of the gods—selling the gold to a collector or melting it down. And maybe give the formula a whirl before he did, just for laughs. I wonder if he's still capable of laughing. His house, it seems, was wrecked that night, totally levelled, and although the officials suspect a gas explosion the evidence does not bear out the hypothesis. No body was found; Matthias is simply gone. Neighbors reported a flash of light in the sky, and there was talk, disregarded by relevant authorities, of an earthquake. Only his house was affected.

When I could, when the investigators had left and local interest had died down, I sneaked in to inspect the site. It was hard to stand there amidst the ravaged remains, knowing full well that something horrible had happened to a friend. I sternly refused to speculate on what that might be. On the spur of the moment I carried out a minimal examination of my own, searching narrowly among the rubble for just two things: the gold sphere and the formula sheet. I searched a long time.

Strange to say, I searched in vain. It could be that someone, this time, has chosen to retrieve those properties. It could be. I could search further, dig deeper for them into the debris—lost Matthias taught me how—but I don't really want to do that.

THE GUARDIAN OF THE GATE

Years ago, when Allen Tolleson first told me the story, he extracted a pledge of silence which must hold firm until he lay still in the grave. Very solemn about it he was, and I have honored that oath, that bond between good friends, in the approved manner. Now that he has passed on, however, I feel that the heavy hand of secrecy can be lifted; my words cannot hurt the departed, and so singular and interesting a tale should not be relegated to the chambers of my own mind, nor lost for the reflection or amusement of others. Now the secret can come out, while the dead rest undisturbed.

I didn't consider Allen intrinsically strange. Many did, later, but without the complete facts they saw only the surface qualities of the man. He had his peculiarities, of course, like all his fellow humans, but those events which so crushed his spirit and disordered his personality formed a really exceptional chapter in his life. He whispered of them at odd, quiet moments when we were alone: the cold, moonlit Arizona desert, the old and isolated house, its sullenly knowledgeable inhabitant; what Allen found there, and what the aged man said it meant; and most of all—that which, above all else, altered permanently the mentality of the man I knew as Allen Tolleson—what he saw when he returned to the house on the last day, and his belief in its profound and horrible significance. I like to think of him not as I knew him, but rather as he described himself from an earlier time: outgoing, boisterous, perhaps a little too forward, and seasonally stricken with wanderlust, an urge to see the world. Always anxious to know more—of the country, its people, their heritage—he travelled in those days to distant portions of the land in search of congenial adventure. Big on folk and regional lore, his subsequent descriptions of visits to out of the way places, curious sights in tiny roadside museums, and quaint dialogues with local spinners of tall tales, could actually bore one with their unending variety.

After his frightful experience, so I gather, Allen changed. The lure of the road and the distant horizon was gone, replaced by a vague dread of strangers, a fear of barren, too-quiet landscapes, of dark corners and shadows. He behaved as though a man in hiding. In his last years Allen became a confirmed recluse, his solitude largely unbroken save, as far as I know, for the sole exception of myself. The vivid contrast to the young, exuberant journeyman was especially notable, as he told it, for the suddenness of its appearance, and I lay it to this massive personality change which forced him to confide in me.

Concerning the story, I can only try to tell it as Allen related it to me, though my calm and remote version won't do justice to the brooding, at times hysterical accounting I used to receive. Aside from that, I must state categorically that I do not believe it. I want that made plain: what I present here cannot be taken altogether seriously, and yet, for the record, I will also state that Allen struck me as a truthful man, and I wholeheartedly vouch for his sincerity. This, I know, is the ultimate paradox, the permanent condition of the sober rationalist when confronted with data outside his experience. I do not doubt his word, yet I simply can't credit the story. The human mind is a curious machine, and we cannot escape from our own ingrained reasoning.

However, to give myself a little credit, I must allude here to Sheriff Lee's report on the incident. This man, since retired, getting along in years, is nevertheless still alive, and I once corresponded with him in order to get the full details. Allen considered the lawman's report the final, clinching proof of his incredible tale, yet on the surface it flatly contradicts my friend's assertions. Allen managed to fit the bizarre pieces together with superficial logic, despite his outrageous accusations against Lee, but the skeptical examiner may quickly dispose of those arguments.

On the manner of my friend's death I have little to say, but as the credulous will find it interesting I offer a short summary. Between one and two A.M. on September 12, 2015 Allen, traveling on foot, was struck and instantly killed by a hit and run motorist. No one observed the incident, nor has anyone yet been apprehended for the crime. Officially a clear-cut case— the police see nothing remarkable about a common road accident—but I do have some questions. What was the victim doing, as a pedestrian, on that unpopulated, wooded lane so late at night? I'm sure he was coming to see me—I live one mile farther down the street, where the houses first begin to cluster thickly—but that was not Allen's way. He seldom left his refuge, any acquaintances (certainly myself) being forced to visit him. If he did intend to see me, why didn't he call? He was prone to doing so at all hours, and his phone was in perfect working order. Why didn't he drive to me? Most of all, why did he feel compelled to set out during the early morning hours, given his all-encompassing fear of the dark? These are questions which can never be answered, important as they may be.

His terrible experience occurred in late 1994. While in Texas the previous summer on vacation Allen had a chance to study the remnants of Indian legend and lore scattered throughout old documents, or preserved in the tales of loquacious natives. Of particular interest was a mass of county records he located in Granton, relating to Indian studies at the turn of the century and before. Fired with enthusiasm, eager for new material, Allen looked westward to the wastelands of Arizona, the center of prehistoric civilization in what would become the United States. In late fall he garnered a couple of weeks off, and November found him in Phoenix, that concrete and asphalt oasis in the desert. Here, like so many tourists before him, Allen found the remains of an advanced culture which flourished a thousand years ago, only thinly overlaid by the burgeoning white civilization. He took in the museums of the city, noting the exquisite archeological treasures unearthed in the last century; moving on, using Phoenix as a base, he explored the central and northern regions of the state. Armed with maps and tourist guidebooks he strolled beneath the towering fortress of Montezuma's Castle, high in its rugged cliff caverns. Likewise he probed the gloomy, narrow chambers at Tonto, carved into the upper crests of a beetling mountain, overlooking the blue expanse of man-made Lake Roosevelt. Other wonders he found, all calling to mind a long-vanished people, a vast trading empire stretching from Colorado to the Peru of the Incas; a way of life destroyed by the ever-spreading desert before ever the conquistadors came to slaughter and enslave the few surviving inhabitants.

Later in the week Allen transferred operations to Flagstaff, the mountain city, famous for the observatories of Percival Lowell which loom above on Mars Hill. He journeyed to nearby Walnut Canyon, where the native Americans once dwelt perched on the steep, unapproachable slopes in tiny, claustrophobic stone rooms. He saw Barringer Crater, gouged from the Earth's crust twenty thousand years ago, and did not wonder why the Indians wove such strange and forbidding tales concerning that ancient extraterrestrial visitation. Pushing toward the east he stopped off at Petrified Forest National Park, absorbing the impressions of a bygone world, and stood before Newspaper Rock, the hidden block scrawled with a language which no living human being can decipher.

On November 14—a date burned into the young man's memory—Allen started off north from Flagstaff, seeking the copious ruins at Wupatki, protected from the depredations of looters and scavengers by their designation of National Monument status. Here, on a dry, ravine-slashed plateau encompassing six hundred square miles, are the remains of over eight hundred Anasazi villages, apartments, citadels, and way stations, baked, blasted, and crumbled by the ravages of time and the elements. Allen surveyed this reminder of perished humanity and felt a chill from some other source than the nip in the air. The landscape was too desolate, too still, silent save for the interminable wind. Over all loomed the southward rise of Sunset Crater, a slumbering volcano, its low brown mound crowned with the fiery red stone from which it draws its name. It seemed the sentinel of a vengeful god's wrath, the funeral monument to a people who dared to defy a death-dealing land.

To the east lay a brooding sea of sand with multicolored islands of angular sandstone shimmering under the failing afternoon sun, which called to the adventurer with its kaleidoscopic splendor. This, Allen knew, was the Painted Desert, one more product of that Nature's artist who ran wild in northern Arizona. Abandoning his car on the overlook by the gravel road, he followed the descending contour of the land in what was meant to be a short excursion. Allen drank in the riot of color, the orange, pink, and crimson shot with blue and gray; he studied the intricate, distorted sculptures of stone protruding from the plain, thrown up by primeval forces which even now bubble and seethe beneath the bedrock. Here and there, now and then, he noted the creatures of the desert, small, hardy beasts lurking in the shunned region, the only living things able to survive here. A black scorpion scuttled past, its menacing claws and deadly stinger held high. A furry blob leaped from rock to rock, fleeing the sun; a tarantula. A cluster of beetles with huge mandibles dispersed at Allen's approach and fled into a crevice between two boulders. All of these sand dwellers were predators; Allen wondered what they ate.

Night falls rapidly in the desert, and while Allen was not caught entirely unaware the sobering event occurred rather faster than he liked. Night wrought curious changes in the scenery: the sharp contrasts of light and shadow by day gave way to a bleak, colorless world of muted images and weird shapes. It is easy, especially for an amateur explorer, to get lost. Allen did.

Disturbed, but not disheartened, he gingerly picked his way over the hills and rocks toward the west, bracing against the encroaching cold, hoping to cross the road at some point and find the car. The stars in their thousands shone brightly, Polaris low in the northern sky, a flickering gleam in the roiling air, so direction was no problem. In the dark, however, the desert seemed more alive than before. Strange calls, muffled croakings broke the stillness, and a myriad half-seen things scampered out of his path or stood their ground, daring him to pass. Once something quite large lumbered by, about fifty yards to the left, and though Allen could not determine the source he resolved to avoid it at all costs.

Presently he detected a faint shimmering of luminosity not in the sky. Peering intently through the gloom, Allen made out tiny rectangular shapes low on the southern horizon, brilliant quadrangular beacons of yellow light. The proximity of human habitation filled him with joy; he was not so far off the beaten track as he had thought. He turned toward the distant, inviting windows.

The house was set into an obsidian cliff face, somewhat reminiscent of the ancient Indian practice, sheltered on three sides by an unscalable cul-de-sac, and even in the dim light Allen did not like what he saw. The house was very old and decrepit, a ramshackle two-story structure of rough lumber. A fenced-in strip of greenery meandered along the cliff's base, terminating at the toolshed in rear of the building. Clearly illuminated by the windows, the sandy front yard bore a disagreeable quantity of rubbish, broken bits of metal, decomposing remains of recent meals, a rusted, dead Chevrolet by the apparently functional pickup. All was dark except the two upper windows, to which Allen now called hopefully. Receiving no reply, he mounted the steps of the porch to knock at the screen door. It jarred open at the touch, but no one came. After a minute of alternating knocking and hopeful pausing he pushed at the wooden door, nervously glancing about in fear of an irate, shotgun-toting farmer. The door swung inward and, muttering to himself, Allen entered.

He felt around in the darkness for a wall switch, discovered instead an oil lamp on a hall stand. Lighting this, he found himself in a large den, replete with old and unfashionable furniture, brick fireplace, quaint ornaments, and massive volume-packed bookshelves along the oak-paneled walls. This sight, in remarkable contrast to the dingy exterior, raised Allen's expectations of aid. However, no one appeared to resent his intrusion.

Scarcely trusting his own boldness, he began a systematic exploration of the house, calling out frequently lest he surprise the hypothetical inhabitant. Porting the oil lamp, he examined a small reading room down the main hall, and to the right found the combination kitchen-dining room, which bore evidence of recent use: a newspaper for the twelfth, washed dishes still damp by the sink. Beyond the dining room a stout door opened on a crude stairwell descending to the cellar. Retracing his steps Allen trudged up to the second floor, consisting of two bedrooms—one apparently not in use—and another room, in which two lamps burned unattended, containing a bizarre private museum, made up of outlandish Indian relics and yellowed clumps of casually scattered documents. A major find, but this was not the time. He sighed and retreated back down the stairs, making for the cellar.

As the only area not yet explored Allen felt duty bound to investigate it, though he doubted anyone was there. The cellar was without a fixed light source, the rough stone walls, hacked out of the living rock, moist and cold. The lamp flickered as if touched by a breath of wind, probably a draft from an unseen fissure. The creaking stairs ran straight down at a steep angle, terminating at the fifteenth step. No one was present, as predicted. The room was small, largely devoid of accouterments; a number of unmarked wooden crates heaped in one corner, and a rude table and chair. On the far stone wall, set into what Allen believed to be the supporting cliff face, were two rough-hewn doors of oak, resembling those on old storm shelters. Storerooms, probably, or underground cisterns, though Allen did not boast of a familiarity with desert water systems.

Seeing no point in remaining, he re-crossed the dismal space and ascended the stairs. On the fifth step he detected a sound behind him, a low but harsh grating of wood on stone. Icy droplets suddenly stood out on his face, and chill snakes wriggled down his back. Allen turned, the lamp clutched in his fist casting its rosy beam into the cellar depths. Then he gasped, choking back a cry. An indistinctly visible human being stood there, motionless by the far wall, apparently eyeing Allen with equal disbelief. Difficult seconds passed until, maintaining a steady eye on the young intruder, the apparition stepped over to the table and deposited a hefty bundle wrapped in newspaper.

The new arrival spoke. "You gave me a fright, mister." The voice was aged, mellow, heavily accented. An Indian by the sound of him, and when the man stepped forward fully into the wavering light Allen saw this to be true. Of medium height and stout, well-muscled build, with a dark lined face and prominent nose, his long black hair swept back, he was dressed for outdoors in jeans, thick corduroy shirt, and heavy, grimy boots. "What is your business here?"

Allen, stammering, told him in broken sentences as much of the story as he could manage. He was still not recovered from the surprise; presumably the gentleman had been hidden beyond one of the two doors, but this did not entirely reassure him. At the time it seemed as if the Indian had appeared from nowhere.

"Let's get upstairs out of the cold," this man offered reasonably, smiling good-naturedly as if to disarm his guest's fears. Allen nodded dumbly and led the way. It relieved him to abandon the close confines of the cellar.

Introductions were made, a fire was set blazing, and within minutes Allen began warming to his pleasant host, who broke out glasses and a bottle of gin—Allen trusted that it was professionally made—which he gratefully accepted, and a box of fine cigars, which he did not. Allen felt completely at ease; the old man, after all, was hungry for human companionship. He seldom had visitors, and saw other people only during his infrequent drives to Winslow or Flagstaff for supplies.

The ancient Indian's name was Leon Valenzuela, which suggested mixed ancestry, but his manner, customs, and interests held none of the white man's taint. He seemed to revel in native American lore, tracing his lineage back through centuries into the pre-Aztec period, or so he said. Allen had heard such claims before from others, and knew it was seldom more than grandiose bombast, a means of holding on to a vanishing past. This, he noted, was Valenzuela's forte; the young traveler thought of the relics in the room above, the gentleman's old-fashioned airs, and the absence of such basic modern conveniences as electricity or, he shortly discovered, running water. The Indian explained in detail his hard but self-sufficient lifestyle. He raised some cattle and hogs atop the igneous cliffs, and kept a small garden by a nearby sinkhole, which barely met his needs. Valenzuela lived alone. His wife had died in childbirth, and his son had disappeared or gone away (this part of his story was a little unclear) thirty years before. In most respects his life was that of the perennial subsistence farmer, tough yet satisfying.

The old man professed to be one of the few surviving members of the Anasazi tribe, the long vanished prehistoric people who flourished in the southwest until shortly before the coming of the Spaniards, and who constructed the marvelous cities, forts, and temples which adorn the blasted landscapes of Arizona, New Mexico, and Colorado. This wildly romantic belief in his own heritage had led to his all-absorbing interest in the artifacts and legends of the dead race. He was, in fact, a competent amateur archeologist, self-taught in the skills of sorting and digging through buried history. Much of his material came from private diggings near the farm, though on occasion he furtively stole across the desert to probe the federal lands of Wupatki; a serious crime bearing harsh penalties if caught, though he felt no remorse for his actions. Unlike the whites, who looted and destroyed sites for profit, he wished only to preserve the heritage of the Anasazi. Therefore, he ingenuously asserted, the laws did not apply to him. Would his guest like to see his private museum?

Allen heartily agreed, not letting on about his earlier prowling lest he appear ill-bred in the eyes of his host. He had really taken to the old man; a bit weird, obsessed in his isolation, but a great guy nonetheless, sharing so many of his own interests. Valenzuela's collection was truly amazing, now that Allen had a better chance to view it, an extraordinary array of items neatly packed in glass cases. Each was individually labeled in English and Spanish printed on a white card and glued to the glass. Allen assumed this was an attempt at the professional look merely for artistic reasons, as he doubted whether foreign eyes ever saw this. In response to a query the old man admitted that he was fluent in both languages. There was a lot to see, including pottery of several varieties, ornamental, religious, and utilitarian. A bare few retained traces of their original coloration, the selected juices of desert berries and the sap of scrub bark. Shiny trinkets abounded, all glossily polished by an expert hand. No precious metals, but exquisite workmanship. One case contained lumpy brown rubber balls, a far cry from their original state, but clear reminders of a grim past's lighter side. Once these balls figured in tournaments which formed the chief mode of entertainment in the dead villages. Allen was not sure, but recalled that the game was something like soccer, but more violent and ultimately lethal. The balls looked roughly handled, weathering being the likely reason. The mountain of documents, he was told, recounted the campaigns of General Crook against the Apaches in the 1880s. Valenzuela swore that many of his papers, not duplicated elsewhere, contained lurid information not made public by the famed Indian fighter.

Most of the displays were of Anasazi manufacture, with a smattering of Aztec and Mayan. Others, however, defied an amateur scholar's powers of classification. Here sat a tiny metallic figurine, a cluster of leering, semi-human faces; there lay a crystalline plaque festooned with stars and ray-like images; next to it a glittering white column, two feet tall by some inches wide, inscribed in obscure characters, possibly writing. Allen wondered about that language—something very alien about it—beyond analysis. Indeed, this entire portion of the museum defied analysis. It did not seem to correspond to any particular Indian culture. Incan? he asked Valenzuela, loathing his own stupidity and hating to show it. No, not Incan. His guide appeared rather hesitant about this aspect of his holdings, becoming very cautious in his replies. He expounded on cultural mixtures or vague tribal influences, saying much while offering little information. Droning on, mumbling passages, his cheerful tone lowered an octave or two, a curious and disconcerting performance. Performance? Allen thought of senility, dismissed the notion. The man was prevaricating, deliberately attempting to distract his guest from the subject. Allen wondered why, paused to consider the fact that he had done some talking himself. He had let on that he knew something of Indian artifacts, and the old man apparently wasn't pleased, as if dreading the knowledge possessed by his young companion. Had he known earlier, would he have allowed Allen to see everything?

Valenzuela shifted to a beautiful but conventional display. Allen ignored this, his thoughts turning inward. An image of the cellar flashed to mind; the cellar, with its curious doors and the wrapped package on the table. Might something unique lie concealed under that newspaper? The old man spoke of archeological finds near the house; why not under it? The ancient Mayans constructed underground chambers and tunnels, if memory served him right, and it did not totally stretch credulity to assume that the extinct locals did the same. If these objects were genuinely peculiar, a peculiarity born of a fact other than his haphazard training, then even now he stood above the entrance to a forgotten realm practically begging for exploration. The Indian did not appreciate the significance of his property, though he obviously held the artifacts in high esteem. Besides, Allen rationalized, legally speaking these treasures did not belong to Valenzuela at all. Hoarding them from an eager public for his own petty amusement—depriving the world of these marvels—it was positively criminal!

Allen feigned a closer interest in what his host was saying, and having apparently achieved his object the old man gradually perked up, assuming his former good humor. Presently, the tour concluded, they returned to the den, where Valenzuela spoke at length of his western-oriented trivia on the walls. Nothing special there: cheap Remington prints, strands of barbed wire and other rusty knick-knacks, fuzzy photographs of dirty, gawking men and thin, sad-eyed cattle. Allen smiled, nodded agreeably, spoke politely when called on, but his mind sped elsewhere. Two doors? He pondered the meaning of that. One the hypothetical tunnel, winding far into the obsidian cliffs, from which the loot was retrieved. The other a mystery. No, an explanation came to him. Yes, that was it, a storeroom. A hacked out chamber where the truly fantastic pieces were kept, hidden even from such stray arrivals as himself. In that case the trove must be really valuable, perhaps the gold and silver he missed in the main collection. The prospect of something with more than aesthetic worth excited Allen. He began to conceive of possibilities undreamed of earlier, and his thoughts took a new and nasty turn. Of course, he meant no harm, but his adventurous, questing spirit was stimulated by mystery as well as knowledge. Mystery thrived here, and with determination would come knowledge.

Allen faked a yawn when the conversation died and the gin ran low, and the old Indian stifled the real thing. The wall clock struck one, and dying embers tinkled in the sooty grate. Valenzuela announced his retirement for the night, courteously directing his guest to the kitchen for a bedtime snack of milk and apples. Allen thanked him for his kindness, and promised to rise early for the proffered lift to Winslow, the nearest major town via the dirt road, and from there back to his car. With that his host excused himself.

Allen, fully alert, watched him go. He followed with his ears as the old man entered his room, the turn of the lock his signal for action. Hurriedly gulping down the rest of his meal he moved off in search of hidden delights. He slipped into the cellar without trouble, though the creaking door disturbed him more this time. Armed with a lantern seized from the kitchen he descended the stairs on tip-toe, glancing back furtively when the rough-hewn wood groaned under his weight.

He disliked the unwholesome nature of the dark chamber. Patches of mildew coated the walls, and rivulets of water ran down the slick surface. He thought of leaking pipes, insecure sewage, which nauseated him. No matter. Proceeding to the first item on the agenda—the old man's bundle—he began unwrapping. The bundle consisted mainly of paper, its concealed prize much smaller than presumed. The object, when revealed, proved to be utterly unlike anything in Valenzuela's collection, including those curious items which first caught Allen's imagination. Despite evidence of great age he doubted its antique nature. Actually, it appeared to be a mechanical component of some larger device, for the three-pointed structure bore grooves and fittings which implied connection with other parts. The central bar was marked by lines and patterns which suggested, of all things, electronic circuitry. The puzzled young man was inclined to dismiss it as a conventional modern unit, perhaps an engine piece, except for the extreme corrosion of the surfaces, pitted and marred as if by a fierce sandstorm. He could not grasp the trident's function, nor recognize the metal from which it had been manufactured. If it was metal; in this respect his uncertainty matched that concerning the artifacts upstairs. Still, this was not what he sought. Now for the doors.

Whatever interesting mystery might lie back of this house and its wise old occupant could be found behind those doors. To be sure, Allen felt a distinct lack of nerve at this juncture; his prying could lead to trouble, and he was a long way from help. Still, it wasn't like he was a thief, just engagingly nosy; besides, life without risks was not worth living, and exploring new regions, even the cellar of a lonely farmhouse, was the whole point of his trip. He approached the door on the left.

The knob turned easily, though the rusted hinges grated annoyingly as the door swung outward. Within Allen saw darkness, darkness so opaque that even the lantern did not pierce it. He felt around for the inner wall, but the stone apparently fell away to the sides. A spacious cavern, then; getting better all the time. So this was not just a storeroom or cloistered cell, but a room of some dimensions. He stepped forward a few paces, stumbled, and then something happened which caused him to drop the lantern.

It was the greatest shock, the most impossible circumstance imaginable. One moment complete and pressing darkness, the next an explosion of searing white light. Allen could hardly be sure he was awake, for in what manner of reality could a man step through a subterranean doorway in the dead of night into a bright and expansive landscape, with a blazing sun and scudding clouds overhead? Worse, he quickly detected some very ominous signs: the sky was a deep green rather than blue, and the thick, tropical-type plants around him were like nothing he had seen or read about before. Bloated insects darted through the tree-like ferns, and suspicious sounds, as of large creatures moving through the undergrowth, could be heard nearby. Not enjoying this in the slightest, he turned to go, and discovered another marvel. Behind him, hovering a few inches off the ground, was a pitch-black blob, a vaguely spherical gap in the scenery. This, he guessed, was the gateway through which he came. It presented a weird sight, for it was so utterly unnatural that he hesitated to reenter it. His mind was rapidly made up, however, as a massive beast, looking for all the world like a ten-foot lizard, slithered through the ferns before him. Forgetting the shattered lantern, he leaped through the opening.

Four strides through darkness, and then he was back in the cellar, facing a furious Leon Valenzuela. "Did you learn what you wanted to know?" hissed the big Indian.

A moment passed before Allen could speak. "My God," he gasped out. Then, presently: "Am I dreaming?" This drew only a blank, angry stare.

Some time later, back in the den, when Valenzuela had calmed down and the focus of his ire had shaken off the willies, the two men had a long talk. Allen wanted information, Valenzuela wanted a promise of silence. Allen agreed conditionally, and the other party agreed to the conditions. That out of the way, the old man's story unfolded.

Many years ago, long before the invasion of the conquistadors, Valenzuela's people had dwelt in the land now known as Arizona. One of countless splinter groups of the Anasazi family, they settled this barren region after volcanic activity fertilized the soil. There, on the plateau of Wupatki in the shadow of newly risen Sunset Crater, they tilled their fields, raised their crops, hunted their game; lived, died, and multiplied during the good years. The devastating drought of the 1400s finished them off, though even today a handful of survivors eked out a marginal existence on the reservations.

Those were terrible years, and as the earth grew too arid to support the teeming population small bands broke away to struggle on their own. Most trekked south into the Verde River valley, mingling with other tribes and disappearing as a distinct ethnic unit. Some went north toward the great canyon. Valenzuela's ancestors journeyed into the Painted Desert, in search of fabled green lands beyond. They did not go far; scarcely had they begun their migration when the little band discovered the free-flowing springs at the base of the obsidian cliffs. Here, isolated by the untraveled sands, they set up a community, clinging tenaciously to the scalding land, somehow managing to live right through the Spanish conquest and the later depredations of the United States settlers. In the time of Valenzuela's grandfather several families still made this spot their home, but political fallout from government policies of the 1890s necessitated their removal to the Navajo reservation which spread over the north-eastern corner of the state. Only Valenzuela and his close relatives remained.

The desert oasis yielded another discovery, of course, one which irrevocably altered the psychology and religious customs of the tribe. Legend told of a man named Maker-of-Idols, a stone carver, who actually made the find. While cutting stone from the cliff face, he uncovered the mouth of the first gateway, the mysterious and unimaginable corridor to other realms through which Allen had stumbled. Further exploration revealed another close by, and when fully exposed opened up whole new worlds to the superstitious primitives. They quickly styled them the pathways of the Gods, who walked in shadows and dreams where no man treads. Now, due to an oversight or favor of the Gods, the people could walk there, and the bold ones did, bringing back tales of delight or horror to their wives and families. Religious rites grew up around the "tunnels," with offerings and even sacrifices (not human, the Indian assured his audience) being rendered.

The divine gates, Valenzuela explained, were portals in time and possibly space, the entering of which carried the traveler to strange and exotic lands. One path led into the past: the doorway Allen had chosen. The old man did not claim to know precisely the epoch reached by the dark doorway, but he felt it to be a period roughly two hundred million years ago. This he had deduced from books and a study of the flora and fauna. He often travelled through that gate, and in his younger days had journeyed extensively in the early world, admiring the chaotic jungle growths which coated the Earth. On occasion he observed, spying from a safe distance, the precursors of the dinosaurs, whose fossilized bones were common in Arizona and from which sprang such legends as the famous "Thunderbird."

And then there was the other gate. He hesitated to speak of that black opening, for matters were quite different beyond its fabulous mouth. It was, he supposed, the pathway to the future, though no books or tribal tales could verify that. Experience suggested that conclusion, but it was not a world for exploration. Few had visited there, and fewer still had returned. Those who did described it as the home of the Gods, where They still walked corporeally on Earth, as They had in the olden time, even assuming the form of men when They chose.

At this point Allen interrupted sharply, for he noted a discrepancy in the speaker's story. Had not the old man passed through that doorway, the one on the right, that very evening, bearing the strange artifact which now lay before them on the coffee table? Valenzuela paused, frowned, went on with his discourse without replying.

THE GUARDIAN OF THE GATE

The Gods, he said, were real, as he could attest from personal knowledge, but They were not Their former selves. Past the days of greatness, They lacked the magnanimity which characterized Them in legend, and no longer suffered men to approach. It was They who built the gates in order to walk between the planes of physical reality, flitting through the eons, creating and shaping the land and the sky. That mortal men would dare cross over to mock Their former glory did not please Them, and it was good that the pathways remained hidden to all but the faithful few. Sensing this, the Anasazi elders led the tribe in worship of the fallen but still potent entities, and advised none to pass through that gate or to petition the Gods except in tactful prayers. Certain young men, coming of age, passed through the opening when valor superseded discretion, but most were content to make heart-felt offerings of well-chosen animals.

In order to protect the holiest of shrines the elders devised a special honorary position, the Guardian of the Gate. Only the wisest, most respected men were chosen, and the duty was conferred for life. The lifetime obligation was no light matter, for the position commanded great authority, and the chosen one was barred from the other ranks, a lonely yet satisfying vocation for the right man. Of course, everything was different now; the Nineteenth Century saw the last of the old-style appointments. Valenzuela held the title of Guardian by default, since the 1960s when his son (the one who went away, Allen recalled; or was it disappeared?) vied for the honor, but he took it no less seriously on that account. It meant, in fact, his whole life, and thus the young gentleman should understand why he reacted so violently to Allen's previous indiscretion. The duty was his until he died, and then the rites of centuries would end. The last Guardian, the last faithful Anasazi, wished to bury the forbidden secret with him.

It was well into the morning when the Indian finished his tale and bade his guest, a little more emphatically this time, a good night. Valenzuela still insisted on an early rising, and naturally seemed anxious to rid himself of the young meddler. After the glasses were put up he marched Allen to his room and saw him in, extracting a solemn oath against further night ramblings. It was dangerous, he repeated earnestly; the young man could thank the Gods that he had chosen the door on the left for his unwarranted snooping. To cross over the other threshold unprepared, without all the facts, gambled more than mere life. Danger to the soul lurked there.

Allen was impressed by Valenzuela's words, though certain aspects of the story troubled him. He mulled over the details as he collapsed onto the ancient iron-frame bed for a few hours rest. He was digesting more information than he could handle, and parts of the puzzle left him stupefied. The old man's tale was true enough, as far as it went, but surely more remained to be uncovered. The explanations for the gates rang true, though he assumed the answer lay in the realm of science rather than superstition. If the time corridors were of artificial manufacture the creators strode, not the fairyland of heaven, but the visionary world of the future. The Gods? Yes, they would appear as gods to a backward tribe of illiterate dirt farmers. Allen did not understand the discreet references to the Indian's missing son, nor the unaccountable dread felt by the natives for the gateway denizens; he would have thought them deliriously happy to meet their supposed masters. Of course, primitive peoples were historically moody in their beliefs. To worship from afar was one thing, to meet the great ones face to face might be an unnerving experience.

He awoke from a fitful doze when the cock crowed. Sleep had not brought rest, only compelling dreams. As his eyelids unsealed the events and discussions of the night rushed upon him with crystal clarity of purpose and anticipation. A faint wash of red shone through the window drapes; morning already. Allen realized that time was slipping away. The moment had come, his last chance to explore the dark and inviting world of the second doorway. It was a crazy determination, yet one impossible to resist. With firm resolve he sprang to his feet, listening intently for sounds of movement from the other occupant. Nothing stirred yet. Almost frantically he pulled on his clothes and unchained the bedroom door. Still no noises from the adjoining room. No time to lose if he wanted to avoid interception; the old Indian, if he chose, could make matters very hard for him.

He again recalled the old man's warnings. Probably sheer nonsense, but he would be careful, merely a quick survey if things looked bad. On pins and needles he opened the door and crept down the hall, slipping by the room of his unsuspecting host. Down to the first floor, across the kitchen, moving without a light, he trusted to memory to guide him, jostling furniture in his wake. Came the sound of movement overhead. With feverish haste Allen bounded down the cellar stairs. A shout of surprise and outrage reached his ears. The game was up, but there was the dark doorway, the second entrance, the one on the right. He jerked it open. A black hole. The darkness, the inviting darkness, and beyond—the sound of running feet above, the dreadful grind of the cellar door, sudden radiance—and Allen plunged through the wondrous corridor, seeking the marvels of the future.

He was slow to realize that he had passed the gateway; slower still to realize what was the matter with him. He felt strange. The air: yes, the air was pitifully thin, difficult to breathe. Allen's chest felt constricted, his head light. In a daze he peered about into a landscape of eerie gloom only slightly less dark than the gateway. Dry, chill breezes fanned him, leeching the warmth from his body. Cold, dark, barren, and silent save for the bitter wind:

this was the world Allen found.

He stood on a vast mesa or table rock thrust by the Earth's forces above a steep gulley. Beyond, almost at the limit of vision, rose another solitary plateau. In the extreme distance a low range of mountains could be seen, although Allen did not trust his eyes that far. It might be clouds on the horizon although, now that he examined the sky, he saw no clouds above whatsoever, only a full moon appearing smaller than it should. The stars shone splendidly bright, far surpassing those of the Arizona desert, with no hint of atmospheric distortion. They did not twinkle, nor did they form any sort of recognizable patterns. The familiar constellations were gone, wiped away by the randomness of time. Whenever he was, Allen felt that it was an incredibly remote epoch of the future.

No traces of living creatures could be discerned, but Allen's attention was drawn to the uplands across the ravine, where a lattice of non-natural shapes beckoned. Perhaps something could be found there. He set out, cautiously descending the dangerous slope, tramping down the crooked channel, pausing now and again to gulp at the oxygen-starved air. The trek seemed interminable, though it was really not so far. A few hundred yards at most, yet this atmosphere, the cold (and he underdressed for the occasion), and the rugged terrain took their toll. All the while he considered the circumstances, the ghastly lunar landscape about him, and its implications. What had happened to cause this? A war, a natural disaster of untold magnitude? Solar flares, possibly. How did this jibe with Valenzuela's story? The scarce atmosphere: blasted away or otherwise depleted. Whatever the cause, and assuming his surroundings were representative of the entire planet, the catastrophe had been complete and final. Apparently nothing had survived to carry on the world's history; no animal, insect, blade of grass, no microorganisms from the look of things. No people.

His goal resolved itself into a scattered collection of broken blocks, disintegrating towers, and sinking foundations. As he progressed uphill by moonlight the ruins grew denser, until at last Allen knew that he trod upon the remains of a sprawling metropolis, a futuristic city built eons before, presumably by his descendants. Certain portions were in remarkably good condition, the weird dwellings and skyscrapers retaining the shape of their alien architecture, joined by strands of crystalline stone which spanned the narrow lanes like a gossamer shroud. Other regions contained only dust and toppled piles to mark where human beings once lived, worked and played. The few intact chambers into which he peered seemed empty. The general impression was not so much of devastation as of abandonment and corrosion.

Gazing up at the mantle of night with its multi- colored jewels, the air too clear to soften the sharp black dome of the sky, he noted one especially brilliant star: Venus? No, it was near the zenith, impossible unless the solar system itself had been altered. He remembered something at this point. His trip to the prehistoric world last night had led to a sunlit sky; now, a morning journey into the future brought him to a land of awesome night. A coincidence, or some effect of the time journey, hard to say. Allen wished he could learn more, but those who could tell him were gone, and he doubted whether the Indian was well-informed on the scientific aspects of his secret. He endeavored to guess, however, at the meaning of what he saw.

No gods, rather nothingness; this, then, was the fate of humanity. Eventually, long after the relative security of the Twentieth Century had been forgotten, civilization would end, and with it all life. He could only speculate as to the cause, perhaps a man-made catastrophe or astronomical disaster that abruptly drove the human race into extinction. Perhaps man lingered pathetically after the event, succumbing when resources dwindled below a sustaining level. Either way, the glory and the dream had disappeared, and evolution had run its ultimate course. This time nobody won. Nothing to do now but return to the ancient present, bear up under the ire of the obsessed Indian, and go, trusting that the future would never well up to haunt him. A vain hope.

Allen left that city of death and decay, leaving behind the perished memories of a golden age, if such it ever came to be. He followed his own earlier path to support his feeble sense of direction; to get lost in the Arizona wilds was infinitely terrible, but here it was beyond sanity. His bare feet sifted the dust of ages. Presently a tingling sensation of unease, arising from an unknown source, tiptoed down the back of his neck, accompanied by an unconscious feeling of urgency and danger. Something was wrong— seriously wrong—and with difficulty did he resist the impulse to run. He did increase his pace, and found himself concentrating on the ground over which he walked.

The reason became clear when he stopped to closely examine the trail. He saw his footprints, the hollows left by overturned pebbles . . . and other signs. Certain prints were disturbed in a manner which did not suggest the action of the wind. Maybe it was the wind, though, light as it was. All too often, he noted as he continued, the disturbances themselves bore the shape of more recent, distorted prints.

This was bad enough, but in addition a faint suggestion of certain sounds now reached him. Granted that hearing wasn't entirely reliable in that thin air—what with the pounding of his heart, the pulsing in his ears, the relentless throbbing in his temples—still he felt that other, barely audible noises sporadically rose above these and the rasping of his breath. A shuffling, a vague rustling emanated from an unspecified direction. He assured himself that it was caused by the breeze, yet it came too regularly for that, as if someone was trying—and failing—to keep pace with his step.

When he reached the ravine Allen broke into an icy sweat. He had been misled by initial appearances. Glancing sidelong at the abandoned city, he perceived lights, ghostly blue beacons blinking and flickering near the ground, in the standing towers; close to a dozen of them, some moving erratically. Then he saw more, to his horror farther down the ditch near a bend he recognized and which he was approaching. These fresh lights were accompanied by a sound, a kind of chuckling or croaking.

Shaking, but not yet despairing, he ascended the steep bank there and pushed on quickly, circling toward the familiar heights of the mesa. Below he heard the clumping of feet, the sliding of soil, handholds being gripped. Allen dashed up the slope, struggling against a fainting spell which washed over him, brought on by excitement and exertion. He did not believe what was happening to him; it smacked of madness, or of a nightmare from which he might mercifully awake at any moment. Such fantasies were useless, as was the inane thought that he had, only yesterday, been exploring the Arizona badlands on a bright and crisp November morning, his major worry the irrelevant fretting over a vacation almost spent. Of course, this was all wrong; it was not yesterday, but untold millions or billions of years ago, on what might have been another planet as far as his morbid surroundings indicated. His century, his world, did not exist, replaced by another time, and new denizens. These denizens—the Indian had spoken of the tribal deities who walk in darkness—Good God! He had put it down as superstition, as the kind of throwback belief which he shunned in the civilized world. Too late, though, to regret his stupidity and the blindness of ignorant rationality which led him to laugh at the old man. The humans of this age, survivors of a race long past its prime, were closing in on him. Gone the sense of wonder, for he thought only of escape.

Terror struck when Allen mounted the ridge and sought out the haven of the gateway. He couldn't find it! He screamed in frustration as he realized his dilemma. The tunnel had appeared the first time as a dark sphere, readily visible against the green of forest and sky, but against the blackness of night it could not be seen. Horrified, he examined the loose soil for his former trail's point of origin. Without luck, for his prints were obscured among the maze of subsequent impressions. The beings, then, had pursued him for some time, observing and laying their snare. It might well have been chuckling he heard in the ravine. They considered the trap airtight.

Then he saw them: the shapes emerging from the dim recesses below, bearing iridescent globes which irradiated the hellish landscape. Saw them and screamed, and ran aimlessly about, begging fortune to lead him through the mislaid opening, screamed again and again, at a soul-searing vision which he would never later describe, only hint at; a vision which would, during our more intimate sessions through the years, reduce him to sobbing hysterics. "Shapeless forms," "devils," "the eye, the eyes," "not living, never alive," "changing at will": such disjointed phrases make up the totality of his cautious utterances as I recall them, nor could probing elicit more of this scene. Suffice to say Allen beheld that which cannot be, forms and images which the sound brain cannot record without destroying itself. Surely they were not men, or anything resembling men. Perhaps they were the survivors, the last degenerate, evolution-twisted remnants of the bygone past. Perhaps they came not from this world's tree of life, but from outside. Fortunately we will never know. Allen saw them, and it changed him irrevocably. Whether the experience was real, or the phantasm of a diseased mind, I do not wonder.

In one titanic burst of fear, one nerve-rending moment which encompassed the undiluted distillation of horror, Allen felt rough hands seize him from behind, clutch under his arms and yank him backwards. He gagged on bile, his arms flailing wildly, seeing nothing and not wanting to see. A smooth, unyielding surface slid under him, and then luminosity shone through his tightly clenched eyelids. Allen blinked, dreading what he might see, and blinked again. He found himself staring up at a damp stone ceiling and the glowering face of Leon Valenzuela. Instantly he knew: he was lying on his back in the cellar, free of immediate peril, and the old Indian gentleman was his savior. Not an angel of mercy, however. As Allen wearily lay back, shaking his head to remove the inner fog (the inrushing air poured like syrup into his heaving lungs), his companion kicked him savagely in the ribs. Allen yelped and sat up, embarking on a string of heated curses, only to be cut off by Valenzuela's rasped words: "You fool!"

The great oaken door in the wall hung open. Hurriedly slipping the bolt, Valenzuela curtly commanded Allen to rise and aid him. As the young man hesitated the Indian threw his weight against the wood and snarled:

"You've done it. I might have known. I should have known. If I had killed you last night no one would have found out, and the secret would be safe. My secret, and the secret of the door. Get over here. I need you now.

"You didn't listen to me, or you didn't believe. That was a mistake. You crossed over in our daytime, and that was a bigger mistake. It's night there, as you know by now, and that's when They roam about. It's too dangerous to cross over then, as my people learned hundreds of years ago. Thirty years ago my son went over into night—Their night—as you did. He couldn't resist, he wanted to see Them. He didn't understand the Gods, and I couldn't make him understand.

"He didn't disappear. I killed him. Why? Because I am the Guardian. No, I don't protect the Gods—They don't need any help—I protect us. You see, our Lords are not good Gods. They are fallen ones, who exist to destroy. My tribe prayed, not for benefits, but to be left in peace. The Gods are not so wise and powerful as They once were; the sun's rays injure Them in Their true forms, and They lost Their mastery of the gates. They created the gates, but forgot about them. As long as the gate connecting our time to Theirs was hidden we were safe, but if They ever broke through and regained control of it . . . well, They have ways of passing among our kind, clever and evil tricks, and our world would suit them a lot better than Their own.

"My son met Them, panicked. He would have led Them through if I hadn't followed and killed him. Then I had to hide until daybreak, when They crawl back under Their city. But I didn't catch you in time—They discovered your presence too quickly—and now They know the way . . ."

The big man stiffened, grew silent. Allen, now at his host's side, tensed as he felt a steady pressure building up against the door. In a flash he realized exactly what the Indian meant, and what dangers 1ay ahead. On the other side of that door a force had brooded throughout the centuries, awaiting its chance to break through. The entities—call them gods, if you will, or demons, for their potential was beyond human reckoning—knew that the gate existed, and that it was the entrance to a new, fresh world for the taking. The scarred future viewed the bountiful past with covetous eyes, and he had led them to it. He had sensed the evil on the other side, and knew that any crossover would be disastrous for mankind and all earthly life.

As he strained against the creaking wood Valenzuela groaned, muttering to himself, overcome by creeping hysteria. "Foretold long ago," he mumbled thickly. "The elders knew. They would come. I didn't accept it. I thought that one determined man could hold them back. For forty years I've tried. It isn't right—"

The door buckled, the bolt grinding into the jam. Allen saw that the metal bolt was absorbing most of the unseen pressure, but the strength of the others was intensifying. The screws which held it into the stone began to pop; the first whizzed across the room with a clang, the second started jiggling and working its way out of the wall. The Indian gasped, commenced praying in his native tongue, the rhythmic syllables oddly accompanied by the increasing chatter in the gateway.

The next moment the bolt screamed and gave way. Allen shouted and jumped back, whirled and dashed pell-mell for the stairs. Valenzuela, aghast at being abandoned (Allen later regretted his own cowardice, but felt that the situation was beyond heroics at this stage), attempted to break away, but could not resist the powers arrayed against him. The heavy door crashed outward, hurling the poor man to the stone floor, shrieking unintelligibly, his arms before his face as if warding off a smashing blow. Allen's pause at the stairwell was of minute duration, but during that short period he saw enough to deaden his thoughts and freeze his blood. The scene was indelibly stamped in his memory: the rickety table and chair, the boxes, the gaping hole in the wall, the downed man, all bathed in the glow of a sputtering lamp. And the emerging horror, shapes flowing out of the black corridor, swarming into the chamber, clustering about their raving victim. They touched him, enveloped him, and then the change came. Before the onlooker's riveted gaze his former host, the self-appointed defender of the world and its normal history, began to physically alter in a manner impossible to comprehend. His body distorted, swelled, compressed, seethed; portions shriveled like fat in the fire, or expanded until they burst like exploding balloons, spraying a fine red mist into the air. The hideous mutations alternated and rippled across the corrugated body, and all the while Valenzuela, or what was left of him, his psyche intact through it all, screamed and begged for death, for release from unendurable agony.

Allen did not witness the culmination of the horror. He fled precipitately, the torment of the hopelessly dying man assailing his ears. He professes to remember little after that: a long and lonely flight down a difficult dirt track under a hot sun, arrival in the small town of Winona just before noon; frantic talks with the police chief, William Lee, followed by a dreaded, jolting journey with Lee and a deputy in a county car back to the isolated house. This journey Allen pleaded to be excused from, but there was no way to avoid it. He went, and ever afterward lived in the shadow of crouching fear.

Controversy exists concerning Sheriff Lee's report on what the party found at the old house. Of course, the controversy is all Allen's doing, for it was he who made note of the original report's destruction and its subsequent recopying a week later. He was on the scene when the first copy was prepared, and it was his firm conviction that the second draft was deliberately altered to destroy his credibility. It is interesting how the same set of circumstances was viewed by the two major witnesses. William Lee seems a forthright and honorable man, and in my correspondence with him he never gave cause to question his honesty. Lee mentions that the original suffered incineration in a minor courthouse fire, yet he dutifully prepared the second copy within days. The reported facts bear him out, which certainly harms Allen's case. My friend maintained that the original was entirely truthful, in the sense that the lawman reported what he saw and. heard that day. The initial results were not pleasant, but supposedly bore out what Allen most feared. Later, he speculated, the report was doctored and the original destroyed in order to cover up his revelations, and Allen always insisted that he knew why and how it was done. His interpretation, based entirely on intuition, is truly grotesque, but without a single shred of evidence I balk at repeating it. It smacks of rabid paranoia, a key character trait of his, I fear, in later years.

Lee's account, as embodied in the second draft, describes his initial interrogation of a "delirious, possibly intoxicated Mr. Tolleson." He outlines the discussion, which he frankly considered ridiculous, and the trip to the house in the desert. The essence of Lee's story is contained in a single paragraph: "The house was deserted, apparently unoccupied for several years. A very old pickup sat out front, corroded beyond use. The windows were tightly boarded and nailed, as was the door . . . Deputy Manson broke in through a side window . . . and during our investigation found no evidence of recent tenancy. Nor do records exist of said person. The curious artifacts described by Mr. Tolleson were not present . . . The cellar bore no trace of the fantastic features previously mentioned. When pressed Mr. Tolleson tried to pass off his earlier statements as a joke, which we did not appreciate, and I warned him of possible criminal charges resulting from his actions." Sheriff Lee concludes by labelling Allen either a liar or a madman. On this basis I can hardly blame him.

Allen, to me, rejected this report as orchestrated fabrication. Despite Sheriff Lee's testimony my friend stuck by his story, claiming that it was the final revelation which brought about his withdrawal from society, the irrational hatred of strangers, and the ever present sense of being watched or followed. I heard his startling conclusion many times, always deeming it the weakest part of the tale. It makes a terrifying kind of sense if one accepts his entire account. Allen's resolve never wavered; he remained absolute in his conviction that he, unknowingly, had let loose in the world a hideous, irresistible monstrosity from beyond time, a malign power seeking primacy over our race. His wild surmises concerning the weird powers of those supposed creatures staggers my imagination. He convinced himself that they could infiltrate humanity by assuming . . . no, I can't bring myself to go into that, even though these preposterous ideas about replacement carried so much weight with Allen. He considered the cancer deeply rooted and spreading, felt its tentacles closing around him as the penalty for knowing too much. At times he even showed concern for my welfare; if they ever got to him, he might lead them to me, his confessor. This may be why I find his death so disturbing. In his eyes, just before the end, he may have thought it the final vindication. The first, of course, was his experience in the Valenzuela house on the afternoon of November 15.

SCIENCE AND SORCERY III

The house was silent, and when no one answered the knock Sheriff Lee (the "real" Sheriff Lee then, as Allen insisted on styling him) pushed in to investigate, dragging the trembling young man with him. Finding the house as aforesaid described by Allen, with all its owner's curious possessions, they shortly marched to the cellar. No body or obvious traces of a struggle remained and, unbelievably, the gateways had vanished, leaving only a surface of solid stone. Dumfounded, Allen probed with his fingers into every hollow and crevice, stammering incoherent replies to the Sheriff's increasingly hostile questions. Propped against the stair rail as if, Allen said, they were no longer necessary, stood the two wooden doors, their hinges broken, the oak cracked and marred with peculiar scars. Humiliated, sniped at by his doubting companions, Allen already verged on breakdown, when his roving gaze was arrested by the sight of a shadowed human figure descending the stairs. He shouted and the two lawmen jumped, whipped out their revolvers and trained their flashlights on the half-seen shape. With the figure revealed in the focused glare Allen felt his heart stop, his brains turn over in his skull. His knees buckled and he slid into a dead faint, never more to behold the cause of his physical distress.

One can almost wonder why he fussed about the two reports, for if the mythical first one followed his tale it must still have been a painfully awkward situation for him. Even if that moment unfolded as Allen—and only he— claimed, the horror that shocked him so could stem solely from what was inferred, rather than any tangible fright. The man on the stairs, his lined face impassive, his expression inscrutable, was none other than Leon Valenzuela.

THE HOUSE AT THE END OF THE WORLD

We spied the house from afar, high atop its precarious perch projecting into the sea, and as the lateness of the hour required some thoughts of shelter we hastened to attain it. Fifty miles and more we had traveled during the preceding week, Robert and I, through wild, rugged, unpopulated terrain seldom breached by man. All the remote splendor of the partially forgotten wilderness had graced our vacationing journey, all the magnificent scenery of a primordial arboreal land: rolling, forested hills, dense cane-break jungles, putrid gurgling swamps, shadowed creeks splashing over rocks or fountaining over falls; and the inhabitants thereof, creatures scarcely touched by the civilization pressing harshly against their domain. All this we had seen, and more, but despite our wonder and fascination we were in truth glad to emerge from that thriving vastness, to burst forth once again into the open air and sky, to find some portion of the humanity we left behind. Far ahead that house loomed, and from a distance it looked inviting.

The Sun, now dazzling when not glimpsed through masses of twisted branches and Spanish moss, glowered in the final half of its mundane progression, a delightful sight but mercifully behind us since we did not have to march into the glare. The pervading light revealed an interestingly low-key, almost somber landscape, and once we surmounted the seaward bluffs we possessed a sweeping view of the area. To the west stretched the wide forest barrier we had painstakingly crossed, to the east the foaming blue ocean. North and south, roughly, ran the coast, and toward the extreme limit of vision to our left appeared the muted, shimmering outline of a small town which, according to our best estimates, did not appear on our maps. Directly ahead the coastal bluffs bulged outward, extending a narrow peninsula into the swelling waters, and at the very end of this huddled the house toward which we proceeded with all possible speed.

Where the land narrowed we drew close to the shore, crossing the pitted, gullied remnants of a disused dirt road, and during the remainder of our hike we trod close by the steep descent to the water's edge, where undeveloped sand beaches lay pristine and silent save for the lapping of the waves and the raucous screeching of diving gulls. This peninsula, in stark contrast to the surrounding green region, seemed curiously lifeless, a bleak, sere outcropping of dry, stony ground mixed with hard red clay. It may have been my imagination—although Robert mentioned it too—that the birds seemed to avoid this lonely spit, but the absence of significant vegetation was a fact beyond dispute. Only a few stunted trees, low-lying scaly shrubs and tough native grasses clung to the perilous slopes or clutched at life on the central plateau, and even these hardy pioneers or survivors appeared to be waging a losing battle against the elements and the obviously impoverished nature of the soil.

Seen from a near remove the house's invitation, its sense of beckoning, lessened dramatically. First we noticed that it was deserted, then that it had clearly suffered from long vacancy. Much had fallen, and much was crumbling, but enough remained to indicate that once this had been a structure of marvelous proportions. The mammoth dwelling, chiefly constructed of stout oak, with huge stones forming the base, rose two stories from the plain and sprawled across most of an acre. A multitude of gaping, unpaned windows eyed us blankly, windows encased by heavy, archaic wooden shutters still marked by random traces of paint. The immense two-piece door, wide and tall enough to drive a car through, stood improbably intact, especially considering the oval-stained glass portals on both halves. These portals, dusty but unmarred, gleamed faintly in the sunlight, with a deep emerald reflection. We wondered how they had lasted. Certainly the mansion itself, at least the initial structure, judging from the ornate fixtures and tell-tale architectural signs, must be close to two centuries old.

Although this revelation dashed our hopes for hospitality it did not depress our spirits, rather marking one more adventure to add to our list. A big abandoned house out in the middle of nowhere; who knew what we might find inside? Divesting ourselves of our backpacks and camping gear we scampered off around the house, pausing now and again to survey the interior as illuminated through the empty windows. Little could be seen, and less recognized due to the thick dust which shrouded every exposed surface. Frolicking like kids we raced around back to see what we might find there . . . and saw something which caused us to stop abruptly short.

The back yard, if it could be called that, stretched monotonously down to the steep cliffs overlooking the surf. This familiarly gray, blighted waste supported only one object, a tall, corroded tower of roughly hewn granite stabbing up at the very edge perhaps one hundred yards from the house. The bulk of the mansion had hidden it during our approach. In shape it resembled a stubby lighthouse, possibly fifty feet high, but certain peculiarities immediately caught our eyes. The covered cupola of stone on top seemed cramped from our vantage point, not at all the sort of place a lighthouse keeper would occupy. Except for a square hole cut in the stone where a door had once been no openings existed, and this one faced land rather than sea. Definitely it was not a lighthouse. Another odd feature was the rusted iron stairway and railing, winding up the outer face of the tower rather than the inside, as I supposed it would in a real lighthouse. The odd bits, the form as a whole militated against this simple solution and suggested some other purpose unperceived by us. My companion, unfortunately, is given to acrophobia, or we would have climbed it right then. I made a mental note to follow up the challenge after we explored the house.

Upon that course we promptly embarked, breaking through the splintered timbers of the back door and entering into a lofty hallway draped in disintegrating tapestries and cobwebs. Once inside the wealth and standing of the bygone inhabitants revealed itself in limitless numbers of aged wall paintings, furniture of a master craftman's design and quality, and myriads of priceless crystal and porcelain artworks. Most of the ground floor was inaccessible to us due to frequent collapses and burials from the upper story, but what we could traverse astonished us. In those days, at least, people knew how to live. Those days, judging from the objects around us, meant the early part of this century, although neither of us claimed to be experts on such matters. Here and there we came across a staircase ascending to the ruins of the second floor, but only one of them still stood in good condition. We equivocated a bit before we made up our minds but eventually we clumped up those creaking, groaning steps, grasping firmly the wobbly bannister every time the peeling, worm-eaten boards beneath our feet lurched under our weight.

As it happened only two rooms were available for exploration, the others cut off or actually fallen through the lower ceiling, and one of those turned out to be a bedroom, a rotted mass long exposed by a rent in the roof. The next, however, proved otherwise, and had been given over to an entirely different function. A library or study, apparently, replete with the typical articles of a gentleman's lair, but the type and quality of the books we found there showed that the man had been no ordinary country squire. The majority of these books, while not exposed to the wind and rain, had decomposed through the actions of time and mold, but enough held together to allow our handling them, albeit gingerly. The shredding leather covers revealed little—some were in Latin, others blank—but the contents of the English texts shocked us. A handful of philosophical works, a couple of treatises on antiquated scientific or natural topics, and an overwhelming number of books, manuscripts and pamphlets on occult subjects made up the set. Some of the bulkier tomes, printed in Latin or German, all much weathered, were very old, one volume on witchcraft bearing a publishing date of 1583. The pamphlets and bound papers, while extremely aged in themselves, and of a similarly loathsome nature, were written in English with modern writing pens which indicated a date within the last hundred years. These covered a multitude of subjects, all strange, some ghastly, but I could scarcely make sense out of them. The unspeakably dry and turgid compositional style repelled adequate perusal, but examples from the headings will offer some idea of the contents: "The Spheres Beyond," "The Gateway of Knowledge," "The Entrance to the Other World," "On Certain Signs Received During the Fifth Ceremony." Weird stuff, all of it, inscribed by hand, and wretched penmanship too. Many of the frontispieces bore the signature of the compiler, Jonathon R. Tolleson, whom I presumed to be the past owner of this place.

After a time we left the books, regretting that we lacked the means to cart them away, and having descended to the lower level once more we exited through a side window, as debris blocked our progress to the front door. We ate a late lunch from our trail rations, speculating on all we had seen, romancing on the imaginary histories we conjured up for the house. Robert had seen enough and was for pushing on to the dimly glimpsed village to the north, but I had that tower in mind. At length we decided to pause until I had displayed my heroic abilities and climbed the thing. My friend, of course, would remain below.

As is always the case the reality of climbing is more difficult than appearances imply. Scarcely had I set foot to shifting iron than I suddenly realized how tall the tower actually rose. Too late to back out now, not with Robert waiting impatiently for my report from the top. Up I staggered, clinging madly, creeping cautiously forward, ignoring my sarcastic cheering section below. Round and round wound that rickety stairway, the dreadfully thin metal rungs sagging at every step. The wind whipped around the circular structure, curiously cold for the season, but I assumed this was due to height. Halfway up that vertiginous ascent, pinned between coarse granite and yawning sky, I detected a sail on the ocean, barely above the horizon. It seemed so peaceful out there, in contrast to my present predicament; what I would have given to be lounging on that boat rather than defying death on those stairs! Still I climbed, glancing down only once and chastising myself for that foolishness, seeing Robert staring up with his hand shielding his eyes, in an attitude of concern. Fortunately the next revolution brought me to a cranky iron ladder, a terrifying sight not noticeable from the ground, but I clambered up and, gasping for breath and shivering from fear, leaned limply into the gouged cupola entrance.

To my dismay the interior did not offer much comfort. Instead of the expected stone platform where I could recover from the climb I found a narrow walkway encircling a wide, irregular hole in the floor. Enough light passed through the entrance to illuminate the room, so I inched forward, again wishing I were elsewhere. The hole did not even possess a guardrail to provide the illusion of safety. Back flat to the inner wall, I surveyed my surroundings. The interior was, if anything, more crudely constructed than the exterior. The stone blocks, though cemented tightly together, looked the work of an amateur. The walls bore traces of what appeared to be words or runic inscriptions which I could not make out, at least not in that gray half-light. A closer inspection revealed odd circles, arrows, pictographs representing eyes, hands and various unidentified creatures. The walkway was paved with uneven flagstones which projected jaggedly over the rim in the center. All in all the space spanned ten by ten feet or thereabouts, although the available room was roughly half that.

Toward the hole curiosity impelled me, very slowly. Lying full length, with my feet dangling through the doorway, I just managed to look down into a pit of some kind, an upright tunnel plunging straight down through the tower. I saw nothing but darkness, and regretted not having a flashlight; or was I relieved? Although nothing was visible I felt overcome by unpleasant sensations, as though I hung over a well with no bottom, a sheer drop to the center of the earth. I hastily drew back from the pit, shut my eyes, tried to think consecutively. For the life of me I could not fathom the meaning of this tower or its pit, or the uses to which they had been put, but the memory of those horrid books and the sight of those weird glyphs on the walls suppressed my eagerness to know more.

As I had exhausted the possibilities of that tiny chamber I crawled around and out the door, pushing a reluctant foot toward the upper rung of that damned ladder. I could not bear to look down but I could look out, at the upland scenery, at the rugged coastline. This side of the peninsula, I noted, bore the full force of the tide and surf; the wave-pounded shore had lost its sand beach or never had one, instead harboring a jumbled collection of gigantic boulders among the tidal pools. The cliffs rose almost vertically from the water, drenched in salt spray, carved into fantastic shapes. From my lookout post I could discern the silent town in the background and, most unexpected, a solitary human figure struggling up the slope in the foreground.

I called down to Robert that somebody was coming, heard his puzzled reply and immediately set myself the task of getting down. That was a real nightmare, but to make a long story short I did it, experiencing the greatest difficulty in getting back over the ladder. I finally made it down, treading cat-like on buckling steps, having sworn en route never to attempt such a harebrained stunt again, and was just in time to greet the approaching interloper.

"Good afternoon, young sirs," the man called, an extremely old man exhibiting a voice cracked with age and a frank cheerfulness which quite put us at ease. In out of the way places strangers are frowned upon, and both Robert and I had vaguely suspected trouble. This old-timer, however, seemed to have nothing of the sort on his mind.

"Caught you at a bad time, I see," he chortled, eyeing me speculatively. "Been touring the wonders of the Tolleson Manor, have you? That's a rarity. Can't remember the last time a body passed this way." Despite the gentleness of his speech the intruder presented a dubious appearance: incredibly old, his leering face creased and lined as if erosion had been at work upon it rather than age; his body scrawny and withered, spindly legs and puny arms protruding comically from the filthy sack he wore in lieu of clothing; and dirty grayish-white hair, thinning at the top, hanging in a thick, matted mop over his sunburnt brow. Bright, active eyes, though, revealed a lively, inquisitive personality.

I explained to him how we had hiked across the inland forest and had unintentionally come upon this old wreck. That intrigued him.

"A camping trip, that what it is?" he said, repeating my words, peering directly into my face as if for evidence of falsehood. Apparently he accepted us. "A good place for it, those woods. Lots of things to see and do there. Been a long time since I traveled. Haven't even been through the woods in more years than I can count. I used to get around a lot." He said this wistfully, as if recalling the bygone days of youth, a fading recollection for one so advanced in years.

I made introductions, giving him a little information about ourselves, but my words might have been the wind for all they registered with him. "And what is your name, sir?" I queried.

"See anything of interest up there?" he asked me. Obviously the old guy was completely senile. He could not do us harm of any sort.

"Guess it's not the proper time," he mused aloud following my reply. "Mind you, if it was the proper time you could see plenty, and you wouldn't stand around talking about it. You'd run, is what you'd do, get out of here as fast as your legs would carry you; if you could, which I doubt."

All along I had puzzled over the mysterious nature of the tower, and the strange impression I received of the individual who once dwelt in the great house. This old man, though he seemed to have trouble uttering his name, apparently knew something about the place.

"Tell us about it," I requested, seating myself on the bottom step of the tower. Robert did likewise. The old man stood silently staring at us, before shifting his gaze to the ruined house behind him. He faced us again, pondering, then shrugged.

THE HOUSE AT THE END OF THE WORLD

"Might just do that, just for something new to do. It's quite a story," he said soberly, "the oddest story you'll ever hear. I never told nobody—nobody left to tell—but I guess it won't hurt to tell you, seeing as how you're pushing on anyhow. Have you been in the house yet?" he asked.

Robert affirmed this. "Did you manage to see those books?"

We both verified this. "Well, I wondered if them books were still around," he drawled. "It was them that started it all. Belonged to Old Man Tolleson, the gentleman who originally built the manor house in 1826. Wasn't a town here then, wasn't anything, but he imported a bunch of workmen to build for him and after a while they sort of settled down out there. He wasn't too keen on that, I guess—came here for privacy, or so everyone thought—but he didn't mind so long as they left him alone.

"Plenty of privacy, all right, but that wasn't why old Gregory Tolleson came. He had his own special reasons, reasons other folks wouldn't understand or like if they did. He was a scientist, you see, a researcher, just a tinkerer but in those days they all were. Every man of learning dabbled in something, just to amuse himself, or keep busy, or impress his friends, but some got carried away with it. That was Tolleson to a tee; carried away, so sure he was on to something that would change the world and make him famous. Considering what happened later I suppose he was right, but not the way he intended.

"As a young man he got hold of those books, and they gave him ideas. He decided one day that there was more to the world than most people know or care to know about, and he was going to be the one to find out. He thought (how can I put this, not very clear to me so how can I say it) he thought what everyone called one world was really many, but most of them were invisible or hidden from us, and it took more than a good pair of eyes to see or find them. Those other worlds had people too, though they weren't exactly people in the sense we take it to mean, and if he could get in touch with them he might learn things as would shock the smartest folks. Mind you now, this was all before he came here—about the turn of that century, maybe—anyway, he was rich, money meant nothing, and he was unattached, no relatives to speak of, so he could devote his whole life to the search.

"He was looking for a spot on earth where the different worlds came together, where a body could actually cross from one to the other, and to find this he roamed the globe tracking down stories and following up old clues. Based on what I know I can tell you he found some such places, but most were in high mountains or unfriendly countries, some even at sea. Nowhere he could stay and work, except here. Here he found what he was looking for, and here he came to stay.

"Look there, good sirs," the old man spoke, indicating the broken terrain along the north shore of the peninsula. "Down among those rocks is a cave.

SCIENCE AND SORCERY III

Tolleson knew this place well from sailor's stories, said to be haunted or whatever, and he fastened on that little evidence and tracked it here, then to that cave. That was the way, the gate you might call it, to the other world, but it didn't do most people no good because they didn't know enough. He did, though, and seemingly found what he wanted. He had the house built, eventually married, begat a son and all that, and continued his studies close to the source."

Some of the statements of that superannuated tale spinner nagged at my mind, although I did not interrupt. That cavern among the rocks, for example; had I not seen him, from the cupola, trekking up from that general area? I rationalized this as coincidence but hoped he might consequently shed more light on the matter.

"Well," he continued, "eventually old Tolleson died, without having done much except pick up a lot of information which he held close to his vest, and write a couple of books he didn't publish and no one hereabouts wanted to read. By that time his reputation, maybe his sanity, had slipped a little, so his ideas didn't carry much weight even in his own family. His wife, a pious girl, fussed about his 'evil' doings, and she brought up their son Thomas to feel the same way. So the books and the papers went down in the cellar, the cave was left alone and Thomas made the Tollesons a typical, respectable family in the area. In his day a road connected this place—the town was named Gregoryville, believe it or not—with the mainland, as they called it because you might as well be on an island sometimes. At that time all the roads were dirt, so this one was as good as any other. Easier to get here by sea, though.

"For a long spell all the Tollesons were like that, decent folks like everybody else, only richer. Thomas' son, Roger, made another fortune in cotton—who didn't, then—and once upon a time they were an influential bunch, here and elsewhere for hundreds of miles. Roger's eldest, Peter, carried on the tradition, the old man totally forgotten although people still said the place was haunted. Lots of unexplained happenings, day and night. You know what I mean: people see things, ghosts or devils, hear things, now and then a body disappears. What with one thing or other the town never quite caught on, couldn't attract many outside settlers. I suppose it was dying even then.

"Everything got turned around by Peter's second son, Jonathan—oh, the name ring a bell?—that's a wonder. Oh, I see. Nosy, ain't you? No offense, I'd a done the same thing in your place, once. Yes, good old Jonathan, born in 1931. The eldest, that is Peter Junior, got himself killed in France by the Germans in 1944. Lots of long faces after that, but not Jonathan's. He knew he'd be second fiddle all his life, and that made him kind of moody. Didn't get along much with nobody except his pets. Animals liked him. Used to sneak about a bit by himself, stumbled across the books and things in the cellar one day and it changed his life. Spent all his time studying, learning the things his great-great-grandfather knew and waiting for Peter Senior to pass on. By this time, understand, Johnny already had big ideas, and he didn't expect his father to go for them. So he had to wait until he inherited everything. Impatient like, but he could wait if need be.

"Peter died suddenly in '53. No one ever figured out what killed him, best of health one day, gone the next." Although I must have been mistaken I could have sworn that our speaker chuckled smugly when he said this. "Johnny made some quick changes, laid down the law, like. He told the old lady, his own mother, that she could leave or not, but she better keep out of his way—that didn't much matter because she died early next year, I guess of the same ailment killed her husband—and told his two sisters likewise. One of them, Theresa, got married off and out of there right quick, and Althea finally got a job up north, although her brother gave her most of his free money, but she hung around for a while, probably from curiosity. Tolleson Manor had plenty of servants in those days, didn't cost much then, and they learned the new rules fast or were thrown out. Most of them stayed 'til the end.

"The new heir set himself up royally, hauling all the books and things up out of the cellar and storing them in a fancy study that was off-limits to everyone else. I expect that's where you saw them. By the time he was master Johnny already knew just about everything his nineteenth-century forefather had known, and since he was educated well by a good tutor he picked up on things real quick. For all his learning, though, he hadn't actually put any of his secret knowledge into practice, and that was the one thing he most wanted to do. The first thing he had to do was check out that cave, which Thomas had blocked off and where no right-minded folks had ventured for a hundred years.

"I won't try to presume too much, my friends, but I'll tell you to the best of my ability what he found there. Jonathan knocked down the log barrier, entered that gloomy cave mouth, disgusted by the terrible fishy odor and worried by the high tide lapping up into the tunnel for many yards. Armed with an oil lamp and accompanied by his favorite dog, a retriever named Wolf who always followed him everywhere, he picked his way past any number of obstacles, rocks and pitfalls, pointed stalactites, crumbling slopes and sucking mud. Things slithered beneath his feet, and once something soft squirmed against his leg; he had half a mind to give up right there, but it was just an octopus. He went on anyway and soon came to a dry room, a sort of raised stone cubicle where the sea never reached. Wolf didn't like the place much, sniffing and whining around the walls, barking at the air. Jonathan tried to shut him up but that gentleman didn't care for what he found either. He couldn't be sure what troubled the dog—he supposed the animal smelled something—but Jonathan saw enough to disturb himself. On the walls were drawings and carvings, some of them in a modern style which must have been put there by Old Man Tolleson, but others were done up strangely, a different kind of drawing harking back to the Indian days of long ago. Pre-Columbian, he thought. My memory doesn't hold too good for things like that, but I do know he recognized the newer drawings—they were like those hieroglyphs you saw in the tower, only these came first—symbols they were, ancient power symbols which only a scholar could know and fear. The old carvings were mainly pictures, pictures of nothing you ever saw on earth, and he didn't care for them one little bit. Still, he wasn't the sort to be afraid of pictures, not when he thought he was really on to something.

"In the cavern wall, far in the back where the room recessed, he spotted a hole, the entrance to a narrow tunnel about a foot across. Too small to crawl in, but that wasn't necessary. Jonathan knew about that hole from the old writings, which described it—let me think—as a speaking tube or something. Those other worlds, he figured, don't always overlap neatly. Things are as likely to pop out of the ground or the air as walk up and shake your hand. It was enough; for a sane man too much, but I don't want to cast aspersions on young Mr. Tolleson. Sane he was, if a little too forthright and driven. He wanted to learn, that's all. Then, that is.

"Well, imagine to yourself how he went about this. Jonathan sat down cross-legged on the floor, taking out a certain book and some bottles of powders and such he carried in a bag around his neck. The powders, which were mixtures concocted from those Latin and German volumes, dull reading but informative, these he blew into the hole, taking care not to inhale any. Some of them would have killed him speedy, and others done awful things to him. Then he opened the book—a big one with a funny foreign title, scribbled by a fellow named Jacob Bleek, so old and mildewed that the pages were falling out and the cover was glued on—and began reading certain passages in there which were underlined for him.

"The key paragraphs in that monstrous book were a series of incantations which allowed a person to communicate with those beyond, if those were willing to communicate. Apparently only certain types of men would do, them with the proper thoughts. You can believe Jonathan fell into that category, never was such a dedicated man. Acquaintances—he didn't have close friends—used to talk of the fire in his eyes, the way he spoke, how he always seemed to be thinking of more important things no matter what was going on. So when he started chanting in that musty cave, with his lantern wedged between two rocks pointing at that hole, and poor Wolf, a loyal companion if there ever was one—been with the family thirteen years—prancing and pawing and whining but not deserting his master, with all this results were to be expected. And you wouldn't be wrong assuming that.

"About midway through the chant the room began misting up. At first Jonathan thought steam was pouring out of that hole, and maybe it was but that didn't explain the further effects. Everything started going dim, as if it was growing darker—the lamp didn't cut through the gloom—or the air itself became opaque. Soon he couldn't see anything, and only by touch and hearing could he be sure he was still in the same place. He could feel the cool, damp stones, hear Wolf padding behind him, acting frantic.

"Suddenly that young man knew he was not alone. The sensation made his spine tingle, as did the furtive rustling which rose up on all sides. Something brushed past him; he thought it was Wolf for a moment but he could still hear him somewhere behind, barking now, and then another invisible thing squeezed by on the other side. Then he felt them rushing by, heard the dog scream. Blood curdling, that cry, not a bark or a whine or a whimper but an honest to God scream of mindless terror, and pain, pain so intense that Jonathan felt it, sympathetic pain. The animal shrieks went on and on, got louder, trailed off like down a tunnel, and finally he couldn't stand it any more. Dropping everything he ran out of that room, somehow not meeting up with Wolf—impossible to miss in that tiny space—and fled down the passageway. He still couldn't see anything, although when his feet sunk in mud, tripping him, and he crashed against a boulder he knew he was moving fast. That horrible blind journey didn't never seem to end, but in the end he heard the last gagging, choking howls fade out and the roar of the sea all around, and felt the warm rays of the sun on his face. While he crouched there by the shore his vision crept back by degrees, and before nightfall he was as good as new. If you overlook the fact, of course, that he was a sorry sight, cut, bruised, spattered in mud, and he had lost his magic articles and a best friend. He tried not to speculate what the dog's fate might be.

"I'll tell you the aftermath because it leads up to something important. In the morning, out back of the house, a servant discovered something that sent him running to Mr. Tolleson. Jonathan, still not quite recovered from his ordeal, dashed down to see what the shouting was about. He found a very shameful thing. Overnight a hole had opened up in the hard clay, a big puckered hole opening onto a wide cavity farther down, and the little bits of scraggly turf around it had been pushed up as if the hole was dug from underneath. Lying by this hole was another thing, a pile of unknown substance without any obvious form. All the others hung back, wouldn't go near it, but brave Jonathan snuck up on it for a look-see. What he found plain ruined his day, and his sleep for a long time after that. The shapeless heap, although it lacked certain parts and seemed to be rearranged a bit, turned out to be all that was left of Wolf."

SCIENCE AND SORCERY III

The old man paused in his story, scratched his scabby scalp, then ran a grimy hand over his forehead, wiping the thick damp hair into his eyes. I thought he endeavored to recall the scene fully in his own mind, and I utilized the moment to wonder how he came by so much knowledge. Had he been a servant to the Tollesons? Or was the entire story a jest or figment of an addled brain? Apparently he considered it the solemn truth; perhaps, despite the pretense of solitude, he made a habit of waylaying strangers in order to relate his lurid yarn. Would he ask for money afterward? Robert shot me a wink and a nod; I winked back.

The old man cleared his throat, after a slight hesitation resumed. "He also found that hideous volume, the Bleek manuscript, lying there by the remains. Two of the hired hands left right then, said nothing like that ought to exist around decent folks. I don't blame them now, especially since after that everything was different, more so than it already was. Jonathan got more stand-offish than ever. You got close to him at your own risk, and if you dared inquire about his business . . .

"He didn't tell anybody what he was up to in those days but I'll tell you, seeing as how it can't work you no harm, not if you're leaving. A week after he found and buried—no, burned—poor old Wolf, Jonathan hired a number of townsfolk for a new project. They didn't fancy coming near the place but the master promised to put bread on their table, and in that town with the sad state of the times that's a mighty strong inducement. I don't know if I mentioned yet that Tolleson Manor, even in the good days, was none too popular. People didn't like the way nothing grew there, and some of them remembered stories of the original old man. As I was saying, he called them in for a big task, and that was to build a stone tower on his land. He didn't say why and they weren't prone to ask. Afraid he might answer, maybe. So they set to it, cutting stone out of the cliffs, chopping it square and sticking it together the way he ordered. Took them three months from start to finish, a long haul but they completed it.

"That's right, sir, I know what you mean, I'm speaking of this very tower here. Now, don't jump so you two, it's not going to bite you. Well, I didn't mention it before because it wasn't here before. Year of '54 he built it, and it looks like it will last longer than the main house. Wouldn't have thought so sixty-odd years ago.

"The spooky thing is that he put up the tower right where his dog was found, over that hole that opened up for no earthly reason. The workmen weren't allowed to fill it in; actually, the whole idea was to protect it. That isn't a normal tower, as you may already know. It doesn't have any insides. Hollow all the way to the ground, and you might ask how far the hole goes below that. Properly speaking it doesn't go nowhere at all, but in another sense it goes to the end of the world. That's how Tolleson saw it.

136

THE HOUSE AT THE END OF THE WORLD

"Jonathan put it up because the cave was inconvenient, and he soon learned this new opening was just as good. He also didn't want to get too close to those things roaming inside, which is why he ordered a tower rather than a simple shed. That way he could stay high up, maintain his distance but still keep in touch. Wasn't too smart on the face of it. Things as could do what he suspected they could wouldn't think nothing of climbing up a sheer wall, but Jonathan was human. He could be wrong too.

"In the old days the ultimate aim was knowledge—he wanted to astound the world like his great-great-grandfather tried to do—but as he learned more the scholar saw practical possibilities in the offing. There was knowledge to be had, all right, but power too, if you was willing to pay the price. He was, or was willing to make others pay it for him. The first to be missed was Harold, the garden man. He never had been much use, not here of all places, but people got uptight about it all the same.

"But I'm not explaining it correctly. Those others from that secret place hankered after a slice of the world for their own reasons, Jonathan discovered, and they didn't mind giving him a chunk for himself if he helped out and didn't get in the way. He never found out why, but those shadow folks liked to get a hold of humans and do things to them, kind of like they did to Wolf. Nobody ever saw any traces after the fact, but Jonathan knew what happened to the victims, and while he didn't care much he tried to ignore the matter entirely. Maybe he figured he could do something about it when he learned enough. That might be why Old Man Tolleson never got too far along in his plans; he would go so far and no farther, unlike Johnny. I don't know, it was so long ago, but I think that's it.

"Before long quite a number of people had vanished, and you can bet the good citizens gave Jonathan trouble, but there wasn't much they could do. He claimed innocence, convinced the right people, other gentle souls, and the problems died down. In the meantime he was working on his studies, dealing with some information he got other than from books. By '56 he was probably the smartest, as well as the cleverest, man in the world. At least he thought so. Started boasting about what he aimed to do to anybody who would listen, said he was getting the earth ready for the others, who meant to shift or eliminate most of the population, and the rest would do what they were told and like it, maybe be put to good use in ways they couldn't imagine. Anywhere else he would have been locked up as a crazy man for that wild talk, but Gregoryville had been too cut off for too long. Folks couldn't see what was right in front of them. They'd rather accept anything but the truth, which they wouldn't understand anyway.

"By then most of the servants had left or disappeared, but in March Althea finally threw in the towel and lit out with the last hangers-on. Jonathan thought she ran away because of an especially revealing speech he made to her about the future, and what her place in it might be. He meant to flatter her, but them things he said made her sick. She took a ship—there were a few that put in here—and went north like I said earlier. Never saw her again. Now that I look back on it, though, I wonder if it wasn't something else that made her run. Around then noises started to be heard in the house, down in the cellar, as if things were moving around and clawing at stuff. Hard to live in a house like that, out here all by itself, with Master Tolleson carrying on about 'infinity' and 'black gulfs' and how this place was at the end of the universe we know. Give her the creeps certain, and it wouldn't take much after that.

"There sat Johnny all alone, not realizing until too late what loneliness is. Never saw nobody now, and got to talking to himself to pass the time. He—"

"How do you know that?" Robert broke in. He beat me to the question; this rambling dialogue seemed more and more a macabre fiction, the kind we would tell around the campfire.

The old man waved Robert silent. "Let me finish. He got so involved in his labors that nothing else counted, even his own comfort. With no servants he couldn't keep up the house so he took to sleeping and eating in the study. When he wasn't there he was in the tower, making signs and shouting chants down the inside. Sometimes he got answers, sometimes he saw things, the way you see things in dreams. In that black room, if he waited long enough and kept his eyes on that hole leading to nowhere, pictures would float up, images that weren't real but printed in his head. He saw the other world, the one beyond the edge, which few mortals can see even if they know where to look. It isn't really there, see, not like this tower or that house, but it's all around us everywhere we go, and things happen there that sometimes affects what happens here. He saw cities of black stone, obsidian it's called, and other materials not found on earth. The cities were colossal, stretching from horizon to horizon under unknown suns of many colors. In those cities, if he saw clearly enough, things moved in the shadows, and he didn't always care for their appearance or activities. Indeed, for all his hardness and experience he saw something once that shot his hair gray through and through; and he still in his twenties! That was during a vision of a far away place with people on it a lot like us, who were slaves or subjects of the others. He actually saw what happened to some of them and it shook him up bad. That's important too; after that he wasn't quite so sure of himself, started having doubts about the whole thing. Of course he was in it up to his neck so he couldn't back out, and didn't particularly want to, not yet. That came a little later.

"Other visions included endless desert landscapes, silent scenes of desolation with half-buried ruins rising up out of the sand. Others looked like those funny paintings artists do now, or did in my time: squares and triangles and fuzzy shapes moving about, no sense or order to it. He supposed those were places so . . . so alien, that the human eye couldn't take it all in properly. Now and then they showed him pictures from space, but even there ghost-like things drifted around, meaning it isn't so empty and safe up there as we think. After a long spell of this Jonathan got jaded, tired of it all, afraid finally, but he couldn't quit. It was like a drug to him, if he didn't get it he would die. What else was there, I ask you? He'd walled himself off from his peers, disdaining any normal contact.

"Come June the outer beings were ready to begin. It was time to start working on the earth, but Jonathan was at last giving them the what for. Seems he'd done a lot of thinking and come to the conclusion (he should have known this from the first) that he was just a tool for those creatures, and once they were finished with the general population and had broken through to stay they wouldn't need him no more. No great leap of the imagination to figure they'd treat him like all the rest, a fate he couldn't abide. He began making plans, putting off his so-called allies with no real idea what to do, but hoping he could delay them until he found something in the old books that would help. He was still hunting that night they came out.

Oh, young sirs, I don't want to bend your ears or disturb your upcoming rest, but that was the most terrible night in all of human history. The things they did, the suffering and mortal agony, has to be experienced, not told, although I wouldn't wish that on my worst enemy. They came, they got among the folks in Gregoryville and . . . they did what they said they would. Poor Jonathan watched it all from the big front window in the upper story of the mansion, the one that's fallen in now, and he saw it happen. Couldn't make out the details, not at that distance, but he could see the fire in the sky, the lights bobbing over town, fancied he could hear the screams of men, women and children being done to in a fashion worse than death. That's the worst of it, you see, they didn't die, couldn't die from what those devils did to them. Death is a heaven-sent mercy compared to what those folks got that night. I'll bet they couldn't believe what was happening to them; it wasn't right, it wasn't real, but it was and it wouldn't stop. Maybe those creatures use them up after an eternity or so, maybe they find peace after an age of burning and torment, but if so that's the only thing good to say about the whole business. Human beings never thought such thoughts as those beasties did, nor ever found a way to put their meanest desires into practice. All those people taken away, every one except Jonathan."

"This is too much!" I cried with an explosive laugh, leaping to my feet. " It won't be Halloween for a while. What do you take us for?" Robert forcefully echoed my sentiments. "If everyone was killed how can you be here telling the story to us? Did you get your facts from Tolleson? What became of him?"

"I'm telling you the truth," the oldster wheezed pleadingly, backing off from our hostile mockery. "I swear it. Look down there—" he indicated the shabby skyline, now shrouded in shadow—"it's dead. I'm not making it up. Do you see smoke, hear cars in there? No, because it's all gone. One night of horror wiped out near a hundred God-fearing folks like they never were. Outsiders picked up on notions of fires causing an explosion, but it weren't anything like that. Believe me, sirs, I know."

He continued quietly when he saw we would not interrupt again. "Come morning Master Tolleson, he rode down to the village, against his will, but he had to see for himself. He found it deserted, empty of people at any rate. Here and there he felt eyes on him, not a pair in a head but other kinds of eyes as don't bear talking about, and he stumbled across traces of what went on the night before. It seems those others didn't always need all of their victims and tended to leave worthless parts behind if it didn't cause trouble. They'd never done that before, but that day Jonathan got an eyeful. All those parts were twisted and changed so that you wouldn't recognize them at a glance but have to scrutinize them real close-like. That he did, and after he got over throwing up he decided this was all he could stand. Some of these parts reminded him of what they did to Wolf years before, and now he finally came around to the idea that it wasn't very nice of them. At the time he thought it was a necessary sacrifice, but now he wondered if it weren't plain meanness. Sounds funny, I know, but that was Johnny. That dog meant more than all those folk, and he'd act on account of the dog if nothing else, for memory's sake.

That very night he found what he'd been looking for all the past month. A paragraph in that damned book by Jacob Bleek, the one he once carried into the cave to start this mess, and which those others kindly returned; an old spell which the author, a sophisticated looney from the Middle Ages, said might work on outside influences. He'd found it too late to save all those pathetic folk in Gregoryville, but if it worked he might save the rest of mankind, which was fair enough since he knew everything was his fault.

"He couldn't kill the things; they weren't alive in the manner people or trees or beetles are alive, and nothing he ever read specified whether they didn't just carry on forever in their own world. He couldn't kill them but he could keep them off our planet permanently. The reason is that here on Tolleson Manor we have the gateway between the different worlds, as I've said. In such places there is always a little cross-over, but Jonathan had opened that gate wide and the things on the other side were set to pour through. He could close it again, put it back the way it was before, if he hurried. He had to act fast because once they came through in earnest the boundary, the wall between the worlds, would dissolve. Our world would blend in with theirs and no amount of spells and chants could ever put it right. The elimination of Gregoryville was just the first step, sort of a test to see if things worked properly. Now they knew that, and might come through at any time. Once Johnny understood this he moved smart, racing out of his house and up the stairs to the top of the tower, dreading every wasted moment. His biggest fear was that he might be too late by seconds, to get there and find that they already had their foothold. Time was precious.

"Once in the meeting room he hurriedly drew his magical diagrams, the secret symbols necessary for the job, and got down to business. He opened that evil book to the marked page; by the way, you didn't see it when you nosed around upstairs. He destroyed it a long time ago so no one else could ever learn the way to open the mystical door. I hope there aren't any more copies lying about in ancient libraries anywhere. That book couldn't do a body any good. So, he found the right words and without more ado began reciting them. The words; they was in Latin, but I . . ." The speaker trailed off, screwed up his features, then got back on track. "No; I don't remember my Latin, but I know parts of it in English. 'Here, as on the dawn of days, when all things in all realms first flowered, hear my voice. By the power of the Cirellian Seal, the Altar of Niblith and the Icon of the Interstitial Wanderer, call to bear the forces of Being to shut the timeless door into eternity, the path to the Seventh Level, the ultimate road to inevitab1e . . .' Well, best not to get all the way into it. You get the idea. He said the words, and by all that's holy he was allowed to finish. The entrance closed, and for what it's worth the world is back like it always was.

"But—" both Robert and I exclaimed simultaneously.

The old man nodded, wagging a decrepit finger in the air. "Sit still, give me time for a breather. I got a finish, maybe it's fair; maybe it's not, but it ain't a happy one. Not for the

suffering hero. Tolleson, you see, saved the earth, I hope, but he found out too late that the ancient words didn't carry no account for saving himself. He was right here at the focus, where the evil and sin from beyond could grab him, and that it did. They didn't kill him or change him like they did those others. Why I don't know, guess those things got a whimsical streak in their natures, but they worked him over good. They sucked him down that hole into their territory, he fell and fell forever in the dark until he lost consciousness. Next thing he knew he was crawling out of a pile of rubbish and cinders in his own cellar, and later saw that the house was tumbling down like a cyclone hit it. As you see it now, the house that is, most of the ruin occurred in a single day. Jonathan was a ruin, also a shell of his former self. They'd scrambled his brains while they had him, made him a half idiot so it hurt to think or remember. But that wasn't all; before they let him go they stamped their mark on him, burned it into the skin of his forehead. A strange mark, like one in that old book, the sort a red-hot fork or trident would leave if you laid it up against bare flesh. It meant he could never leave, and would always be cut off from his fellow men. Seems kind of cruel, doesn't it, to strand him here 'til he died, but that was their parting joke. Some people'd say he had it coming."

At that the speaker fell silent. Apparently that was all he had to tell, but eerie thoughts and suspicions raced through my mind. I forced out one more question: "When did Tolleson die?"

The old man stared blankly, shuffled uneasily, then shrugged his slumping shoulders. "Jonathan . . . lingered," he replied, nothing more.

Enraptured by this morbid tale, Robert and I had scarcely noticed the passage of time, but now we realized with a start that the sun was hidden by trees against the horizon and dusk was falling swiftly. The violet of evening darkened perceptibly as we watched, the dying rays silhouetting the embattled, grimly foreboding house against the sky. The mild sea wind had temporarily abated, the only sound intruding on the scene being the perpetual rushing of the waves below. The old man noticed also, and for a moment his mild countenance spasmed erratically. "Day's getting on," he muttered weakly, pulling himself together. "I got to be getting on about my business. What be your plans for the night?"

Robert looked at me strangely, stammered out, "We had considered camping here until morning." The announcement sounded rather half-hearted.

Our host reacted strongly. "No, no," he declared, "you mustn't do that. I don't recommend it at all. It isn't safe here, not within walking distance. You see," he feverishly explained, "the gateway isn't really like a door, or a solid line like a wall. That's just a figure of speech I used. It . . . it diffuses all over the region where the spheres meet, at the ends of both. While you stay here you're not in the real world, nor in that other, but somewhere in between. It's like a corridor between two rooms; you want to get yourself in the right room, not hang about out in the hall.

"Don't even think about staying in that house, for whatever comfort it might still hold. I wouldn't live there anymore; too many things went on there. I keep myself mighty nice in the cave. Oh, don't you worry, the back's all blocked off again, and I get all the fish and crabs I can eat. If you'd showed up earlier I might have offered you some.

"No, you can't stay in the house. Better it fall down completely. There's things as walk that shouldn't, and if you stay you might meet up with them. Same goes for the town. A good thing you didn't pass through there before talking to me. I might not have had the pleasure. Good sirs, my advice is to make tracks south, fast as you can, and cover as many miles as you can before you drop. There's a fishing village down that way—I guess it's still there—

with a fine paved road that'll get you home. Where did you say you lived? Oh yes, I remember, a wholesome city, not like where I grew up. Traveled there once with my father as a boy. I suppose life goes on out there.

"Well, I've said my piece. You better scoot while you got time."

We were convinced; something, perhaps only the lateness of the hour, led us to take him very seriously at that moment. The three of us trooped around that ugly, vaguely threatening house to the front where Robert and I collected our packs and extraneous gear, where the old man saw us off. No long goodbyes; our tense mood and the waning sun, no longer visible through the decayed fingers of trees to the west, urged us on, south and away from that dreadful scene of related tragedy. Later, much later, the two of us discussed that strange and terrible story, declaring it bogus with sneers and snickers, but at the time we both felt curiously indisposed for conversation. We were weary from a long day's march, and we had a long way to go.

Robert, occasionally trembling but fiercely resolute, never looked back, but I did, catching a fleeting glimpse of that old man as he trudged haltingly over the hill past that hateful, crouching pile of fractured oak and blasted masonry. That old man, who had lived here all his life? Who remembered so much, who in his decadent, childish fashion recalled that which it was humanly impossible to know, and through whose coarse chatter occasionally gleamed the disused speech of a learned, cultivated man. That pathetic old man, who wore his shaggy hair long over his forehead, from under which his bright eyes scarcely showed. Robert admitted afterward that—purely as a joke—he had felt the urge to reach out and brush away that dirty mop, to see what lay beneath on that hidden flesh. I am glad that he did not. As matters stand, we can still laugh at the story.

A SIMPLE SOLUTION

"I tell you, Vorchek," said Tobias Bentley, "this terrible mystery has become too much for me. I try to live a quiet life here with my books and my manuscripts, but this ugly business has wholly disordered my affairs. Bad enough it was when my beautiful new wife died—Sheila, in the spring of her years, poor child—only now my servants are dropping dead as well, the two healthy young women I had hired from the village. In each case death was without apparent cause. Three bodies, no explanation; an insupportable situation. Soon I shall be alone here to fend for myself, if this goes on. You must help me."

"I will, for the case intrigues me," suavely replied Professor Anton Vorchek, investigator of the arcane and the uncanny, in his precise, well-modulated, slightly accented speech. He had come at the urgent bidding of his friend—a near hermit, not prone to receiving or entertaining guests—dilettante scholar and wealthy denizen of isolated, forest-cloaked Oak Creek Manor, where they now sat sipping drinks in the Tea Room, Bentley restless and nervously puffing a cigarette, Vorchek casually reclining and easily drawing on his pipe. Said the professor, "The lack of physical wounds suggests poison, yet you imply that all normal avenues have been explored by competent medical authorities. Does that imply all natural avenues? That, now, would impress me. I take it you have never experienced the unusual here before?"

"Absolutely not," Bentley assured him. "My life has been entirely normal in its relative seclusion, my household happy and conventional."

"Incorrect," Vorchek noted, "at least in part. Besides the two remaining servants I have met, there is one other personage at the manor who is passing strange."

"You mean good old Orvin, of course," said Bentley. "Why, the fellow has been with us as butler, the tyrant of the house, since my father's day. True and steady, the salt of the earth, is Orvin. Besides, he is the only human being here who can not be suspected of foul play."

"Because," Vorchek observed, "out of the goodness of your heart you keep your butler in a box."

"It is the only way, my friend. Since the unfortunate accident last year that cost him his arms and legs, he has necessarily transferred his mobile duties to others. His brain remains intact, however, and from his odd throne he still governs with an iron hand. Oh dear; you know what I mean. Anyway, I or the other servants cater to his every need."

"I wish to see him." Vorchek's host led him through the twisting passageways of the vast house to the cavernous hall or den where antique furniture and priceless paintings created an atmosphere of comfort and quality. To the right a fire burned fiercely in a yawning granite alcove. To the left a wide and massively solid marble mantel upheld, along with valuable gold and silver and crystal trinkets, a huge, standing oblong box of mahogany, open to the front, with its ornate door, never shut, hanging wide. Within lurked Orvin, a gray, wizened, Roman-nosed head surmounting a trunk wrapped shapelessly in a heavy black robe.

Bentley performed polite courtesies of greeting, to which Orvin rasped in a harsh but ostentatiously genteel voice, "My pleasure, Professor Vorchek. It has been long since you called upon us. Sadly, I can not see to your needs as once I did. Life has been hard to me, but I make do, and still contribute after a fashion. May I be so bold as to inquire what brings you to us this day?"

"My old and learned friend," said the master, "shall get to the bottom of our sorrows. You know, Orvin, his credentials and background. If anyone can help us, he can."

"You flatter me," Vorchek muttered with a tight smile."

"Those of us who survive must be pleased beyond measure," said Orvin. "It was my understanding, however, that proper procedures have already been undertaken by the relevant officials."

"I know more than they," replied the professor, "of curious matters. Rest assured, good Orvin, that within twenty-four hours I will have solved this case, and taken the necessary steps to defeat the mysterious menace. Now, sir," he said to his host, "I would refresh myself, for I had a long drive up here, and it grows late. I must ponder and sleep before I act."

Bentley and his guest dined on lamb curry and rice. Afterward, over a bottle of Mentothelle '83, Vorchek questioned his friend concerning various seemingly random particularities of recent life at the manor. He ascertained that the late and latest Mrs. Bentley had died eight months before, some weeks following faithful Orvin's tragic accident; that the lost servants had been new hires who proved less than stellar, never living up to Orvin's rigorous standards. Vorchek asked Bentley about his current research into matters ancient and profound, to which came the reply, "It does not go well. Orvin was always by best and brightest assistant. With him largely out of commission I am often at loose ends. These past years I've devoted myself to occult interests, an analysis of rare sorceric texts, very much in your line, yet on my own I found myself routinely stumped." Vorchek then exchanged words with Mr. and Mrs. Stoob, cook and maid, man and wife of long standing at Oak Creek Manor. They could tell him nothing of overt value, preferring to focus on squabbles among the staff, the departed and the still living. After this conversation he took to his prepared bed.

That night he experienced a strange visitation. He woke, suddenly, into what he briefly deemed the continuation of dreams. Out of darkness a hideous phantom form, a gigantic glowing face of indescribable savagery, hovered before him in the bedroom. It closed upon him, shrieking silently and mouthing unheard curses, then merged with him, bathing him in ghostly radiance. A vise seized his heart and daggers pierced his brain, which Vorchek knew for an attack unto death. With all the powers of will and secret knowledge the professor fought to repel the devilish assault. Perhaps the contest raged for mere minutes, but the battle felt endless, a murderous campaign, a seesaw struggle for life. The phantom demanded his death, ordered him to succumb; Vorchek steeled himself to resist and survive. He did so, gaining strength by desperate degrees, until such time as he sprang from bed with a victorious shout and sensed the baleful influence receding. The nightmarish phantom vanished on the instant.

The victor collapsed back onto the soft sheets, entirely spent. Some time elapsed before Vorchek regained full control of his motor functions. Once his subsequent weakness had passed he felt the need for nutritional succor, rang the bell pull for aid. No one came. Wearily he rose, lighted a lamp, made his way into the hall. At the far end a window emitted a trace of reddish dawn. Vorchek groped downstairs to the servants quarters, knocked briskly at the door of the room shared by the two remaining ambulatory servants. Receiving no response, he pushed open the door. He found the Stoobs in their beds, obviously dead. A quick examination revealed no wounds, but the staring, rigid masks of their sunken features told all. Death had come to them this night, as it had been intended for Vorchek.

A horribly grim possibility occurred to him. He raced from the death chamber, charged up the stairs, stormed into his friend's bedroom. His surmise had been correct, his intentions far too late, if there had ever been a chance. There, in the antique bed where kings had once slumbered, surrounded by books and scattered parchments and lurid artifacts gathered from the corners of the world, lay Tobias Bentley of Oak Creek Manor, deceased. The death had come to him some time before, perhaps even as Vorchek had wrestled with the insidious horror. It was much the same as with the Stoobs, though with greater evidence of a struggle. The corpse sprawled half off the mattress, the covers thrown wildly back, the teeth tightly clenched, the mouth contorted in a fearful grimace. That made sense to the professor. His friend had known a thing or two of arcane lore—not so much as he believed, unfortunately, nor had his amateurish knowledge prepared him for confronting the grotesque reality—enough, apparently, to afford him a clue when evil struck, providing him a chance, however feeble, to fight back. Bentley had fought and failed, while the devoutly studious Vorchek had triumphed.

With that the professor knew all. He marched solemnly to the great hall (after a short detour to the supply room) to seek the only other human being still living in the house. There in his box hunched Orvin, no longer pathetic to behold, but ghastly, for his face was distorted by maniacal fury; precisely the face of the malicious, murderous vision. Yes, Vorchek had recognized him, only it was not intended that he live to utilize the knowledge. Thus spake the professor:

"Before I slept last night, Orvin, I had already deduced that you were the instigator of these dreadful events. You had lost the use of your body, which must rankle an active and masterful man, yet you were privy to Bentley's studies in ancient sorcery. He told me that your keen mind was vital to his work. I could guess, then, that in the absence of physical locomotion you would turn to developing the powers of your mind. This you did, only power was channeled through rage, focused by hate. That you railed at uncaring fate I understand, yet I would know the reasons for the earlier three killings."

"The last Mrs. Bentley," croaked Orvin, "was nothing more than a gold-digger, but she I would have tolerated, had it not been her earnest desire to rid this house of my sad carcass. My ruined form sickened her, so she implored Tobias that I be put away. That I would not allow. Those foolish girls were trouble-makers who mocked me with simpering smiles, knowing winks and nods, and they were poor household resources to boot. I did my master a favor by removing them."

"You did him no favor this morning," Vorchek observed, "to put the case mildly. Of course you must attempt to destroy me, for you suspected that my investigation meant the end of your monstrous empire. I am trained in the age-old methods of psychic attack, however, through years of study and experience, and therefore defeated you. But the others, Orvin, why the others? Why must you slaughter Bentley and the Stoobs?"

"I lay the blame at your door," hissed Orvin. "The fault is your own. I can send out the claws of my mind, but I do not yet consider myself a proficient. When you, quite unprecedentedly, rebuffed the sending of my ire, I could no longer maintain control or direct it. It acted as an entity unto itself, lashing out at any and all victims at hand. You must realize that I did not mean to destroy them, for they were useful to me."

"Quite so," replied Vorchek. "All is explained. Only you and I remain. Now I must act as the instrument of justice." Orvin screamed, his lips twitching repulsively as he bellowed hostile syllables of antique magic. That crazed face swelled fantastically and lunged through the intervening space at Vorchek, who merely laughed and, with a mental shrug, dismissed the apparition. "Too late," he said. "I am onto your game. Your force cannot affect me. I can imagine many productive solutions to this problem. I choose the simplest." With that Vorchek swung shut the big door of Orvin's box, produced hammer and nails, driving the latter through the rim of the door into the thick mahogany frame. Orvin squealed and begged for mercy, but his words were muffled, nor did the professor care to hear them. With the deed done Anton Vorchek left the confines of Oak Creek Manor, confident that natural causes would resolve the situation in due course.

THE SOUTH FACE OF MEDICINE MAN MOUNTAIN

This isn't some kind of oddball tall tale from the good old days; it just recently happened to me, and I tell you it's true—that part I can relate of my own knowledge, anyway—and as for the rest, you're free to sneer just like I did, and to explain it, just like I didn't. So, here goes. There were four of us, Bob, Lenny, Jake, and myself, and we determined to climb the south face of Humphrey's Peak, the way nobody else ever does it. Most people, the tourists of course, go up the good trail on the west side from the ski resort, then brag about scaling the highest mountain in Arizona. The hardier sorts go up the steeply sloping north face, or scramble over the subsidiary peaks from the east, but we would do what nobody does, at least not since Malvin did it back in '54: make our way up the sheer cliffs of the southern side, a trek incorporating a more than thousand foot climb requiring roping and spiking, running out and belaying at every step. We'd do it because we knew we could do it, because we lived to dare that kind of thing.

Already we knew the big mountains of the Southwest, including the icy standards of Colorado and New Mexico. This was different, because the San Francisco Mountains are different: jagged peaks looming starkly above a great bowl-shaped valley, the Inner Basin, relic of a super-Krakatoa that blew itself to smithereens a million years ago. The terrain is unique, the exposed rock surfaces unconventional in their composition, a mix of igneous and primordial granite. We planned our expedition to a tee, made a big deal out of it, even got some local press coverage of our boasts in the weeks leading up. Lodging for the night in Flagstaff, we drove out in the SUV over that wretched mountain road through the firs and the spruce to the meadows, where we parked and hiked with all our gear into the Basin through an eruptive gap in the old volcano's wall. There, on the northern edge of the wide grassy plain forming the bottom of the extinct caldera, we camped by the tree line at nine thousand feet, relishing the view of the ringing peaks that encompassed us, especially that of Humphrey's, which pressed down on us from over twelve thousand feet like a stone tidal wave about to drop. We took it easy that afternoon, for the morning would bring back-breaking labor.

There, at dusk, by the light of the fire that cooked our hearty meal and held off the infringing chill of that high altitude summer evening, we met Professor Anton Vorchek. He came trooping into the radius of flame-flicker about eight, with a big pack on his back and a skinny young punk in tow staggering under his own burden. "Hail and well met," he called in a pleasant kind of foreign voice, introduced himself and his companion, a Toby Gastolf, said they were up from a Phoenix college, asked who was in charge. "That would be Mark," said Jake, which I acknowledged, inviting the pair to join us. "That is precisely what I had in mind," replied Vorchek. He was a big man, smartly dressed like for a movie safari, wearing a broad floppy hat that shadowed his eyes.

He came to the point right quick, after graciously accepting a paper plate full of skillet-fried chicken and barbecued beans. "I see by the papers," he said, "that you gentlemen propose to climb the south face of the peak tomorrow. My student, Mr. Gastolf, and I wish to accompany you." That was out of the question, we needing no tenderfoots underfoot. "I am willing to pay you for the privilege." There was still some very negative muttering from my ranks. "And I will pay in cash," he added, naming an impressive figure. I called him on it, he produced the lovely colored paper. Okay, so they were coming with us. My buddies still grumbled, especially Lenny, who had no use for strangers on this outing among friends, but a fair distribution of the profits quieted lingering concerns.

"This isn't a common hike," I warned. "This is the real thing, a genuine cliff-hanger, for which we have experience. Once you get onto the higher, comparatively even slopes you'll be all right, but if you've never dangled on the end of a rope, with a killing plunge into space beneath your feet, you're in for a shock."

"So are we," said Bob sourly, "if you panic and take us down with you."

Toby said, with that ubiquitous television-inspired patois of his, "No problem, man, we're only tagging along. We'll take it as it comes. We're, like, engaged in serious scientific enterprise," and he laughed. He was the typical, shabby sort you get in school these days, with a careless attitude, but he seemed tough enough for heavy duty stuff. Vorchek was an older guy, with a little beard and fussy manners, and he worried me.

The professor cut in hastily, saying, "We recognize the risks. We ask for no allowances, being willing to carry our weight. As good Mr. Gastolf suggests, our reasons for venturing thither differ from your own. Indeed, it is of no importance to us that we reach the top. Rather, we ask for your aid only so far as the cave, from which vantage we shall look to our own devices."

I didn't get that at all. "What cave?" I cried. "There is no cave, none I've heard about, and I should know. It's not the proper kind of rock layers for caves."

THE SOUTH FACE OF MEDICINE MAN MOUNTAIN

"I know something of strata," Vorchek replied with an amused air. "I refer to a volcanic pocket, blasted by gas emission in elder times. My sources assure me that it exists." He paused, made a long to-do of producing a pipe and lighting up. Puffing lazily he said, "To explain: I am engaged in studies of an anthropological nature, following the trail of certain esoteric historical reports relating to the aboriginal inhabitants of this country. Years of research have led me to this place, which I have endeavored to explore, off the beaten path, that I might confirm unusual claims pertaining to odd matters."

"That's clear as mud," quipped Lenny.

"It's going to sound crazier," said Toby, laughing again, a stupid snorting noise.

Vorchek smiled patronizingly at his fellow traveler. "This much I can tell you. Early oral sources from pioneer records, as well as documented Spanish accounts going back to the period of the Conquistadors, all refer to still more ancient Indian accounts of a curious tribe antedating the Yavapai and the Anasazi, who dwelt in this land long before Columbus, and who, according to primitive legend, practiced magic and the dark arts among this volcanic desolation. Something about this spot, some emanation from this particular landscape—its strange features, the mysterious energies lurking latent here from ages vast and unrecorded—served to heighten the mental powers of their keenest minds, that they might perceive the higher reality normally hidden behind the material plane. As they described it, they talked and walked with the Gods, their perniciously grim and harsh Gods, who at times, without clear reason, chose to bestow boon or doom as They saw fit.

"This antique cult centered on a cave, shunned by lesser mortals, said to reside on the southern facing cliffs of the great peak they styled the Medicine Man Mountain, the highest of the so-called Ring of the Old Ones. Gentlemen, my perusal of yellowed papers and crumbling parchments, my interviews with surviving Indian worthies who remember scraps of fading lore, convince me, beyond question, that Humphrey's Peak and Medicine Man Mountain are one and the same."

"The deal's off," said Bob.

I chuckled. "Not necessarily. It sounds like fun. Professor, that cliff is a mile across. Suppose, even granting it exists, we don't find your cave?"

"That is my problem. In such case, we go up, we come down, having enjoyed the stimulating exercise."

"Suppose we do find it?"

"Should that transpire," said Vorchek, with the utmost seriousness, "Mr. Gastolf and I shall no longer require your expertise. We can handle ourselves quite nicely from that juncture. I assure you, that troubles me not one iota."

SCIENCE AND SORCERY III

From all this you must get the idea that Vorchek was a really dedicated, first-class kook, probably with the papers to prove it. If I'd had any sense myself I'd have sent him packing, only I didn't really believe he meant everything he said, and furthermore he was being remarkably generous solely for the privilege of keeping company with us. I told myself that he'd most likely give up before we were well into the approaching ordeal.

An unlikely source fed my self-serving conclusions. This Toby of his, a guy I was made to dislike, sidled up to me while I prepared my bedroll, eager to ingratiate and, it turned out, distance himself from his erstwhile mentor. "Don't take old man Vorchek too seriously," he said. "He's bats, all right. I'm getting additional credits out of this, or I'd be home partying now. I'm surprised he hasn't conked out already. We spent the last two days camping at Trident Rock, with the professor deciphering the Indian pictures there on the stones."

"Nobody can read the Indian petroglyphs," I pointed out. "I've seen that batch. They're wild specimens, for sure, but they don't mean anything to anybody living."

"I'll take your word for it," Toby said indifferently. "I don't care. Old Vorchek says he can read them. He's got a pile of notes, claims to be onto something big. He'll probably give up tomorrow morning, cook up an excuse for why he got nothing. I'll have passed for the year, the only thing that matters to me."

In the morning we, the six of us, commenced the assault on the south face. Normally I would deliver now a blow by blow account of the climb, filled with stirring anecdotes of scrabbling over rotten rock and treacherous stone shards, finger holds on shelving with the wind whipping, ropes played out loose or taut, spikes biting stone and boots digging for perch. This time, however, I'm telling a different kind of story, so I'll skip the conventional details.

My immediate concerns were the opposite of reality. Professor Vorchek took to that slope like a mountain goat, scarcely retarding our progress at all. Either he had experience he hadn't mentioned, or he was one determined fellow. I'd go for the latter, for his technique didn't impress, just his grit and stamina. Toby, on the other hand, proved a hopeless klutz, and weak-kneed at that. The climb scared him. Hardly had the ordeal begun before his face turned white and he lost his speech, stayed that way so long I expected him to soil himself.

We went up the most likely way, inching from one narrow ledge to another, and Vorchek truly seemed to understand the theory of the thing. By the time we reached the three hundred foot level, in the latter half of the morning, he was anticipating our route, even offering suggestions. They were good, I thought, save for the last. "No," he said, "over there, to the right: that gully should open onto a fine shelf." I nay-sayed him, ordered a shift left, but he pushed on as I spoke, springing recklessly up a flight of crumbly natural stairs toward his invisible ledge. I pursued, meaning to collar him, drag him back, but when I caught up with him at the top of the gully I saw he was right, that the shelf existed, a wide one, the most substantial yet, precisely where he appeared to expect it.

I'll be damned, but there we found the cave, with Vorchek somehow managing to lead us right to it. "The ancient records are murky," he said, "but they do not lie." When the rest of our people caught up we explored the site. It was Vorchek's cave, no question about it: a sheltered cavity within an igneous protrusion, shielded from sight by a massive granite overhang. There was stuff inside it, too, that supported the strange professor's ideas to an amazing degree.

Inside that big chamber, into which the several of us could easily walk and stand, we found smoothed walls covered with exotic petroglyphs, mainly symbols I've heard described as astronomical—star-bursts and pinwheels and spirals—along with swaths of smaller scratchings that resembled weird letters. Vorchek seemed mighty taken with those. We found much olden debris mixed into the dusty floor, bits and pieces of chert tools and obsidian blades and shreds of decayed woven fibers. In the back, where it was pretty hard to see, Jake spied the oddly flat, blank circular patch of wall, bare of drawings, blackened with prehistoric soot. Painted white arrows pointed to the spot, which was surrounded by a gigantic spiral image. Lenny spotted what was on the floor in front of it.

"Looks like somebody didn't make it," he said in a funny voice. They were bones, old yellow bones, with burnt bits, a jumble of them crammed into a minor crevice between two triangular boulders.

"Human sacrifice," Vorchek murmured. "That was the only way to satisfy, to appease, to placate the fierce beings of mystery they called their Gods."

Something else puzzled me more than anything we had found. "Tell me," I demanded, "if you can, how the Indians found this place and got up here?"

He said, "They did not climb up the way we did; of that you may be convinced. Truly, that beautifully confirms the hypothesis. Now, if my translation is accurate, I may establish the rest." I thought him talking more to himself. The professor blinked, pushed back his hat from his eyes, stared at me in the gloom. "This cave was the destination of old and feeble men, the medicine men, the scholars of yore. They learned secrets from their masters. They knew how to get here and back without effort. Yes, that was the only way."

"You're not making sense," I snapped.

"Not to you, perhaps. Now, sir, I shall, predictably confuse you the more. My young friend and I can dispense with your services here. We go no farther. We have attained our goal, can make our way down unaided."

"You're crazy," Bob snarled.

Toby agreed. "Jesus, Professor," he whined, "we're on the side of a cliff, ten feet from quick death. We can't make it back without them." My buddies and I joined in with our loud arguments. Vorchek just smiled, sort of a creepy grin, like he had it all figured out, and we were dummies for not knowing better. He said in a suddenly snaky way, "Dear Mr. Gastolf— Toby—if you wish to sever our relationship, if you choose to accompany these gentlemen instead, you may do so. You are, after all, a free man, a citizen in good standing by the lights of this age. Gentlemen, how far is it to the top? Another seven hundred feet to walkable terrain, I believe? More than two thousand rugged feet of ascension beyond that, I calculate. I know Mr. Gastolf is eager to carry on." Toby blanched even more, shook all over, quivering like the frightened jelly he was. He almost screamed, "I can't do that. You guys, take me back down now. Come on, give me a break!"

We wouldn't. By God, I'd explained the risks, and there was no way we were going to quit this far along. "We continue the climb," I declared. "You come with us, or you wait here until we pass by on the return."

"If you do come back this way," Vorchek drawled.

"I don't guarantee it," I added.

As it fell out, Toby decided to stay, although he was the unhappiest little squirt I'd seen in my life. I should have felt sorry for him, but I couldn't be bothered. My views were seconded by the rest of my bunch. This wasn't fun and games to us, not down deep. One can't scale a face like that with a light and kindly heart.

After a few more minutes of pointless chatter we left the two of them there, considering them stranded. We went up, and still up, and before evening (to make a long story short) we got off the southern cliff onto better sloping ground and made camp, the intimidating part of the climb behind us.

Thunderstorms rocked the mountain that night. In the morning we fashioned ourselves a relatively easy trail to the mist-shrouded top, stood on the wet summit of Humphrey's Peak, took our pictures and called out to the world via our cell phones. We dawdled the day, camping near the top that next night, a clear one giving us limitless views of far horizons and blazing stars.

Yacking among ourselves, we decided it was the least we could do to retrace our steps and collect those two bozos before they got themselves into

THE SOUTH FACE OF MEDICINE MAN MOUNTAIN

worse trouble. I knew they had food and some water, but they'd have a pathetic time waiting for rescue from outside. So, on the following morning we descended, naturally making better time, being sure to drop back onto the cliff where we had emerged from it, thereby ensuring that we should avoid bypassing that spooky cave where our temporary comrades undoubtedly still tarried, much the worse for wear. I imagined Vorchek amusing himself with his goofiness, poor Toby crying himself to sleep. To be honest, I laughed at the notion. Would they be deliriously grateful when we showed!

Here's the ominous truth of what happened when we got there. We recognized the spot from above, called out to them before we dropped onto the shelf, received no answer. Proceeding to a point where we could see the cave, we spied something dark lying before it on the ledge. Examination quickly established the ghastly fact that a human corpse lay there, badly burned, chiefly vestigial in its remnants, consisting more of blackened bones than charred flesh. There were, nevertheless, intact tatters of clothing, and the tell-tale boots, which immediately identified for us the body as that of Toby Gastolf, late student of Professor Anton Vorchek.

We searched the cave. The interior was greatly disordered, far more so than previously noted, and it was Lenny who opined that the petroglyphs looked altered, or that—this became our consensus—fresh ones had been drawn or painted upon the surfaces around the smooth wall in back. We found no trace of Vorchek, assumed he had tumbled to his death or, improbably, made his way down the cliff to at least some lower level.

Our cell phones would not communicate to the outside world from within the Inner Basin, so it was very late in the day, well into evening, before we reached bottom, hiked out of the caldera, and drove out of the mountains to the plains where we could contact Flagstaff. We learned, to our amazement, that Vorchek had indeed returned to civilization the day before, duly reporting that his companion had been instantaneously killed by a lightning blast. There it was. The explanation made sense, nor did I or my friends think to question. Really, what puzzled us most was how old Vorchek had gotten himself down off that cliff. Anyway, the big effect on us was that we derived less coverage than expected for our successful climb of the south face of Humphrey's Peak, our story being secondary that week.

That is just about all I can tell you of my own knowledge. Everything I have written so far is true, facts the result of direct observation. Most of what follows I picked up from another, which I repeat for what it's worth.

Two days later, while we were getting set to pull out in the morning, I coincidentally ran across Professor Vorchek, dressed to the nines, sitting at lunch on the patio of an upscale Flagstaff bistro. He wasn't alone, rather sharing his meal with a young, pretty, fashionably dressed girl, they deep in conversation over a ragged pile of papers. When he saw me he gave me the coldest glance, then grinned slightly, waving with a beckoning flick of his fingers. He touched heads with the girl, whispering something, at which she jumped up and disappeared into the restaurant. I joined him, pulling up a chair.

"A pleasure, sir," he said. "That was another student of mine, a fine girl, one unable to accompany me on my latest venture. Probably for the best, that, given what happened. You have heard, I take it, the disagreeable news?"

"I have; a terrible pity."

"Quite." He seemed oddly jovial, heedless of the tragedy even as he blandly mouthed the story as I'd heard it. After a few minutes of commiserating I pressed him as to how he had saved himself from that dangerous perch. This is what he told me, as I recollect it.

By way of introduction he beamed joyously, shook his head and said, "I am dying to tell someone, and why not you? It can't matter, since neither you nor anyone else would believe me. I tell you, sir, that I learned a great deal up at that cave, that I achieved my goal to the ultimate degree. I proved the veracity of the ancient Indian legends beyond sane doubt.

"Never did I tell you all about those legends, obscurely transmitted to our own day. According to the Yavapai, the shamans—the wise medicine men—of old communed with the Gods in that cave, but all accounts insist that those elderly gentlemen did not require mountain climbing skills in order to reach the site. Oh no, these archaic myths brag that the native scholars of long ago perfected, by the blessing of the Gods, a means of stepping from any point in the material universe deemed sacred by the Old Ones, to another point in the celestial spheres, the planes in which the Gods walk, and then stepping back into our cosmos at that or another sacred location. That, so all of my information claimed, was the secret of locomotion which allowed them egress to the cave, without any physical effort whatsoever. The medicine men performed this feat by utilizing esoteric spells of awesome power, and by satisfying the apparently hungry Gods with a chosen victim; in other words, a species of human sacrifice.

"I intended to duplicate their feat, or their arcane machinations, thereby confirming or falsifying their claims. You must admit, sir, that it constitutes a remarkable and gratifying line of study. I possessed already many records containing key phrases of the shamanistic spells, and I gained still more from the inscriptions at Trident Rock, which only I of all living men have read and understood. Think of how many archeologists and tourists have gazed upon those stones, gawking mindlessly. I understood the hidden words, but they too were insufficient. My only hope was to reach the cave on the south face of the Medicine Man Mountain by commonplace means, there perhaps to uncover the missing links of the logical chain.

"That I did! With your invaluable aid I made it, found there the inscriptions that completed the vital incantations. Once you and your good fellows were out of the way, it remained only for me to reproduce the exacting methods of my intellectual forebears. I ignited the measured flames, drew on the walls the critical images that focus the otherworldly energies, spoke and sang the words of power as they were spoken and sung in past eras. This I did as did those men of lost centuries, and I, as they, hurtled headlong out of the tedious confines of this despicable patch of ephemeral flotsam we call 'everything,' into a strange, indescribable world of shocking otherness that represents no less than the conjectured planes and spheres of the most high Old Ones.

"Nothing more I can tell you of that incomprehensible land. The memories shall terrify and confound me all my days. Imagination has carried me far, yet I confess to a dry and static mind, like so many of my colleagues. Still I can not grasp fully that which lies beyond the ken of mortal man. Regardless, I aver that, at a time of my choosing, I returned to this world, stepping out of the mystic void to the desired locale, the sacred rock floor within the structure of Trident Rock. Victory, sir, decisive success was mine. I had proved all.

"It matters not that others will not accept. I know, which appeases my lust for knowledge. In time, I pray, I may learn much more. There you have it, my friend: why I joined you, how I came back without trained human help. That is the whole of the story."

It wasn't, but I say now that I shouldn't have pressed further. I refuse to believe what he told me, will not grant any of it, especially the last and nastiest bit, but I'd rather not have heard it. I can hear his hatefully triumphant, sickeningly pleasant voice as he responded when I asked him about the sad accident that took Toby.

He actually laughed, that Vorchek. "Accident, sir? That thunderstorm was a convenient happenstance, I admit, but dismiss its relevance from your mind. You have not attended to my words, or else you fight against the obvious, lest you accept a conclusion which tramples upon your bargain basement, discount morality. You truly think I took with me that oaf because I required his mind or his brawn? No, indeed, I traffic not in such expendable sorts, save when I may utilize them for my needs. The olden accounts were definitive, and for my own sake I dared not tamper with those anciently approved methods. I needed a sacrifice, had to have one that I might feed the Gods—whatever entities They be, They must eat, like all else in this creation and beyond—and Mr. Gastolf, whatever his mental limitations, beautifully served that turn."

THE BIG SEDONA BASH

I got the word that Jerry Ethelred had breezed back into town when I received the ornately engraved invitation to his homecoming dinner party. He was one of Sedona's hotshots, had been for years since he cleaned up in real estate—forcing a sale on that choice wilderness land west of town, smack in the middle of National Forest territory, where he built that big ticket resort—after which he devoted his time to further speculation, punctuated by global ramblings. Back from Europe, he wished to gather together his old friends to celebrate his return. Well and good, because Jerry always threw a fun party. So that evening I arrived, just a little later than on time, with a girl in tow I've already forgotten (no I haven't, really, but she was forgettable, so forget her), at his boxy southwestern style mansion on the high top of Schuerman Mountain south of town. Jerry and his loud third wife cordially greeted us at the door.

The night's circus was in gear by then, with a lot of people crammed into the expansive downstairs entertainment hall. The interior was baroque, garish, pricey, Jerry's way all the way. I knew some of the people there, a few from earlier fetes, more from hobnobbing about Sedona, where most of us scratched a living from the tourist trade. Restauranteurs, owners of expensive curio shops, lesser peddlers of housing plots dominated the group. I, for instance, sold semi-precious stones dug up in the outback. Like most, I got by, proclaimed satisfaction, envied Jerry's success. Especially notable, as it happened, was the presence of Morton Challot, the operator of one of those ubiquitous jeep tours that roamed the countryside pointing out the lovely wonders of the unique surrounding landscape.

The party was already noisy, smoky, and liquor drenched. Jerry regaled us with commonplace observations derived from his travels, a typical tale interspersed with snide comments and ostentatious winks from Eileen (Mrs. Ethelred, part three). In the midst of this Theresa Delaney arrived, a gorgeous young blonde whom I ever appreciated seeing only because she was great to look at. Dressed like a classy fashion model, she made the other women look pathetic and mousy, but she was the snooty, stand-offish type who'd never given me the time of day, scarcely willing to grant minimal civility, except perhaps to her partner that evening, a rather tall, mature fellow introduced as Professor Anton Vorchek. I'd never heard of him, nor did he sound like he hailed from those parts. With his little beard and his old fashioned suit and broad floppy hat he exuded an air of the Old World, which his mellow, faintly accented speech did nothing to dispel.

Dinner commenced, some kind of French extravaganza laid out on the huge, endless oblong of an oaken table. The food was pretty good, although I didn't recognize much of it. Certain local culinary experts critiqued the fare in low tones. The rest of us yacked about anything that came to mind, with Jerry butting in and taking charge of conversation if the topic appealed to him.

I heard him saying in his booming huckster's voice, from down and across the table, "No, Schuerman Mountain isn't a vortex site, whatever outsiders say. I'd never be that crass, to put a house atop one. I must cater, after all, to regional proprieties." He laughed, Eileen squawked, and I chuckled politely, though I didn't know at what. "Might raise the property values at that," he added with a smirk, "if I advertised." Obviously someone had alluded to one of our city's prime attractions, this tiresome business of the Sedona vortexes.

This is it in a nutshell: back in the weirdo Sixties a bunch of oddball hippie types descended on the vicinity, charmed by the starkly poetic marvels of the famed Red Rock Country—that mammoth jumble of weather-worn sandstone spires and water-carved canyons encompassing Sedona—and declared, on the basis of, I guess, hazy historical report, that there was magic in the land, an enchanted force soaring above the crude materialism they'd chosen to reject. This force was concentrated, they claimed, at especially scenic spots, said concentrations becoming known as 'vortexes,' places where the burgeoning advocates of the New Age Movement could commune, or get in touch, or seek the beyond, or whatever those people do. I knew that much about the vortexes and their strangely dogmatic believers, because I pandered to the latter all the time, but otherwise I'd never paid much attention to their folderol, nor did the majority of my fellow citizens. There were exceptions, of course, since over the years numerous folk had moved there solely in order to connect with that beneficial cosmic power.

Professor Vorchek sat directly across from me, with Theresa on his left. I caught her eye, grinned, made a cheery remark, received a frosty stare in return. She hadn't changed a bit. She whispered something to Vorchek, who smiled and glanced at me. Then he leaned forward, muttering conversationally, "Actually, you know, the appropriate plural is 'vortices.'" I nodded, supposing he would know.

Morton spoke up harshly at that point, distinctly audible from way down near Jerry. "It isn't a con," he declared, responding to a statement inaudible to me, "I'm not just in it for the money. It's for real, all of it. I'm engaged in worthy public service." He sounded like he meant it, which simply convinced me he was a locally grown kook. You see, unlike much of the competition, Morton's jeep tours (you'd recognize his vehicles on sight, all of them painted chartreuse) were billed as "spiritual expeditions," focusing solely on visiting locales where vortexes—excuse me, vortices—were said to exist. He hauled around the dedicated New Agers from place to place, up and down the bumpiest roads in the area, to get them to their Nirvanas on earth. Apparently he sympathized with them to a greater degree than I had realized. Well, big deal; what did that matter? Sedona attracts all kinds.

Maybe—I see in looking back on that night—maybe it was some kind of a big deal, to somebody.

Jerry was saying something to him, when Morton leaped from his chair and exclaimed, "I can't stomach skeptical minds, closed minds that won't admit the truth. The force is out there, the presences are out there. I know, I've felt them, I've made the connection too." Now there came a lot of muted disagreement and lightly jabbing chatter back and forth. Morton sat down, but he didn't shut up, carrying on a vague argument with no one in particular. It sounded like both camps were well represented that night.

Then I heard Theresa saying, "Oh, come on, Professor, give it a rest," but that fellow, in a quietly commanding voice, announced, "The pseudo-scientific mind, while occasionally touching upon a morsel of reality, operates too completely estranged from critical thought to ever wholly achieve a state of clear understanding vis a vis the unknown. This intriguing problem of the Sedona vortices connotes a dramatic case in point. My research indicates the existence of a genuine, if poorly defined, phenomenon, yet one which relates rather weakly to the views expressed by our self-aggrandizing true believers." His words carried clearly to Morton, who started as if shot, turned red. I pushed out a laugh, facetiously called down the table, "I guess you can close up shop now Morty, at least until you go back to school. You need to learn the real stuff." Jerry burst into laughter, picked up the joke, drove it home farther than I intended. "Vortex 101," he roared, "the kindergarten level." Eileen chimed in, "You can carry your folks in little red wagons instead of red jeeps."

Morton rose again. Now he was evidently angry, keen for a scrap. "You, Mr. know-it-all—Vorchek, is it?—who are you to tell me? I'll have you know I've studied, I've read a bunch of books on the subject. I've got the straight dope from published researchers, professionals like Kagan, Luther, and Ney. Ever heard of them?"

Vorchek replied, barely turning in his seat, "I have; quacks and mental midgets, the lot of them, nor a professional degree among the lot." Theresa cringed, almost spewed her mouthful from suppressed laughter, managed to say jocularly, "Here we go."

"So you say," snapped Morton. "I've also read Bleek, Jacob Bleek. Did your education take you that far?"

Now it was Vorchek who visibly reacted. He blanched, turned for a full view of his opponent, said, "I know Bleek very well, as well as anyone can. Jacob Bleek, the mystic researcher of yesteryear, is, as you might say, the 'real deal.' I possess fragments of his works in my collection, know something of his intellectual prowess. He was, of course, a self professed wizard—in fact a scholar—of a far land and far time who never heard of Sedona, though his unusual ideas may bear upon the matter. I confess myself puzzled, sir, by your acquaintance with his writings."

"I got one page," Morton explained, "sold to me for big bucks by a foreigner who translated it for me in exchange for transport to some very out of the way sites. The original was old, a ragged sheet of yellow parchment; must have been centuries old. I knew I was on to something right away."

"If genuine," Vorchek shot back, "then you should dispose of it without delay or, better still, give it to me for safe-keeping. Bleek's teachings, so far as they are understood by legitimate students of elder lore, are not for the unwary or the fanciful."

"Got you running, don't I?" said Morton. "I have the page on me right now."

"That's a coincidence," Theresa said brightly.

Morton ignored her. To us all he said, "Folks, these truths are so important that I carry them around with me at all times, just to soak them into my brain. The words of mystery raise consciousness by their very presence. Here it is." He fished a wadded sheet from his wallet, not parchment, of course, but plain paper, presumably his translation. "This, I am assured, is a bona fide magic spell, an incantation of secret words that makes things happen. I swapped for it because these words are designed to open the mystical gate that separates our world from the world of the cosmic beings who dwell on the other side. Those people, or whatever you call them, are the sources of the power that flows through the vortexes. It is they who I and many other earnest delvers have long tried to contact. This is spooky stuff, so I've hesitated, but I've a good mind right now to try this out, see if I can break the barrier and finally greet the great ones."

"Utter foolishness," cried Vorchek, who rose at last to face Morton.

"Might does not imply benevolence, nor desire, truth. Granted that the words on that page are genuine, how do you know what you will confront when you smash the barrier which holds us apart from them, and them, I assert, apart from us? That spell, as you deem it, may tear asunder your final defense against forces which you, an ignorant mortal, can not comprehend."

"I'm going to do it," Morton said hotly.

"Some other time, then," Theresa suggested, with a bored toss of her golden locks. She nonchalantly lit a cigarette, puffed absently. "Get over it, bub. You can't do anything now. Don't you have to be at a vortex to make it work? That's the gate you're planning to open, isn't it? Well, you heard what Jerry said. This isn't one."

Jerry, who was enjoying every minute of this, said, "That's what I told you. I've heard the issue debated, though, had plenty of fingers wagged in my face. What do I know?"

Morton said, "Schuerman Mountain is a vortex site, that's for sure. All the initiates know it. There was lots of fuming when Ethelred desecrated the summit with his gaudy house."

Jerry frowned, grinned evilly after a beat. "Okay then, Challot the clown, why don't you put on your act for my guests? Prove what you've got is more than a one way ticket to the loony bin. Stage your magic show, let us see how it's done. Talk to the vortex, make it open for us. I'm extending my dinner invitation to our visitors from the other side."

"That," said Vorchek, "is a remarkably stupid idea."

The upshot was that Morton determined to undertake his weird experiment immediately, before the whole crowd. Jerry gleefully took charge of organizing the event. Under his deft management we, once dinner was complete, gathered at one end of the hall where, at his direction, we shifted furniture to provide Morton with a cleared space, an impromptu stage on which he could operate. Eileen hustled some excess drapery and streams of black and orange crepe to festoon the designated area, make it resemble a bit more the kind of place where a master magician (or a clown) would perform. Morton, with a sullen air, went along with the festive trappings, dividing his time between perusing his paper and boasting of coming exploits. Professor Vorchek stood aside, looking glum, with Theresa by his side cool as ever, appearing faintly amused. I sidled over to them through the tangle of guests with drink in hand.

"It's no big deal," I said. "Everybody has his quirks. This is Morty's. I'll bet you he's doing it for a laugh. He'll have his fun, we'll give him a big hand, and then get down to some real partying."

"Don't be a boob," Theresa replied. "The professor's worried about something. He says this stuff isn't for amateurs. I guess he ought to know."

SCIENCE AND SORCERY III

"I wish I knew what to expect," Vorchek growled. "Miss Delaney, do me a favor, if you please. Speak to Mr. Challot, ask him if I may read his paper before he takes action." She blandly accepted the charge and strode away. The professor said to me, "If it be genuine, I would recognize the words without effort. Bleek's endeavors constitute a fond sideline of mine."

The girl returned, said with a sniff, "No go, Professor. He's mad at you, says seeing will be believing. Look, Morty's getting ready."

"In that case, my dear," he replied, "be so kind as to assume a station by that door leading into the kitchen. Wait there until the deed is done." Theresa shrugged, but she obeyed. Without further word to me Vorchek strode away, taking up a watchful position from before the main door, the only other exit from the room save the closed windows. I figured what he was up to, making ready to catch out Morton in a scam.

Jerry insisted on turning the lights down low, to heighten the spooky atmosphere, but I could still see Morton plainly enough, a vague but unmistakable silhouette. He groused about not being able to read his spell properly, received from someone a pen flashlight. One hand and the ragged sheet flared into clarity. He began to read.

There's no point in my trying to recount what he recited. It was English, so I can tell the gist of it, only it was mixed up with a lot of bizarre ten and twenty letter words, weird conglomerations of syllables that didn't sound like any real language. I guess those didn't translate well. One comparatively simple word he repeated often, the term "Zennofor" (don't call me on that spelling), which seemed to be a person or being he was attempting to contact. Morton wrapped the reference with a bunch of odd flattery and mention of power, like that character was a big important type who had to be spoken to respectfully. So, what was he saying? "I beseech you, Oh great master, king of the old ones, ancient creator and destroyer;" stuff like that, then a pile of fifty dollar words, and "Open the gate, that I may gaze into your face;" more meaningless cant, followed by this, more or less: "Take my hand, that I may walk with you among the crystal spheres." There was plenty more, with considerable repetition, but that's the general idea.

Somebody—I guessed it was Jerry—must have been playing tricks with the lights, because as Morton intoned the crazy phrases it grew harder to see him, or much of anything. Also, the window curtains fluttered, and a warm breeze played about me, as if a fan had been turned in my direction. When Morton came to the end of his recital I gather he snapped off the flashlight, for suddenly the room grew almost inky dark. There was dead silence for a moment.

He began again to speak, in a hushed tone as if his voice came from far away, sounding hollow, as if the words reached us through a long, faintly echoing tunnel. He said, "It works! My friends, I commence the passage into the beyond. The illusion of your reality recedes, as I move without effort through brightening mist; no, a vast void, limitless space to which my eyes are painfully adjusting. I see no form, just light and shadow, shifting, advancing toward me. If you can hear me still, I tell you that I've crossed over into the cosmic planes beyond the gate. It has truly happened, is happening to me. I shall behold that face behind eternity, behold and adore!"

Somebody in the group mumbled, "Give us more light." Others chimed in, and a cigarette lighter flickered, then another. I still couldn't see anything for certain, except that Morton had obviously moved, for where he had been standing was vacancy. I scanned the hall for him, attempting to detect his outline slinking away.

At that moment the lights flashed, or a light did, a hazy reddish glow emanating from the stage. That was the moment I expected the culmination of Morton's big put-on, because the image revealed indicated funny business. Instead of Morton on his set I saw a tangled web of unusual shadows, stark shades of light and dark in rapid motion, overlaid upon that end of the hall. It was a light show of grotesque forms, pretty awful from what I could make out. Of course it all passed in the matter of an instant, and I couldn't be categorical about what I was viewing, but those shapes, while they lasted, looked noxiously unpleasant, and I began to think that Morton carried his comedy routine too far.

A shrill scream rocked the room. I lost my taste for the joke in that instant, for it was too realistic of an agonized, mindlessly terrified shriek. It seemed to come from everywhere at once, reverberating about the hall. Enormous hubbub and commotion ensued, folks moving and making all sorts of noise, yet over that could be heard Morton's voice hollering, now sounding impossibly distant and tinny, like he was speaking over a lousy telephone connection. "Oh God, save me, save my soul! They are demons, monsters from the pit. I must get out—which way?—there's nothing here but these horrors, closing in. Why do they laugh? Better death than—"

A voice I recognized as Vorchek's roared, "Turn on the lights now!"

I thought I heard Morton one more time, scarcely audible, saying, "Must find the gate—"

The lights came up to full intensity, an ashen Jerry at the dimmer switches. Nothing had changed, except that Morton wasn't there, wasn't anywhere in the room, as a couple minute's hunt established. Instinctively I turned to Vorchek, saw him curtly catching Theresa's attention with a gesture. She shook her head. I paced over to her, she wrinkling her nose as I neared. "Give me a break," I said. "I want to know, too, if he made his exit this way." She replied, "Not a chance. He'd have to knock me down."

Professor Vorchek sauntered up, after first stooping to retrieve something from the floor. He said, "Not by the doors, I conclude. Our devoted host, Mr. Ethelred, appears to be taking these developments hard, but I can not rule out the possibility that he was in on an arranged parlor trick. That would delight his supposed sense of humor. On the other hand—" here he smoothed the paper held between his fingers, studied it intently—"these peculiar scribblings left behind by Mr. Challot are, I suspect, no phonies, nor copied from the latest silly paperback. I do believe they are verily extracts from the grim researches of the infamous Jacob Bleek himself. Many of these phrases could be known only by strict devotees. I, also, would pay big money for more of the same from the mysterious purveyor, if I knew who he was. If—when—Mr. Challot rejoins us, I shall pump him for full particulars."

"Something stinks," I said.

"It is this sheet," he replied. "That is most odd. It bears traces of a foetid, tarry residue."

"Residue of what?"

"Organic matter, I would say. Indeed, I must have that talk with Mr. Challot."

"Leave your card," advised Theresa. "This big bash isn't living up to expectations. Let's blow the joint."

They did, presently, as did we all, sooner or later. That was a while ago, and good old Morty hasn't turned up yet. I admit that, at the time, I was a little shaken by events, but in retrospect I can imagine Sedona's favorite tour guide off on holiday somewhere, enjoying a grand chuckle at our expense. Of course he would carry the stunt too far (so much so that the police have gotten into the act, currently seeking his whereabouts), but no one accuses Morton of subtlety. I don't mind. It was the one amusing incident in an otherwise forgettable night. Theresa the ice queen was right; despite my high hopes, it really wasn't much of a party.

YARDREELA

West by Luxor amidst the shifting sands on the fringe of the lonely Egyptian desert the excavations continued under the watchful eye of Professor Anton Vorchek. That keen minded man, explorer of the unknown and the mysterious, driven by the logical calculations of his research, had chosen to dig here, in a territory ignored by previous scholarly delvers, a decision spurred by fragmentary records suggesting the presence of hitherto unsuspected burial sites dating from the earliest dynasties. His youthful and lovely assistant, Theresa Delaney, devoted her cunning to tabulating accounts, which kept her in a perpetually grimmer mood than her mentor. Said she, with a toss of her long blonde hair, "It's bad enough that we have to maintain a gaggle of party animals disguised as graduate students, but these native workers will shortly put us out of business. I thought they were supposed to come cheap."

Vorchek paused to light his pipe, stroked his short, manicured beard, and replied in his pleasantly modulated, slightly accented speech, "The days of cheap foreign labor, Miss Delaney, are long behind us. In the good old days of Petrie and Carter the local hired help indeed constituted a dwindling fraction of costs. The natives, however, have caught on to the archeological game, having acquired a taste for high definition televisions and fancy cell phones just like the folks back home. Still, I will grant you that this bunch seem prepared to put aside a stash at one go for early retirement. It can not be avoided. If I had to rely on my students, I would be sunk."

Immediate developments dispelled their gathering gloom over expeditionary finances. A throaty-voiced Arab bawled unintelligibly and urgently from the pit, and the pair scuttled and slid down the dune, Vorchek looking tall and commanding in his big floppy hat and loose fitting garb like something picked out for an old time safari, Theresa appearing pretty and dainty in her overly fashionable outfit of blouse and wide skirt and high black boots, more like something out of a movie safari. They stumbled down into the narrow L-shaped hole, where the raggedly (and typically) dressed student Jake Weston accosted them.

"Found something," he grunted at Vorchek. "I'm knocking off for lunch."

After he scrambled from the pit Theresa made an acerbic comment about the frequency of work breaks—none of the other Americans were currently in sight—but Vorchek paid no heed, having attention only for what pickaxes and spades had exposed under the thin layer of bedrock. He pushed past the muttering Egyptian workers, peered intently through his wire-rimmed glasses. "It appears to be a portion of wall," said he, "crude yet stout masonry, quite common to a wide range of olden Egyptian architecture. This slight projection on the right may be the edge of a door. With luck, my dear, we have struck the wall of a tomb."

"It better pay off," warned Theresa.

During the remaining daylight hours Vorchek directed his team—newly galvanized, including his five graduate students—to dig to the right, excavating and clearing away the debris of dark centuries heaped against the subterranean structure. Despite his mature years he labored as much or more than the rest. After the others had retired for the evening he and Theresa mused over what lay revealed by flashlight.

"It is truly a door," he observed, "and truly a tomb. Miss Delaney, console yourself, for I think we have hit the jackpot. The mortar seals appear unbroken, and the inscriptions about the casing are intact. It may be that grave robbers of yore missed this one. My, these carvings look pristine. The elements have left them untouched. Despite the archaic script, I do believe I can hazard a translation of their meaning.

"If you would please, hold the light there." Vorchek studied for a lengthy period of silence, once admonishing Theresa not to fidget. "A non-standard funereal hymn," he whispered at last, "much less praise for the entombed than is the norm, considerably more by way of warning. Do not desecrate, do not disturb, do not do anything but quickly abscond. This is odd: explicit mention that there is nothing of material value deposited within. A notice to thieves, most like, if honest too bad for us, but surely a weak lie."

Theresa crowded her face into the circular glow, pulling aside her hair to stare at the (to her) meaningless symbols. She shrugged her discouragement. "It's got to be true."

"On the contrary," Vorchek said crisply, "already I discern light in darkness. Do you see the three symbols in this cartouche?"

"If you mean in that oblong drawing, yes, I see three little pictures, like all the rest."

"Oh, my dear, this is good old fashioned Egyptian script, of syllabic nature, denoting a language like any other, and the enclosed carvings represent a royal name, according to long-standing custom. Follow with me as I translate. The stick figure of a man holding a scepter: 'Yar;' the long-lashed open eye: 'dree;' the two wavy lines, perhaps the stylized image of flowing water: 'la.' Yar-dree-la; Yardreela, an uncommon name, yet one known to experts on antique history."

"You've heard of that name?" Theresa asked. "It's somebody important?"

"Fantastically so," Vorchek exclaimed. "This connotes the coming to life of legend. Let us return to camp, where I will explain to all."

They did, and he did. Surrounded by an arc of gasoline driven electric lights, and before a fire which warded the evening desert chill, Professor Vorchek joyously pontificated to his entire crew. "One of the most intriguing tales descending to us from the age of the formative dynasties," began he, "is the story of Yardreela, the evil princess who sought to cheat death. Something like genuine history presents a scathing account of her vicious enormities, but it is around her passing from this world that myth accumulates. Not for her the glories of the afterlife promised to the pharaohs and their kin; nay, she rejected that speculative boon in favor, we are told, of a more material longevity. According to hoary tradition—well known by the time of Rameses the Great—she conspired with sinister magicians and dark priests from an unknown foreign realm to preserve her conscious mind in bodily form through the ages, potentially forever. We are told that at the approach of natural death she suffered burial not of her corporeal frame, but of an esoterically detached element of her soul. That was entombed within her chosen grave site, after which the priests ceremonially destroyed by fire her still living body. Sounds risky, does not it? She must have sincerely believed in this dreadful method.

"Where the presumed benefit? In exchange for the destruction of her body the remaining fragments of her soul would pass into, seize and take over the body of another, and she would thus live another span, a hateful species of reincarnation. In the fullness of years she could repeat her fiery end, at which point her broken soul would move on to another victim, and then again after the period of that life, and again, on and on throughout the ages. This legend, we know, endured unto the reign of the Ptolemies, a brief mention of it being found in Caesar's *Commentaries*. So, the tale was told throughout thousands of years, with similar but greatly distorted versions cropping up during the Classical and Medieval periods.

"Ladies and gentlemen, we have uncovered the tomb of Yardreela! Down there in the pit we shall excavate the true essence of the tale. Of course what we will most likely find inside is a conventional mummy, but there should be valuable ornaments and jewels, and more importantly funereal inscriptions that may suggest a real world basis for these morbid traditions. We have achieved a rare find. You should all feel honored to take part in this work.

"Tomorrow, my friends, we open the tomb."

Come the morning Vorchek did not have to struggle with rounding up his lazy staff. They crowded into the dig, necessitating that one eager shift be forced to stand down and watch from the lip of the pit while the regular morning crew, fully manned, willingly labored. At the professor's beck they widened the trench before the door, creating ample work space for strenuous operations while also clearing that entire side of the tomb. Hammers and chisels were produced, applied with gusto to the engraved door jam, Vorchek constantly cautioning against wanton destruction of the carvings.

"There couldn't be anything to the Yardreela legend," asked Theresa, "could there, Professor?"

"Probably not," he replied. "As you should know by now, Miss Delaney, that is my stock answer to every puzzle, until a finding be established. The Egyptians, as well as other forgotten peoples of yesteryear, were mixed up in strange doings. I do not casually believe, but I put nothing past them."

The seals were broken, the massive granite door wrestled from its position. A gush of rancid air caused the laborers to recoil.

It was then that Doctor Obermann appeared at the top of the pit.

"Doctor Lenore Obermann," she called down, "of the University of Heidelberg. Come up here, Professor, that you may explain yourself to me." Vorchek frowned, shading his eyes against the sun, grudgingly obeyed. Theresa tagged along. They confronted a sharp-eyed, hard-faced woman of middle age, very thin, with pale, skeletal visage, dressed in drab, darkly utilitarian attire. Everything about her was cold and gloomy, save for the gaudy star-bursts of sculptured jade that hung by large gold loops from her ears.

"Explain yourself, madam," retorted Vorchek with thin grace, as he dusted off his jacket and trousers. "I do not know you, and I am an extremely busy man."

"But I know you, sir, and what you do." Her icy manner, her haughty voice (rather lacking in definite accent) repelled even as they demanded respect. She did condescend to extend a bony hand for shaking, which the professor accepted. "I understand that you have discovered the long lost resting place of the Princess Yardreela."

"It is her tomb," Vorchek frostily replied.

"By what right do you disturb it?"

YARDREELA

"By the right of scientific investigation," said he, "the right of knowledge."

"And we've got the proper permits and everything," Theresa interjected hotly, "so you can just bug off."

Doctor Obermann smiled condescendingly. She studied the girl at length before addressing herself solely to Vorchek. "I have long sought the tomb of Yardreela. In addition to my own research, I have kept careful track of other expeditions such as yours. Those previous attempts at discovery came to nothing, so I did not then intrude."

"You refer, I take it," said Vorchek, "to the efforts of Drs. McKilliam and Handsley. I heard something of their missions. As I recall, they experienced difficulties and gave up the task."

Doctor Obermann nodded. "The former, I seem to remember, suffered casualties among his staff; the latter, I do believe, perished suddenly. That was most unfortunate."

"Yes, I too remember that. Believe me, good woman, that I expect no untoward complications. By luck or cunning I have succeeded in making the find, and shall indulge myself in strenuous analysis."

"I know of you," she replied, "thus expected no less. Also I expect, Professor Vorchek, as a favor to a colleague, that you allow me to observe."

"Agreed. Call your people."

"I have no people."

With Vorchek in the lead they entered the revealed chamber. It was small, dark, noisome. Despite the murk it did readily prove distressingly bare of desired artifacts. Theresa said, "The warning was right. This is going to be a bust." A graduate student, Sally Perkins, chuckled and said, "I get my stipend either way." The professor seemed wholly cheerful, his attention seized by more wall carvings and a short, inscribed obelisk of obsidian which rose from a squat pedestal in the center of the room, the only object in the room.

"These hieroglyphics," he announced, "will tell tales. These on the walls direct at us conventional threats, described with uncharacteristic gusto. This obelisk, on the other hand—" He perused the ancient writing by flashlight. "There is, in fact, no claim of this site being a tomb. I am astonished, but it does appear that the traditional story of the princess dates back to her time. That intrigues me. It says this—this 'holding place'—this 'house,' perhaps, guards the disembodied *ka* of Yardreela, held here alive that she may have life of a sort with the remainder of her soul. The wording is peculiar, but I get the gist. There must be more here. Examine the walls. Seek another door."

Easier said than done, for the small chamber was quite crowded at that point. Vorchek ordered out unnecessary personnel, retaining only Theresa, the husky student Mark Turner, and Doctor Obermann. They looked all over. It was Theresa who, feeling with her fingers, detected a barely perceptible ridge in the stone floor. Vorchek cried, "Excellent, my dear. There is a trap door. It is below that we must go."

A short delay saw the requisite tools provided, the professor and Mark attacking the square slab, scraping away dust and crumbled mortar. A narrow gap soon lay exposed which called for the use of a crowbar. The slab slowly rose. The unpleasant odor intensified. "There's something dead in there," Mark stated. He reached into the black aperture to lift the stone aside. As it fell to the floor he sprang back, groaning and sucking his thumb. "It's got a sharp edge to it," he complained.

Vorchek peered into the lower level. "There is something down there," he said. "I see angular shapes. There we will find our treasures." He was all for diving in immediately, but his attention was distracted by a curious development. Mark Turner suddenly screamed, doubling over, falling heavily and thrashing spasmodically.

"My goodness," Theresa said. Instantly they gathered about, Doctor Obermann solicitously kneeling to attend him. Feeling of the now silent prone figure, she shortly intoned, "He's dead, Professor. I trust that you have students to spare." Vorchek examined the edge of the removed block. "Tiny prongs," said he, "little needles of copper, encrusted with traces of a black substance. There was more than sealant here. This was a defensive measure against intruders."

Doctor Obermann said solemnly, "We must remove him. The authorities will have their say."

No more work was done that day. The local officials proved stridently tiresome, appeared much impressed by the doctor's suggestion that excavation be suspended while the tragic case was investigated. Professor Vorchek was fit to be tied. That night he communed with Theresa, sitting in lounge chairs before their tent after dinner, bemoaning ridiculous complications. "Of course it is too bad," said he, "but why should my useful life be put on hold? Here is another example for which we must long for the good old days. My forebears would have bought off these petty dictators with cheap bribes and drink." He took a long swallow of his own.

Theresa sat quietly through the tirade, introspectively working on her cigarette. Then she flicked it into the sand and said, "This Obermann person didn't help much. You ought to chase her out of here."

"I can not, as a matter of simple courtesy. She means well."

"Maybe. She'll be weller when she gets lost." The girl leaned toward him to gain greater secrecy, that the infrequent passersby might not hear. "I ran an Internet search on her. I came up with a handful of privately published articles, goofy stuff—you would call it 'arcane,' I guess—but found no reference of any connection to the University of Heidelberg. I grant she sounds the part, but the facts don't add up."

"That perturbs me," said Vorchek. "I shall quiz her if she reappears."

"She will. She's camping alone in the next gully."

Next day, and the next, the authorities ruled the pit off limits. Vorchek engaged in earnest negotiation with the police. His native laborers began wandering away, which troubled him little, for their task was mainly done. The remaining four graduates annoyed him more, for two of them spoke darkly of leaving, having (oddly, as he thought) lost interest in the enterprise, and all indulged in reckless and embarrassingly noisy drinking binges. He feared that none of them would prove helpful henceforth in furthering his schemes.

Doctor Obermann reappeared, commiserating with Vorchek on what seemed the breaking down of his expedition. The professor sneered at that, desiring instead to interrogate her as to her professional qualifications. She said, "You are correct, that I'm not actually employed by the university. I was a long-time assistant, however, of Doctor Hilda Morgensturm, whose writings on Egyptian myth you must know, and who taught there for decades. After her untimely death I continued her research at the library and museum, from which I drew the information for my own publications."

Vorchek said, "I see. All is understood. That being so, why the inordinate interest in a minor player like Yardreela?"

Doctor Obermann smiled thinly. "Your question embraces a point of view. The princess appeals to me because her story, as told, extends beyond the realm of antiquity into latter days, perhaps even the present. Call it superstition, but I would not wish the tenets of the tale ignored or needlessly trampled upon. We must, of course, record the evidence—that is mandatory—but we need not molest the enclosure beyond bounds. Let us, I say, learn what we can, then seal again the chambers. We will have what we require, while her soul, if it be sheltered there, will live on safely."

Returned Vorchek, "My studies have led me to many strange matters, but never do they force me to suspend skepticism without due cause. An old saw translated from tatters of papyrus or tomb scratchings does not augment belief. Acceptance derives from evidence in the here and now. I shall have my way. The artifacts within, whatever their value, must be gifted to the world."

His extremely polite, even fawning dealings with the police eventually bore fruit. Their restrictions removed, the delving into the tomb went forward. With his team in disarray Vorchek paid off his native workmen, sent his two recalcitrant students home—they having muttered something of their conversations with the German lady scholar—and proceeded with the residue of his people. Doctor Obermann still insisted on observing. Her host acquiesced, though with less civility than before.

The poisoned block had been taken away to a forensic laboratory. The dark hole in the floor of the first chamber yawned invitingly. So Vorchek thought, though he asked Loretta Potts to lead the descent. She demurred, but catcalls from Wally Mason drove her down the makeshift rope ladder (fastened to the obelisk's pedestal) into the lower darkness. Flashlight beams preceded her, aiding her footing on the ladder and initial landing on the flagged pavement.

"Not much here," she shouted. "A big box like a coffin, and another thing, don't know what it is; might be an urn."

Vorchek scrambled down, followed by the others. This was a larger room, wholly lacking in ornamentation, merely a brick chamber with stone floor on which rested the sarcophagus and the other item. The coffin, for such it surely was, nevertheless sported none of the beautiful inlaid wood and jewelry attributes commonly found in royal interments. It was just a gray stone box, like the walls missing the usual inscriptions. The chamber seemed entirely solid. This time extensive investigation revealed no more beckoning doors.

"This looks like it," grumbled Theresa. "Slim pickings after all this, hardly worth dying for."

"I counted on much more," Vorchek ruefully agreed. "It makes me wonder if this entire tomb could be a blind, the outer writings emplaced merely to lead robbers on to nothing, perhaps diverting them from treasures elsewhere."

Said Doctor Obermann, "Most astute of you, Professor. That appears likely. There is no evidence of former grave offerings, no signs of previous entrance and removal. I think we have wandered down the wrong alley."

"I acknowledge the possibility." Vorchek strode about the plain coffin, poking at its bland surface. "Here is the real test. That lid is not sealed. The heavy stone alone holds it in place. The five of us can push it off. It may be that all of the princess's wealth resides with her mummy. I will settle for that."

The suggestion became the deed. They all came to one long side of the box, and strong or weak they gathered their powers and pushed. The thick granite lid squealed and ground horribly over the thick granite sides, grating by fractions of an inch, until it toppled with a reverberating crash to the floor. Collected flashlights probed the interior. Nothing lay inside.

"Confirmation of hypothesis," Vorchek muttered. He sat down

morosely against a featureless wall. "This entire structure constitutes an ancient attempt to lead us astray."

"Meaning the whole thing's a phony," Theresa said confidently. "The popular rags won't give us the time of day for this one."

Wally said, "Professor, if nothing's doing, I'm going to get a bite." Loretta went with him, their loud, convivial chatter trailing away as they made their way out.

Eventually Doctor Obermann spoke up, breaking the drear silence. "It does look like a dead end. That can be explained. This complex may not be so old as we assumed. It may have been built in a later dynasty as a monument to the story, rather than being the source. The Egyptians, after all, were fond of their myths, as are we."

Vorchek rose, rubbed his hands briskly. "That leaves out," he said, "the factor of the poisoned stone. That trap was rigged for a reason. Somebody wanted to keep us out, to keep anyone out. I ask why? What is the point? There is that story, and there is still this thing." He indicated the only other object in the room. It was a massy copper shape atop a large square block of stone situated a couple of yards from the empty box. The metal piece, about a foot high, was figured as a thick round shaft surmounted by a globe, so big that, as the professor found, his two hands would barely fit around it. It was, he now noted aloud, the sole location of inscriptions in that chamber.

"Here again I spy the familiar cartouche," he observed. "Yardreela, and here the word '*ka*,' and a series of fire-breathing threats. Is it possible that tomb-robbers beat us here, leaving no trace of their despoliation? There is not so much as dust in that sarcophagus."

"Maybe they cremated her," Theresa suggested. "The priests changed their minds about mummifying the princess, put her ashes in the copper thing instead. It's an urn. That would sort of fit the story."

"The Egyptians of the olden Nile kingdoms did not burn their dead," said Doctor Obermann. "That would be sacrilege."

"The case of Yardreela is different," said Vorchek. "Her people—the Egyptians, that is—would have intended to mummify her, yet according to the story she came to favor another approach, recommended by mysterious foreigners, thus the unused coffin. Miss Delaney, you may be on to something."

"Of course I am." She approached the thing, fiddled with it at various points. "I don't see any way to open it, though." After Vorchek tried his luck, to no avail, she said, "We can take it with us, check it out. There might be a few baubles inside."

The professor attempted to heft it. "It is remarkably heavy," he declared, "far more than I would expect of copper. And yet—" He rapped the metal globe with his finger. It rang faintly. "The structure is hollow. It should not weigh a great deal. Let me see." He stooped to examine the join between metal and stone. "Why, it is welded to the block! It is not made to move, any more than it is designed to open. Either we destroy the urn in cutting it from the stone, or we remove the entire mass, block and all, which will be a difficult task. I do, however, favor the latter course, which will allow us to open the container scientifically. I would not be charged with vandalism."

"So that is your intention, Professor?" queried Doctor Obermann. "I do not approve. You have logically reached the end of the road. There is nothing here for you, nothing requiring disturbance. Write your notes, take your pictures, seal the enclosure and the pit. Move on to green pastures. This worthless excavation wastes your abilities."

"I complete what I begin."

The woman's brow furrowed, her features assuming a cast more decidedly unpleasant than before. She spat the words, "An unfortunate attitude. Is it your last word?"

"It is. I will figure out a way to move it."

"For the time being, then," said she abruptly, "I take my leave. I would be no use to you in that kind of manhandling." She gingerly climbed the ladder, leaving Vorchek and Theresa to themselves.

He whispered, possibly to himself, "I do wonder about her. I detect a curious angle to her presence and motives."

"I'm glad to be rid of her," said the girl. "What do we do now?"

"It is our turn to depart," said Vorchek, "for the nonce. We will need all that is left of our pitiful crew to have a chance of shifting this thing. That block must weigh two hundred pounds. We will have to drag it across the floor, haul it up to the next level, then pull it out of the pit. That sounds like a work-out."

Theresa laughed. "That sounds like a positive nightmare. It'll keep until tomorrow. Everybody else is dodging duty. Just for once, why don't you and I do the same?"

They returned to camp to learn that Loretta's latest meal had disagreed with her. To be plain, it had killed her. Wally was also in the process of collapsing, half deliriously proclaiming to the world of a gastro-intestinal crisis. Before he passed out he mumbled as well something about Doctor Obermann having joined them for lunch, providing herself the entree.

Modern cell phone technology brought the authorities pounding. Wally they whisked away. He survived, after a sound stomach pumping, caught a plane out of the country a few days later. Meanwhile, Professor Vorchek was beside himself. As Loretta's body was being removed he explained to all who would listen, "It is that woman, Doctor Obermann. She did this. She opposes me in all things. She wishes me to fail." Even then it had been hard for him to grasp, but Theresa put a bug in his ear right away, experiencing no doubts herself. "That witch is a wrong one," she said. "She's up to something nasty."

The Egyptian cops searched, found the site of her abandoned camp, no sign of the suspected woman. They advised Vorchek and his remaining companion to pull out for their own good. It might be unwise to stay, they pointed out, if a fanatic was on the loose, and besides, they were surely going to lose their permits now. A civilized country, they said, did not condone such antics, even in the name of science. The professor might be blameless, yet trouble hovered over him like a dark pall of evil, or certainly inconvenience.

He staunchly refused. "Here I stay," he declared, "until my worthy labors be finished." Theresa shook her head, but she stood by him. She always did. They would stay *in situ* until further arrangements for carrying on could be made.

Evening fell, then blackest night. A fire blazed in the center of camp, illuminating the circle of tents, most of them empty now. Above the great dome of sky mounted darkly, pierced by a plenitude of cold, winking stars. A chill wind blew, rustling canvas flaps and thrumming tent cords. Vorchek, strained and wearied, had retired. Theresa sat hunched in her chair before the fire, a sweater thrown around her slim shoulders. She did not care for the situation, nor for the place in which she found herself. Nothing good had come of this venture, quite a bit bad. Somewhere out in the darkness, she felt, lurked a lunatic driven by unguessable motives, keen to do harm to her and the professor. The police had assured them that the area would be patrolled, the culprit caught if still in the vicinity. That had satisfied Theresa's mentor. It did not satisfy her. She imagined Doctor Obermann creeping about the drifting sands, subtle and sly, furtively closing in on her next victim.

Theresa was right. Although she doubted her own fears until that moment, Doctor Obermann suddenly appeared before the girl, her skinny form cloaked in a long shapeless dress of black, bearing in one claw-like hand a five liter can. "I feared that he would stay," said the woman, setting down the can on the sand. "I could not count on his instinct for self preservation. Nor could I explain myself. It is a pity, for all I desired was to be left alone."

"You'd better get out of here," Theresa snapped, springing to her feet. "You ought to know you're in big trouble. I'm calling the police right now."

"You're not doing anything, not ever again." Doctor Obermann pointed with her right hand at Theresa, extending two stabbing fingers, while making a weirdly convoluted sign with her left. She spoke a strange word, the likes of which Theresa had never heard, a conglomeration of cracked vocal sound which did not resemble human language though it issued from human throat, syllables indusive of painful aural properties. The effect of the utterance was immediate: Theresa froze in place, helpless, speechless, as if her mind had lost its connection to her corpus.

Said Doctor Obermann, "Eternal life with a fractured soul isn't all it could be—I didn't count on the wearisome internal limitations, the mental decay underlying the dark priests' smiling promises—but it's better than nothing, and after all these centuries it's all I've got. To think that I, the glorious Princess Yardreela, should be reduced to scrambling to survive in this silly world, generation after generation, ever fearing those who would desecrate the sacred chamber and expose my *ka*. That would be the end of me, so periodically I must return here to ward off the threats.

"The tomb, so-called, must be maintained inviolate, lest I die; and what awaits me then? I have gone too far, offended too many gods, even if the dreams of spiritual immortality be true. I meant to hold onto this body longer—those inevitable moments of transfer are so risky!—but my crimes, clumsy due to haste, have become known. Your Vorchek is no fool. He would eventually divine my secret, as did that meddling Doctor Morgensturm, and therefore he must perish as did she. First, however, my dear Miss Delaney, I beg a favor of you, that I may borrow your fleshy shell."

Doctor Obermann, who called herself Yardreela, launched into a crazed sing-song chant, compounds of grotesque words akin to her former utterance, reciting them as by ingrained, unforgettable rote, without intonation or inflection, and as she spoke she lifted the hefty can, unscrewed the cap, proceeded to pour the liquid contents over her own head and down her own body. Thoroughly soaked, she steeled herself, turned from the immobile young girl to face the belching flames of the camp fire. "Once more," she said, "through the unendurable wall of agony, thence another stale but necessary measure of existence."

Professor Vorchek emerged from his tent, fully clothed, blinking against the light of the flames. Donning his glasses, he demanded, "What goes here? I smell gasoline. Doctor Obermann? I thought I recognized your voice. My brain has been in a whirl of speculation concerning you. I insist that you justify yourself."

"Too late, Professor." So saying, Doctor Obermann strode straight into the fire, instantly exploding into dazzlingly bright, hellish fury. Shrieks as from the legions of the damned tore from her charring, bubbling lips. She collapsed into the fire, thrashing madly, her flesh disintegrating and boiling. Vorchek raced to her without delay, yet he could not approach that ghastly mass of cooking meat. He turned to Theresa, who had stood motionless and silent throughout the horror.

And she turned to him then, her features distorted by unspeakable passions which did not belong on her lovely face, and smiling a cruel, sneering smirk she snarled, "Too late, Professor. I have found lodgement. Once settled, the splinters of my soul retain tenancy until the dissolution of this ephemeral dwelling. It is mine, and there is nothing you can do about it."

"You are Yardreela!" he bellowed. "Indeed you are. I laughed at myself for my insane suspicions, yet all the while that grisly old legend haunted me. So you have survived. Release my friend."

"Don't be stupid. What I take is mine. If you know what's good for you, you'll leave here now. Go complain to the police if you like."

Vorchek came at her, his hands raised as if to grab and shake her, but he stopped, confused and uncertain, listening to that familiar voice, so unnaturally harsh, spouting its unfamiliar craziness. At length he cried, "There may still be a way." With that he whirled, dashed into the darkness toward the excavation.

From out of Theresa's mouth came a fierce shout of "No!" and she charged after the man, spitting maniacal curses. "Those who cross me die!" she raged. "You haven't a chance. I won't allow it!"

Vorchek reached the dig, fumbled amidst the gloom among the tools lying discarded in the sand. He picked up the crowbar, slid down into the pit, groped through the outer door. As he passed through Theresa appeared above, hissing her venom—in her uncontrollable anger screaming at him in another tongue than English, ranting in what sounded to his ears as excellent Old Egyptian—then raised up in two small hands a pickax. She scampered down after him.

Vorchek in his haste almost fell through the trap door, dropping the iron bar as he clutched at the rope ladder. The metal rang on the stone floor below. He ducked as the ax swung at his skull, more clanging of metal on stone. He hit bottom heavily, groaning against the pain in his ankles, recovered the crowbar and lunged forward. Theresa, dangling from her free hand, dropped more lightly behind him. Within the lower chamber brooded endless night, the dark of ages, the dark of ancient morbidity. Nothing could be seen.

Theresa screeched, "You mustn't! I won't let you! You can't dare strike at my eternity!" The professor stumbled against the unseen sarcophagus, took bearings as best he could and lashed out blindly with the crowbar. The invisible pickax gouged stone within inches of where he stood. On his third frenzied swing Vorchek's weapon impacted yielding substance. Something noisily shattered, and Theresa gave vent to a despairing wail.

SCIENCE AND SORCERY III

Out of that infernal blackness Vorchek beheld a curious wisp of slightly luminous vapor spurting into the air. It dissipated rapidly. He heard the sound of metal hitting stone again, this time with lesser force. He nerved himself to ask, "Do you hear me, Miss Delaney?" After a frightfully long pause he heard Theresa's voice, speaking in normal, if plaintive tones, "Is that you, Professor? Where am I, and how do I get out of here?"

Later, in the more suitable surroundings of the deserted camp, Vorchek said, "She was not yet seated firmly in the saddle. I had only one chance, to liberate the sealed kernel of her spirit, thus, presumably, breaking the charm. It worked. Your soul had been thrust aside by hers, yet not entirely banished. You were able, perhaps by the narrowest squeak, to regain your rightful body."

"That makes sense," Theresa replied, gulping down a glass of wine, her second. Reaching again for the bottle she added, "I guess it does. Too bad about the expedition, though. It's a dead loss. It's even too bad about Yardreela."

The professor puffed alight his pipe, grinned. "I am surprised that you would say so."

Theresa shrugged. "Well, she had a pretty good thing going for her, or should have. It's a pity that, in stories where a fabulous wonder is granted, it so often comes in the creepiest possible way, to the creepiest possible people. Life's no great shakes at times, but it looks like the alternatives are worse."

THE MAN WHO SOUGHT BLUG

P rofessor Anton Vorchek received an invitation to a "business dinner" from one Jarrod Flenberg, self-billed as "an amazingly profitable and incredibly influential" Hollywood director, and who proclaimed himself in immediate need of Vorchek's "unique services." In mysterious tones Flenberg hinted, over the telephone, at an offer which should prove "lucrative, thrilling, possibly terrifying;" and, as the director would be flying down to Phoenix from the Sedona Film Festival at very short notice—"my time is valuable—" he left it to the professor to make the meeting arrangements. Vorchek, intrigued despite himself (for he knew nothing of the man, had little use for recent movies, indeed disdained popular culture on principle) agreed, reserving a table at his favorite Scottsdale restaurant, the Aragona, where he repaired at the appointed time with his absolutely gorgeous young assistant, Theresa. They arrived, precisely punctual, were seated side by side. Flenberg had not shown.

"Perhaps the matter is not that important to him after all," Vorchek mused in his cultured, faintly foreign voice. He had removed his trademark hat, unbuttoned his jacket, settled himself cozily with a glass of wine. "The way he spoke, I thought—"

"What I want to know is," said Theresa, with a toss of her ample blonde locks, "is who's paying for this dinner: him or us?"

"The manager assured me that the bill is already covered."

"Then let's eat." They ordered, and the food arrived after a sensible period, and it was excellent, as always. Theresa made the most of the wine, with repeated helpings draining much of the bottle. Vorchek, still nursing his original glass, remained out of sorts.

"The fellow has a bad habit of speech," said he, "as of snapping orders to minions. I do not approve. I trust that he considers the value of my time."

"Something tells me," Theresa mumbled, gulping down a mouthful of highly seasoned beef, "that's him now."

The new arrival attracted attention. Smartly dressed in an overtly casual, youngish fashion, he appeared about forty, with a head of full jet-black hair. He moved quickly, his dark eyes flashing as they gazed across the room. He spoke briefly with a waiter, gestured in a promising direction, then darted rapidly to their table. Vorchek and Theresa rose.

"You're the professor, right?" snapped the stranger. Receiving a courteous nod, he then demanded brusquely, "Lose the babe. This is personal stuff."

Vorchek smiled tightly. "Mr. Flenberg, may I introduce you to Miss Delaney, my private secretary. She is involved in all of my business, and is no less discreet than myself."

"Private secretary, eh?" Flenberg examined the girl from head to foot, obviously enjoying the scenery. "How private?"

"Very private," Theresa responded coldly.

"I see. All right, let's sit down." Flenberg did, opposite the pair, Vorchek following. Theresa ostentatiously looked over her host, with a very different expression from his on her face, then slowly seated herself, as if to make the point that she did so not as a result of his command.

"The cuisine here is a treat," Vorchek observed amiably.

"Coffee," said Flenberg abruptly, snapping his fingers at the waiter who hovered nearby. To his guests he added, "I'm not hungry. I'll take your word for the food. Now, let's get down to business."

"As you please," said Vorchek.

"You're paying for it," Theresa chimed in, with a false grin.

"So I am, and time is money." The coffee set before him, Flenberg, without acknowledging the waiter, embarked upon a speech. "First, in case you don't know, let me tell you a little something about myself."

That he did. In fact, he told them an awful lot about himself. They learned that he had attended film school on a scholarship, and had directed his first professional feature length film at the age of twenty-four, a film which had proven quite successful and quickly put his name on the map. He had gone on to direct, later produce, one blockbuster movie after another, until he had reached the point that his name in the title credits, alone, was sufficient to guarantee box office triumph. His movies were now praised and technically analyzed in "how-to" courses, and he asserted that all of the current crop of "whiz kid" directors were merely following clumsily in his footsteps.

He told them more. He recounted, in great detail, the endless flow of blessings which he had derived from his success. He bragged about the money, the inexhaustible inpouring of cash granting him everything that a man could seriously want in this life. He described his houses, his cars, his servants, his jets, his yachts; he described his women—the famous, the comely, the famous and comely—who existed to satisfy his every secret passing craving, and in the telling he left little to the imagination. He spoke fervently of wild, outrageous parties—orgies, mostly—days and nights of sybaritic pleasure. He related the mechanics of his crude business practices, how he had managed to get the better of them all, how he had shown them all, beaten them all at their own game. Flenberg talked through two cups of coffee, the third arriving before he finished with a complacent smirk.

"What do you think?" he asked. "I've got it all, don't I, Professor?"

"You have plenty," Vorchek replied evenly. "My ways are not your ways but, I suppose, we all seek satisfaction in life after our own lights. By your standards, you must be a supremely happy man."

"Happy?" Flenberg laughed bitterly, savagely. "What rot. I'm talking about desire, power, influence, all that really counts. I never mentioned happiness, nor would I. I didn't call you here to discuss such an outmoded concept."

"Which leads to the big question in my mind," Theresa said primly, "of why we are here. Surely, Professor, it isn't to listen to this."

"Are you sure, honey?" asked Flenberg. "I thought you might be personally interested."

Theresa paused to allow Vorchek to light her cigarette, exhaled slowly, looked the Hollywood man dead in the eye and said, "Think again."

"What about all the money, the goodies?"

"I have money."

"What about me?"

"No comment."

"No matter. Do I make myself clear, Professor?"

"To a degree," Vorchek said wearily. "I presume there is some point to telling me all this. I must warn you, however, that the point escapes me."

"I'm coming to that. I've told you about my career and my life, and I've given you some idea what kind of man I am. How would you characterize me?"

"You're a big, worthless, empty phony," Theresa cried, "only you're too stupid to know it. You're a joke on two legs."

"Miss Delaney, please," Vorchek cautioned.

Flenberg laughed again. "She's right," he said, clearly amused. "She's almost right. I'm not a phony. I'm the real thing, just like everybody else in this rotten world, only I'm more of it. I don't try to fool myself, that's all. I'm corrupted to the core; always have been, always will be and if anything, I'm getting worse. I know all too well that there's nothing wholesome, decent, sane, or valid in my life; and knowing that fact, I revel in it. That's Jarrod Flenberg, big man, hotshot, in a nutshell."

"Very good," said Vorchek. "A most entertaining account, worthy, perhaps, of a free dinner, but little more. For some reason you persist in ranting about yourself, but you do not say why. If this be all—"

"It isn't," Flenberg grunted, "not by half. I've laid the groundwork; now I get to the heart of the matter. I've told you what a crummy guy I am. I'm telling you that I know it. I'm perfectly aware of what a vacuous travesty I am. I state for the record that my life lacks value. I'm a virtually soulless human being, and I deserve whatever I've got coming to me, and what I've got coming is . . . punishment."

"Why don't you just straighten up?" Theresa demanded.

"Because I don't want to do so," Flenberg sneered. "I love what I am, I embrace it, and I deserve to suffer eternal torment for it. You see how simple it is? I'm a bad boy, and I can't pretend otherwise. I won't. Instead, I intend to see to it that I pay for my—crimes, if you will—certainly my moral failures. Anton, buddy, you can be instrumental in making that happen."

"Nodding acquaintances address me as Professor Vorchek; nor am I your 'buddy.' I regret that your achievements have failed to content you, but that is none of my business. You should not be talking to me; rather, for all this confession, you should find yourself a priest."

"I must find myself a god," Flenberg corrected. "It must be the right god, though, the real thing for real people like me. I won't waste time on children's stories of atonement and salvation. All educated people know that Jehovah is a tall tale, a puppet manipulated by human cunning for human ends. That notion is an empty shell."

"Says who?" Theresa snapped.

"Says everybody who counts. Also, I feel it in my heart. On the other hand, I've come to realize that there is a true god, a god who can speak to me, and my whole life has now come down to finding Him. Vorchek, you must help me." Gone, suddenly, was the arrogance in Flenberg's voice. "You know things, things other people don't know. I've asked around, tried to locate the man who could point the way, the man with the big mind and broad ideas. You are that man."

"I, a lowly professor at a small Arizona college of no great repute?"

"I'm telling you I've investigated. You're keen on weird stuff, you research phenomena other scholars won't look at. Also, there's nothing fake about you. In your own tiny circle—and I don't mean academia—you're considered the expert." Flenberg paused, then leaned forward and lowered his voice. "Vorchek, I seek Blug."

The professor did not reply for a long moment. Then he muttered, "I did not expect that name to arise in the course of this discussion."

"Now you know why I came to you."

"I suppose I do."

"I don't," said Theresa. "What is 'Blug?' Is that someone, or something?"

"He is everything," said the director. "He is the true ruler of the universe, who reigns from his throne in the Black Swamp at the center of creation. He is my god; He has called to me, and I choose of my own free will to go to him. You, Professor, must get me there."

"To the Black Swamp? You overestimate me. Perhaps your knowledge of geography ranks superior to my own."

"Don't patronize me, Vorchek!" Flenberg growled. "I know very well we aren't talking about a place that can be found on a map of this world, or any world. I've done my homework, you see."

"He—called to you—did he?"

"In a dream; a vision, it was. This was years ago, but I've never forgotten a single detail. I found myself in a place of utter darkness, and yet light seemed to radiate from me, so that I could see nearby objects. I was splashing through a shallow, weedy marsh, on what might have been a path enclosed by denser growth, damp moldering trees and fat, clinging shrubs. I could smell the place, smell it in a dream. The odor was like a compound of everything detestable and unclean, the reeking odor of decay, of death, of excrement, of vomit. The liquid, oily slush underfoot teemed with vermin, and larger, shadowy creatures rustled, not quite out of sight, among the nearer bushes. I was terrified, yet nothing could have prevented my pushing on; and I seemed to know where I was going. The trail served to an extent, but there came occasions when I would deliberately, yet without conscious thought, crash my way painfully through the dank growths. It was as if I followed a homing beacon.

"The sense of delicious horror mounted as I proceeded, growing extreme when I began to hear the sounds. I detected a thumping and bumping, and a grumbling of many voices—low, unpleasant voices—gabbling in rough unison, and punctuated by shrill cries. It sounded like a crowd in motion. I passed through a wall of bent, twisted trees to behold a freakish sight: a clearing, a wide circle of stinking muck, and within the circle a small island, a dryer patch of ground where a vast, unimaginable horde of monstrosities swayed and danced and chanted around a dimly seen central mass. I waded through the ooze, without the slightest hesitation, climbed up onto the island to join them. There, in close proximity to the beings, I quivered with disgust and loathing; I felt nauseated, and in one or more fashions I think I soiled myself; yet I joined them willingly.

"They weren't human. Many—most of them—might once have been so, but except for their general outlines all had long ago departed from any state of passable humanity. I thought they'd been dead for centuries, then dug up and animated—that gives you some idea what they were like—but whatever had happened to them, they were far gone down the road to decay. Some were dry and brittle, others as liquid as the swamp. They jostled one another, and as they did so bits and pieces broke or sloughed off. They kept on dancing, however, and through their moans and their sobs they laughed. Others moved among them: things that had never been human. I can't describe them, although I remember they wore curious drab vestments and bore corroded iron crowns on the sodden lumps which might have been their heads. It occurred to me then that they were priests. I still think they were."

Flenberg paused to swallow dryly and clear his throat. Perspiration beaded his brow. "A voice called to me from the dark mass ahead. Funny that I still couldn't see it properly; I was close enough. This voice, if I can call it that, this dripping filth in my brain said, 'Jarrod, come to Me.' I pushed blindly through the dancers, I trampled them down, I crushed them into squirming jelly beneath my feet, in my haste to approach. I beheld a kind of throne, a high-backed platform composed of crude, unmentionable items, and upon that throne squatted a vast, black, amorphous mass of degenerate matter, a ghastly blob so foul that it made the rest of the swamp and its denizens seem clean and wholesome by comparison. It was the concentrated essence of everything nasty and putrid and indecent in the world; the culmination and the source, the beneficiary and the First Cause of squalor. Then I knew. Perhaps that voice of trash explained. This was great Blug, the God of the Black Swamp, the true ruler of that obnoxious, detestable jest we call life.

"And I went closer. I spied, protruding from His dark, heaving, gelatinous corpus, numerous, practically uncountable swellings of greasy pale substance, which pulsed and throbbed invitingly. I recognized them for what they were. They were teats, only they moved, expanding and contracting in rhythm like stubby fat worms. I recognized them, and I knew what was expected of me. I knew what I must do. I wanted it, I wanted that more than anything in my life, more than life itself. I wanted it . . . and then I woke up."

After a long, shocked silence, broken only by the routine noises from the surrounding restaurant, Theresa managed to gasp, "Yucko."

"Well said, Miss Delaney," observed Vorchek. To Flenberg: "Is that all?"

"That's my vision, in its entirety." Their host produced a monogrammed handkerchief to mop his face. "As I said, that was years ago. Since then I've devoted every spare moment to learning of the sordid reality behind what I saw and experienced. I've done the research. I know exactly what it means."

"You're still one up on me," said Theresa.

"What about you, Professor?"

"I am sorry to admit, that I do understand."

"That's fine," said Flenberg. "We're operating on the same level. I've got to get back to the Black Swamp. That's all I have left. I've tried on my own, persistently—via meditation, altered states, dream therapy—and learned I can't do it alone." He sighed. "It always feels tantalizingly close, but it never happens. You can do it, though. You can get me there."

"You have in mind a form of physical transference," Vorchek thought aloud, in a tone he more often utilized in the lecture hall. "A removal of the cellular body, complete with its thoughts, memories, and personality, from the material universe into what some call the Invisible World. Not a blind, exploratory transfer, however; in this case the spiritual location or geography is all important."

"Of course it is," Flenberg snarled. "I couldn't care less about cosmic joyriding. I don't want to go somewhere; I want to go there. Can you swing it? Is it possible?"

"Very little is impossible. It is a tricky business, however. Breaking through the dimensions can be accomplished. Miss Delaney and I have undertaken experiments along those lines—"

"It's not something to look forward to," she pointed out, "if my experience is any guide."

"But it is doable," Vorchek continued. "I would have to carry out a great deal more work on the aspect of precision. Which begs one very important question, Mr. Flenberg: why should I? What is in it for me?"

"Fifty thousand dollars," came the reply, "cash, in advance, plus whatever you need for expenses. Agree, and you'll have the money tomorrow. I'll have to trust you, and I'm pretty sure I can. I've interviewed just about everybody who knows you. Fifty thousand, Professor."

"We don't need the money," Theresa said. "I'm rich. If you don't want to fool with this, Professor, I'll write you a check for that amount."

"Miss Delaney, your bountiful generosity has made it possible for me to continue my advanced studies, and for that I am grateful. On the other hand, I would never want it to be said that I am living off of you. When I can, I prefer to earn my way. Mr. Flenberg, for reasons that have nothing to do with you, I accept."

The director sagged in his seat. "Good. Thanks. You'll get your money pronto. I'll stay in touch, and I expect you to keep me informed. I'll be waiting, and I'll be ready."

"I'm ready for dessert," said Theresa.

***

In his private laboratory, situated in back of his lonely old house on the

189

high hill overlooking the desert, Professor Vorchek busied himself, in stained white smock, with the novel mechanical apparatus which had occupied his attention since that night at the restaurant. Theresa lounged nearby, overdressed for the situation, leaning over a heavily laden work table as he fiddled with circuits and wiring. At intervals he would demand a certain tool or a specialized reference book; she would provide it. They had been buried in the laboratory now for several days, with infrequent breaks, Vorchek happily, Theresa somewhat less so.

"I don't get this Blug business, anyway," she was saying. "Flenberg is just a goon, with too much money and, for all his self-hatred, too high an opinion of himself. I don't see why you need take him so seriously."

"Miss Delaney, please minimize the distractions," suggested Vorchek, "and hand me that particle meter." She did that, with a mounting frown. "Thank you. Now, plug in the cord."

"Why can't I know things, too?" she whined. "You're supposed to be the professors' professor. Teach me!"

"It would take too long. I am at a critical stage."

"Every stage is critical, according to you. Give me a capsule summary."

"These tiresome impositions," Vorchek rumbled, but he laid down his tools and faced his companion. "All right, my dear. I've told you that Flenberg is not a fool—at least not a fool of the garden variety—and that his scheme is, theoretically, capable of operationalization. That should be enough for you; however, if it will further your education, I shall make clear to you just how strange his intentions really are."

"That's more like it," Theresa replied. She plopped herself into a seat, like a good student (which she could be, when interest compelled her), lit a cigarette and waited expectantly.

"Of all the myths and legends of olden times," began Vorchek, "few have proved more persistent or universal than the myth concerning Blug, the great god who dwells in the mystical Black Swamp. It is strange that this concept should be so pervasive, for it offers none of the commonplace attractions of conventional religion. In Blug the true believer finds no hope, no glory, no consideration; no salvation. Despite this, Blug worship has been traced all across the Earth, throughout the ages, in definite, recognizable forms, with surprisingly little variation. Although never establishing a broad cultural foothold anywhere, the myth has endured, whispered devoutly into one ear after another, with its logical substratum remaining intact. You may live a long life and never hear of it, but it is always there. Mr. Flenberg, a man of boundless resources, has tapped into that covert intellectual stream, and has learned sufficiently to realize that it is more than the latest dark twist on New Age nonsense.

THE MAN WHO SOUGHT BLUG

"Indications, hints, may be found in the most ancient of records. It was, however, a rather late Egyptian sorcerer, Artocris, who first wrote extensively of this matter, during the reign of the Ptolemies. His findings are contained in his shunned work, *The Seven Gates of Hell*, as it came to be called during the Dark Ages. Most scholars prefer the original title, *The Substance of Life As Revealed to Artocris*. That is by the way. I read his volume as a young man but, except for the purpose of acquiring background information, never followed up on it. It did not occur to me in those days that I should ever require such morbid knowledge. Lately, of course, I have thoroughly refreshed my education, reading everything I can get my hands on, and have corresponded with some impressive gentlemen who paid more heed to this subject. Apparently I have been missing out.

"So, genuine research begins with Artocris. He deduces, from personal observation, that the universe is a vile, terrible, and toxic realm, that the bedrock of living existence is horror and nausea. Make no mistake, Miss Delaney: he lays it on thickly; I'm cleaning this up for your sake. His first chapter consists of a catalogue of every crime, disease, atrocity, and disaster which can befall mankind, or living entities in general. Then, working from his first principles, Artocris concludes that this unbearable universe is in the clutches of, is controlled by, a supreme god who approves of all this nastiness. It stands to reason, so he assures us, that the intentions of the maker can only be understood by examining his fruits. The Egyptian actually employs a phrase which could be translated as the old standard tag, 'Ye shall know Him by His works.'

"Blug, we are told, is the universal Lord of Filth and Decay, the Master of Depravity and Squalor, who derives joy from everything foul and degrading. Those who 'believe on Him,' as the expression goes, are the lowliest specimens of humanity, those utterly convinced of their own degeneracy, beyond hope or pity, secretly craving to be treated according to their dim lights. The mindset of such pathetic people may not be understood by you or I, Miss Delaney, but they are out there; we recently enjoyed the dubious pleasure of conversing with one. I am convinced that Flenberg is the genuine article. The others must be similar. Blug's acolytes are not allowed the luxury of pleasant illusions; they know that they are lowly and worthless, that their God deems them so, and that He desires nothing but their destruction, preferably by their own hands. To the believer, the greatest human good—the only good—lies in finding one's way to Blug, abasing oneself at His feet, and seeking justice at His hands, or what passes for such. The Egyptian leaves open the question of what that justice entails: the questing soul finds oblivion, or is devoured by his Creator, or in some horrendous fashion becomes one with Him. Whatever the mechanism, the outcome is not a happy one.

"Having logically established the existence and sovereignty of this deity, Artocris set out to find Him. He writes of his travels through seven magical gates—openings in the space-time continuum, I would style them—and what he discovered on the other side. Each journey is a matter of interest, but through one of those gates Artocris claims to have located the Black Swamp. He describes the place in terms which are familiar now to you, thanks to Mr. Flenberg's account of his dream or vision: the stinking ooze, the rotting growths, scuttling parasites and grotesque creatures, and the central island where Blug holds eternal court. Artocris is strikingly reticent about the doomed dancers and the physical form of Blug Himself; but then the writer, having no desire to destroy himself, tells us that he maintained a sensible distance. He saw enough: the dead-alive souls of the believers, the venturing near of the brave to a half-seen mass; and then he recalls, or will recount, no more of the scene.

"Such is the tale of Artocris. Like many reputed wizards of the elder times, he is remarkably stingy with his practical lore. He never quite gets around to explaining how he found the right gate and passed through it. That is our specific, money-making goal, so I have had to turn to other worthy sources. I believe I have found the answer in a more recent author, the evilly wise Jacob Bleek. That mage of all mages, during his extraordinarily long life (I assume he is dead now, though records are vague and contradictory), wrote about every bizarre and magical topic you can imagine; that I can imagine, for that matter. Well aware of Blug worship, in his infamous *Black Book* he addressed the issue on numerous occasions. Unfortunately, my copy of Bleek is sadly incomplete. I have never been able to track down a whole copy; nor, I gather, has anyone else, at least no one who will admit to it. Still, what survives in the material available to me indicates an answer, one which has led to my current work.

"In a ghoulishly obnoxious chapter, oddly entitled 'Those Who Drink of Blug,' Bleek attempts to chart a course for those despairing mortals who would dare the journey. He says little of magic gates or spells; Bleek can be rather modern in his thinking and writing style. He states that certain rare crystals, in combination with other precious elements—which are desperately difficult to get hold of now, and must have been virtually impossible to acquire in his day—will turn the trick, by opening up vistas of other worlds and dimensions. It is not quite along the lines that we have attempted before, but close. Utilizing his process, he claims, one can peer into these forbidden realms through cracks in space and, if one be bold, the cracks may be sufficiently enlarged to allow bodily passage. Bleek precisely identifies the dimensional stream down which one must voyage in order to reach the so-called throne of Blug (which makes his knowledge fabulously useful to me), and admits that, while he chose not to undertake the harrowing journey himself, he did send several involuntary subjects through that time-space gap, and recorded the results.

"Most of them did not come back. Two returned, one of them in an incomplete state, from which he rapidly expired. The surviving subject came back in his entirety, unless one counts his mental condition, which had tragically disintegrated. Bleek got his story from the man, but it was so broken and disjointed that it did not materially add to what Artocris had reported in a former age.

"Nevertheless, I have most of Jacob Bleek's analysis before me, and so armed with his wisdom and the fruits of his quasi-scientific delvings, I have made a stab at living up to the terms of our contract with Jarrod Flenberg. This machine, which you see here taking shape, is the practical result."

Vorchek referred to the spidery apparatus of crystal rods and wedges, embedded within a complicated matrix of spiraled wiring and metal circuit boxes. "It relies on an atomic power source," he pointed out. "I would love to know how Bleek ever deduced the existence of such energy, much less put it to work for him. He must have done, and I expect that it will function for me."

"I don't care for that," Theresa protested, examining the contraption with distaste. "It sounds horribly dangerous. Surely, Professor, you don't intend to test it on yourself?"

"Lord, no," Vorchek exclaimed. "Once it is completed, I shall guarantee that the mechanisms function. There will be no field tests, however. Mr. Flenberg is the only man who shall utilize it in the manner for which it was designed. That is, if he does not abandon his scheme, which still might be a possibility. Anyway, I have included a cunning fail-safe feature which will prevent future unpleasantness on the part of the unwary. This machine will operate, fully, only once, and then it will irretrievably break down. I will make clear to our generous employer that he gets just one shot at it."

"Why does he need a machine?" Theresa expostulated. "If these sickening stories be true, many people have just—well, gone—gone on their own, by wishing themselves there, I guess. He thinks he's done it. Why can't he keep wishing until it happens again?"

"That is why he is paying us the big bucks, my dear; to remove the element of chance. Perhaps Blug enjoys toying with his victims, making life harder for them. No matter how wretched the quest, it should not be too easy. Flenberg wants it easy, and he is willing to pay for a smooth ride."

"Maybe he'll chicken out," Theresa mused. "Flenberg's a blowhard; I spotted that right away. It might tickle his fancy to dabble with such craziness, but I can't believe he'd be stupid enough to carry it out."

***

On the contrary, as the weeks passed Flenberg grew more insistent, demanding by mail and telephone to hear of Vorchek's progress, almost begging that the experiment be completed immediately. Toward the end he became frantic, and the professor could almost bring himself to pity a man who so desired self-destruction or worse. "I can't stand it anymore!" Flenberg screamed at Vorchek one night over the phone. "You have no idea what's it's like for me out here. All seems useless; getting out of bed in the afternoon"—those were his words—"is torture. Give me a date, or I can't function much longer."

"The device will be ready when it is finished."

"Not good enough! I tell you, I'm falling to pieces. I'm currently working on a big movie project, the biggest yet. It's garbage, of course, but it ought to be a gold mine. You can guess, Professor, how little I really care for that, but I want to get it done anyway, want it badly. It's my swan song, my last trivial statement to a pointless world. I want to rub their noses in it, cackling at them as I go. I can do it, I think, I can hold out, but I can't go on until I'm sure you'll come through for me. Promise me!"

"You have my word," said Vorchek. "My project will work. Be patient a little longer, sir. I am very close now."

Dozens of adjustments remained to be made on what he styled the "Bleek Machine" (and what Theresa called, with more feeling, "that creepy gizmo"), but Vorchek adjusted merrily away, before long being able to report his satisfaction with the final result. He notified Flenberg by telegram that the machine was ready, inviting the movie king to come to the desert laboratory, at his convenience, in order to make his peculiar personal arrangements. The professor received a registered express letter the next day:

"It is done? Good, it's time. I've almost got this ridiculous movie off my back, and then I'm all set. I can't tear myself away from here, though. Travel now doesn't suit me. Bring my machine out here at once. Enclosed is an additional check for $10,000 to ease your way. Come immediately. Bring the thing straight to the studio. Don't keep me waiting. I can taste it already."

The extra ten thousand dollars overcame a considerable portion of Vorchek's irritation. In order to collect the utmost data from the process, he had intended to carry out the experiment in a controlled laboratory setting, with monitors operating. As much as he desired this, he realized that he worked for hire, and would have to bend his rules. That being the case, he quickly responded to Flenberg, agreeing to the condition while demanding one of his own. He insisted on a slight delay until the director could send a certain item of equipment for inclusion into the Bleek Machine. Flenberg went berserk, as testified to by a forthcoming late night call.

"I have no need of that!" he screamed.

"I do," said the professor.

Flenberg soon calmed down to a degree, grudgingly accepting the new terms after asking several questions, which Vorchek artfully declined to answer. The equipment arrived by private van, the professor incorporated the requested item into his device, and two days later he and Theresa conveyed the completed apparatus by van to Hollywood, arriving after an early morning drive.

Work had, meanwhile, been wrapped up on Flenberg's latest cinematic extravaganza. The cavernous sound stage, where the final scenes were filmed, stood empty, and he had the big crated object taken straight into it.

"There must be no disturbances while the machine is running," Vorchek told him. "That is most important. I do not care for such a public place."

"This studio is my private property for a few more days," Flenberg snapped. He looked older, more worn; his edginess had increased. Tension had been eating at him, rendering him perilously close to collapse. "No one gets in without my say-so, and they don't get that."

"That is acceptable," replied Vorchek. "I will set up the machine for you. Everything will be in place. At the moment of your choosing, all you will have to do is throw a switch and sit back. Then the machine takes over. At that time you must be alone. No one else can be within range of the energy field—a diameter of a hundred feet or so—or the process may fail. Do you understand?"

"Loud and clear. Set it up."

"As you wish. Miss Delaney, this will take some doing. Would you give me a hand?"

"Yes, Professor."

Flenberg stood aside as they worked, staring as if at a far horizon. "It is coming," he said gently. "At last, bliss; the bliss of consummate degradation."

***

"Indeed, Mr. Abernathy, I quite understand your position," Vorchek was saying, "but it puzzles me that you should travel all the way out here, into the wilderness, just to speak with Miss Delaney and me of this matter. I do not see how I can contribute."

"It's no trouble," replied the addressed gentleman, who sat with his host and hostess in the cozy den of Vorchek's isolated desert retreat, the professor's black cat Claudia rubbing curiously between his shins. He exhaled a puff from one of Vorchek's expensive cigars. "I flew into Phoenix and rented a car. I'll admit that was something of a drive, especially after leaving pavement. I was sure I'd lost my way."

"On the contrary, you have found it, but, perhaps, to no purpose."

"More tea, Mr. Abernathy?" offered Theresa, who poured without waiting for his answer.

"Thank you. Ah, good little kitty; she takes to my trousers. Off you go. Well, that I would undertake such efforts may surprise you—it isn't often that a studio executive finds himself in such unusual surroundings—but Flenberg is important to us, and since his disappearance I've grown somewhat concerned. He left hanging numerous administrative matters, which don't necessarily require his approval, but could stand his attention. I thought, Professor Vorchek, that you might have some idea of his whereabouts."

"Why would you think so?"

"I know, from documents, that you had extensive dealings with him in the months before he vanished. Large sums changed hands—the financial records are most irregular—I can't quite make out the connection. You built something for him, a machine, which I found left over on the sound stage. Some kind of special effects machine, I take it?"

"It was intended to produce special effects."

"I don't know that he used it. Fortunately he finished his film before he went. I attended to post-production editing myself."

"What did you think of the movie?" asked Theresa.

Abernathy chuckled. "Between you and me? It's a piece of crap, like all his movies, just a bunch of noisy computer images strung together, tied up with a collection of silly pop songs. His usual result, but the video game crowd love the stuff."

"Who stars in this one?" she persisted.

"If you'll pardon me, I haven't time to go into that at the moment. I really do want to track down Flenberg."

"Have you involved the police?" asked Vorchek.

"Absolutely not!" cried Abernathy. "This isn't the first time he's taken off on us. He's most likely on another tear, bingeing aboard a yacht wandering the Mediterranean, or some such foolishness. He's never remained out of touch so long, however, and the last time I saw him his behavior was strange . . . I mean stranger than usual. Also, I'd planned to cobble up another movie deal with him, and I can't do that until I hear from him, can I?"

"I can't imagine the police being interested," Theresa said sullenly.

"Of course not, but I am. Professor Vorchek, have you no idea where Flenberg is right now?"

"I can tell you," replied the professor, "that I have no idea."

"You could tell him that," Theresa muttered under her breath, "if you were lying through your teeth." Vorchek nudged her into silence.

"That's it, then," sighed Abernathy. After a lingering pause he went on, "Professor, about that machine: I can't tell from the documentation whose property it is. Do you want it back?"

"That would please me. It is nonfunctional now, but I may be able to do something with it."

"Over my dead body," Theresa whispered.

"More importantly, the apparatus contains a roll of sixteen millimeter film, which Mr. Flenberg should have exposed for me during the operation of the machine. I desire that, as quickly as you can get it to me."

"The film!" Abernathy nodded and shook a finger in the air, as if remembering a minor point which he had forgotten. "Yes, I'm familiar with that, although I didn't appreciate its significance. I'm sorry to tell you this, but I had it destroyed."

"Did you?" Vorchek looked suddenly crestfallen.

"What film?" Theresa wondered. "Professor, I never heard of this."

"I failed to mention it to you, my dear. It was all part of the experiment. Mr. Flenberg sent out a movie camera, which I set up inside the Bleek machine. Mr. Abernathy, you might think of it as a sort of test footage."

"That's exactly what I did think," came the reply. "That being the case, I can assure you the test was a failure. The film didn't develop properly, or for whatever reason didn't come out right. There wasn't much to see."

"You viewed it yourself?"

"I did. I thought it might be footage related to his latest movie. It plainly wasn't that, and didn't appear to be good for anything. It was just crazy stuff, so I junked it."

"Good sir," Vorchek said earnestly, starting forward, "you would be doing me a gigantic favor if you recalled, in all possible detail, what you saw on that reel of film."

"If it matters that much to you—" Abernathy hesitated, studying the eagerness of his host, and something other than eagerness in Theresa. "I recollect it well enough. It wasn't professional footage by any means. It looked crude, amateurish, grainy, and very dark—I mainly see in my mind the darkness—as if badly lighted, or using natural light. I knew it was test footage because no name actors appeared in it. The star, you might say, was Flenberg himself. Under those poor viewing conditions I could barely recognize him.

"Apparently this was a location shoot, for the scenery was like nothing we'd put together on stage. Flenberg, usually seen from behind, was walking swiftly through wet, broken terrain. There were endless shots of that, all close up and fuzzy, without much in the way of detail, although I noticed images of damp, dripping plants. Could he have filmed this in the rain? That might explain the scene, and the poor conditions.

"Suddenly there came a long shot. The camera—which held steady throughout; none of his typical handheld tripe—opened upon space, a space of pitch darkness, at first. Then I realized I was looking at a crowd scene, very poorly done; not up to his standard, I would say. There were lots of people in a small area, but I couldn't make out who they were or what they were doing. They seemed to be running around aimlessly, going nowhere in particular. Flenberg dived into the group at a run, and the image followed him, but I still didn't get a decent look at the others. Maybe it was a trick lens; they looked distorted. I couldn't make much of that. By this time I was ready to give up anyway."

"The psychic capture actually worked," mumbled Vorchek.

"Excuse me?"

"Nothing. Go on."

"There isn't much more. This was a short film. Flenberg pushed through those people, rather roughly, and made his way to a black wall or mound. The picture was especially bad here. Due to a trick of the light, the black mound seemed to move; or maybe it was an effect. If so, it didn't impress me.

"If Flenberg was trying to make a point, I haven't the slightest what it was. I could barely make out the finale. I caught a glimpse of his face: he was rapt in ecstasy; obviously having a good time. He got down on hands and knees before the mound, and crawled to it. I could see more detail; the shaky mound wasn't—what's the word?—homogenous, that's it. There were big, damp, whitish bumps all over it. I thought they were growing out of it, getting bigger as he raised his head to them. And then—this mystifies me— he did something weird. Flenberg stretched forward (I'm sure I saw this correctly) and took one of those odd bumps in his mouth. The camera held on him while he appeared to suck on that ugly thing, and then the image blanked out, and the reel ended."

Theresa sprang to her feet, and without a word to either man ran from the room. They stared after her, until Vorchek smiled and said in his most suave manner, "Without warning, nature will call. Thank you, Mr. Abernathy. You have done me a great service. I must detain you no longer."

"That was helpful to you?" Abernathy asked as he rose.

"Indubitably. I regret that I am not able to aid you to the same degree. Good luck on your search, however. Be sure to give my regards to Mr. Flenberg, when next you see him."

ALL EXPENSES PAID

I.
SEASIDE VACATION
ALL EXPENSES PAID

Dear Mr. Cravitt:

We are pleased to announce that you are a winner. Your entry has been selected as one of our grand prizes. You will receive an all expenses paid, five day vacation for one at the exclusive Caltel Ocean Resort. Enjoy your holiday in elegant, old-fashioned surroundings:

Relish the fine accommodations

Bask in the healthful sea air

Swim in the sparkling surf of a clean, white sand beach

Dine heartily on the masterworks of our acclaimed Old World chef

Mingle with others in an intimate setting

Enjoy peace and quiet, without maddening crowds.

All this is yours, but you must call now!

"All Expenses Paid" means no travel charges, no taxes, no surcharges or hidden fees of any kind. This amazing vacation is free to you, if you call now!

In order that our staff may provide the very best service, we choose to limit the number of resort guests at any one time. Vacancies are few, demand is high, so if you are interested in this once in a lifetime opportunity, we urge you to make your reservations immediately. Our customer service representatives are standing by to take your call.

The page closed "Sincerely, COR Enterprises," followed by an illegible penned signature. The flip side contained a telephone number and unusually strict conditions on when to call. The offer pleased Martin Cravitt, although he had numerous questions, and it surprised him as well. The statement seemed to imply he had entered some sort of contest. He remembered nothing of the kind. He never fooled with contests because, in times past, he had never won any of them, no matter how trivial. The brochure bore no return address. It contained no pictures. Other than the beach location, it gave no indication whatsoever as to geographical whereabouts. He had never heard of the Caltel Ocean Resort. The whole thing was an enticing, tantalizing mystery.

In a tentative, offhand fashion he asked around the office to find out if anyone knew anything about it. No one did. That night, alone in his small, Spartan apartment, he phoned the provided number during one of the narrow windows of opportunity. A pleasant, vaguely mannered female voice answered. The conversation proved remarkably noncommittal. The representative, who failed to give her name, had no new information to impart, but did offer to arrange an appointment at the firm's local travel office. Cravitt jotted down the unfamiliar street address and pertinent details, wondering all the while if he intended following up the contact.

He did so, at the set time, on the morning of his next off day. His destination, it transpired, was a decrepit strip mall on a run-down street on the cheap side of town. The look of the area—classic urban blight—didn't fill him with great hopes. However, when he got off the public bus he spotted right away the bright, fresh "Travel Office" sign, over a refurbished store front which appeared much superior to the dingy shops around it. He asked himself if he had gotten the time wrong. The voice had been most specific, but everything in the vicinity seemed closed, much of it permanently. He tried the door; locked. He hesitated, observed the locale with a jaundiced eye, gave half a thought to fleeing, and then the door suddenly swung inward.

"May I help you?" asked a brisk, youngish man. Cravitt briefly explained himself. "Of course, Mr. Cravitt, I was expecting you. You're my first customer of the day. Come right in and we'll get started."

A perusal of the interior revealed the hallmarks of a bare-bones operation: a counter, a single large, plain table, scattered with generic literature, several metal folding chairs and a handful of colored posters promoting exotic locales on the walls. There was no one else present, not even a secretary. Nothing he saw connected to his postal offer.

"We've handled many bookings for the COR people," said the agent, by way of explanation. He introduced himself as Bob. "They don't go in for a lot of fancy advertising. They're an exclusive outfit, and they want their customers to know it. Let me tell you a little something about their operation." He did so, but nothing he had to say added materially to Cravitt's pre-existing store of information. It all sounded, however, most impressive. The resort was down south, on a secluded, unspoiled stretch of coast. It had been a going concern for ages, but only in recent years had anyone been invited to vacation there. As part of their traditional, and rather unique policy, they didn't allow many guests at one time. Bob didn't have any photographs of the property—a lamentable lack—but he had seen it for himself, and waxed effusive on its quaint, rustic charm.

"Only certain dates are still available," Bob pointed out. He listed certain week-long blocks extending over the next couple of months. "What period would be most suitable for you?" Cravitt chose one, far enough in the future he could confidently predict getting the time off. "Thank you, that is perfect. Now, would you be so kind as to fill in this form, please?" It required just name, address, telephone number, and a few statements of personal taste and, as it happened, that was it. Bob assured him the resort folks would be in touch to set up the final travel plans, all of which they would handle for him—a good thing too, since he didn't own a car—and he need have no further worries. He was "in".

When he returned to work Cravitt suffered a brief scare due to employer intransigence. His boss of many years, a fellow who had joined the firm after he did, was inclined to be troublesome. That hurt him. Cravitt had always been a stolid, dependable employee, never asked for any special favors, nor inclined to press issues. He took so little time off he seldom used up his annual vacation allotment (he couldn't afford big plans, and sitting around a stale apartment didn't suit him).This was the first occasion on which he'd requested a specific time frame. Others did as a matter of course, and routinely got away with it. For once Cravitt felt obstinate.

"I don't know if I can work it out now," said the office manager; ridiculous; now as ever. "It might conflict with scheduling." Yes, vacations were prone to doing that; so what? "Give me time to think about it." There was nothing to think about. Cravitt had done the thinking. Resistance fueled desire. He would take this trip. He took a hard line, at least in his own mind—he couldn't assert himself too much—it didn't come naturally to him, but stubbornness saw him through. He didn't quite raise his voice, but he didn't leave the manager's office until he had obtained the jerk's surly acquiescence. His boss shrugged and let it pass, as if the subject were of little consequence anyway. Cravitt got what he wanted. He was dismayed, though, to discover with such clarity, just how little respected he was in the workplace. He had always assumed, without testing the proposition, that he mattered more.

One week before the day arranged, he received a call from an unnamed COR representative, who informed him that on the awaited morning a chartered bus would come to his residence, at nine o'clock on the dot, to pick him up. He could bring as much luggage as he could carry. "There will be plenty of room for your effects," said the pleasant, vaguely mannered female voice. Well, he would carry one large piece; that was all he owned, and surely no more would be necessary. The voice approved of his decision. "We at COR Enterprises promise you an entertaining and rewarding experience."

Came the big day. Not knowing what was expected of him, but always desiring to look his best despite limited means, he dressed for the occasion: jacket and tie, and shined shoes. He was ready by eight, too nervous for breakfast, and spent the final hour peeking out the window every five minutes. Moments of doubt had arisen during the long wait. He wondered what he was getting himself into with this vacation. He never did anything like this. He had heard of theoretically free trips being offered to the unwary—all too often, as it turned out, sold to suckers—but had never put much faith in them. They usually seemed to end up at gambling casinos, which most likely justified the deal to corporate sponsors. What was the justification in this case? What was in it for the investors behind COR?

Perhaps his ride wouldn't show. Just then a large unmarked van, or rather a small mobile home pulled into the parking lot. One of those super campers, he thought. It stopped, and a young man emerged wearing a cap and what could pass as a uniform. He took from his shirt pocket a note pad, flipped through it, looked up at the building. This wasn't what Cravitt expected, but something told him this was it. He dashed out of the apartment with his suitcase and down the stairs, accosted the man.

The fellow grinned, said, "Hi, I'm John. You're Mr. Cravitt? Good. Any time you're ready—" John opened the back doors, revealing a roomy interior that could seat six. No one else was inside. "I'll put your luggage here." He ushered his charge inside. "Make yourself comfortable." Cravitt chose a seat by the left window. "If it's all right with you, I don't plan to make any stops. It shouldn't be necessary, as you'll see. We'll drive right through. It ought to take about two hours." He shut the doors, returned to the cab, and they were soon underway.

Cravitt soon learned what the driver meant. A snack bar held fruit juice, soft drinks, and sandwiches. A narrow door in one corner opened upon a chemical toilet. So, no need to stop for necessities. He resumed his seat and relaxed to enjoy the drive.

Their route wound through town, then out onto the highway. He'd thought they might stop somewhere anyway, to pick up more passengers, but it didn't happen. Having traveled west for a spell on the main highway, they turned onto a secondary road and headed northwest through farmland, which gave way to increasingly dense wooded territory. He still wasn't so far from home, but Cravitt wasn't familiar with the area. He had never explored a great deal, due to lack of time and funds. There were some fine country drives, he'd heard, in these parts.

Also, he couldn't make much sense out of the direction they were going. Possibly he should have paid more attention, but he couldn't understand how this route would take them to what he presumed to be the destination. Were they, after all, making a detour to collect others? His concern grew when they came to the intersection with another rural road, one which provided a distant view of the ocean, and took the turn due north. That didn't seem right at all. He rose and rapped on the pane separating him from the cab. John reached back and opened the window a crack.

"I'm not scheduled to pick up anyone else this trip," John said. "South? No, the resort is north, straight north from here. We aren't too far away now. I'll have you there in a jiffy. Somebody must have gotten your information confused." Cravitt supposed he might have made the mistake, although the direction to the place was one of the few facts he thought he remembered clearly. It really didn't matter. He ate a ham sandwich, drank some orange juice, and dismissed it as just one of those things.

The road wound through steep hills, then down into a broad valley, at the bottom of which lay a little village. Cravitt caught the name—Tellmee— but it meant nothing to him. Prosperity, development, and a good chunk of the previous century had passed this place by. The road became the main street, and kept running north, but they turned onto an asphalt-patched local lane which led off to the west, toward the sea. The village immediately vanished behind them, while the road degenerated into a dirt strip consisting mainly of potholes, these obstacles occasionally reinforced by protruding stones of threatening size.

The road—or path, as he deemed it, so bad did it become—dipped among wind rustled trees, then wound down through a kind of gully or ravine gouged into the earth. Dirt walls rose up like a gorge. At one point they passed through a dilapidated entrance, with the road gate hanging open. Cravitt noted the rusted black on white sign: "Private Property. Keep Out." Onward and downward they bounced and jostled. Now another sign appeared on the right, a brand new one constructed of railroad ties and brightly painted red. "Welcome to the Caltel Ocean Resort" it read, and underneath, in smaller letters, the words "Established 1922". Beyond that they came to another fence and open gate, a padlock hanging loosely. Then the trees and the heaped banks fell away, and he saw the lovely blue ocean and the wide beach of gorgeously white sand. The van turned sharply to the left onto a smooth gravel drive, just at the edge of the sand, and there before him lay the resort.

SCIENCE AND SORCERY III
II.

Cravitt gleaned his initial impressions in the few seconds required to pull up to the main building. Okay, so this was what a resort looked like. This place looked old, suggestive of an historic relic rather than a thriving establishment. It could never have been fancy, although it might still possess a certain elegance. Everything was wooden. The key structure, before which they parked, was obviously the hotel. A two-story affair, whitewashed, not extremely large but long and narrow, presided over the hillside like a beached ship, with a peaked roof. Such a building couldn't hold more than a score of rooms, he reflected. Those on the ground floor didn't have outer doors, only windows. Those on the upper level opened onto a railed walkway or communal balcony, with stairs at the ends. A single small window above the rest suggested an attic. A raised boardwalk, almost like a pier, jutted from the seaward side and extended down to the water's edge. He glimpsed other structures beyond, but at present didn't get a good look at them.

He dismounted with his suitcase. Another van and two regular cars were parked in the gravel lot. That was all. John appeared, whisked the case from him and cheerfully led him—"Right this way, sir"—through the yawning double doors into the lobby. The exterior might be quaint and functional, but the interior was stylish and ornate. Paneled walls bore impressionistic paintings (prints, maybe) of beach holiday scenes of long ago, hanging rugs and atmospheric nautical artifacts, such as driftwood, naval ropes and stuffed gulls. One wall contained a large stone fireplace, unlit. Plush carpet, worn with age but clean and attractive, covered the floor, which creaked slightly where he trod. The vaulted ceiling rose high overhead, peaking at a tremendous chandelier which gleamed brightly through a million facets of cut glass. Every wooden surface appeared polished and varnished to a deep red, and looked hand carved. The sweet aroma of incense filled the air of the room.

A check-in booth beckoned from across the lobby, but Cravitt never made it to the counter. Two people came to meet him: a stout, red-faced older man with an easy, good-natured countenance, and an aesthetically thin, middle-aged woman who exuded an appearance of being all business. Both were well-attired, especially the man, who sported an expensively fashionable suit. The woman wore a long black dress which brushed the floor. The man spoke briefly to John, enunciating his words with a mild foreign accent, in an attitude of genial command.

"Take Mr. Cravitt's luggage up, please, and be sure his room is prepared. Good morning, sir," he said loudly, turning to Cravitt and clapping his meaty hands. "Allow me to welcome you to our hide-away resort. I am Mr. Hartmann, the general manager. This is Mrs. Drexel, the hotel's housekeeper, as well as my oldest and most competent assistant. She will administer to all of your needs during your visit."

"How do you do?" she said, in a pleasant, vaguely mannered voice.

"We wish you the very best during your stay. To us, your happiness here is paramount. Enjoy our facilities as you please. When you get about the grounds, you will see the horse stables and the boat house. Beware the sun; very bad for the eyes. On the ground floor we have a large dining room and a cozy lounge. The latter is available to you at all times. There is plenty of good food, a well stocked wine cellar containing the best French and German vintages, even a classical library on the English pattern. It is early yet, but everything we have to offer will be available by lunch time." Cravitt thanked him for the kind words. "It is my pleasure, sir," Mr. Hartmann replied. "I trust that you will enjoy the company, company of people with whom you have much in common. At the moment we have only one prior arrival, but we expect the other presently. Mrs. Drexel, would you show the gentleman to his room?"

"If you will follow me, sir?" She motioned toward the stairs to the left of the counter, up which John had disappeared.

"We appreciate your acceptance of this opportunity," said Mr. Hartmann. "Make as much of it as you will. Until later, then."

The woman mounted the stairs with Cravitt in tow, a lingering smell of incense wafting after them. As they proceeded she commenced, as on cue, a running monologue on the history of the Caltel Ocean Resort. "The building was erected as a private summer residence for Thomas J. Dashauer, the oil tycoon, in 1912. He is famous for being one of the very first billionaires. Dashauer's Retreat, it's still called in Tellmee. The property was bought out after his death, the building extended, opened to the general public in 1922 as the Seaview Hotel. The resort's original incarnation closed during the war years, not resuming business until 1947. The previous owners sold the property in 1953, and for some years it once again became a private home. In 1962 the present owners acquired the resort, gave it its current name, and have been operating it on a restricted public basis ever since."

Two flights of steps brought them to the second story, a long gallery which spanned the length of the building. No adornment up here, dim hall lighting, simple and inviting. "Number 21, sir." The door stood open, Cravitt's suitcase just inside. She gave him the room key.

Mrs. Drexel recited a few more salient facts. "Breakfast is served at eight, sir; lunch at noon, dinner at seven. It is usually very little trouble for the cook to prepare snacks, for between meals or outings. That is handled by special arrangement. All meals are served in the dining room. You may take breakfast in your room, if you so order it. Drinks shall be provided at any time at your request. Is there anything I may do for you now?"

Cravitt had a question, based on a puzzling statement made by Mr. Hartmann.

"That is correct," she replied. "We are expecting a total of three guests only. One other is already here; a young lady, a Miss Carswell. I believe she is out walking the beach at present. I beg your pardon? Oh, it is a strict policy of our establishment. Neither more nor less than three at any given time. Sir, we do not concern ourselves with such crude matters as profitability. We have bountiful resources of that kind. Your pleasure, right up until the last moment of your stay, is our goal. I can assure you that we derive an absolutely enormous degree of satisfaction from our endeavors here." Then, after almost fawning parting formalities, she withdrew.

Cravitt entered and perused his room: small, as would be the norm for an old place—and with its atmosphere rather cloyed by the ever-present perfume, which they laid on pretty thick—but possessing every comfort. To be precise, every old-fashioned comfort: no television, no video or DVD player, no microwave oven—no great loss. He had those back in the tiresome real world. He didn't need any of those things here. What he got (for free, he reminded himself) was a big, fat four poster bed, which might have belonged to a king or a captain, a small table with two cushioned chairs, an awesome chest of drawers, a writing desk, several lamps and some other convenient odds and ends, all tasteful, encompassed by paneled walls bearing paintings or prints similar to those below. A window, framed by curtains, revealed the sweep of the beach, with light surf, terminating in white foam in the distance, beneath rocky bluffs. Bright, fresh shag rugs of geometric design sprouted from the hard wooden floor. Two adjacent doors opened onto a small clothes closet and a tiny bathroom with shower. Another door by the window gave onto the balcony, with groups of chairs spaced at irregular intervals. And on a small table, an ancient telephone, which might have been installed in 1922.

It was all refreshingly unconventional; perhaps charming was the right word. He could get used to this place. He could relish five days here.

Cravitt sat down on the huge bed. He laid back. The bed enveloped him. So, what now? For the first time in a long while he had nothing to do, so naturally his mind revolved unbidden, considering his options. Case the joint, he said to himself. He got up, refreshed himself in the bathroom sink (which amused him with its antiquated, noisy plumbing), went prowling.

He returned downstairs and examined the facilities. An unknown older man acknowledged him in the lobby, but let him wander alone. Apparently most of the first floor was given over to services. He visited the dining room, a fancy, rather cavernous place for the number of guests who would be occupying it. There were at least a dozen tables, only three of them laid. Three tables for one. Something about that image irritated him. Surely he could do better than that on such a vacation. He was scarcely a mingler, but he desired company when opportunity knocked. Swinging doors led into the kitchen. He could hear someone banging around in there.

He peered into the library. He had no idea what "English pattern" meant. It was small, crammed with books. They looked musty and old, like the stock in an expensive used book store devoted to collectors. There could be interesting items awaiting him there. It impressed him the place kept books for the guests. Was that often done? He wouldn't know.

Next he passed an office or utility room, and beyond that, the lounge. It was set up like a reading den, and in practice most likely functioned as an adjunct to the library. Periodicals in attractive piles and a number of boxed games were stacked about. He noticed the lounge was occupied, and after a moment's hesitation crossed the threshold to introduce himself.

"How do you do? My name is Martin Cravitt. I believe we're going to be neighbors," he said, addressing a young woman, fresh-faced and somewhat attractive, if a little plump, as was the fashion nowadays. The easy chair dwarfed her, as she smoked a cigarette while leafing through a magazine. She was dressed rather cheaply—not coarsely, but with a bit too much by way of garish feminine adornment for his taste—and sat beside a big, gaudy handbag—all of which projected to his mind a notion of wild or uninhibited character. He wasn't quite willing to accept this as company with whom he had much in common.

She lowered the magazine, puffed smoke, rose halfway from her seat and shook his outstretched hand. "Hi. I'm Diana Carswell. I just got here a little while ago. Did you win a free trip, too?" She slipped back into the seat.

"I don't know how, but I did. May I join you?"

She seemed slightly uncomfortable, pensive. "If you like."

"Thank you." He took a chair which wasn't too close to hers. "You beat me here by just a little bit. I'm given to understand that we aren't going to be a large crowd. What do you think of the resort so far, Miss Carswell?"

"You can call me Diana," she giggled.

"Very good. I'm Martin. How does the place strike you?"

"I don't know. I've never seen anything like it. I suppose I'll be in a better position to judge later."

"True. I expected more hustle and bustle."

"You got that right. There aren't many people here."

"You do know we're two-thirds of the clientele?"

"So I heard. I can't believe it."

"I still haven't seen much of the staff."

"There are six or seven of them," Diana said, counting with her fingers. "The top dogs, a couple of waiters, drivers. I met Hartmann—"

"As did I."

"He's all right. Then there's Mrs. Drexel."

"Indeed," cried Martin. "Now that I think of it, there's something about her. For some reason I feel I've run across her before, that I should know her."

"Maybe she's Dracula's stepdaughter."

"No, I don't mean anything like that. I'm sure she's very nice."

"If you say so. She gives me the creeps. Don't you think this place is creepy?"

"It hadn't struck me that way," he chuckled. "Of course, I haven't seen much of it yet."

"I mean how isolated it is, and how old it is, and how—" She shook her head. "It smells funny. Did you notice that? They use a lot of air freshener, but it doesn't work always. I think they've got mold somewhere." Now that she mentioned it, Martin was aware of this. In certain areas, like in the upper hall before several rooms, the hint of an unpleasant mustiness, possibly akin to that of the library, possibly not, had affronted his nose. The girl went on, "The whole set-up is improbable. How do these people make a living out of giving a few strangers free vacations?"

"This would qualify as the off season, wouldn't it? Maybe they do a booming business during the tourist months."

"That isn't how I heard it. I got the impression it's always like this, giving out a handful of freebies. I'm supposed to have won a contest, but it's news to me. Mine came out of the blue. Yours did too? So there. Somebody with deep pockets must be propping up this operation."

"A philanthropist."

"I guess. That's someone who gives away a lot of money? It must be like that."

They discussed the possibilities of a resort as a charitable institution. Martin figured they'd chosen well in his case. During the conversation he learned she had not been offered a choice of vacation weeks, but had to accept the only one still available. He had been lucky. He asked her what she had been reading.

"An old magazine. Look at it: 1953. Have you ever seen anything like it? People used to read this stuff all the time. I kind of like the pictures. They're colorful. Now it's falling apart. Most of these magazines are the same way."

"Some of these might date back to the war. That could be a thrill. I don't see anything—"

"It's a pile of women's magazines, fishing guides and boating stories."

"I hadn't heard about fishing."

"Do you fish?"

"Not yet, but I'm ready for anything."

And so forth. He learned she hailed from his city—lived only a few miles away from him—and visited the same travel agency. Soon Diana took her leave, leaving Martin to his own devices until lunch. He chose to while away the minutes by extending his tour to the grounds. He exited through the side door onto the railed boardwalk, and followed it down to the shore, descending the steps at the end. It appeared badly in need of repair. In spots entire planks were missing, and others shifted underfoot. The ocean looked glorious, however, and the air smelled salty and clean. Fleecy white clouds scudded over the sea in a deep blue sky.

Over to the left stood the boathouse, a dingy building with part of the roof gone. Beneath a sagging overhang at a decrepit corner he recoiled from a scanty web in which dangled a creeping black widow spider. Through the windows he could make out, within the gloomy, trashy interior, a mid-sized sailboat, whitewashed and looking ready to sail, wallowing within a narrow trough of water cut into the sand. Massive wooden piles supported the front of the shelter, facing the sea, where wide doors allowed ingress and regress. Martin knew nothing about boating, but assumed someone on the staff could pilot it and offer rides.

Up the beach he found a locked building, without windows, which must be some kind of tool or storage shed, quite large, also extremely dilapidated. He heard a thumping sound, as of some mechanism in action, emanating from within. A cable stretched from the roof to the ground, then across the sand to a corner of the hotel. Beyond loomed the stables, a better kept structure, although desperately in need of paint. He saw four horses inside, well-groomed animals. Horses for three, and one for the guide. The powers that be had planned to a tee.

From what he had observed Martin gained the impression the hotel had been extensively refurbished, possibly in fairly recent times, while the rest of the resort had yet to undergo such costly work. Mrs. Drexel hadn't said anything about really new management, but that might explain current conditions, and answer some of Diana's questions, which he thought rather sound. While no expert on these things, Martin couldn't help but conclude the Caltel Ocean Resort united maintained splendor with historic decrepitude to an astonishing degree. Perhaps COR Enterprises was starting up the place again after an indeterminate hiatus.

Close on noon, he circled back to the hotel, passing around and entering through the front. Once more he met the unknown man, who now introduced himself.

"Nylstrom, sir. You must be Mr. Cravitt. Begging your pardon, but I was busy before, and got myself in a hurry. Lunch is served. Miss Carswell and Mr. Horton just went in this minute. The dining room is this way, down the corridor." This Martin knew, but he allowed himself to be led.

Diana and the heretofore unseen Mr. Horton were dining separately, as he expected. Nylstrom placed Martin at the table between them. Quick as a wink a young waiter in white jacket bustled out and deposited before him a plate of pot roast, green beans, cole slaw, rolls with real butter, and cantaloupe spears. He offered a choice of beverages, from which red wine was accepted. From the kitchen door a heavyset man also in white, wearing a stereotypical chef's hat, studiously observed the proceedings.

"I'm Thomas," said the waiter, "and that's Maurice, our cook. He's an honest to goodness French chef. He can't speak a word of English. He prepares everything on site. In our circles he has quite a reputation. He keeps lunch simple, but he will amaze you at night. His dinners are a feast for the eyes as well as the palate. Eat hearty. If you want more, just call." Thomas slipped past his boss into the kitchen. Martin nodded to that worthy. He nodded back without speaking, then withdrew.

Martin indulged himself with gusto—having skipped breakfast, and taken only the snack on the drive up, his belly was becoming insistent—but he did not forsake the social graces. "Diana, hello again." She waved back, her mouth full. "And Mr. Horton, I presume?"

"Wallis Horton. My friends call me Wally. You're Martin. She's Diana. It shouldn't be hard to keep our names straight."

"Not if we're the entire passenger list on this ship."

"I'm glad to be here, but we couldn't make up a hand of bridge."

Wally was a genial, smiling, quiet-voiced fellow, somewhat past middle age, far gone into baldness. He looked flabby and soft, without being especially corpulent. He seemed tired and gray. Martin fancied he might be suffering from ill health. He wore a shabby suit too hot for the season's daylight hours, and too tight by a size.

"Then we will have to find other things to do," Martin replied, "unless we can convince Mr. Hartmann to join us."

"That's worth trying. He's a very friendly sort."

"You are, of course, here as a special guest, all expenses paid?"

"There's no other way they would let me in the door." Wally explained how he came to be there, which was by now a familiar story. He motioned with his laden fork. "This is good stuff, isn't it?"

No question about that. Without any pretense of French cuisine—at the moment, at any rate—Maurice knew how to whip up a satisfying meal. The others agreed with his assessment. Martin contemplated seconds.

He very much wanted to engage Diana in further conversation. One of his hopes for this vacation was to meet many new and interesting people. As it had turned out, there wasn't as much scope for that as expected—amazingly less—but he wanted to do the best he could. He had doubts about Diana, but she was the only girl in town, and it would be wasteful of the opportunity not to try ingratiating himself. He had so few chances, under normal circumstances, for social contact, not to mention romantic.

Martin wasn't skilled at gay banter with females, however, and Wally's suppressive presence (through no fault of that gentleman) tied his tongue further. Also, the more he thought about it, the more absurd seemed this seating arrangement. The staff were only being considerate of the privacy of a random collection of three strangers, so he supposed, but the ice had to be broken, and pushing the group together—placing them at one big table, for instance—would have served the purpose. He thought of leaping up and urging them to relocate in unison. He didn't, the moment passed, and eventually lunch broke up. Diana had said hardly a word.

He might have pursued her afterward, for this was his holiday, and he would do what he really wanted. On the heels of such a big meal, however—he had ordered more, leaving not a crumb—he felt like taking a nap. That magnificent bed called to him. He surrendered to the call for a couple of hours, time he regretted upon awakening, although the rest had thoroughly refreshed him. Now he could get himself into gear.

He went for a longer walk this afternoon, intending to explore the limits of the domain. He didn't see the other guests as he set out. To the shore, then right, up the coast, he strode. Shortly he stopped, removed his shoes and socks, then continued, splashing through the surf. The water chilled his feet and calves. This might not be the best time of year for swimming, despite what the brochure had said. He'd give it a try anyway; might as well put that old bathing suit to use.

Before he progressed half a mile the beach narrowed and ran out at the foot of the steep bluffs, which towered at least fifty feet overhead. A wall of trees crowned the top, and he could see a fence stretched along the cliff edge, marking the boundaries of the property. He returned, hugging the boulder strewn bluffs, the top of which gradually dropped down to meet him, so by the time he reached the road he was walking along the fence. He kept going, past the hotel and the outbuildings, for something over a quarter of a mile. In this direction the beach narrowed, too, although it didn't come to a point of clear-cut termination. The fence bent inward onto the beach and ran into the ocean, a warning line of rotting wood and corroded strands of barbed wire. Here his kingdom ended. Beyond, for as far as he could make out—not so far, for the coast turned out of sight—the beach continued empty, quiet, devoid of human artifice or life, devoid of all life save for the wheeling sea birds.

Isolated was the word. The irresistible encroachments of modern development, overrunning everything in their path, hadn't reached this region yet. That pleased him. The vacation package pleased him. No crowds marred the landscape with their oppressive presence, their raucous noise and commotion and screaming children. When he had thought—often—of getting away from it all, he had imagined a spot just like this; more like this, at least, than what he knew of contemporary popular resorts with their glitzy plastic and chrome and over-computerized conveniences. He had surely found what he sought. Rather, it had found him; out of the blue, as Diana put it. It relieved him to discover such a place could still exist in this busy world.

From this end of the resort property the return journey was a matter of a very few minutes. Martin meandered back, making his walk last. Presently a rider on horseback appeared from behind the buildings and headed his way. Diana, mounted on a stocky, reddish-brown mare, pulled up as she passed.

"This is Cherry," she said. "You know something? Learning to ride a horse isn't so hard. I got the hang of it in no time."

"Surely their horses are chosen for sweetness of manner," Martin observed. "It wouldn't do to have them bucking the guests."

"I guess not, but I was afraid, at first. There's nothing to it. Nylstrom equipped Cherry, and offered to take me out, but I wanted to ride by myself. I've already been all over that way"—she indicated the larger expanse north of the hotel—"right to the edge. Did you see anything down this way?"

"More of the same: sand, ocean, and trees."

"Boy, we have really fallen off the edge of the world." So saying, she rode on. Martin wanted to say more, but couldn't think of the words. She had changed clothes, he saw; changed into a tight blouse, short skirt, and high boots. Gold (or gold colored) bracelets, necklaces, and anklets glistened in the sun. He still discovered something outré in her taste, but had to admit certain baser aspects of her costume appealed to him. He really needed to make more of an effort to get to know her. After all, they had been acquainted for whole hours now.

Entering the lobby, he found Mr. Hartmann and Mrs. Drexel conversing in animated whispers. They broke off abruptly and approached.

"Mr. Cravitt, sir, taking the sea air?" asked Mr. Hartmann.

"Is everything to your satisfaction?" asked Mrs. Drexel. Upon receiving assurances to that effect, she continued, "Don't forget that you won't have to wait for dinner if you get hungry. Our Maurice is always standing by to serve. He can make up something filling in a hurry. If the mood comes over you, don't hesitate to let me know. It isn't every day we can eat all we please."

"Your eyes are never too big for your stomach here," Mr. Hartmann said jovially. "We would not want to see you waste away."

"It does me good," added Mrs. Drexel, "to see a body eat. One must not let the moment pass. We must make the most of our fleeting opportunities."

"You only live once," quoted the manager. "Strike while the iron is hot; or, in this case, the oven. Mr. Horton has been availing himself of our largesse, if I may say so."

"Making up for lost time."

"And none of us wishes to lose time. He's in the lounge now, sampling our sweeter fare. You must try it. Eat hearty, Mr. Cravitt. It's all on the house."

Good of them to be so solicitous of his welfare and pleasure, thought Martin. They did seem a tad insistent about it, though. Surely he didn't appear in need of such advice. They talked like he was skin and bones! Sadly, there was too much of falsity in that deduction. Left to himself, he often ate a lot of junk, cheap snacks and fatty tidbits. He would rein himself in one of these days; perhaps after his vacation. He had no intention of fretting about diet now.

Nor, despite entreaties, did he feel hungry at the moment. Company agreed with him. He sought Wally, finding him in the predicted location, engaged in the predicted pastime. He was savoring a creamy confection—a heaped plate of quivering richness—it might be a slice of exotic pie. It looked sinfully good.

"Hello, Wally. Am I disturbing you?"

"Not at all, Martin, sit down. Join me. Let me tell you, this is a remarkable pastry. They don't exaggerate Maurice's prowess. It takes a master to create this. I love to eat fine food. I don't get many opportunities anymore, so I indulge my palate when the occasion comes along. I ate a big lunch—hope I didn't make a spectacle of myself—that should have been enough to satisfy me. Mrs. Drexel—quite the overbearing type, isn't she?—practically begged me to try this."

"That is exactly what I would expect of her."

"I could have refused, but she did press so, and that isn't the hill I want to die on. Isn't that right? I gave in, and am none the worse for it. There is plenty more."

"Maybe later."

Wally ate in silence for a period. His brow darkened, as if he were deep in thought. Then he said: "In one respect, this place disappoints me."

"How's that?"

"There's nobody here. No offense to you, of course, or that moody little girl—"

"You expected livelier surroundings," Martin interjected.

"I did. Didn't occur to me that it could be otherwise. It's a funny kind of resort. I'd almost believe they opened it just for us. I wanted to see people, lots of them, even if I'm no good at, well, interacting. Sometimes I get a craving for human company, on any terms. I thought to satisfy it on this trip."

"I understand your position very well."

"My wife died many years ago. I had always been devoted to her, to the exclusion of all others. I didn't know anyone; she had friends, but I lost track of them afterward. Then I had to sell my business and retire—for health reasons—and my life shrank even more. I've lived simply, on a fixed income, ever since. I don't know people, I don't do anything. I have no family—no surviving relatives I can trace—no friends, and precious few opportunities to make new ones. It gets old after a while."

"This is the most amazing thing!" exclaimed Martin. "To a degree, my situation is similar to your own. I haven't lost a wife, fortunately—you have my sympathy—I've never been married. Not even that. I have no family. I never had brothers or sisters, and my parents were killed in a car crash when I was quite young."

"That's terrible."

"That's life. Not being the outgoing sort, I've never made up the lack. Along the way I took a wrong turn—I can't honestly describe it any other way—and now I find myself in a dead-end job, going to work and coming home every day, without a break. The sameness appalls me. I tell you, Wally, it does get old; it gets maddening."

"Isn't that a strange coincidence? Both of us have come here—if I may say this—looking for something new and fresh; a change of pace and scenery, at least. Speaking for myself, perhaps I seek a reason for living."

"It does seem a great deal to bear at times." Now Martin grew absent, silently reflecting. "I want to make the best of this chance. Vacations—all expenses paid—don't drop from trees. Perhaps we could make this more of a group enterprise."

"That sounds promising."

"For starters, why don't the three of us get together for dinner? It won't be long now."

"That suits me."

"There's no sense in boxing ourselves off. I'll discuss it with Mrs.

Drexel, or whoever will arrange it. Oh, and if you run across Miss Carswell—Diana—before I do, mention it to her. Surely she will agree."

"I'll do that."

"You'll see. We're all going to have a good time here." With their business concluded, Martin took leave to track down one of the staff.

He came across John, who directed him to Mrs. Drexel in the office behind the check-in booth. At his knock on the open door she rose courteously and greeted him. He outlined his request.

"Of course I can arrange that, if the other parties . . . second the motion? The happiness of our guests is paramount. The others want this?" She seemed oddly reserved, as if the request were unexpected or unwelcome. Martin, getting ahead of the facts somewhat, assured her all three desired the new seating scheme. "Then it shall be done."

He felt funny about assuming even that much on Diana's behalf, but he especially wanted her to join in. Now, if Wally should take ill and drop out? No, he didn't mean it. That wasn't very nice—just a random idea, of no importance—forget he thought of it.

As it happened, everything went wrong, and the grand design almost didn't come off. Martin didn't meet Diana again before dinner; evening closed in, and when he appeared at seven o'clock sharp, she wasn't in sight. Only two settings were laid at table. Wally was there, in fact had already tucked in, but he had no report to make.

"I haven't seen her since you brought it up," he explained, adding ineffectually, "I presumed you had taken care of it."

"I heard something about her intending to dine in her room," said Thomas the waiter.

Martin dashed out, met Mr. Hartmann and Mrs. Drexel just arriving, and told them he wished to place a call to Miss Carswell's room.

"That is possible," mused Mr. Hartmann. "We do not wish to disturb her, though."

"Is she awaiting your call?" asked Mrs. Drexel. Martin hinted it was likely.

"In that case, use the telephone at check-in," the manager advised. "Mrs. Drexel, please accompany him."

Martin assured her that wasn't necessary, but she came anyway, and a good thing too, because he had to ask her to dial, since he didn't know the room number. Number 25, it was. The telephone was another period piece, a real antique, affixed to the wall. The housekeeper continued to hover nearby, solicitude he did his best to ignore.

"Diana, this is Martin. Yes, hello. I had a great idea, which I meant to mention to you earlier." He laid it out for her quickly. "I thought it would be a lot more enjoyable for us, make it a lot easier to get acquainted. Oh? I see—if you're already eating—you aren't?—well then, why not come down and join us? It would be a great pleasure to all; I would appreciate it very much. You will? See you there." He disconnected and handed the earpiece to Mrs. Drexel, who hung it up without a word.

Martin left her there, priding himself on a job well done. Diana had sounded pleasant enough. He hoped he hadn't irritated her. He hoped she took his request in the right spirit. He hoped—he hoped too much, perhaps, but for now he'd settle for getting her downstairs.

Returning quickly to the dining room, he requested of Thomas a third setting be prepared. Mr. Hartmann was there, and he cheerfully hurried the waiter along. While that was being seen to, Martin took his seat at last.

"I took care of it," he told Wally, with a trace of smugness.

"I'm glad it worked out. Now, catch your breath. Look at all this!"

Maurice obviously put all of his talent, effort, and devotion into creating his dinners. The center of the table, and an adjacent tray, were loaded with silver platters, several of them still covered. Those uncovered already contained more food than any three people could ever handle. Beef filets dripping with au jus, roasted chicken pieces swimming in thick gravy, little baked birds in orange sauce, steaming cream soup, creamed vegetables of various kinds, sliced French bread, rolls, a mountain of butter; this was only what Martin could see and recognize. Besides the viands, an iced wine bucket with three bottles added to the potential for cheer. The good dishes and eating accessories had been replaced by the finest china and silver.

"I hardly know where to start," Martin said.

The waiter, having completed his errand, now deftly served his guest. Meanwhile, Diana made her entrance, with an air of haste. Martin rose politely as she took her seat.

"I'm glad you could make it," he said.

"I didn't have a chance to clean up. Am I out of sorts?"

"You look great." She smiled, the first time he had seen her do so. Much better. "So, here we are together."

"Dig in!" urged Wally, who was well through his first course. "It's powerfully good."

They ate, and not one found scope for complaint. It was an incredibly rich meal; Martin had never indulged in anything like it. His fellow diners echoed the sentiment. No sense counting calories here, where such a repast must break dietary records. Presently they talked. Martin instigated this; Wally was too wrapped up in sampling everything, as a rule, to converse in more than monosyllables, and Diana required considerable drawing out to get her going. He employed his withered social skills as best he could to achieve that result.

"Let me tell you what I did today," he began. "So far . . . " He ticked off the few items on his list, trying to make them sound more exciting and adventurous than the actual circumstances allowed. Then he pressed Diana for her day's itinerary.

"I didn't do a lot," she replied. "I went horseback riding, as you know, and I guess I saw everything there was to see. It's pretty country, and I love the ocean. There are some cute rocks and stuff. Still, there isn't much to it. It's the beach, with no people, and the water is too cold.

"You, know, I've really had trouble keeping myself busy. I've flipped through the magazines in the lounge, and they don't go a long way. They're fun for a while. The library is full of old stuff, too—very old stuff—it all looked too heavy for me. I didn't pay much attention to it. I don't read much anyway."

"This might be the time to start," Martin suggested. "A good book can kill a lot of time. I haven't checked out the library yet. I enjoy old books—so often they aren't run of the mill fair—new books these days all read the same to me. I should look into it."

"If you like old books, you'll love it."

"I like to eat," said Wally, in one of his rare intrusions, "something other than the crap I make for myself at home. I generally live on cans of soup. Therefore, I'm in heaven now. I'd just as soon take it easy anyway, when on vacation."

"He's got a point," said Martin, addressing Diana. "We can enjoy the peacefulness of this resort. There's plenty to go around."

"I'll say. No television. Not even a radio. It will take getting used to. I'm not worried. One day isn't a fair test; and it does feel good to get away from the world for a while."

During dinner the contents of each platter received some attention. It wasn't possible to even think of eating it all, nor did that apparently concern management or staff. Thomas swept by periodically—Maurice looked in at times from the kitchen only to stare—Mr. Hartmann and Mrs. Drexel appeared at separate intervals, to make sure everything about the repast was absolutely perfect. A rich, sugary cake filled with chocolate cream rounded off the meal. Only Wally made much of the dessert; the others nibbled. Coffee followed, a thick, sweet foreign blend with whipped cream on top. And the wine kept flowing. Somewhere along the way another bottle had appeared. Diana lit a cigarette and sank wearily into her seat.

"I'm going to die here," she said with a grin.

"Not until the end of the fifth day," Martin recommended.

"Bury me inside one of those cakes," said Wally. "There's room enough."

Mr. Hartmann entered once more, to ask if anything else could be done for them this evening. No one could think of anything.

"It is excellent that you are satisfied with the cuisine," he cried. "I can not tell you how it pleases me to see you all happy. We take pride in the fine dining we offer to our very special guests. If only we could do it more frequently. Ours is a small operation, as you may have realized, but we emphasize quality to a degree that the biggest and most popular resorts can not match. The lunch suits you? Very good. The dinner—it takes your breath away—I trust so? You will see that breakfast starts off your day properly. Of course, all this is as nothing, in comparison to the gala feasts with which we shall celebrate your Big Nights."

Nobody, Martin realized, looking round, understood the reference. This moved him to ask for clarification.

"The Big Nights? But, surely, that was adequately described in the extremely detailed brochures you received from the travel agency long ago?"

Once again, blank stares. Comments from all proved to Martin he wasn't the only one to have been left largely in the dark, prior to arriving here.

"Unbelievable!" stormed Mr. Hartmann. "If I had only known!" Then he shrugged, threw up his hands, and said in mock sorrow, "You can not count on anyone these days, can you?" His guests chuckled. "So, I took you by surprise? How about that. If I had known, I would have kept it a total surprise. You might have appreciated it. Do not you think they would have, Thomas?" The waiter, busy clearing the dishes, merely grinned and turned away, shaking his head. "Well, as it stands, we must not keep them in suspense, eh? The agony would be unbearable. *Lieber ein ende mit schrecken als ein schrecken ohne ende.*"

It took time to pin him down, and then Mr. Hartmann wouldn't tell all—he kept chortling about the element of surprise, and the added delight that factor would foster—but what it all boiled down to was this. "You each have coming to you a Big Night of your own, when each of you will be taken away individually in turn to be fêted at a magnificent banquet hosted by our entire staff. You will find this a no-holds-barred extravaganza, a once in a lifetime event, at which it shall be made clear that you are the most special person in the world. It is the least that I and my assistants may do, to thank you for gracing the Caltel Ocean Resort with your presence.

"It will be the final honor to you," he burbled, with acutely painful sincerity. "If we succeed in our plans, your Big Night will be the high point of your life. Never again will you experience anything like it."

Martin didn't know what to say, and neither, obviously, did anyone else.

ALL EXPENSES PAID

He wanted to be polite and acknowledge the idea, but he sat mute.

"The only thing more I will tell you now," continued Mr. Hartmann, after a frozen pause, "is that the schedule for your Nights has been arranged. Mr. Horton, yours will be the third evening of your stay here; Mr. Cravitt, yours the fourth; Miss Carswell, we are saving you for last. Yours will be the fifth evening, the ultimate and the best. I can hardly wait, and I speak for everyone here." He nodded and left them to muse among themselves over his revelations.

After that there was scarce little left to say; eating was unthinkable, and drinking had surpassed respectable limits and verged on the dangerous. The party broke up. Martin felt he had reason to be pleased with the developments of this night. He could have stopped there. Under normal circumstances he would have. Something—perhaps the change of environment—gave him greater courage than usual. He nerved himself to inform Diana he intended to sit on the balcony for a while in order to wind down and allow his meal to digest. Could she—that is—would she join him? Yes she would, thank you. Wasn't that something? It could be so easy, when everything was just right.

She came to him there after taking a detour to freshen up and change her top, donning a loose-fitting, airy blouse. Not bad. She wore another necklace, a jingly gold thing which looked too big for her. While she smoked they discussed the view, although all was dark, with no moon. A myriad of dazzling stars peeked through scattered clouds. Below, lights could be seen far off, from otherwise invisible ships at the invisible watery horizon. This was peace, the material embodiment of the concept. Martin made some such comment, and—feeling uncharacteristically loquacious and open tonight—contrasted the present moment with the less than edifying course of his regular life.

"What has your life been like?" she asked him sharply. So he told her—he told her everything—he held back nothing. He whispered of the high hopes and great expectations which had steadily dwindled, of the disappointments and failures which had inexorably mounted, until he had reached the point of not knowing what the future had to offer him and, more and more often these days, not caring. It was quite a monologue, made easier for him because it felt as if someone else were speaking, or as if he were speaking of someone else. Diana sat silently throughout.

When he had finished, and after a quiet pause ensued, she seemed to overcome some inner struggle, steeled herself, and told him the story of her life. It was not a pretty tale. Even allowing for the exaggerations of youth—who always feel everything strongly—she had suffered some hard knocks. Much of it sounded like the dreadful stories he read in the newspapers, usually written up in statistical form: broken homes, thoughtless mothers, overly friendly stepfathers, squalid neighborhoods. Then there were the more private affairs of the heart, or of the broken heart, as she told it. He gathered there had been in her short adult span too little of the right kind of solitude, and too much of the wrong kind of loneliness. Now she lived by herself (not counting a pet cat) and worked a low grade job at a department store. To a degree Martin could relate—oh brother, could he!—although he would never have described such experiences so strongly, nor in such graphic detail.

What she had to say shocked him, distressed him. He found it difficult to accept all he heard. Such was the modern world, he reminded himself. He chose to sympathize rather than recoil. He took her hand; she didn't resist. He kissed her cheek. She didn't pull away. He could do no more, for now. Soon the night air grew too cool and they went their separate ways, she to her room, he to his. Thinking about her delighted him, but his thoughts were hazy and unfocused. The goddess of slumber beckoned to him, and he went quickly.

One item of her story nagged at his fogging mind before he dived into sleep. Diana's mother was dead—of a drug overdose—she had no father to speak of, and no siblings or close relatives. She belonged to that same sad fraternity as did he and Wally. It was the most remarkable coincidence.

III.

Martin awoke the next morning, after a long, restful night, with—he could scarcely credit this—a headache. Once he threw off the thick blankets his room was quite cold. Desiring to employ the luxurious services of the resort, he called down to the office for orange juice, aspirins, and a newspaper. The first two items were on the way as he spoke. The latter was not available. No newspapers, not even the local rag, were delivered to the hotel.

Perhaps they carried "getting away from it all" too far. The juice and the pills arrived, hand carried through the wilderness by the faithful Nylstrom. Martin thanked him, sent him on, took both and collapsed back into the warmth of his bed.

What about this isolation business? There had to be limits. No, there didn't have to be, but there ought to be. Peace and quiet required the avoidance of crowds, but not a complete ban on information. He chose to withdraw from the world for a while, live for a handful of days without the tedious cares associated with "out there"; that didn't mean he found it necessary to pretend it didn't exist. Suppose the country were swept away by a nuclear holocaust? He would want to know about it. All right, so somebody would mention that to him. Earthshaking matters would, presumably, seep through regardless. Still, he saw no need for a wall of silence. A moderate policy would serve just as well.

It hurt to think too much. Why worry? He hadn't had it so good in a long time, if ever, and he shouldn't spoil the mood by quibbling. Perhaps one of the staff, for a tip, would fetch him a newspaper from Tellmee, if such were sold there. Was that where they all lived? It hadn't occurred to him before, and no wonder, for it seemed unlikely. Where did these people, or those not on duty, go home to at night?

Presently he felt better, and the room warmer. He checked the clock: only seven-thirty. He'd thought it much later. Breakfast was about to be served! That would do him up nicely. He rose gingerly and spent the next minutes preparing himself for public display. He used plenty of hot water, sought the temperature control for the room, didn't find it. He guessed that was another example of the old-fashioned approach.

Memory functioned slowly, but had not failed him altogether. He recalled fully his tête-à-tête with Diana. In that corner of his mind, warm thoughts abounded. He hoped she remembered it the same way. Both of them had done a lot of talking—looking back on it, he surprised himself— but he didn't see any cause for regret. Quite the contrary. That might be the big selling point of vacation resorts like this: they were places where things happened, even things that could change one's life.

Before parting, they had made a date to go boating today. It was an obscure plan—he knew nothing about sailing, or how the COR bunch handled such business—but he looked forward to working it out, if she didn't change her mind. He refused to consider that possibility.

He came down for breakfast sporting a fresh shirt and tie, noting with pleasure the blaze in the fireplace. In the dining room he found Wally had beaten him again, and had already started on hot rolls, butter, honey, and choice of jellies. This time, without prompting, one table had been laid for three. Henceforth, Martin realized, that would be the standard.

"Are we getting our money's worth this morning?" he asked.

"It's continental style," Wally informed him. "These big rolls, straight out of the oven, all the goodies to put on them, and as much hot tea or coffee as you can stand. When we run out, Thomas will bring more. Simple, but effective. After a night like the last one, I think it for the best. How are you feeling?"

"I'll recover. Pass the butter, please."

"There you go. I tell you, Martin, I haven't abused myself that way in years. It was sheer joy. We must do it again tonight."

"I'm not sure we have the option. They're eager to stuff their guests. If we refuse their generosity, they may start charging us. Should you splurge again, though? Don't you want to save room for your Big Night?"

"My Big Night! I'd forgotten all about it. What miracle can they perform to top what they already offer? I shall see, as will you when your turn comes. Maybe I'll tell you about my party; that is, if I'm not supposed to keep it a secret."

The waiter had brought more of everything before Diana showed. Her lateness had alarmed Martin, but here she was, a little ragged, dressed in shabby tee-shirt and shorts, but here. He smiled; she grinned sheepishly, and joined them.

"I'm still alive," she announced. "Is this what we get?"

"It is, and it's good," he said.

"Look how big the rolls are," said Wally. "They're light and fluffy, just what you need, Diana. They go down smooth."

"That's the ticket. I'll take one. If I can keep it down, I'll eat another." She did, and she did.

"Life just gets better and better," Wally enthused, polishing off another one. "Our hosts really must watch out; I'm getting used to this treatment. Already I feel as if I were born for this. It will be painful to leave. If I could only figure out some way to spend the rest of my life here!"

"Perhaps that can be arranged," said Mrs. Drexel from the doorway. She approached, flashed Wally a frigid smile. "I'll be sure to pass on your kind words. I trust that all is in order?"

"As always."

"Then I will leave you to yourselves. Mr. Hartmann is still abed. Please ask for me if you need anything this morning." As she turned Martin rose and, making an excuse to his companions, followed her out. In the corridor he asked her about his taking out the boat with Miss Carswell. "John can pilot you both," she said. "After breakfast? I will speak to him at once."

Martin returned to the dining room, saying nothing. Presently, when he and Diana had eaten their fill, Wally—going strong on his sixth roll—withdrew temporarily to relieve himself. That was Martin's chance, but Diana pre-empted him.

"Are we still going sailing?"

"I've taken care of it."

"Good." Good indeed; she remembered, she remained interested, and she seemed—like himself—eager, in a well-intended fashion, to exclude Wally from this little jaunt. If she had chosen to raise the subject before, it might have proved necessary, for the sake of politeness, to invite him. Martin hadn't been willing to risk it. Their mutual friend might not be the sort who could read between the lines and bow out gracefully.

ALL EXPENSES PAID

Diana went upstairs to pull herself together—"I won't be a minute"—while he went out to attend to the boat launching. He ran into Wally on the way.

"Finished so soon?" asked the latter. "I'm keen on one more helping."

"I'll make up for it at lunch. What are your plans for the day?"

"They are lazy plans, I can tell you."

"Have fun."

Outside he saw the sailing vessel already floating in front of the boathouse. Some fellow—John, presumably—was aboard. Martin lingered by the hotel, waiting for Diana to emerge. It looked like a perfect day for boating: an azure sky, specked with white puffs and softened by wisps of cirrus gauze, light winds bearing a hint of coolness; made to order. Gulls hovered and squawked along the shore. Something—fish, or larger creatures (did they have seals or sea lions in these parts?)—broke the surface of the smooth sea. And the surf melodically grumbled its eternal susurrance.

Diana didn't show. Chronic lateness might be an ingrained characteristic of that girl. For whatever reason, she was consistently the last to appear. Then he offered her more credit; perhaps, while he'd chatted with Wally, she had raced ahead? Not likely, but worth finding out. He strolled down to the shore, passing the boathouse. More forcefully this time its squalid condition struck him. It was a plain eye sore. He didn't get close enough to check for spiders. Martin hailed John (it was he) when within calling distance.

"No, Mr. Cravitt, I haven't seen her yet. Yes, we're ready to go."

Back to the hotel he went. He hung around outside for a spell, not wanting to miss her if she came out the wrong door. Still he waited, ever patient, but with increasing frustration. Considerable time passed. Finally he reentered to look for her. He found the door to room 25 wide open, Diana inside, dressed for their excursion, but in no hurry to leave. Her belongings, the contents of two suitcases, were spread on the bed. She seemed harried. He heard her cursing to herself. Indeed, her vocabulary was remarkably earthy.

"May I come in?"

"I'm going nuts," she informed him. "I can't find it anywhere."

"What can't you find?" He entered and examined the mess.

"My cell phone. It was here, now it's not."

"Did you unpack it?"

"No. I didn't have any need to yesterday. I told a girlfriend of mine I'd give her a call when I got here. It wasn't important—just something I said—but I thought I'd go ahead and get it out of the way this morning. Now I can't find it."

"I don't own one myself, or I'd loan it to you. Maybe you forgot yours."

"I never go anywhere without my cell phone," she said crushingly. "Normally I carry it in my purse, so I have it right at hand in case anything comes up. This time—this time—I packed it in my green suitcase, because, since I was traveling, I didn't have room—oh, that doesn't matter—what matters is it was here, and now it's gone!"

"Are you absolutely certain you brought it?" Martin poked at the scattered items, mainly clothes, some of which he found bizarre, if enticing. "You've looked through all this?"

"Twice."

"And all over the room?"

"Every nook and cranny."

"If you're right, this is a serious situation."

"I am right. Someone stole it."

"Then let's do something about it." She might be correct, unpleasant though that would be (and he still harbored doubts); such things did happen, in the best of places, and it might have happened here (despite what he deduced to be her inherently suspicious nature, which made no allowance for error on her part), although it seemed an odd object of theft. Cell phones were handed out like candy these days. Who would think to look for it? And weren't they traceable? At the first attempt to use it . . . "Take a moment and make sure nothing else is missing."

As far as Diana could tell—she stated this with certainty—the rest of her belongings were intact.

Martin felt the helpful and possessive firmness welling up within him. He would not let her down. "Then let's go have a talk with Mrs. Drexel."

He led the way downstairs to the lobby. Not finding anyone there, he rang the buzzer at the counter, several times. Nylstrom appeared.

"I want Mrs. Drexel at once," Martin demanded. The man scurried off; within the minute the housekeeper replaced him.

"Is anything the matter, sir?"

"Something very definitely is the matter, Mrs. Drexel. A most troublesome situation has arisen. Miss Carswell cannot find an object of her personal property; a cell phone, in fact. She knows, beyond question, she had it with her yesterday, on the premises. Today, she can't lay hands on it. We instituted a most careful search of her room, but it isn't there. From this, we can draw only one conclusion."

"Mercy," cried Mrs. Drexel. She shook her head vigorously, her whole being a picture of embarrassment and concern. "That isn't possible. Nothing of the kind has occurred at Caltel in all the years of its operation."

Probably not true, even if she believed it. "It does happen, madam," Martin declared with intentional pomposity, "and it has happened now. As you can imagine, the loss has caused Miss Carswell a great deal of distress. She wants something done about it."

"It must be some kind of mistake—"

"There is no mistake. Theft is evident, as is the aggravation. You understand how this puts a damper on our holiday. We don't want to bring away memories of this kind."

"Of course," she replied, "of course not. Such an act, if it actually occurred, cannot be tolerated. I would rather have my eyes out. We must repair the situation immediately. I wish to assure you, however, our staff are noted for their integrity. We don't hire our people off the street. They must all account for their backgrounds. It is difficult for me to suspect a single individual—"

"Nevertheless—"

"Mr. Hartmann will be advised when he wakes. Meanwhile, I shall undertake a search of my own. I will examine every inch of the premises. Fortunately, there is no possibility of a presumed culprit getting away with his deed. If the object has been stolen, then it remains here, hidden by the perpetrator."

"How do you know that?" Diana interjected.

"Because no one has left here," explained Mrs. Drexel, "since the three of you arrived."

"I don't understand that," said Martin. "Don't you people go home when you're off duty?"

"No, sir. We all live on site during open season. We allow no outside influences. Also, the resort was fully stocked with all necessary supplies prior to your arrival. There are no tradesmen coming and going; no outsiders of any kind, Mr. Cravitt. The thief could only be someone here, and he could hardly hope to escape detection."

"In that case, your task should be an easy one. In the meantime, Miss Carswell can use the hotel telephone."

Mrs. Drexel coughed apologetically. "Begging your pardon, sir, but the hotel possesses no outside line. It will not be possible to place a call. Nor, unfortunately, are any of these cell phone things carried by the staff. That is not an aspect of our ambience, you see."

"No outside line?" exploded Diana. "That's ridiculous."

"It is an antiquated system," admitted the housekeeper. "It dates back to the original ownership. Our guests, by and large, have tended to appreciate that feature."

"Oh, brother," Martin muttered. "I had no idea it was like that. Did you?" he asked pointlessly of Diana, who shook her head without speaking.

"It is so," said Mrs. Drexel. "However, I'll get on to our problem.

SCIENCE AND SORCERY III

Please continue as you were, and don't waste a moment worrying. All will be well. Miss Carswell, I extend my sincere regrets for this unfortunate development—I speak for COR Enterprises, as well as myself—and I guarantee you that you will not be the loser in any way. I make you a promise, on my own authority. If the object, this cell phone, isn't located, and if, upon returning home at the end of your stay, you don't find it where you might conceivably have left it; if all of that should transpire, then you will be reimbursed for a telephone of equal or greater value without delay. No charge to you, of course; all expenses will be paid by us. You have my promise, and before you leave, if it comes to that, it will be put into writing. Will that satisfy you?"

Diana was satisfied. With such proposed generosity, nothing more needed to be said. Mrs. Drexel did say more—expressions of sorrow and mystification, accompanied by the wringing of hands—but the sad business, for the time being, was settled. Martin reminded the girl the sailboat awaited their pleasure, and she came with him willingly enough. She also said to him:

"I love the way you talk. You handled that very well. I could never have done it the way you did." Which was reward enough for now. He had surprised himself, most favorably. Sometimes taking a stand worked.

So, with major annoyances behind them, they trooped down to the boat, where patient John smilingly helped then in, and off they went into the wide blue sea. Diana provided sunburn lotion—Martin hadn't thought of that—and they both applied it liberally to their exposed skin. Everything was just right. They naturally gravitated away from the navigator, sitting by themselves at the bow. A sail granted the liberating illusion of freedom. The shoreline receded; the hotel and its outbuildings dwindled to toys. Even more so than before, it seemed as if the entire world had dropped out of existence. They said little at first, and when they did begin to converse in earnest, by tacit agreement they spoke in whispers.

Diana lit a cigarette and sighed. "I just don't know," she sighed.

"What are you thinking?" Martin queried.

"About my cell phone. Could I have left it behind? I don't think so. Maybe I did."

"Anything is possible."

"It would be crazy for anyone on the staff to take it. I have to admit, that is so."

"Do you suspect Wally? He looks shifty."

"He doesn't. Nor do you," she added with a grin. "I don't know what happened."

"You'll find out, and you can't lose on the deal; Mrs. Drexel gave you her personal guarantee."

"What is that worth?" She laughed, a little. "I don't know these people. She gives me the creeps."

"You said that yesterday. I'd hoped you might be able to put such an idea out of your mind."

"It's still true." She grinned, but her tone conveyed seriousness. Whispering could do that. "She isn't for real. Maybe Mr. Hartmann isn't, either. They're like characters in a movie. I'm trying to convince myself this is real. None of it makes sense."

"By the standards to which I'm accustomed, no, it doesn't. I don't have wide experience, though. Perhaps there are places like this all over, run by people like them. It's a big world, and there are all kinds within it." Martin mused on that point for a moment. "It's an odd set up, no question about it. You know, it wouldn't occur to me to press the matter, because I'm not inclined to look a gift horse in the mouth. On the other hand, in order to satisfy curiosity, it wouldn't hurt to ask them. They might be pleased to tell us what they're all about, and how they can make a go of an operation like this. I sure haven't figured it out."

"I suppose you're right, but they haven't told us yet, have they? It's a secret. I like to know what is going on around me. I wish I could make a telephone call. I'd like to know how I came to be here."

"Now that is a puzzle. Yesterday, when we spoke of that, I wondered—" He stopped short. He slapped his forehead, an action which drew John's attention. Martin smiled at the man and continued, in a lower whisper. "I just recalled something—it came up last night, while we were talking on the balcony—it had slipped my mind."

"I don't remember a lot from last night," Diana said teasingly. "Only the good parts. I drank a tad too much for my own good. Was it something I said?"

"Sort of. Yes, I remember how amazed I was at the time. I still can't get over it. It's nothing, of course—"

"Do tell!"

With some reluctance, but with a desire to thrill her with his revelation, Martin explained his discovery that they and Wally shared a striking life trait: they were completely alone in the world, without strong personal or familial ties of any kind. "It's rather strange how it worked out, our coming together like this."

He didn't much care for Diana's reaction. At first she stared at him, open mouthed, as if stunned. Then she turned away and brooded silently. She moved her lips, from which no words issued. Then she faced him squarely, thrust her face into his own, and declared:

"That isn't coincidence. That's deliberate—it's purpose—we were selected!"

"Can such things be?"

"Of course they can. Don't you see it?"

Of course he did. The realization had stolen upon him as he slipped into sleep last night; a strange, unsettling feeling; and there had been more. It came back to him now.

"I dreamed about it," he told her. "I don't recollect the details, but the thought haunted my night." And then he cast it aside. Why? Because of the kind of man he was, or had been, all his life. He always gave the benefit of the doubt to others, always questioned himself. It had been his way since the dawn of consciousness. In this case, he had refused to connect three obvious clues because the necessary conclusion he derived from them opened a door unto mystery, and too much of the world mystified him already. He hadn't been prepared to face more, not here, not now.

"Oh, I'm a big dreamer," Diana was saying. "I have plenty of them. I'll dream about this, mark my words."

"There probably isn't any reason."

"Don't you think dreams are meaningful?"

"Not especially. They're just collections of inner thoughts, derived from shreds of reality." Martin wiped perspiration from his brow. He hadn't noticed the warmth before. "There is a reason for what we've learned. It may be no big deal, but now that it's come out, I'd like to know what it is."

"Me, too. Why don't you ask them? I'd be afraid to."

"Afraid? What kind of talk is that?" Martin laughed, loudly enough to draw John's attention again. "There is nothing to be afraid of. You'll see; it's some goofy explanation. They're a church group, let's say, and they concocted this whole scheme in order to establish a fancy lonely hearts club. Not a bad deal, from my point of view."

Diana giggled and stroked his hand. Then she frowned and said, "For three? That is poor planning."

"Perhaps someone didn't show up."

"And people who otherwise are—well, what can I say—we don't have much else in common."

"No harm, but you're right. That isn't the answer, but just wait and see. It's something off the wall like that."

"What bothers me," she said, "regardless of reasons, is their knowing so much about us. They must have researched us."

"It isn't difficult to dig up facts about people these days," Martin pointed out. "Every detail of our lives is on record, on paper, or in a computer network. We leave behind us an inescapable trail. If it matters to anyone, they can pick up on it, follow the traces. It would be far more amazing if that weren't so."

"Well, nobody asked my permission."

"They never do."

He promised to pursue the question later, and she seemed content, although he sensed her mind was still racing. With the dying of conversation, they both grew bored with sailing, and presently Martin signaled they wished to return to dry land. The boat turned away from the endless ocean horizon, and soon the hotel loomed, looking like an ancient schooner plowing through the seas toward them.

Back on shore, Diana indicated she wanted to take a lie-down. She wasn't sure if she would be down in time for lunch. Sure enough, she didn't appear. That irked Martin. He wished he hadn't brought up the peculiar subject, which must still be plaguing her. He lunched with Wally, who also, as it happened, didn't own a cell phone, and who chuckled at the minor mystery. Wally didn't appear troubled by anything. He seemed livelier than ever, not so tired and gray. He had found himself here. Wasn't that sufficient justification?

The lunch was, again, thoroughly satisfying. Afterward Martin wandered the halls, looking for Mrs. Drexel, whom he considered the font of knowledge on the Caltel Ocean Resort and its doings. She was nowhere in sight. He guessed she was asleep—all the staff must be staying in the first floor rooms, for they never appeared upstairs except on business—and temporarily unavailable. He crossed paths, however, with Mr. Hartmann, who would do just as well.

"Mr. Cravitt, it is grand to see you," exclaimed the manager, who beamed with what must be genuine and unflappable good humor. "You look fit, healthy, contented I trust. It must be so. I read it in your eyes. Your happiness is mandatory."

"I appreciate your attitude. I'm fine. I do want to ask you about something, though."

"I was afraid of that. I heard about the contretemps this morning. It is dreadful that even the suspicion could arise. Simply dreadful."

"Oh, that? We're not concerned. The phone will turn up. Mrs. Drexel handled the matter most professionally."

"She is my eyes. I count on her for everything," Mr. Hartmann said solemnly.

"And right you are to do so. I was just wondering: how, exactly, did we three come to be chosen for our free vacations?"

"How can that be unknown to you? It has been discussed. The contest, you remember. That was explained in your initial notification."

"It didn't explain anything," Martin insisted. After some prompting, the host expanded on his answer, without materially adding clarity. The guest didn't leave it at that. "Were there any special criteria involved in the selection, certain unique rules?"

Mr. Hartmann professed not to know what he was talking about. Martin pressed, but didn't come right out and ask the question he specifically had in mind. For some reason it seemed important that Mr. Hartmann volunteer the critical information. He did not do so. He even appeared uncomfortable with the probing. That might be Martin's imagination, but the man had nothing to say of consequence, and as a matter of politeness Martin dropped the subject and moved on, vaguely dissatisfied.

Martin took the liberty of dialing Diana's room from his own. She answered. She was fine, just a little tired. She would definitely be down for dinner. He assured her he'd only wanted to hear the sound of her voice, and rang off. Hours lay before him. He decided to acquaint himself with the wonders of the library.

Equipped with a drink provided by Thomas, he entered that room and began to browse. To those who had no regard for the wisdom of the past, it might appear a forbidding place. Every volume in the collection must be older than he was, and most of the items, judging by wear and binding style, dated back to the Nineteenth Century. Even the furnishings predated those of the guest rooms. A stately, elegant odor of mildew emanated from the surrounding shelves, perhaps from elsewhere about the room. That was an odd note, yet for the moment Martin loved it. It was a restful, old-fashioned place, where he could think old-fashioned thoughts and get away with it. There weren't enough of those left in the world.

He discerned no rhyme or reason to the collection—a whole bunch of books jammed in tightly wherever they fit, making best use of limited space. The types of subjects suggested erudition of a limited sort. There were general works of history and politics, a few of which were familiar to him; dry, outdated stuff, bearing on issues which had lost relevancy ages ago. He cracked a volume entitled *The Great Dilemma*, read a long and excruciatingly tedious paragraph about the gold standard, closed it and put it back on the shelf. There were numerous works of philosophy, none of them by authors known to him; perhaps minor thinkers of their day, who had impressed their readers for a time and then passed into dust. *Principles of Happiness; The Carpenter's Message; Fulfilling One's Goals In Life; Daily Readings On Virtue;* and so on, all undoubtedly worth perusal, some other time. These were dry indeed, pitifully earnest, no doubt chock full of magnificent insights, but not for him, not at this moment. Study didn't interest him at present, only relaxation.

Another brand of reading material offered unusual possibilities. A number of titles constituted exposes or reports of the activities or claims of secret societies or other shadowy organizations, mostly from the Classical or Medieval periods, but some dwelt on forces at work in the modern day. Many of them were apparently written by true believers, and were quite laudatory in their presentation of Theosophist, Holistic, and Uranite movements, all outfits devoted to good works and self-realization. In short, mainly philosophical. Not all writers were so keen on their subjects, however. One volume, *Barbarous Survivals within Contemporary Society*, painted a rather different, and lurid, picture of secret doings. Some of the claims attested to within its fragile, yellowed pages were so grotesque Martin ended up skimming the entire book.

He noted one other major category which caught his attention. Several books consisted of what might be called travel or true adventure tales, compilations of accounts involving daring explorations or terrible disasters. A lot of those sounded fun. Many involved tragic stories of the sea, others accounts of primitive horrors lurking in mysterious jungles and wastelands. They were scattered throughout the shelves, with one especially large grouping in a prominent position. Now he was looking for them, he realized what a very large number of them there were.

He examined a small volume entitled *Doom on the Horn of Africa*, which dealt with a trading ship wrecked by a storm in that region. The surviving members of the crew had ended up on a desert island off the coast, a dreary, lifeless patch of rock. In sight of the mainland, but with their lifeboat wrecked, they had attempted to subsist on tidewater mollusks and the occasional sea bird. That source failing them, and growing increasingly desperate and quarrelsome, they began to consider a grim alternative. Then one of their number had perished—ostensibly through accident, although the author suggested otherwise—and the unspeakable alternative became reality. A week later they were rescued. The frontispiece, a colored picture, showed a ragged band of unshaven men squatting around a fire, gnawing meat from cracked bones. Martin flipped through the last chapter, which discussed the damage to their moral fiber and threats of legal action which never materialized.

Pleasant reading fare, this, on a full stomach. A nearby book, more recently printed, turned out to be the first hand account of a Spanish conquistador who took part in the expedition of Cortez against the Aztecs. Martin had read excerpts of this in the past, or secondary works derived from this text. The pious author dwelt with horrified fascination on the abominable culinary habits of that once powerful nation, whose people carried to absurd and disgusting lengths one of the worst vices ever to sully the annals of the human race.

SCIENCE AND SORCERY III

Another book proved disquietingly similar. The rather charming title, *One Year With the Palungas of Borneo*, belied the squalid nature of this early anthropologist's tale of fieldwork among a murderous tribe of bloodthirsty headhunters. Living in remote and unproductive territory, the shunned Palungas preyed upon their somewhat more civilized neighbors, harvesting heads rather than crops. Being practical types, they didn't waste the rest of the body. Grainy black and white photographs of stony-faced natives, stiffly posed, hinted at their cruel character. The author had much to say concerning nutritional requirements and the social implications of their behavior. He provided long descriptions of uproarious ceremonies, and a chilling relation of the ways in which these heathen monsters alternately honored and tormented their victims prior to the kill. In attempting to explain the superstructure of ritual which had developed around their dining activities, he almost came across as if he meant to justify it, or somehow approved of their abhorrent lifestyle. Martin thought it an example of bad taste or desire to shock rather than sober scientific analysis.

This one sounded different: the history of a party of settlers in the era of the covered wagon, which boldly set forth across the untamed continent in search of their Manifest Destiny. He skipped toward the back. Wait a minute; he knew this story. Trapped in the mountains by a fierce blizzard, their supplies ran out, and they were ultimately reduced to the last extremity of . . .

Having been exposed to a random sampling of works from this set, Martin was no longer convinced of their entertainment value. He had thought the common denominator to be adventure, but it seemed to be something else. Surely they weren't all like that; he'd simply made bad choices. He scanned the shelf for a volume which might promise more, and removed one whose title intrigued him.

Something by way of biography, this must be; a hefty volume, with an ornate binding containing gold leaf scrolling. The amusing name on the binding had caught his eye, but the first page gave him the full title: *The Curious History of Sawney Bean and His Unusual Family*, written by one J. Allen Hathaway, F.R.S. (followed by various other initials). The book had been published in England in 1883 and, judging from its physical quality, no expense had been spared.

The opening statement in the first paragraph of the introduction indicated to Martin he was once more on dangerous ground. "Gentle Readers may feel that apologies are due from this Humble Author for his daring to undertake the composition of a history so vile, incorporating themes so ignoble and of such a destructive nature to the sensibilities of the decent and the young; for relating a tale which, in the interests of truth, must needs be builded out of the most vicious components of crime, madness, and evil; for offering, as if for the edification of the learned, a book whose real subjects, who walked the earth in an age not widely separated in time from our own, inaugurated a reign of terror the likes of which have not disgraced our fair shores since, conceivably, the darkest phases of the lowly Palaeolithic Era. Rest assured that the purpose of this volume, its enduring value, resides in the enlightenment it may afford, rather than the base titillation that the undiscerning may seek from these pages." More followed, which didn't convince Martin of Mr. Hathaway's good intentions, rather leaving him wondering what kind of story he'd gotten his hands on.

It didn't take him long to find out; *The Curious History* purported to be a genuine chronicle of the most nasty, perverted doings imaginable. He might have chosen to disbelieve the tale, except it was based on a mass of official court documents dating from the Fifteenth Century. It transpired that Sawney Bean was a Scottish gentleman who had fallen on hard times. Financial and personal difficulties had so multiplied for him he was no longer able to maintain himself and his wife in their home at any reasonable standard of living, or apparently by any standard at all, for his solution to his mounting hardships was most peculiar. Rather than join the King's forces or sell himself as a serf to the local lord—the commonly available options, according to the author—Esquire Bean chose another, less socially approved avenue, one perhaps more befitting of his gloomy temperament. He withdrew, with his devoted wife, from all civilized habitation, into the murky fastness of the Scottish wilderness, where they found a new abode in a dank cave by the seashore. It was described as a picturesque region, of sandy beaches, flourishing forests, and rocky headlands (thought Martin idly, much resembling the location of the Caltel Ocean Resort). From there the embittered Mr. Bean waged a one man war upon the world he had rejected, or which had rejected him, earning a precarious living as a murderous highwayman. As awful as that despicable trade might be, it was only the beginning of the depths of depravity to which Sawney Bean would sink.

His reaction against the land and the people he had known reached such extremes he came to have no use for their company at all. Theft proved an unstable income, and he shunned the towns and their folk, so the ill-gotten gold and other monies he acquired provided nothing for his sustenance. Travelers seldom carried enough food to justify the risk of assaulting them, and the locale Bean had adopted for his home possessed few possibilities for agricultural industry or hunting; not that he was the sort to excel at either.

A shiftless disposition, the desire for easy solutions, combined with a strong will, led him to the elegant, if harrowing answer to his problems. Sawney Bean graduated from common murder to something else; his victims became, in themselves, the source of wealth in that ogre's private paradise. They became human livestock, cornered and slaughtered in expert fashion by a man who recognized no boundaries to conduct. Over time his system worked. He and his wife waxed hale and hearty, and they beget children, a multitude of them, and all grew up fit, and strong, and innately evil. In time the children beget children as well, necessarily the products of incestuous union, and it came to pass that three generations of the Bean household, scores of individuals, dwelt in their underground kingdom, a veritable portal to hell, issuing forth in search of the unwary whenever the monstrous craving overtook them. Eventually this perfect system collapsed; an unfortunate accident led to exposure; the King himself, with all his horses and men, intervened, tracked the Bean family to their filthy lair, fought them, rounded up forty-eight survivors and marched them all off to their well deserved deaths. The men were hacked to pieces, the women and children burned at the stake.

Thus endeth the lesson. Martin cared for this book not at all. As he read through the highlights he discovered, to his disgust, Hathaway's work was profusely illustrated with finely delineated engravings, pictures which, despite a certain quaintness of style, left nothing to the imagination. Could the events, as described, actually have happened? Was man—even late medieval man, which surely couldn't make that much difference—capable of such enormities? Considering some of the barbarities nowadays, he wouldn't rule the story out of court. Better just to forget it.

How did such books come to be here? Based on the age of most of them, he provisionally deduced they once belonged to what's his name— Thomas Dashauer—the hotshot who originally owned the place. That made sense. He must have been a man of morbid tastes. On the other hand, not all of the offending volumes seemed old enough. Perhaps the collection had been added to by others subsequently. He wondered why.

One afternoon had cured Martin of his desire to while away his time in the library. There were other books, many others, but a disturbing proportion of them bore titles which, based on his recent experience, suggested unhappy reading in store. Goodness! Without realizing it, so absorbing had the material been (he shamefully admitted) he had passed hours here. Against all expectation, dinner approached.

He returned to his room, dressed, then went below, with several minutes to spare. He walked out front to take some air. Here the sun shone, the birds called, the surf murmured. Away from the suffocating cloister of the library he felt better. The outdoor freshness lifted his spirits; he hadn't noticed how depressed they had become. He noticed now, idly, most of the vehicles were missing. The few cars and the other van had gone; only the one van remained. So some kind of traffic moved in and out of here after all. That might be good to know. He did long for a newspaper.

Wally had beaten him to the table. Diana wasn't yet present, but he expected to see her presently, if she kept her word. Already the three of them had established a routine. Every society evolved its own rules which must be obeyed, whether it be this one, or that of Sawney Bean and his gang of carnivorous troglodytes. Scratch that—banish it from his mind—there would be no such thoughts while dining; especially not then.

Diana arrived and sat next to him, closer than before. "Where have you been all day? I came looking for you a while back. I wanted to talk to you." She reacted to his answer with mock outrage. "It didn't occur to me you'd be hiding from me in there."

Dinner was magnificent, again. Thomas bustled about his duties, while Maurice observed silently from his post, making sure all went according to plan. The three guests chatted amiably among themselves: Wally in soaring spirits, Diana seemingly recovered from her latest blues, Martin joining in when called for. His companions had to speak to him twice on occasions, or to repeat themselves; he joked of being tired, but inwardly confessed his thoughts had taken to running off into unbidden channels of their own. Still, a fine meal—one of the best he'd ever eaten—and there were several more of the same caliber to which he could look forward.

After desert had been stuffed down, Wally removed from his pocket and lit up a monster cigar. He grinned devilishly and said, "They're on the house, Martin. You ought to take advantage while you can."

"I don't smoke."

"Too bad. This place has everything. Do you have any idea what this one cigar would cost, if you purchased it over the counter? If you could find it, that is. Mr. Hartmann was handing them out earlier. He gave me an entire box."

"He, or somebody, must be rolling in dough."

"It must be that way."

"We've already guessed that much," Diana said wryly. "Have you a light, Wally? Thank you. It's everything else that puzzles us. You know something? This is a grand old place, and I suppose it's everything it can be, but when my five days are up, I think maybe that will be long enough. Do you see it that way?"

"Me?" asked Martin, realizing he was being addressed.

"You, Mr. Moody. You aren't very talkative tonight."

"I'm not moody. I thought that was you."

"What do you mean?"

"Nothing, really." That was the truth. He shook his head. "I suspect when our days here are behind us, we will look back on them fondly. I can't think of any solid reason to doubt that."

Mr. Hartmann put in a brief appearance, only to verify the standards of the Caltel Ocean Resort were being maintained. There were no overt complaints; Wally was ecstatic in his fulsome praise. He jocularly asked about monthly rates. The manager laughed. Martin asked about the library collection. Mr. Hartmann didn't laugh.

"It is just bits and pieces, assorted items, gathered at random," he explained. "I hope you found something there to hold your interest. I hope you all look into it before your time is up. That would suit me perfectly. A quality library can be a most useful element in an operation like this one. It serves its purpose. A well chosen book is an eye through which we see the hidden truth. Mr. Horton, perhaps you will find an occasion to explore its treasures tomorrow, before your Big Night."

He left them, pleading pressing business. Diana wondered aloud what business here could possibly press. Wally enthused over the unknown splendors of his upcoming event. Martin said nothing.

After dinner he and Diana took a walk along the beach. At this hour a crescent moon hung above the waters, a lovely symbol of the new. The girl was immensely talkative this night, and seemed eager to tell him about her likes and dislikes. At an appropriate distance from the hotel he kissed her— a good one—and then they walked arm in arm. For the first time Martin stated plainly they ought to continue their acquaintance—their relationship, he called it—when they returned to the world. She agreed with alacrity. That pleased him immensely. Everything appeared to be looking up for him, as if all the pieces of his life finally had a chance of coming together. Overall, a good feeling. It ought to have been a joyous one. They stayed out late, under the moon and the stars, and all was well, until the increasing chill drove them inside; but his mind wouldn't rest. He wondered whether anything that happened here was real.

IV.

In the morning Martin woke with an active and clearly functioning brain. He knew immediately that a great deal about his current situation troubled him. He hadn't slept well, but that was just a symptom. Things weren't right; they weren't obviously wrong— no one factor stuck out to say, "Here is the key; now I've deciphered the riddle"—but every little item, when he tried to add it up with others and connect the whole, gave doubtful or problematical answers. What was it that bothered him so? The isolation; to a degree, was exactly what he had bargained for. The financial mystery; what was that to him? The cell phone—nothing, simply a mistake on the part of his girl. The presumed evidence the guests had been investigated prior to selection might be incorrect. The library; well, no point in making a big deal out of it. That nettled him though; one more item in the ledger, in the wrong column. In the main, a grotesque collection for a holiday resort. Why was it here? *Cui bono?* Mr. Hartmann's remarks hadn't soothed him. There was something funny about his response, as if he knew all about those strange books, and thought it important his lodgers know about them, too. Yes, his reaction was somehow off. That was it, more than anything else. What kind of people were running this place, anyway?

Nothing to fuss about and yet he felt a wariness building slowly inside him. He would go about his business, enjoy the resort and his company, but keep his eyes open, pay attention to what went on around him, observe everything. If nothing else happened to perturb him, if the days to come dragged out in their predictable lazy, easy going ways, then he would dismiss the subject. He would not manufacture alarming signs, only respond to them.

A great idea occurred to him now. Breakfast was still an hour away; he had time for a clever scheme, which was well within the power of his hosts, who were here—as they continually assured him—only to please. Martin wanted his morning newspaper. Donning a sweater, he went downstairs and cornered Nylstrom in the lobby.

"I want to go into town," he announced. "I'd like to ride into Tellmee and pick up their morning edition."

"I don't think they have one, sir."

"They've got something, man; one of the big dailies from the city will do."

"That might be available."

"Of course it is. It would only take a few minutes."

"That is true, Mr. Cravitt. I will speak with John. I'm sure he will be glad to pick up one for you."

"Don't bother him," Martin protested. "I'd just as soon get it myself. I need to buy a few necessities, anyway. Why don't you drive me into town right now? We could be there and back in no time."

"The van may be spoken for at the moment."

"By whom?"

"I couldn't say." Nylstrom seemed unhappy about something. "Mrs. Drexel keeps track of everything. I would have to direct you to her."

"I'll talk to her, then. Where are the other vehicles?"

"I don't know that, Mr. Cravitt."

"Get me Mrs. Drexel, please."

"I'll look for her, sir." Nylstrom left him, and Martin didn't see him again, or Mrs. Drexel, before breakfast.

Not satisfactory—making too much of a fetish out of this isolation silliness—but one way or the other he would have his answer soon. He sat in the lounge for the next hour, having shed the sweater as the morning quickly warmed, leafing through the old magazines. They, certainly, were conventional, non-threatening literature.

Breakfast followed the usual pattern. Diana arrived wearing shorts and a multi-colored halter top. Hopelessly out of place, he thought, if practical; yet, despite himself, the outfit charmed him. He wondered to what extent he ought to push matters with her. It would be easier to decide if he weren't so preoccupied. They didn't have much chance to talk at the table. Wally dominated the discussion.

"This is the big day, leading up to my Big Night," he crowed. "It's going to be something, I tell you, like nothing on earth."

"We've got a couple of those coming up as well," Martin said. "Why don't you tell us a little more what it's about."

"I don't know. I'm still in the dark. It's a surprise, you see."

"I don't see," countered Diana. "With what they've got here, they can't put on much of a show for you. Are you expecting them to bring in a busload of dancing girls?"

Wally laughed, snorting orange juice. "If so, I won't argue the point. I really don't know. Twice now, Mr. Hartmann has taken me aside and hyped the event. He didn't say much, as I recall, but he wouldn't puff it up so much if it was going to turn out a bust. After all, the next day I'd be reporting the disappointment to you."

"That's true," said Martin, mumbling around a mouthful of thickly buttered roll. "They don't want to let us down. We'll all find out when our time comes."

"I have to wait until the very last night," Diana said. "Suppose I'm a shambles when they send me home?"

Martin finished before the others. Diana let it be known she wanted to make claim to his time ("We haven't made plans for the day yet"); he asked her to wait in the lounge while he tracked down Mrs. Drexel to ask her about a trivial concern. He found her, as if waiting for him, at the counter in the office.

"Good morning, Mr. Cravitt. It is a beautiful day. More clouds gathering, I notice. We might get a sprinkle. That wouldn't be a bad thing. These light ocean showers can be so refreshing."

"I'll look forward to it. Did Nylstrom speak to you?"

"He did; a few words. He wasn't clear. Something about a newspaper." Martin patiently explained his proposal to the woman, who listened intently, nodding all the while. "I see. Yes, yes, now I understand. I hadn't expected anything like this; hadn't made arrangements—"

"Surely no great effort is required."

"No, of course not. We had no plans to run errands into town, but John would be more than pleased to drive you in, at your convenience. I will speak to him shortly."

"I am very happy to hear you say that," Martin said, feeling much relieved. For a moment he had thought . . . "I'm ready any time. I'm ready now. Why don't I go talk to him?"

"Oh, please don't, Mr. Cravitt. Just at this moment you would be wasting your time, and I wouldn't want you to do that. Let me check with him first—I believe he's down at the shed now, gathering his tools—and find out for you when he predicts that the van will be running."

"Running?" he asked. Icicles broke off from the back of his skull and slithered down his spine. "Van not running? What do you mean?"

"I must clarify." She was looking him straight in the eye, her face an immobile mask of kindly solicitude. "There is some ridiculous problem with the engine—one of those mechanical difficulties, so I'm told—certainly nothing of consequence, for it was running adequately before, but at the present time the van is inoperative."

"A van won't go. All right, that happens. Where are the other vehicles?"

"Sent away. Those were rental units, employed to bring in staff and supplies prior to opening. Having served their purpose, they have been returned. We make do with the one van, which is normally quite sufficient."

Martin wanted to hit her. "It isn't now."

"A setback, soon to be remedied. Everything goes on as before."

"It shouldn't be long?"

"No. I will notify you when I have further information. Enjoy your day."

That was that. He wasn't going anywhere, not at this time, and he didn't know when his status would change. He felt like a prisoner. What if he just started walking out of here? A hike to the village would take hours. It would be foolish to try it. Of course they wouldn't really try to stop him.

John was a mechanic of sorts, he'd been told. He would tinker with the valves, or clean the carburetor, or adjust a battery connection, and all would be well. Not satisfactory, though; definitely not satisfactory. Another item in the wrong column.

And her attitude; it wasn't right—something patronizing in her tone—as if she were humoring him. He'd thought of a mask. Her mask was slipping, exposing the true face of Mrs. Drexel. What lay beneath the mask? What kind of stupid question was that?

Suppose there was something phony about this setup. Suppose—for the sake of argument—they were all playing parts. Could he deduce the reality (however innocuous it might or must be) from observing them? He could make a game out of it, and laugh at himself later. Down the road that would make for amusing memories of his experiences here; how he endeavored to solve *The Mystery of the Caltel Ocean Resort*.

He met Wally coming down the hall.

"So you do have a thing going with that girl," the older man observed. "I suspected as much. Not bad, if you can swing it. Miss Carswell is an interesting type. Anything cooking yet?"

"I'm working on it," Martin said gamely. "Say, Wally, shouldn't you find out more about this Big Night business? Maybe you need to prepare for it."

"That has crossed my mind. They're pretty cagey. I tried pumping the waiter, but his lips are sealed. He just gives me knowing looks. They're damned secretive about it; about everything, in a way. What's the matter? Can't you wait for your own Big Night?"

"I don't see why we have to do each one alone. I'd love to be there with you to join in, and I'm sure Diana feels the same. Since it is your night, perhaps you could pull strings and invite us."

"I like that. I'll ask, but don't be hurt if I hog it all to myself."

"Get back with me and let me know what you hear."

Martin hadn't thought too much about the Big Nights. Still another item in the ledger? He couldn't see how. To be sure, he lacked information. Another strand to unravel, as it might be.

Diana gave him a sour smile when he entered the lounge. "I'm starting to feel like the most unpopular girl in the whole resort."

"Nothing of the kind. I was detained. Have you thought about what you want to do today? Your wish is my command."

"Keep me company. I don't want to be alone." Martin thought that an odd thing to say, yet she seemed outwardly cheerful. She wanted to have a good time—he had let it be known he was eager to provide it—therefore, she expressed herself bluntly. No harm in that; it might even be a good sign. There were many delightful ways of not being alone.

"I'm keen on horseback riding this morning," he said. "Are you good for that again?"

"Surely."

He arranged matters with Nylstrom. Presently Martin and Diana strolled down to the stables, where she was given Cherry, at her insistence, and he took Whitey, a large, dappled animal who seemed to possess spirit. Off they went, he in the lead, heading north, first curving around the front of the hotel. Diana drew attention to the van, which was sitting in the gravel lot with its hood up. Martin explained to her, in a few words, what he had been told.

"I hope he gets it fixed," she said.

He—John—was nowhere in sight. Still collecting his tools, perhaps, or back in the shed, hunting for a replacement part. It could be that. Martin would have preferred to see the mechanic hard at work. They rode on, up the rough road, toward the edge of the trees. Whitey, after all, proved a slow motion conveyance, prone to stoppages unless gently goaded, which his rider did frequently. Cherry passed often, then a kick would send Whitey lurching forward for a time.

"Let's ride up the road a ways," Martin suggested when they reached the tree line. "I didn't get a good look at that territory when I came in."

She nodded agreement, and they pushed on; only, they did not get very far in that direction. Within a few yards they reached the old gate, which was now shut and padlocked. They rested there for a period, Martin staring morosely at the barrier. Eventually Diana broke the thickening silence.

"Are you thinking of a jailbreak?"

"Lord, yes," Martin exclaimed—for some such idea was truly passing through his mind that very second—then caught himself. "It's just funny, that's all."

"Is this place giving you the spooks, too?"

"Not in particular."

"You can talk to me," she said with emphasis. "Even if you can't, do it anyway. You obviously have something on your mind. You seem more a stranger than you did when we first met."

He apologized, sincerely. "I don't want you to think of me that way. I assure you, honey, I'm not the brooding sort; at least, I've never thought of myself in those terms."

"Am I your 'honey' now?"

"Don't change the subject. And what if you are? That isn't a crime, is it?"

"Not at all. I wondered." She seemed to be teasing him, and yet a seriousness crept into her manner.

"What I wonder about," he drawled, "is our situation here. I have never been so completely cut off from everything. I find that I don't appreciate it as much as I ought. It gives me goose bumps. No telephone, no television, no radio, no newspapers—what I've always desired—and yet, not quite satisfying, not here, not now, not in these circumstances. There should have been more people here. That would have taken up the slack. That isn't to say I disapprove of present company, mind you. It's just . . . well, there is the van, our only link to the world, out of commission. It will probably be repaired by the time we get back. Of course it will. That's no big deal, but it is our necessary link. It's supposed to be kept in good shape. And then there's this gate."

"I'm with you so far."

"Why is it locked? Is security an issue? Maybe it should be. It is everywhere else. They don't want intruders sneaking in. Maybe that's a problem. I don't know. I expected this, somehow, and I don't like it."

"Do we jump it or ride on?"

"These horses don't jump."

"We do," Diana said.

Martin chuckled, with an effort. "Let's ride on." They trotted back into the open and continued north, away from the hotel.

"So it's finally getting to you, too," Diana observed.

"What is getting to me?"

"What you said. And everything. How this place just can't be what it makes itself out to be."

"They don't want uninvited guests getting in. That's fair enough."

"I'm not only talking about the gate. I mean all the creepy stuff."

"That's how you sounded yesterday morning," said Martin. "I had the impression you were over that."

"So I fooled you, too," Diana replied. "I hope I fooled everybody. Listen, sweetie"—she emphasized the word, to his amusement—"my opinion hasn't changed. I came here to enjoy myself, and I'm going to be happy if I can, but things aren't right, and I could swear they're getting worse. When you get right down to it, this so-called resort is a dump, and nothing about it makes sense. There's something underhanded about the place. I can't see how it could do us any harm, but it's there. Do you know what I think? I've figured it out. These people are a bunch of con artists."

"Trying to bilk us out of our millions."

"Be serious," she insisted. "That's what I meant: it isn't directed against us; there's no reason for that; we don't have anything they want, unless they collect cell phones. I guess we're okay, if they don't even bother to charge us admission. What they're doing is putting the squeeze on whoever is sponsoring the resort. He's some deep pockets fellow, an unassuming, friendly type. Someone like Wally"—they both laughed at that—"easy to lead by the nose, who they talked into bankrolling their scheme. So, having gotten the organization running on a shoe-string (except, I admit, for all the food), they convince him that they're getting hundreds of guests, and have hired a hundred employees, and are spending all kinds of money, and are demanding that he foot the bill for it. Meanwhile, they're entertaining the three of us, which doesn't cost them much, and keeping the place quiet, so as not to make waves, and skimming barrels full of gravy. That is a great racket, and I say that's what they're doing."

"Diana, you are a treasure. By Jove, I think you've got it." They discussed the ins and outs of the scam at length, in animated fashion, adding various hilarious elements as they went on. Martin liked the sound of it: a real world problem, the sort of thing one read about, clucked over and shook one's head at the iniquities of man. A good, solid, safe explanation, one he could normally live with. If it satisfied her, enhanced her sense of adventure while easing her mind, he might leave it at that. Too bad he did not believe a word of it.

Her idea didn't come close to dealing with all his concerns. He remained convinced the mystery was, in some manner hidden from them, focused upon the guests, rather than a theoretical outsider. He couldn't shake the depressing thought a level of threat existed, nebulous, carefully concealed, and all the more dangerous for that. Lately Martin had fallen into the habit of taking himself to task for being too imaginative. Now he honestly wondered if his difficulty in seeing clearly was due to lack of imagination. He felt that, within a subterranean chamber of his brain, the answer lay before him, if only he possessed the mental agility to marshal the evidence and ask the proper questions.

They rode on to the limits of the Caltel domain, where the high, fenced bluffs crowded the shore. They removed their shoes and socks and played in the cold surf, keeping an eye on the horses in case they were inclined to bolt. The animals stayed their ground, nipping contentedly at weeds. Martin felt better away from the hotel, the center of his amorphous forebodings, and at this point they were as far away as they could get . . . without jail breaking, that is.

Neither having brought bathing suits, they chose to sprawl on the dry sand beyond the reach of waves. That was easier for her, since she wore her skimpy outfit again. The angle of the cliff partially hid them from the hotel. They chatted in good spirits. When he attempted to draw her close, she yielded gracefully. He kissed and caressed her; she responded in kind, and then some.

Martin let it be known, in no uncertain terms, he didn't regret his vacation for a moment; the opportunity to meet her far outweighed other considerations. She accepted his statement of feeling as he hoped she would. They discussed, in greater detail than before, the sorts of things they might do when they got back home. Their views didn't entirely coincide, which was no surprise. Some of her ideas sounded rather tiresome, in fact, activities he might relish only for the sake of pleasing her. So be it. That was part of the deal, always, and he supposed he could do a lot worse for himself; had, in fact, several times in the past. If they continued to hit it off well, he would never complain about this trip, no matter what happened.

As they plotted the future, the present darkened. Fast, heavy clouds were rolling in, unlike the sluggish cottony puffs which had formerly alternated with open sky. The wind was picking up as well; a stiff breeze rustled the trees, livened the surf, and annoyed the horses. Cherry and Whitey grew skittish, began to edge away. Martin had to leave his place, jumping up with alacrity rather than eagerness, to rein in the beasts before they wandered away. Diana joined him. Together they surveyed the scene, which had altered dramatically. Distant specks of seabirds wheeled and raced away, their receding cries forlorn.

"Where has the time gone?" Martin asked. "I didn't notice."

"We were preoccupied," she said.

"A little bit. It looks like rain." He consulted his watch. "Believe it or not, we've missed lunch, by a mile."

"Good," Diana said. "I'm glad. For once we haven't been living according to the Caltel schedule. We did our thing. That's the way it ought to be."

"You're right. That's the way it should always be.. Oh, and since neither of us is hungry—"

"Now that you mention it, I'm starved."

"Let's head back before the storm strikes," Martin advised, "and have ourselves a snack, 'specially prepared, anytime we please', as promised."

"Let's. Wouldn't it be a joke if they made a fuss about it?"

As it turned out, it didn't storm, but a bare drizzle began to patter upon the sand before they reached the dry sanctuary of the hotel. As they approached, Martin noticed right away the van was missing.

"John got it going after all," he said. "I wasted a lot of mental agony on that."

Mr. Hartmann and Mrs. Drexel were waiting at the front door. He called to the riders.

"We were worried," Mrs. Drexel said, with a trace of sharpness in her tone.

"What she means," Mr. Hartmann added, with a cold glance at his associate, "is that we were afraid you might be caught in the downpour."

"Not much of one," Martin noted.

"They come on quickly here, and can be fierce. It would have pained us if you had experienced discomfort of any kind."

"No harm done. The van is fixed, I see. Any chance of getting my newspaper?"

"John took the vehicle for a test drive," Mrs. Drexel said. "I will speak with him when he returns, and gauge the situation then." Not much of an answer, Martin reflected, especially since he'd wanted a lift more than the paper. Still, he would learn how matters stood shortly.

"If you are through riding," said Mr. Hartmann, "leave the horses. I will take them over myself."

Decent of him. Martin and Diana dismounted, brushed past their hosts and went inside. Their clothes were scarcely damp; more gritty with sand than anything. Mrs. Drexel followed them into the lobby.

"You did not appear for the midday meal," she observed. "Without prior notification, I could not be certain that was your intent."

"We were delayed," Martin admitted. "The beauties of nature called."

"We got carried away," Diana said sheepishly.

"Of course, your time is your own," Mrs. Drexel said sternly. "You are here to amuse yourselves as you see fit, however that may be. You must understand that we attempt to prepare for every contingency—"

"I hope we didn't put you to any trouble," said Martin. "As it stands, we're both famished. We could do with something."

"At once, sir, if something light will serve. Would you prefer the dining room, or—"

"We'll take it up to my room." To Diana: "We can eat on the balcony and watch the rain."

"It will be sent up to you, sir," said the housekeeper. She actually sniffed before she strode stiffly away.

Diana waited until the older woman was out of earshot to say, "A bit of a bluenose, isn't she?"

"I'd expect her to be accustomed to everything."

Soon after they had relaxed on a balcony seat, Thomas arrived with ham and cheese sandwiches, potato chips in a round cardboard tub, and cups, with a thermos of hot coffee. Hardly grand cuisine, but it suited the moment well. They watched the dense, roiling canopy of darkness sweep over, never depositing much precipitation, but cooling the air considerably. The salty scent of the ocean mingled with the crisp smell of ozone. As they sat, eating and talking, the thickest clouds blew over and the sky began to peek through again.

They noticed comings and goings of the staff from the direction of the boathouse. Something was happening over there. The building blocked most of the view, but it appeared a large canopy had been erected, atop wooden supports, on the sand by the shore. They could make out the end of what might be a long picnic table protruding around a corner. The Big Night taking shape? If so, it was intended as an outdoor ceremony. Apparently they weren't expecting rain this evening.

SCIENCE AND SORCERY III

For all of Martin's gloom and doom notions earlier, this had turned out to be his favorite day so far. Really, why should he get long in the mouth about trivialities and lurid daydreams when he had it in his power, here, to be so happy? He almost wanted to laugh at himself. A full belly and a nice, fairly pretty girl, so it appeared, could do wonders for a man's frame of mind. He really ought to get his head on straight, and start enjoying life a little more.

"I must check in with Wally," he said presently.

"Stay with me," Diana urged, "and leave him alone. He doesn't want to fool with us today. He has other things on his mind."

"That's just it. I want to hear more about the Big Night. By now he must know everything they're willing to tell. Don't you want the latest information?"

"Maybe I do. What can it be about?"

"A private party. That's all I can come up with. It's more managing of our time, if you ask me. I'm just looking for some idea what to expect."

She consented to come with him. They carried their refuse down to the dining room, which was empty, and left the stuff on a table. They looked in the usual places for Wally, without finding him. Coming back around to the lobby, they met Nylstrom. Martin asked if their fellow guest was in his room.

"He is there, sir."

"Fine. I'd like to call him there."

"I wouldn't recommend it, Mr. Cravitt, for his sake. I understand that he's napping, you see; resting himself for tonight's activities."

"It's like that?" Diana asked. "He has to prepare himself?"

"Indeed. The Big Night is a grand occasion, but a hectic one. All eyes will be on him. As you will learn, in due course."

"I can't wait," Martin said dryly. "Thank you."

Diana announced she needed a shower. He promised to catch up with her later. He went in search of Mr. Hartmann who, sure enough, was just then returning to the hotel from the busy beach site. Martin accosted him at the side door.

"Is everything all ready for Wally?" he asked casually.

"Nearly so. He will have the very best this night." Mr. Hartmann seemed about to push past, but his guest blocked his path.

"You make such a mystery of it," Martin said. "I'm on pins and needles thinking about my night. Can't you be a little more forthcoming?"

"Surprise and mystery are essential elements of the Big Night," Mr. Hartmann said with a tight smile. "They are the 'ding an sich;' do you understand me? No? They are what it is all about, the core of the experience, if you will. To give away the secret would make a travesty of the occasion. Believe me, Mr. Cravitt—I say this to you as a fact, in all honesty—if I told beforehand all there was to tell, then it would greatly lessen your enjoyment when your moment comes."

"Very interesting."

"Also, as long as we are on the subject, I have important requests to make of you and your sweet friend, Miss Carswell. I beg that tonight, for the duration of the event, neither of you will leave the hotel. To remain in your rooms would be best, but I will not insist. Keeping to the premises will suffice."

Martin's blood was bubbling again. What the man was saying didn't sound right; the manner of his saying it sounded worse. He wasn't barking orders, not exactly—no, not like that—but his voice took on a steely tone. It didn't sound like a request at all.

"You don't want us turning up uninvited?"

"That would be inappropriate. I would rather you did not approach the party location for the time being. The entire staff will be waiting on Mr. Horton, from eight in the evening until midnight. He will receive all of our attention. You and Miss Carswell will be somewhat neglected for a period, but that necessary lapse on our part will be more than atoned for later. Please work with us on this, and we will not regret it. You will see."

"I hear you," Martin said vaguely.

"Dinner will be served at six for the two of you. It will not be fancy, but it will satisfy. Maurice, you realize, will be devoting his amazing skills to our star of the night."

"Of course," said Martin. "Thank you for the information. I will pass word to Miss Carswell."

"Please do so. I wish to avoid awkwardness."

Martin stepped back and allowed the manager to pass. From this angle he could see more beyond the boathouse. A long wooden table stood emplaced for a group, Wally and his hosts, every single one of them. They were such considerate folks, willing to spend hours of their time on entertaining one guest. Even by Caltel's murky financial standards, it was difficult to figure out the profit motive.

What were they really up to?

He struggled to formulate a suitably scary explanation which would cover all the mounting weirdness, but failed signally, as before. Too much of this was beyond his experience; an unworldly life, perhaps, had left him lacking when it came to such evaluation; he tended to be quietly reasonable, to make allowances.

And they knew exactly what sort of man he was.

They had chosen him, and the others, for definite reasons of their own. They wanted loners like himself, like Diana, like Wally, people who wouldn't put up a fight when confronted by the strange. People who already considered this world an odd place, and who would bow before further oddities.

Pieces of the puzzle were fitting together.

He still lacked the critical piece, or the flash of insight that would make it fit. Perhaps he would know by morning. By then, maybe Wally could explain the whole thing. Martin wasn't sure he wanted to wait; he wasn't sure he wanted to know.

The sound of a roaring motor drew him around to the front of the building. Here came the van! It squealed to a halt. Two men emerged. Martin darted back, puzzled. John, the driver, naturally. The other man . . . the other looked familiar. Martin recognized him from somewhere, or thought he did. Impossible, of course . . . unless he were a television reporter or some celebrity. That didn't feel right. The second man had disappeared into the hotel before realization came. Bob, the travel agent! Martin had met him once, oh—was it a million years ago?—at the agency. What was he doing here?

Martin walked nonchalantly up to John. "Sounds like your van's in great shape now."

"No, sir, it's running rough. I'll have to work on it again in the morning, when I have time."

"You didn't pick up a newspaper, by any chance?"

John's blank stare told all. But he said, after a quiet pause, "They were all out."

"Pity." That, surely, was a lie. "I haven't seen that fellow around, the one you came in with. Is he a new guest?"

"No."

"New staff?"

John shrugged. "He works for COR, in administration. Just checking." He slapped the hood and went into the hotel without another word.

And another lie. It was Bob, Martin was sure of it. It occurred to him everybody he knew who was aware of the existence of this place was now present. Did Wally's Big Night merit that much consideration?

He knocked at Diana's door. She had finished her shower, wasn't dressed, was primping, would be out shortly. He returned to his room. "Shortly" began to stretch interminably. An idea percolated. He dialed Wally. The man was awake, cleaning up, dressing himself. Might they drop in on him for a while? He was cheerfully agreeable.

"Let's pay him a visit," Martin said to Diana when she emerged. They presented themselves at room 29. Wally ushered them in.

"Forgive the mess," he said, though there wasn't a lot. He had brought so little with him. "I haven't seen much of you two lately. Sit down, make yourselves comfortable. Keep me company. Bring me up to date on what you've been doing."

After the bare necessities demanded by politeness, Martin got down to what was really on his mind. "Tell us what you've learned about your Big Night."

"Nothing, not a thing. Mum's the word. Nor do I care. It won't be long now until I live it."

"I wish you would put your foot down," Martin said, "and invite us."

"No can do. You know the rules. This night is all mine." Wally chuckled. "Don't get greedy, Martin. Your turn will come. I promise not to hog all the nights. I'll settle for one."

"I don't think you should go," Martin snapped on impulse. "Stay in with us."

"Not go?" Wally seemed thunderstruck.

"Just for fun, let's throw a monkey wrench into their plans. Forget their routines and their schedules. Let's get together and amuse ourselves."

Diana, obviously puzzled by the turn of conversation, accepted it and, as if on cue, added, "We haven't seen enough of you. That's our fault. We want to include you."

"I appreciate your kindness, my dear," Wally replied gravely. "Perhaps I can take you up on that tomorrow, during the day. I will not deny myself this treat, however. I've been waiting a long time for this."

"Waiting for what?" Martin asked impatiently. "It's only a dumb party."

"It's my night," Wally said, with warmth. "My Big Night, the only Big Night I've had in my life, likely the only one I will ever have. It's all about me. Do you understand that? I've lived—existed—these many years, but it's never been about me. This is." His face grew red, as if anger simmered. "I don't care what is going to happen. Maybe I will be bored stiff before the night is done. If so, I won't be worse off. That's the story of my life. I don't care. It will be for me, about me. I've dreamed of—I've prayed for—a moment like this. It's going to happen. And you would take it away from me!"

"I'm not taking anything from you. I only thought—"

"You two have gotten so wrapped up in each other—pretty fast work, if you ask me—you can't imagine how it is for me. I need this. I won't give it up."

"I believe that. You win, Wally. It was just a wild hair. Think nothing of it. You will tell us all about it in the morning?"

"If it's allowed," Wally mumbled.

He saw them off with ill grace, scarcely observing formalities. They had barely left his room before Diana was plaguing Martin with questions he couldn't answer.

"What was that about? What were you up to? Do you know something I don't? Aren't you going to tell me?"

"It's time for dinner," Martin said. That was near enough the case. "Let's not be late."

Over a simple, but excellent, meal of beef soup and salad, accompanied by the usual quality wine (to which he helped himself copiously), he had to admit he didn't know what he had been doing. "I couldn't stop myself. I knew it wouldn't do any good, and I don't know why it mattered to me."

Diana seemed to realize that he was more oppressed than ever. After dinner, over which they dawdled, she invited him to the lounge to play a game. Neither had looked at them before, and they spent much time sorting through the aged, crumbling boxes, seeking something both of them could enjoy. He preferred chess. She wouldn't touch it, accusing him of being an expert, which was probably true by comparison. He considered checkers tiresome. They ended up playing a children's game, which consisted of brightly colored plastic pieces, shaped like dogs, cats, birds, and fruit, which marched along squares in a garish fantasy land. Such a moronic pastime embarrassed him; losing at it more so. The game didn't require much concentration, but demanded more than he could give.

It grew late. Night had long fallen. At intervals they had heard distant, muffled sounds, which must connote a riot of noise. Both wearying of the game (although Diana won twice), they went upstairs to the balcony in order to steal a peek at the festivities. Practically nothing could be seen. Bright illumination shone from behind the boathouse, wavering reddish light and shifting shadows. A bonfire raged back there. Occasionally a lancing beam, as of a flashlight, pointed in their direction and swept the hotel. At times human figures could be glimpsed under the canopy, but their actions could not be discerned at this distance. Much was audible, however, at all times. Raucous singing carried on the breeze, and music of a sort—someone blew on a flute, someone else banged on a drum—shouting and laughing. It sounded rather grotesque, but apparently a good time was being had by all.

Diana finally gave out and retired to her room for the night. Martin remained at his seat, immovable, ignoring the mounting coolness for a good while more, until going on midnight. Then he heard the scream, which jolted him from a doze, and he leaped up and ran downstairs. Before his feet touched the chill sand Nylstrom appeared with a flashlight, focusing it into his eyes, blocking the way.

"I thought something might be wrong," Martin said, blinking and turning from the dazzling beam. "Where is Wally?"

"Mr. Horton is among friends, sir, never you fear," Nylstrom said pleasantly. "It's been the night of his life. Believe you me, he's feeling no pain. We'll take good care of him. Good night, Mr. Cravitt."

Martin listlessly went to his room. The noise of partying gradually died away, but it would be a long while yet before sleep claimed him.

V.

He awoke with a start at the sound of the telephone ringing. Despite weariness, his mind was perfectly clear. For the second time running he returned to consciousness feeling alert, and now on the alert. He remembered everything of the preceding night. He rolled over and picked up the receiver, hoping it was Wally. It was Diana.

"Do you have any idea what time it is? You've missed breakfast, sleepy head. It wasn't nice of you to leave me to eat all alone. I'm feeling rejected." Martin apologized, and promised to catch up with her shortly.

He dialed Wally's room. One ring, two rings, three rings, then many more. He formulated an excuse for calling while he waited, then grew annoyed he had no chance to use it. No answer. To be sure, after such a night a man might sleep like the dead.

Did Diana's statement imply Wally hadn't shown up for breakfast either? Possibly not; the man could have eaten and gone out. It could be that. Martin would feel a hell of a lot better after speaking to Wally himself, to make certain all was well, and to glean what information about the Big Night his fellow guest was willing to bestow.

He showered, dressed himself warmly, then left his room and walked down the silent corridor to number 29. He knocked tentatively, then harder after a pause. He waited another minute, then knocked again, without effect. No—to the contrary—a door opened, but to room 25. Diana poked out her head.

"Is he up yet?"

"Apparently not." Martin joined her, standing in the hall. "I take it that you haven't met up with him this morning."

"Not so far. I haven't seen anyone except the waiter, and he was dragging. I guess they're all sleeping it off." Diana opened her door a little wider. She was wearing a pink sun dress, pleasing to the eye. "Are we doing anything today? I know you're spoken for tonight."

"Don't you worry, we'll get up to something. I'm not going to waste an entire day because of a Big Night, when I can spend it with you."

"That's what I want to hear."

He kissed her. "I'll get back with you. I really want to talk to Wally before I make any plans. Don't go away."

251

He went downstairs. No one in the lower corridor, nor in the adjoining public rooms or the lobby. The fireplace was cold, uncleaned. Thomas wasn't in the dining room now. He supposed all concerned were keeping to their rooms. They must have really had a wild time of it. The hotel seemed deserted.

He went outside. The parking lot lay empty. The van was gone. Another road test, perhaps? Maybe this time John would give it a clean bill of health. A cheering development. Martin couldn't care less about the newspaper. Such outside influences must violate local taboo.

He heard a noise, an indefinable proof of activity somewhere in the vicinity of the resort. He walked around and scanned the outbuildings. The sound was louder here. Something was going on down by the boathouse. He would find out what, if no one tried to stop him. They might get fussy about his snooping around down there. Let them; he could make a fuss in return, if he had to do so, and it occurred to him he might find Wally there, basking in the scene of his recent triumph.

He found two men, neither of them Wally; rather, Nylstrom and Bob, the so-called travel agent, engaged in garbage collection around the picnic table beneath the canopy. At least, they were gathering up refuse in large plastic bags, and otherwise cleaning and straightening out the site of last night's festivities. They did not react adversely to his approach; indeed, though both looked a bit droopy, they were all smiles and welcome. Bob waved and hailed him.

"Long time no see, Mr. Cravitt. Are you investigating the scene of the crime?" Bob laughed at his own joke, while Nylstrom grinned broadly and shook his head. "As you can tell, we made a bit of a mess, but we'll have the place ship shape for you. When we're done, it will live up to your expectations."

"Only the best for our honored guest, Mr. Cravitt, tonight," Nylstrom said, as if by rote.

"I appreciate the sentiment," Martin said. "Bob, is it? I didn't realize you were part of this organization."

"I never miss the Big Nights."

"So, are you actually an employee of COR Enterprises?"

"Something like that."

"I'm looking for Mr. Horton," Martin said heavily. "I thought he might still be down here."

"Funny you should say that," Bob observed. "In a manner of speaking, he is. In spirit, I mean. Did you check in his room?"

"He didn't answer."

"Well, isn't that the most amazing thing." Not as much as their evident mirth at these verbal proceedings. They were truly a jolly pair this morning, despite the messy work, which mainly consisted of scraping up the residue from the dampened bonfire. Ashes and charred material went into the bags. "I can't say I'm surprised," Bob continued, "after a night like he had. If I'd celebrated that way, I wouldn't be up walking either."

"It would be most unlikely," Nylstrom said coolly. "I shouldn't expect it, not after last night. No sir, I wouldn't. A body needs a long rest after excitement like that." Bob burst out laughing, and his companion joined in.

"I'll keep looking until I find him," Martin said. "Perhaps he'll let me in on the fun."

"He'd tell you plenty if he could," replied Bob. "That would be a story worth hearing."

Then an odd thing happened. Bob reached for a full bag sitting on the sand, picked it up, then turned it over and, with a laughing oath, dumped its contents on the ground. "I beg your pardon," he said. "What a clumsy fool I am." The maneuver hadn't looked clumsy. Actually, it seemed to Martin as if he had done it on purpose. There were lots of moistened ashes in the pile, and some pieces of paper, and a quantity of bones.

Quite a few bones, many of them small and fragmentary, but a few were of impressive size. There were parts of cracked long bones, and one intact, as long as a man's thigh. Martin stared at them for a period, during which the only sound was the lapping surf.

"Did you cook the horses?" he asked, with a feeble smile.

"Perish the thought, sir," exclaimed Nylstrom. "Those animals are healthy as ever, and waiting for you whenever you're ready to take them out, today."

"I think we can do better than that," Bob said seriously, then laughed once more. The two men began scraping up the mess with gloves and rakes. "Horseflesh! Oh, we'd never live it down. Here at the world famous Caltel Ocean Resort we can provide a very great deal better than that. Take my word for it."

"You can bet your eyes on it," said Nylstrom.

"I'll keep my eyes, thank you. Good morning, gentlemen." Martin backed away, with the same smile pasted on his face, seeing the genuine merriment in theirs until he turned away and strode out of sight around the seedy boathouse. He trudged back to the hotel, his mind in turmoil. He saw someone standing at the corner of the building, but as he closed the figure vanished. When he arrived no one was in sight. Whoever it was had darted into the building.

He leaned against the wall, breathing hard. This was an unnatural place. He truly didn't believe in it anymore; how could he ever have done? This wasn't a resort, it was a stage, a set of plywood and paste board where a play was being performed, by skilled actors, for the benefit of the selected audience. How they would benefit remained to be seen. Martin knew next to nothing about resorts—and it pained him that those surrounding him had counted on his ignorance—but he wasn't blind. He had lacked awareness, but gradually the scales had fallen from his eyes. These people liked to talk about eyes, didn't they? They were always mentioning them in some unconventional context or another. That made him uncomfortable. Perhaps it was meant to do so.

No, Caltel wasn't a proper resort. Where were the tennis courts, the volleyball nets, the live entertainment? The latter might be out of reach for a small establishment like this one, but so much more could have been done with it over the years. However they generated income, it could have been put to considerably better use.

All this presumed their goals were those of other resort operators. If this place functioned for a different purpose, then all bets were off, even if he bet his eyes. Non-traditional concerns might drive them; their motives would justify different actions. What of the isolation, which they carried to such extraordinary extremes? He looked up the road, to where it disappeared among the trees. There were no power lines, no telephone poles. The latter made sense, given what he already knew, although puzzling. As to the former, there must be an electrical generator in the big shed. There could be a water tank in there too, or elsewhere on the property. Except for food, which had been brought in previously, this place might be entirely self-sufficient. It didn't impinge upon the outside world in any way. And, of course, that distant world need know nothing of what went on here. Perhaps it was a critical factor.

He felt exposed, standing there in the sunlight. He went inside. While the idea disturbed him, he thought he ought to eat something, to keep up his strength. With all his crazy ideas, he didn't care to predict what might happen today. The waiter still wasn't in attendance, though—it appeared Martin must wait for lunch—and he wasn't interested enough to make an issue of the matter. He returned to the lobby, and now found Mrs. Drexel. Had it been she watching him earlier? She stood motionless, eyeing him patiently and cautiously from before the counter. She said nothing until he came near.

"It's another fine morning," she said. "Everything is so bright and gay. How do you do, Mr. Cravitt? We're all rather slow today, but that will pass. Breakfast was prepared for you, but you did not show. I understand that Miss Carswell was quite unhappy about dining alone."

"Mr. Horton couldn't make it?" asked Martin.

"Mr. Cravitt, haven't you been informed?" cried Mrs. Drexel.

"Who would inform me, if not you? What about Mr. Horton? Where is he? When can I see him?"

"He is no longer with us," she said simply.

"Wally—Mr. Horton—he's gone?"

"This morning, early. He was called away. Something came up unexpectedly—a family emergency, I believe—so John drove him home. A great pity."

"A family emergency," Martin muttered, "called away. What a shame."

"Isn't it, though?"

"And he didn't even have time to say good-bye. It must have been something serious."

"So I would presume," Mrs. Drexel said. "Otherwise, he would still be here. You know how much he enjoyed himself with us."

"I do," Martin agreed absently. "I certainly do. What a shame."

He returned to his room. He didn't turn on a light. He sat there, in the darkness, on the bed, thinking, trying not to think. What now? Dare he fit together the final pieces of the puzzle? He had hung all his hopes on seeing Wally again, on convincing himself, despite the evidence, all was well. Only Wally, in the flesh, could have turned Martin's mind from the sinister channel down which his thoughts were coursing. Wally, however, had been called away. Indeed, was that how it had happened? Had Mrs. Drexel's lips curled into a superior sneer as she told the tale? It could have been his imagination, but he didn't think so.

The phone rang. He didn't answer. It kept ringing. Later came a pounding on the door, accompanied by Diana's raised voice. "Martin, are you in there? I heard you go in. Answer me!" Presently he did so, opened the door and let her in. She took one look at him and asked, "What's wrong?"

He told her what Mrs. Drexel had told him. "That's terrible," said Diana. "I'm sorry to see him go. I thought of him as a fixture around here, even if we didn't have much to do with him. I hope everything is all right. So, what about lunch? Can I count on you?"

"You can. It is about that time. I'll eat as much as they will allow me. I need some pep. Let's head down and get them moving." He added with a show of mirth, "It won't hurt you to be early for once."

The dining room was empty, but a table had been laid, for one. They won't get their way this time, he thought. Within minutes Thomas appeared, as busy sounds commenced in the kitchen. Martin explained his situation to the waiter, and made clear he required a full lunch today, regardless of the rules of the Big Night. Thomas seemed ill at ease due to the shocking change of plan, but he acquiesced with good grace. Dishes and utensils materialized, and before long the two remaining guests were dining amiably.

SCIENCE AND SORCERY III

Martin was not in a hurry. Save for the Big Night, there was nothing to do here they hadn't already done. His private thoughts dominated the moment, and while Diana chatted around them, the meal dragged on languidly.

"I wore this dress just for you," she pointed out. "Compliment me, if you want to."

He did so, between spoonfuls of creamed chicken soup. Mrs. Drexel is lying, he thought. Everything she told me was a prepared fiction.

"We could take a stab at swimming, Martin, just to say we did. It's something to do. Don't you think the water is awfully cold?"

He feared it was. And a clumsy fiction at that, he noted, as if she really didn't care whether he believed her. It just had to sound barely plausible, enough to keep him going, a frayed rope thrown to a drowning man, offering hope without safety. Remarkably clever how it worked. They could string along the right kind of person forever, until his time came.

"Nobody has said anything about sharks," said Diana.

Bad for business, he observed. A family emergency came up, for a man without a family? That was good. Keep them wondering, but not doubting enough to take action. Wally was called away? How, by semaphore? He pictured them all getting together and laughing about the story, and laughing about his accepting it, on some level, until it was too late. No, they wouldn't mention sharks.

"I'm going to wear my bathing suit anyway, just so you can see me in it. It's one piece, with frilly sleeves, and tiger stripes."

He would enjoy seeing her in that, even if they never touched toe to water. Wallis Horton was dead. He no longer existed. He had died, and Martin knew exactly when he was killed, that sickening moment when the mirage faded and exposed the brutal reality of the Caltel Ocean Resort. He knew the when, he could surmise the how, and as to the why . . . The puzzle was nearly complete. Did he have the courage to slip in that last piece? He mentally held it in his hand. How much longer could he avoid using it?

"I can tell it's going to be another one of those days," Diana said.

"This day will be bloody well different," Martin snapped. His tone startled her.

"You had better tell me everything," she whispered.

Mr. Hartmann entered. He wended his way past the empty tables and, without a word, sat down at theirs, unbidden, across from Diana, next to Martin. Smiling a kindly smile, he spoke directly to the latter.

"It is unfortunate that Mr. Horton had to leave us so suddenly. These things do happen, as much as we may deplore them. I am convinced there is no cause for concern, and he is not suffering in any way. Perhaps, before you leave us, we may receive good news of him, and hear all is well with him and his people.

"His unexpected departure has not been entirely fair to you. I realize that, no matter how we may counsel against it, it would be customary for a celebrant of the Big Night to share confidences with he who comes after. Due to circumstances beyond our control, you do not have that privilege. I cannot tell all, for that would lessen the surprise and pleasure, but I wish to put your mind at ease by preparing you for tonight, in a small way.

"Beginning at eight o'clock sharp, you will be honored and entertained as you have never been in your whole life, and as you never will be again. It will be your night, devoted to you, revolving about you, taking place solely to extol your being here, your being. For the duration of the event, only one human being in the world will matter. There will be no other; only you, with us there for the one purpose of celebrating your life. There will be superb cuisine, beyond your dreams, and singing, and music, all to honor you. The Big Night, however, is not about these things. It is about you, an homage paid to your living individuality; and you shall honor us, by expressing your individuality, to the extent you choose. You may regale us with your ideas, your views, your sense of self and your place in the grand scheme. These matters are important, and we look to you to prove how important they are. This is the time to make the most of yourself, to open your soul to those willing to listen, who will hang upon every word you speak, and promise never to forget it. Do you understand me, Mr. Cravitt? Can you see with the inner eye? Do you grasp how much we are offering you?"

"I shall be crowned king for a day," Martin replied.

"Or for a night. The sentiment is the same."

"There are men who would pay a high price for such honors," Martin said.

"No price is too high, for the one night in which you will be the center of the universe. Few get that chance. I urge you to make the most of it. I shall meet you at the appointed time." Mr. Hartmann rose. "And a good day to you, Miss Carswell." He left them.

"What was that all about?" Diana asked shortly. "It sounded like babble to me. Did you understand any of it?"

"I understand all of it. Diana, it's time we had a talk. Let's go play on the beach for a while, by ourselves."

They chose a spot on the north side, away from the cluster of buildings. Diana splashed into the ocean, then splashed out again quickly. This wasn't the right time of year for swimming, no matter how hard she tried, but it was a small matter. They sat together on the sand, very close to one another, he overdressed as usual in his long-sleeved shirt and tie (with bathing trunks underneath his pants, in case she had insisted), she in her provocative bathing suit, her sandals at her side. This was a lovely place, Martin thought: the pristine beach, the sonorous surf, the clear skies, the gentle sun, the background of ancient, untouched trees. Here he could be happy, always, here all cares could dissipate and vanish forever. Hard to believe anything bad could ever happen here.

"I'm not sure where to start," Martin said presently. "Tell me, Diana, do you feel any easier in your mind about this place? Do you see things differently, at all?"

"Don't beat around the bush," she demanded. "You know where I stand. I have creepy feelings about everything here. We've had this conversation."

"I have more to say."

"Then say it. Don't keep me in suspense. Is it Wally? Has something happened to Wally?"

"I'm convinced that Wally is dead," Martin said. To judge from the sudden alteration of her expression, he had set off a bomb. As she struggled to reply he continued quickly. "You hit the nail on the head. Very good. I ought to congratulate myself for figuring it out. I'm not really the sort of man who can put together tiny pieces of evidence which lead inevitably to a painful conclusion. I shy away from that, always have. I'll usually give anybody the benefit of the doubt, right up until the last moment. This is that moment, or pretty nearly.

"The Caltel resort is a fraud. These people aren't hotel staff, they're conspirators. I don't know how far back the conspiracy goes—I don't know if it's always been this way—but I think it's been going on a long time, and I know what it is now.

"I never won any contest for an 'all expenses paid' vacation, and neither, I presume, did you and Wally. As you surmised, we were selected—they must have their tried and true techniques—as the right kind of people to be lured here for their purposes. They wanted guests like us, lone individuals without ties, the sort who could disappear without too many questions being asked.

"This place is a trap, especially designed for people like us. It's all phony, just good enough to hold us here for a few days, keep us content to stay. More savvy travelers probably wouldn't have fallen for it; they would see through the shoddiness of the set-up immediately and head the other way. Even the travel agency was a blind; the fellow who met us there is here now, part of what's going on. We fell for that. We could be kept quiet until the time came, if all went well for them.

"I wondered what they might really want from us. We asked how such a crazy enterprise could make money. We were on to a clue, but a negative clue. They're not interested in money. Their scheme has nothing to do with robbing or scamming. I wish it did.

"If I've worked it out in time, it is because their plan went wrong in one little detail. You and I came together. That wasn't supposed to happen. We were to remain isolated, from the world and from each other, our thoughts trapped within our self-doubting minds. Of course they stole your cell phone; they handled it clumsily, but they probably don't have much experience with these new gadgets, and they did get away with it. If odd ideas came to us on occasion, we were expected to keep such ideas to ourselves, for fear of making waves or looking foolish before strangers. Given that, it was a mistake to bring you here. I was looking for a young, pretty girl to add spice to my life; I don't know what you see in me, but whatever I've got did the trick. We grew close—we talked—we exchanged ideas, and sharing them made any conclusions we might draw seem that much less ridiculous. I know for a fact that I couldn't have done it without you. I suppose they thought us too dissimilar. In some ways they were right, but fortunately it didn't matter."

"Let's get to the point," Diana urged him. She stubbed out in the sand the cigarette she had been nervously smoking. "I can accept everything you have said so far. It's weird how it all fits. But why are they doing it? It's pretty plain what you're suggesting. You mean they intend to kill us."

"Yes, but it isn't that simple. This is the tough part—" Martin broke off and leaped to his feet. "Look there," he said, indicating with a nod.

Two men, at widely separated points, were pacing along the tree line. The nearest could be identified as John; he waved. The other was most likely Bob, judging from his build.

"Guarding the perimeter," Martin said, nodding his head in grim satisfaction at this further confirmation. "They're keeping a watch on us. Now that they've got the ball rolling, they can't afford to take chances. Let's go back to my room. I can't stand the thought of them spying on us."

He dreaded re-entering the place, but for the moment options were few. They made themselves fairly comfortable, he in a chair, she on the bed, the door bolted. At last, feeling a nervous shock as he spoke the fateful words, Martin got to the point.

"They are cannibals," he said tersely. "It's true. Once the idea struck me, I realized that they weren't really trying to hide it."

"You've got to be kidding," cried Diana. "You can't be serious. This must be a sick joke of yours. Admit it."

"No such thing; I'm deadly serious. They are ritual cannibals, creatures that couldn't possibly exist in a sane and civilized world, but they're here, and they've got us. It's what they're all about. The way they play it—"

"No, no, no—" She shook her head and turned away from him. Martin came to her, sat beside her and roughly took her by the shoulders.

"Yes," he said decisively. "I didn't leap to the notion. They deliberately insinuated it. It's all part of their game, their ritual, you see. Dropping little hints, making suggestions, to create unease while they entertain us. They've played it that way right down the line. Why didn't they invent a more plausible story about how they operate the resort? They wanted it to sound stupid, so that we would wonder. Why the ostensible mystery over the Big Nights? They could have surprised us without all that. They did it like that because it amuses them. Have you noticed how often they make strange references to eyes?"

"I have," Diana said. She appeared to concentrate. "It bugged me. I thought I was being silly about it."

"Hardly. It's their way of needling us, or it may be a private code of theirs, or both. It's all part of the game.

"The library contains volume after volume on the subject. Much of it is nothing more than a catalogue of horrors. No resort would stock such filth; they put it there to torment anybody who read it. It makes for repulsive reading, but I'm sure they've had a good laugh thinking about my poring through it.

"That isn't the worst, however. They killed Wally last night—that was the big surprise he was waiting for—that is the real secret of the Big Night. I heard him die. I heard his scream at the end, when he realized what was happening to him."

"Don't," whispered Diana.

"I must," insisted Martin. "He didn't leave. There was no family emergency, he received no message. You know how impossible that is here. They murdered him, and this morning I saw what was left of him. They made sure of it. They went out of their way to let me see. I saw his bones, Diana; his gnawed, fire-blackened bones!"

"It can't be," she said. "I won't believe it."

"You had better believe it. My turn comes tonight, and then yours. We must get out of here. I intend to make a run for it, and you are coming with me."

"It's crazy."

"There are plenty of crazy things that just happen to be true," Martin observed. "This is one of them."

"But to run out," she persisted, "because of these—"

"It's our only chance. Diana, please listen. I can't leave you here. It wouldn't be right, and you matter to me, so you must come. If we stay, they will take me to the celebration tonight. They will wine me, dine me, kill me, butcher me, and eat me. Then, in the morning, they will tell you some cock and bull story about my suddenly leaving. You won't believe it, of course, but that won't do you any good. You will be alone here, with them."

"Not that!" Diana shrieked, clinging to him. Martin flinched. He hoped no one had heard. "Not that," she repeated quietly. "Oh my God, I couldn't stand to be left alone. You're right: Wally didn't leave us, and . . . and he didn't have a family. I knew that. He's dead. I accept it. The other thing—those bones you saw—"

"No question about it."

"So what are we going to do?"

"That's more like it," Martin said encouragingly. "We will have to wait until dark. We'll stick it out until the sun sets, and then you and I take off. Have you a flashlight?"

"No."

"Too bad. Neither do I. I advise staying here in my room until dinner. I suppose they will expect you at six."

"No thank you," Diana said hotly.

"You will be there at six," Martin said. "We can't arouse their suspicions. I'll be there with you. I might even sneak some food; I have no intention of waiting for their feast. Then we go."

The afternoon crept by, one moment inching into the next as the sun sank lower in the sky. For the time being there was nothing to do, and little more to say. Martin found it ironic: not so long ago, he would have relished being alone in his room with Diana for hours, but the situation wasn't even remotely romantic. He held her once, when she began to cry, but that was all, and she got over it in time. Six o'clock approached.

He escorted her to her room, where she changed back into the dress she had worn earlier, then they descended the stairs, where Mrs. Drexel waited in the lobby. Diana's face was impassive, while Martin feigned a smile and acknowledged the older woman. She was as severely pleasant as ever. They made their way to the dining room, where a single place setting and chair indicated Diana was to eat alone. Martin pulled up a chair, explained himself to the waiter, and imitated small talk with the girl. Mr. Hartmann arrived, only to advise she keep to her room this night, and promising inconceivable splendors for her the next.

"We shall save the best for you, Miss Carswell," he said. "On the last night we try to outdo ourselves. Maurice plans to serve you in an especially grand manner."

Diana ate little, but at Martin's urging got something down. He did cadge a bit himself, and downed one glass of wine. Then they returned upstairs, he loudly proclaiming he was seeing her off to her room. Then, after she collected her jacket, he hustled her into his room and locked the door. He turned on a single bed lamp.

"Just a little longer," he said, peering out the window. Only the faintest trace of redness remained in the western sky. The first stars glimmered. He removed his tie, pulled on his sweater and changed into his sneakers.

Diana spoke to him from the window. "I see people, two of them, walking toward the boathouse. It's Mr. Hartmann and one of the other men."

"The more who head down there first, the better," he replied.

The telephone rang. Both of them jumped. Martin picked up the receiver. Mrs. Drexel was on the line.

"Your moment has come, Mr. Cravitt," she said. "I congratulate you. Your Big Night is being made ready for you. If you will meet me in the lobby, I will walk you over."

"Thank you," he said. "I'll be down shortly, at eight sharp."

"We wish to get started by eight. By the way, Mr. Cravitt," Mrs. Drexel added, "I dialed Miss Carswell's room, but couldn't reach her. That concerns me. Is she well?"

"She said something about going to bed early," Martin told her. "You understand, since she couldn't take part in the festivities—"

"Of course. Please hurry, sir."

To Diana he called, "What do you see now?"

"Two others, carrying boxes. One of them is Maurice."

"That is four out of the way," Martin mused. "We can charge out the front and head for the hills."

A knock came at the door. Diana tensed, looked to him. Saying nothing, he motioned her into the bathroom, then cracked the door. Nylstrom stood without.

"It is your time, sir," he said agreeably. "I was asked to make certain you were prepared. We wouldn't want you to be late."

"Quite right," Martin cried heartily. "Can't be late. Give me five more minutes, and I'll join you."

"I will be happy to wait—"

"No need. As soon as I'm ready—"

"I will wait right here, sir," said Nylstrom, in a tone which brooked no argument.

"Very well. Five minutes." Martin closed the door, locked it again, then retrieved Diana. "We're getting out of here now, down the back way."

"They'll see us," she hissed.

"There is no easy way out of this mess." He turned off the light. "Here we go, slowly and quietly, at first."

He eased open the balcony door, swinging it by infinitesimal degrees. The oiled hinges made no noise to speak of, but to his ears they sounded like an intolerable cacophony. The air was balmy. The sky was now completely dark, save for the stars and the crescent moon, somewhat larger than when he last saw it. He had forgotten about the latter, but it didn't put out too much illumination yet. A faint glow, however, was rising from behind the boathouse. The sight—and the thought of what it meant—horrified him.

He went before, holding Diana's hand, both creeping hunched over along the balcony, then down the outside stairs, which creaked maddeningly. They stepped into sand. So far, so good. From the corner of the building Martin could see their enemies busy around the mounting bonfire. He and Diana edged around the hotel, away from the ominous view, then took off at a run through near total darkness in the direction of the trees, angling toward the road.

They hadn't gotten far before a ray of light reached out to them, cutting a swath across the beach. There came a shout, answered by another farther behind the flashlight beam. Then a series of calls and cries in the distance. By the time they reached the road, close by the trees, three fingers of light were pointing at them, zeroed in on their position. A shot rang out. Someone on the staff would be armed. They darted under the trees. Another shot, followed by a sharp report in the branches overhead. Martin helped Diana over the fence, scrambling over himself scant yards ahead of their first pursuer.

Within the instant, pitch black gloom swallowed them. Without signposts, without landmarks of any kind, all they could do was crash through the trackless forest at all possible speed, heedless of direction, their only goal to evade the deadly tongues of radiance which winked at and stabbed after them. It was a difficult, harrowing business. Undergrowth clutched at them and tripped them; stones on steep slopes slipped beneath their feet; trunks of great trees rushed at them out of the darkness and smashed into them. Onward they ran, veering right when a flashlight beam flickered from the left, to the left when a too familiar voice bellowed from the right. Those voices chased them as surely as did the lights. Once Martin thought he heard Mr. Hartmann calling to them, saying, "You must come back! We cannot proceed without you!"; and it must have been Mrs. Drexel's voice crying, "We're your friends! The best friends you ever had!" If the painful scratches, the growing exhaustion, and the shortness of breath hadn't been so terribly real, he might have taken their mad flight for a vivid nightmare.

They struggled on, against the rough terrain and the sapping chill of the night. Diana was getting weaker, her legs buckled under her, and he had to devote more of his dwindling energies to holding her upright. Despite this, they seemed to be pulling away from their pursuers. Those ghastly voices no longer assailed them, and the harassing flashlight beams grew feeble with distance. Once they came out upon the dirt road leading to Tellmee—it had to be the same one—and a glimpse of the moon, low among the treetops, served as a crude compass. For all their wandering, they had been heading in roughly the right direction. They left the road, for Martin expected someone to be patrolling it, staggering through dense, thorny thickets which tore at their skin and clothing, and burst into a rocky clearing.

There a flashlight blazed into their faces and a gruff, unknown voice barked, "That's as far as you go." Diana gasped and screamed, collapsing onto Martin. He blinked against the light, holding the girl with one hand, wiping perspiration from his brow with the other. Did they confront a new tormentor? He stared. Maurice, the big, burly French chef, speaking English without even a trace of French accent, stood there holding the flashlight in his left hand, and a pistol in his right.

"Both of you, step back out into the road," he ordered, "and no sudden moves. I don't want to have to kill you now. That should be done properly, the olden way, with the festival and the feast. We're especially looking forward to the feast. You won't be able to take part, but we'll all take parts of you. That includes you, missy. Maybe we'll have you tonight, with your boyfriend; or maybe we will hold off on you until tomorrow night after all. It would be a new twist, keeping a little girl like you all that time, and you knowing every minute what's coming."

"How can you do such things?" moaned Diana.

"What sort of people are you?" demanded Martin.

"What does that matter?" Maurice sneered. "The old folks are true believers of some kind. I never paid much attention to that; I'm a connoisseur of unusual flesh, a professional with a demanding palate. The eyes are the supreme delicacy. I always take those. The young punks are nothing but criminals, mental cases. They get a kick out of it. Does that satisfy you? Consider yourselves enlightened, and get moving." He gestured with the gun.

Martin jumped him—the gun roared—he felt the burning sting in his shoulder, but felt no sense of risk or fear whatsoever. Maurice had been momentarily incautious, a mistake when facing a man who has absolutely nothing to lose. Then Martin had him down, was on top of him, pounding the life out of him with his bare fists, while the big man raged, then begged for mercy. Martin tore into Maurice until he stopped groaning and went limp.

Light shone from behind. Diana had picked up the flashlight. Martin asked her to put it out, while he collected the gun and rose wearily to his feet. His shoulder had gone numb now, but that would change as his adrenaline rush faded. The wound didn't seem too serious. He would deal with it. "Paid in full," he whispered. The human predators had miscalculated. They hadn't known who they were dealing with this time. "We're going to be all right, Diana," he said, and meant it. "Let's just keep moving."

They continued on their way quickly, staying off but within sight of the road, until they heard new signs of pursuit, at which point they cut across country again. The sounds and the lights died away. They still had a long way to go, but Martin knew they would make it. He felt the power within him, as if he were finally in charge of his own destiny.

VI.

Morning light found them in the middle of uncharted country, but another hour brought them within sight of Tellmee, which did not seem like such a bad place once they got there. Whatever its faults, the minuscule village possessed a semblance of a police force, and an adequate telephone service, which soon brought in the big guns. Martin was almost past caring; his shoulder wound had worn him down during the night, and now he having trouble staying on his feet. He sank into unconsciousness shortly after arrival, and his direct experience with insane matters came to an end. Diana stayed by him until he was transferred to the city hospital, and she was the first person he saw when he awoke.

At a later date, feeling considerably improved, he, along with Diana, attended the final ceremonies honoring Wallis Horton. They were the only mourners present at the cremation of what little remained. A pastor said something good about him, and then various technicians performed good, fast work. Then Wally was completely gone.

An enormous amount of police effort went into the case, and Martin remained in touch with them for a considerable period, and a vast amount of coverage in the press—sensationalized coverage he was tempted to call it, except that was impossible—but in time he lost interest, because he never learned much more, and what he did learn eventually led nowhere. The authorities reached the scene in short order, to find the birds had flown the coop. The resort staff, having apparently given up on recapturing their chosen prey, had made their getaway, taking off in the van with most of their book collection, and perhaps a few other items, leaving the rest. No corpse was recovered from the woods; either Maurice still lived, or the search overlooked him, or his comrades had carried him away.

The horses had been abandoned in their barn. The animals had been rented from local stables, so were returned to their owners. The initial investigators examined the hotel from its disused attic to its basement (where they found a water tank with heater and pumps, but no wine cellar). They made one curious discovery which reflected on the overall quality of resort accommodations. Most of the rooms on the ground floor, clearly those of the staff, were in good order, though empty of personal effects. The three rooms formerly occupied by the guests were, naturally, in the same adequate condition. Otherwise, all the rooms were nothing but hollow, dilapidated shells, with sagging ceilings and collapsing floors and bare, rotten, odorous walls, the fruit of scandalous neglect. The place could not have been operated commercially for a very long time.

In fact, it never had been so used. The history of the property, as determined during the subsequent investigation, proved startlingly different from the story with which Mrs. Drexel had serenaded Martin on the first day. All the precise dates, for example, were sheer fantasy. More of their evil games, he realized. The site had been built up decades before by a fairly wealthy man, but not one as imposing as the mythical Thomas J. Dashauer. It had passed through the hands of several private owners and tenants in years gone by, before finally being left to crumble into ruins. About a decade ago it had tumbled into the lap of a holding company, which oversaw minimal repair work on the structure and stabilized the foundations, but otherwise did nothing with it.

The Caltel Ocean Resort was a complete chimera. COR Enterprises actually existed, although it came as no surprise they possessed no known offices, and could no longer be contacted. COR sprang into official being six months before Martin first heard of them, when they applied for incorporation. Addresses of company officers proved false. COR had leased the ocean side property as well as a ramshackle location in the city, which temporarily styled itself a travel agency, although it had never conducted documented business. COR had run up sizable bills in restoring what they ultimately passed off as a grand old resort, always paying in cash through third parties. Some of their most recent bills were left unpaid. The record made clear they had opened the locale only for the one occasion.

All vehicles on site, including the sail boat, were leased, and the cars and one van were returned during the period of the guests' stay, as Mrs. Drexel had said. Apparently she had told the truth, once, perhaps by mistake. The van which remained, also a rental—the one with convenient engine trouble—was found days after the escape of Martin and Diana, ditched on the other side of the country.

Which leads to the final question: what became of the bloodthirsty staff of the ephemeral Caltel Ocean Resort? Mr. Hartmann, Mrs. Drexel, Maurice, Nylstrom, Thomas, John, and Bob; who were they, where did they go, and what are they up to now? No answers have been forthcoming to the present day, and the police have no leads. The authorities were unable to match the names or descriptions to any known persons. Martin and Diana, looking back on their ordeal, have convinced themselves, if no one else, this was not the first foray into unspeakable bestiality by that bloody crew, or at least its ringleaders. They were too accomplished, too sure of themselves, to be amateur fiends. Martin urged the police to look into the possibility of similar atrocities elsewhere, but he never heard back anything of substance, which he considered profoundly dissatisfying. Those creatures existed; they were real beings in this world, and yet they came out of nowhere, they went far in carrying out their unbelievable charade and their loathsome crimes, and then they vanished from the face of the earth, as if they had never been.

About the author:

A degreed anthropologist, wilderness enthusiast, and photographer who makes his home in Arizona, Jeffery Scott Sims is a writer of fantastic and weird fiction with over 100 literary credits to his name. He is the creator of popular characters such as Professor Anton Vorchek, investigator of strange mysteries; Jacob Bleek, the ever-questing medieval wizard; Sterk Fontaine, hard-boiled protagonist of supernatural adventures; and the combative and colorful heroes of ancient Dyrezan.

His publications include the dark fantasy novel, *The Journey of Jacob Bleek*; the short story collections *Science and Sorcery, Science and Sorcery II*, and *Eerie Arizona*; plus many dozen short stories of the bizarre and the macabre, set in extraordinary locales ranging from the cosmos of the far future to imaginary lands of the distant past.

The author maintains a literary web site, *The Weird Writings of Jeffery Scott Sims*, which in addition to providing useful information on his works also offers a vast collection of entertaining essays devoted to unique or unusual topics related to the weird tale. This material may be freely accessed at http://jefferyscottsims.webs.com/index.html

www.ingramcontent.com/pod-product-compliance
Lightning Source LLC
Chambersburg PA
CBHW021953190626
46807CB00005BB/2145